From the Neck Up

From the Neck Up

By

Erik Flores

ISBN 978-0-578-02352-6

Chapter 1

This year's Performance Power catalog of Martin Romaine merchandise, titled:
Obliterate All Obstacles

T-Shirts
"The Classic." Show your tremendous drive with the wildly popular "I Do It Like the Successful People Do It." T-shirt. Now available in ¾ sleeve.
"Awesome." The design and eye-catching colors of the new "The Colossal Power Rules All" T-shirt makes it a definite attention grabber.
"POWER." The artist rendering of Martin Romaine by renowned painter Leroy Neiman captures the world-famous speaker in action!

And with the explosion of twenty Chinese New Years, staccato drums and convulsing laser beams, Martin Romaine, swinging Tarzan-like from a rope, flew over the beaming faces onto the stage, slashing through the bannerized replica of his latest book (a symbolic gesture of breaking through barriers he would mention five minutes into his speech). The tattered banner was swept away followed by victorious punches into the air, each accompanied by white light explosions from the corners of the stage. He finger-shot Roman candle blasts tracing high over the audience's heads. Passages from the cannon of epic soundtracks woven together and backed by a techno beat exactly the speed a running man's heart shook the stadium. Mr. Romaine tore off his jacket and leapt from the stage. Security guards flanked him but he wouldn't slow down, darting this way and that, easily evading their clumsy bulk to engage the audience. Through the aisle his sister had strolled only ten minutes earlier he sprinted, high-fiving the wheat field of outstretched arms, shouting enthusiasms to the men, hugging the women and lifting the children high into the air. His name ignited in a pinwheel of spinning fire on the stage. Strobes throbbed. Fireworks burst overhead. Cameras popped. His motion amongst the first thirty rows was marked by a wake of audience clamor. He stopped long enough to climb atop the sound stage and gesture wildly to the upper balconies. More fists in the air. Shouting. People hundreds of yards away stretched closer to make out what he was saying. What was it? Certainly not the obligatory, "yeah," "whoo," or "thank you!" but rather conversing with an old high school buddy from across the room at a party, making plans for drinks later. He laughed to himself as if hearing an intentionally bad joke, leaped from the sound stage and took off. High-fives. The security guards parted the crowds as he sprinted up ten stairs to the stage. Miraculously, while he mixed with the audience, the entire stage had been transformed with props, a new banner, a microphone and an oversized novelty replica of his new book *The Colossal Power Rules All! My Personal Journey to Self-Grandeur.* He spun around to face the audience, and with a blinding supernova explosion of light and sound, raised both arms commanding an invisible sea to part. Ka-Blam! The music stopped and a single spotlight shone upon him. He breathed heavily and ran his fingers through his hair.

The pulsing applause was unceasing. Martin Romaine waved, strolled about calmly as he sipped from a glass of water that waited for him on a simple small table next to the microphone stand. He shrugged in disbelief to an empty side stage. As the cheering seemed like it was about to die down, it erupted again. Martin Romaine smiled and nodded. He then raised his arms high and held them there as he scanned the audience. Finally letting them fall, the stadium hushed.

Martin took in the silence of the stadium, interrupted by random shouts of, "I LOVE YOU!" and whistles, and then greeted the audience with a tremendous, yet somehow bashful, "HELLO!"

Mona couldn't see her brother as she sat backstage with the trained doves, but the words emitting from the PA system that echoed throughout the stadium made him more present than if he were standing right in front of her. Martin Romaine was words. Vibrating vocal chords. The exploding fireworks and fanfare that preceded Martin's appearance were fine, but it was the words that reached her in addition to millions of people throughout the world. In the old days, with nothing fancier than a hand-drawn banner in a rented out hotel conference room, up to five seminars in a day, she didn't have much to do but listen to her brother's speeches and book the next appearance. Now it was different.

After a lengthy empowerment phrase—quoting Winston Churchill: "However tempting it might be to some when much trouble lies ahead to step aside adroitly and put someone else up to take the blows, I do not intend to take that cowardly course, but on the contrary, to stand to my post and preserve in accordance with my duty as I see it."—Martin squatted on the stage to catch his breath. The stadium was silent. They could have stayed like that for hours, hanging there waiting. And they knew he was generously offering them a gift, a gift he gave though it thinned his life's blood with exhaustion. The audience sat with tight-clenched hands; stunned at the swelling power they received. Tears flowed. Children comforted their quaking parents. Raised arms with out-turned palms acting as satellite dishes for more. Each of the five senses dedicated to the absorption of Martin Romaine.

*

Despite her status in Romaine Enterprises, sharing Co-Presidency with vast decision-making privileges, Mona's handled the doves, two dozen of them intended, "to lift off towards the heavens, in an arc like that of the human drama, separate but together..." That was the final sentence of her brother's opening speech, the trigger to release the snowy birds over the heads of 35,000 people. The speech wouldn't go exactly like that (it never did). Martin worked best unscripted. The exact words didn't matter; Mona could sense the impending crescendo of his address coupled with the sinewy tension of the masses before him. It was palpable to her. Years of touring had taught her a few things about timing and showmanship and the appropriate moment of release. To withhold and reward.

But the doves weren't so certain. During the speeches, they like the audience became wound up amongst each other, and Mona worried that they would refuse to burst from their pen or worse yet swoop down in the middle of formation and peck out the eyes of some poor old lady, resulting in a gargantuan law suit. She sat holding the pull cord, waiting anxiously like a boy with a glowing punk in his hand for the formal announcement of the Fourth of July.

The doves were one of Martin's ideas that would quickly evolve into another one of his distracting crusades. To get her brother back to the task of creating soul-stirring speeches (and because she was certain someone else would screw it up), Mona took care of everything: transferring the birds from the cages to the silvery sparkled release box, wheeling it to the side of the stage, leaping back after their release into the air, and finally waiting as they flew their thirty-second formation (her nerves jangling over something horrible happening like the doves getting sucked into stadium vents and spat bloody out into the audience). Every time, however it was a success. Without fail, those birds delighted all with their clockwork choreography. As a reward for a job well done, Mona would let them peck grain out of her hand. The one responsibility she freed herself from was cleaning the glittery release box of dove turds. She assigned that duty to an intern. Doves leave a hell of a stink.

The stadium was filled to capacity and bloating. Merchandise booths inside sold T-shirts, videos, CDs, posters, bumper stickers, books, 8x10 glossies (framed and unframed), and related items: books and cassette tapes by other speakers under Martin Romaine's publishing company, Performance Press. Outside more booths sold cheaper, lesser-quality unauthorized T-shirts with the inevitable bleeding colors as well as bootleg copies of previous performances; even ones from as long as ten years ago when Martin and Mona toured California alone in a K-car. The tapes were generations old, so the sound quality was definitely off. No comparison to the 24-track studio recordings available inside the stadium, in stores or through mail order. But still, fans were fans. The opening speakers had a half-hour time slot. The children's choir sang three long numbers. The Supi Indian drum circle had forty-five minutes.

The late morning sun edged into the stadium during the opening speakers performances. A common thread ran through them all; the anchorman, the retired general, the actress declining in popularity: They punctuated their deliveries with thanks to or mention of the headliner—Martin Romaine. Though everybody in the stadium knew what they had spent from seventy-five to upwards of three hundred-fifty dollars on, his name was constantly mentioned on stage, in passing and in praise—sometimes even in winking jest. The last opening speaker and regular on the Romaine circuit, a former Mr. Universe from twenty years ago and currently a successful car dealership owner, put on his sunglasses halfway through his speech when the morning sun reached his eyes. He kept his presentation dynamic to hold the audience's attention, punting his briefcase or asking a thin-legged mortgage broker to come on stage and arm-wrestle him. Thirty five thousand people aren't easy to keep engaged. Folks were still filing in, finding their seats, picking at fries bought at the concession stand, inspecting their freshly purchased merchandise. "Hey, that's Randolph Shuron," they said and went back to their T-shirts. And it wasn't rudeness on the part of the audience; they were simply saving their emotional energy for Martin. He demanded it.

Mona left the dove box and went into the audience. She walked halfway up the floor aisle and turned to the stage. The ex-bodybuilding champ spoke with natural ease, his size seized attention. The sun gleaming down on him, though, was unfortunate. Instead of spotlighting him, it washed him out. Thin clouds formed above and that helped. Mona looked around the stadium to get a feel for the place as she had always done before her brother hit the stage.

A nearby couple occupying choice aisle seats were kissing in gasps as the huge man on stage waved his arms, equating winning the Mr. Universe title to succeeding in the automotive selling industry. "What you want from your quadriceps," he said, "is a perfect compliment to your gluteus." Mona watched the two lovers, and they didn't hold back, lip-locked as if they had just resolved their first major argument as a couple. Children pointed. Mona smiled, feeling somewhat indirectly responsible for the public display of affection, as if, in a small way, she added to the romantic ambience. But it was really her brother, Martin. His presence and charisma encouraged all sorts of weird behavior. He performed weddings, gave the opening speech at a Squash tournament, showed up to say some words at funerals for dead people he had never met or heard of. He was even asked to perform a circumcision. The man could do anything. He spoke Swahili. He carried a third degree black belt in Tai Kwon Do. He owned an island and homes in three continents with landing strips he was trained to land on. He had flown himself to this show on his private plane named the "The Commander," and he was going to fly back to his Florida home at the end of this leg of the tour.

Seagulls had made it into the stadium. Not many but there they were. They better not get in the doves' way, better not interfere with their formation or join the group. Mona thought of picking them off one by one. The stadium was too cluttered for the birds to angle in for dropped popcorn or half-eaten hot dogs. They hadn't grown that bold in their evolution of scrounge. The sun rose to a reasonable height with Randolph Shuron no longer fighting the glare. His voice grew more animated with punctuated shouts that briefly seized the audience's attention before going back to their sticky concession stand meals or programs as if a false alarm had gone off. A surprisingly pleasant smell hung in the stadium, remarkable for the amassed humanity. Sweet and mild. Was it the churning cotton candy? Or perhaps the sex of the young lovers? Mona was thrilled. Another great show lay ahead, she knew it. The seagulls rose and sped off in a formation that impressed her. Folks shouted, "ahhhh!" Rapid heartbeat. Mona never allowed herself to get swept up in the combustible fray of the audience—unprofessional, this was a business—but permitted her brother's amplified words to swirl about her each night as she sat backstage with the box of birds.

The sun would soon be perfect for Martin Romaine, a pillowing haze to frame his speech. Faces bright and upturned, a hush between syllables, everyone lunging forward for his next utterance.

Mona met Mr. Shuron as he left the stage behind polite applause. She thanked him and patted his back to send the giant muscleman on his way. It was always at this time, just before the main event, that Mona became an unstoppable commanding and organizing force. She snapped the road crew to attention through last-minute commands on walkie talkie. Her threats of what would happen if she received anything short of perfection were never subtle. "If something goes wrong, everybody will burn!"

*

Any problem in the office and it's, "Let Joe the human resource guy take care of it." I'm Joe. Everyone has their designated tasks clearly defined—from the receptionist all the way to the CEO. Mine however, because of the built-in ambiguity of the word "human" in my title means that I'm the go-to guy in situations like this.

I'm supposed to count people's hours, keep tabs on their sick and vacation time, occasionally organize a company picnic, but often I'm regarded as the human custodian. This is what happens when a company that trains businesses in employee conflict resolution has a conflict itself. They call me, and I'm not even trained in what we specialize in.

Two specialists from the training division of my company, Conflict Control Systems are brought to my office. From time to time, the management feels that our conflict resolution strategies need to be re-vamped and kept fresh. Mostly it's just minor things like terminology (the word "intercede" gets replaced with "mediate," for instance), and less frequently it's a major overhaul of company policy. In any event, our conflict resolution training experts periodically need to go in for re-training themselves. It's along the lines of a new/improved dishwashing liquid, obligatory in keeping the public's interest.

So an old timer with the company, Curtis, is called in with his (much) younger supervisor, Alan. They sit down before my desk knowing full well what this meeting is about, and from the look on Alan's face, he seems pleased to finally have it addressed. Curtis, on the other hand, asks if we're going to be long, he's got work to do. From the get-go, he ties this into the issue at hand—he doesn't want to waste time going through the new training. He's been with the company for fifteen years, even before it had morphed from workplace efficiency training into conflict resolution training. He says he does just fine with the old methods and finds it absurd to change just for change's sake. I like him. But I also empathize with Alan, immensely uncomfortable about the power foisted upon him.

"It's a fact that companies evolve," Alan says. "And their employees have to evolve along with it."

Curtis just sits there in his sky-blue shirtsleeves and fifteen-dollar haircut, refusing eye contact with his supervisor. He looks at me though glasses with scratched-up lenses, but I say nothing. I have overheard a few conversations in the halls about how this is done, and glanced at some of our literature from time to time. As a mediator, I should say as little as possible and give no opinions. So I stick to protocol.

Alan is in shorts and sandals, and it isn't even casual Friday. He launches into a rehearsed speech with no pauses. "Curtis, I have no control over the major decisions that are made in this company. I am here to make certain that our policies are upheld. Ask anybody, in any line of work: all employees need to keep up with the changes that are made, and sometimes that includes training."

Curtis speaks, but addresses me as if I am to translate to Chinese for his boss. "My skills are just fine. I've had nothing but success with them. Look at my track record. I would rather do what I do best with the few years I have left."

"But, it's policy—" Alan says.

"Screw policy!" Curtis's face tightens.

"Now let's watch the language," I say.

Curtis keeps his eyes on me. "Can't you see how stupid this is? I mean, come on. What would you do? Then this guy," he points his thumb at Alan, still refusing acknowledgement, "comes along and tries to tell me I'm not doing my job right."

I'm at a loss for something to say and luckily Alan butts in. "Curtis," he says, trying to get eye contact, "I feel that you have very little respect for my authority."

"Ah, shut the hell up with how you feel."

I speak up. "Now let's wait just a second and try to address the matter at hand."

"Please," Curtis says. "I know how this works. You need to," he forms quotes with his fingers, 'Assist in clarifying the issues that created the conflict/concern.'"

"I realize—"

"Then you need to, 'Provide information regarding available options.'"

Alan says to me, "See what I have to deal with?"

"What do you mean, 'deal with?'" Curtis finally looks at Alan menacingly.

"I'm just saying, we need to come up with a solution that will—"

"That everyone can agree upon," I say.

I sit before them, hands folded on my desk, praying for this to end. I'm supposed to count hours, hand out birthday cards, deliver paychecks, and rarely (thank God) conduct interviews. This is not in my job description.

Curtis turns to me. "I know everything I need to know, and just want to stick with it until retirement."

"That's not the way it's done," Alan says.

"Give me a break!" Curtis laughs.

"It's true."

"Hah! If that's the case, I'd do this instead." Curtis keeps looking at me, but thrusts his arm out with the middle finger turned up about two inches from Alan's face.

"Hey!" I call out.

"See?" Alan says to me.

"See what?" Curtis looks to Alan calmly.

"See the insubordination I have to put up with. It's usually more subtle."

We all sit there silent. I'm aching at a loss of words. It's fifteen minutes past five. I would almost be home by now, dammit. I see my girlfriend Misty digging into the pint of double-fudge chunk we bought last night, not bothering to wait for me. Curtis speaks up again.

"Just let me do my work!" he says.

"It's not a matter of you just doing your work. It's a company, Curtis, a team."

"Don't talk to me that way!"

"I wouldn't if you didn't act like this."

"Like what?"

"Like a child!"

I stand up. "Please, you guys know better!" But I may as well be out of the room standing in the conference room juggling staplers, because now they're standing facing each other.

Curtis looks to me, "Yeah, what do you know, anyway?"

"I know that you're both acting unprofessional," I say but with the conviction of a dead party balloon.

He turns back to Alan. "Everybody in your department thinks you're a chicken-hearted yes-man."

"Yeah?" Alan says. "Those same people are sick and tired of cleaning up after the sloppy work you do."

Curtis swings. Smack! It isn't a square blow but he catches Alan's cheek. Alan grimaces and swoops forward with a punter's kick into the knee. I yell, "Stop, you shitheads!" Curtis grabs his leg and looks up, "A kick? You kicked me?"

I leap from my chair and my thigh catches the edge of my desk. Leg stinging, I limp between Curtis and Alan. Curtis is throwing punches over me trying to reach his supervisor, and manages to graze my head a couple times with the sharp bony edge of his forearm. Alan has his other arm, smashing it against the wall as if knocking a gun from his hand. Curtis screams and lands a solid one on Alan's temple. It sounds like a potato being stepped upon. A trickle of blood comes from Alan's ear. I see this and instantly the air leaves me and my legs disappear. From the floor, I grab the phone and call downstairs. Alan kicks Curtis again, this time right in the gut.

Chapter 2

Sweatshirts

"The Heat." Yes! You can take the heat, or the cold, or anything that comes your way with the stylish fall sweatshirt, the distinct Performance Power (PP) logo stitched on the left pocket.

"The Outdoorsman." Go to your favorite sporting events, concerts... or Martin Romaine seminar in this rugged new sweatshirt. The color says "performance" while the style says "outdoors."

My full name is Joseph Ashe Median and I have been given my first homework assignment since college fifteen years ago—reviewing Martin Romaine's new book, *The Colossal Power Rules All! My Personal Journey to Self-Grandeur*. Conflict Control Systems (COCO) told me to look into him, as our sales figures were 3.7% lower than the previous year due to, according to the board of directors, low morale. The kind of morale that also led to the fight in my office with bloodstains still visible in the carpet. Because of COCO's Fortune 500 status, I was given a hardcopy pre-press release, a thick, heavy book with tons of pictures. I didn't bother to read his first one, the best seller, *How To Do It Like the Successful People Do It*. Too instructional. I did however flip though it with its pie charts, outlines of downward-spiraling behaviors, cartoons and famous quotes from long ago. George Eliot: "If we want more roses, we must plant more trees!" It contained very little about the author himself.

Some higher-up in the company, my supervisor Bill Emmons I bet, was probably watching cable late at night in his penthouse; the t-bone from dinner upsetting his stomach and keeping him awake, even after half a bottle of sauvignon and movie sex with his stunning wife. I imagine him flipping through the channels and stopping at Martin Romaine sitting at one of his beach houses bantering with a fill-in-the-blank superstar or instructing a World Series-winning manager on how to win. Click. The gears turn in Emmons' head, and on Monday the board hears and approves his proposal.

Look at that cover. They don't skimp on the design. It's gilded in some kind of gold-like lame. Hmm... The title is below the name in smaller letters. I look closely but can't tell out whether his skin is really that perfect or an airbrush has swept away the inevitable blemishes. Tie and jacket with sharp gray lapels. The man's glance. I see where the charisma comes from. Almond eyes. Very inviting. The type of guy who wants you to think he's new to confidence, like saying, "Can you believe this? Me? I'm no different from you, but here I am." That and the gap-toothed grin, though not quite goofy, deflates any reservation you may have that he's an approachable guy. A slight tan. Not much of an upper lip there; a bit out of proportion with the lower. But the hair. Wow. I see what they're talking about. It's stunning. A dark chestnut, short on the sides, and swept back on top. You can make out the individual locks. The widow's peak is perfect. I look at him, and then I gaze at myself in the mirror: comb-over hair, pudgy midsection tucked in tight like a sausage, and a soft face completely lacking intensity.

Opening the book. It's dedicated to the bodybuilder Randolph Shuron. "To Randolph Shuron, who's taught me as much as I've taught him." I flip to the table of contents. It's his autobiography all right. It runs through his life in chronological order, each period given an abstract title or quote describing major events. "Reaching up and Pulling Down the Stars." The final chapters seem to lapse back into his philosophy and teachings.

Chapter One. This section covers his family's history. There's a portrait of his parents as a young couple. Happy, but a little stiff. He doesn't look like either one of them. The father is thick around the neck while his mother's eyes are almost exact inverses of her son's, dropping at the corners. Perhaps if you squint real hard you can see Martin's hair in there somewhere. Below is his birth house. A small bungalow surrounded by other small bungalows. Next page he's a baby reclining in the arms of his older sister Mona. His hair isn't anywhere near its current magnificence, merely a thin cloud of fuzz. His sister is looking straight at the camera, penetrating in her Prince Valiant haircut. I guess she's worked for him all along. She's his personal assistant or manager or something like that. Below the baby picture is a shot of him in a scout uniform. No older than twelve but his hair has already matured into its full glory. There he is, proudly clutching a small trophy. His chest is covered in scout regalia: badges, patches, beads. Underneath the picture is a caption that reads, "This is a picture of me after I was accepted into the Eagle Scouts. I was the youngest member of the troupe." There's a copy of a newspaper clipping covering the young achiever, Martin Romaine, who managed to lead a fundraising drive to save and restore an old flagpole that was erected shortly after the Civil War. Sheesh.

Martin had accomplished more as a pre-teen than I have in over thirty years. I take a breath and flip to the next section of photographs. The adolescent years are omitted. Now in his twenties, his hair is intact and here to stay. He's outside standing at the top of marble steps, grinning and shaking hands with a senator I don't recognize. Below that is a shot, artful in composition, of him in the throes of a small seminar. His eyes are wide, hair mussed, collar open, with clenched fists as if entering a melee. He's not directly facing the audience, so the shot contains both the speaker in full force as well as the hypnotized spectators. A few of the audience members are smiling as if sharing a secret joke with the speaker. A very nice shot, indeed. Ah... the photo credits in the back say the celebrity photographer Lois Rosenthal took it for a Newsweek special on motivational speakers. This triggers a memory from the eighth grade of a speech I had to give about walruses. I was so petrified of speaking in front of my classmates that I threw up all over the podium. Even the teacher shrieked. The janitor brought in a dripping mop and said to me, "I oughta make you do it." I can still taste the Chicken a la King.

Returning to the book. Martin is smiling; expansive and welcoming like an Italian grandfather before a family feast— "Come. Join us!" he's saying. This page effectively portrays the speedy rise in his field that a lifetime of constant success had prepared him for. Another shot has him pitched forward, pointing at no one in particular, jaw set. There's one of him in a karate outfit, standing before a cinder block about to be chopped in half. Next page, a wide shot from the rear of a seminar with a couple hundred attendants. They're illuminated from the glow of an overhead projector casting a pie chart on the wall. Martin is standing beside it, mouth open and patient. I feel like I'm punishing myself somehow by pouring over every picture. The final section portrays him really coming into his own. Now we have actors, pretty ones, elder statesmen, famous sports figures, an Army General. They surround him both formally in suits and ties or lounging in Adirondack chairs at his home on the beach. It really is something seeing a four-star General in shorts entranced by this tanned fellow in linen. What can he be saying? Finally, there's a photo of Martin Romaine from behind, arms akimbo, in front of a stadium filled with listeners, surveying his land.

I close the book and read the synopsis of his career printed on back. Also listed are a few of his accomplishments as well as quotes from authors and other famous successful people. An actor calls him a "Life Master." There's a blurb from the author who wrote *Turn Yourself into Anything You Please* that reads, "Mr. Romaine has taken the word 'Successful,' analyzed each contributing element and instructs us how to take the diverse parts of our lives and combine them into a sum of greatness."

Again to the front cover. A speckled maroon background behind Mr. Romaine, black trim around the edges, the letters in white with gold flourishes between the author's name and the title and elsewhere. Those are the colors of success. The title, *The Colossal Power Rules All!* is placed so the word "Power" is next to his head. The subtitle, *My Personal Journey to Self-Grandeur*, begins at his left shoulder in smaller print. A golden #1 for its National Bestseller status sits glowing in the upper right-hand corner like a sun. I feel its heat.

Instead of collapsing for the usual after work nap, my eyes blink in squirrel-like alertness. I lay the book beside me on the couch and flick on the television. In mere moments however I feel guilty about it, like I should be doing something more productive. No doubt Romaine's fault.

*

Crackling peals of applause followed Martin Romaine as he jogged off the stage. He whipped back around, for the third and final time, and sprinted back into it. He skidded to a stop at the far front edge of the stage and gave his trademark two-fisted punch in the air. The audience burst open in frenzy; whistles and screams and the stomping of feet shook the stadium with a menacing tremor. Martin did it again to sustain the hysteria. People were on their feet and chairs mimicking the two-fisted salute, long after Martin Romaine left the stage for good.

Mona patted her brother on the back as he passed. Backstage, dozens of special guests gave a restrained applause respective of their social standing. Randolph Shuron crashed forward and swallowed Martin up in an inescapable brotherly bear hug. He was getting more touchy-feely with each performance.

Brother and sister rushed to the dressing room for debriefing. Martin wrapped a wet towel around his neck and collapsed into a Laz-E-Boy. He reached over to the snack tray, grabbed a banana and seltzer water and closed his eyes. Despite the continued flood of staticy applause, Mona got down to business.

"You fooled 'em again," Mona said.

"Thank you," Martin said, eyes still closed.

"There are, however, a few details which ought to be addressed while they're still fresh in our minds."

"Give me a moment to catch my breath, won't you?" Martin exhaled slowly. Mona looked down and silently counted to ten. "Well, I—"

"I know what you're gong to say," he piped up.

"Yes?"

"The time it took getting into the sweatsuit before the third act." Martin cracked the water and took a gulp.

"Yeah. Too long. The audience was getting impatient. How did you know that's what I was gonna bring up first?"

"There's others?"

"Of course."

He threw up his arms this time not in triumph, but in exaggerated despair. They flopped down at his sides. "What is it?" he said.

Mona said nothing. This forced Martin to open his eyes. His sister sat forward, looking at him expectantly like a mother waiting to get the truth out of her impetuous child.

"Mona, I saw the look you gave me when I was coming back from the dressing room."

"What?"

"The 'hop to it' look." He leaned back into the chair.

The post-event milling about and emptying of the stadium brought the noise down to a low hum. Mona had determined that it takes between forty-five minutes to an hour for a stadium to empty. It was during this time that they debriefed; the way it's always been done, from the rented-out Holiday Inns all the way to the Astrodome.

"All right, Mona. Let's move on," Martin breathed out.

"Okay. Starting from the beginning. You took too long waving to the folks in the nosebleed seats when you ran to the back of the stadium. It's chaos for the people on the floor as they try to follow you," Mona said.

"Tough for them. They get to see me up close for the entire show," Martin said with a mouth full of banana.

"Now don't get all uppity on me, Martin. You don't have the same perspective on this as I do."

Martin sat up in his chair. "Why don't I just cut that whole segment out, then?"

"My goodness. You must be tired," Mona said, pen and pad neatly set upon her knees. "That's not what I'm saying at all. Running around the stadium is a wonderful trademark of yours. It shows your willingness to get up close to the people, no matter where they sit."

"What, then?"

"Just try and make it more organized. Don't scurry this way and that. It gets hard to follow you."

"It's fine the way it is." Martin rubbed his eyes.

Mona stood up. "You really need some sleep. I think I'll just—"

"Come on. Let's finish this," Martin said.

Martin Romaine still had twenty minutes before stepping outside to sign autographs. He raised his arm to his sister in a weak beckoning gesture. "Sit down."

Mona sat and immediately went back to it. "Okay. It's not just the crowd I'm concerned about. Mostly it's the cameras. They told me that they're having a hard time following you when you run around like that. We almost have enough footage for the new video you know."

Martin gave in. "All right. I'll see what I can do. But you know," he pointed at her, "I still have to make it look spontaneous."

"I've got it," Mona said. "We'll choreograph that entire sequence, write it up and give the plan to the cameramen."

"So I've got to run the same pattern every time?"

"Well, yes," Mona said.

Martin slowly breathed out. "All right, if it'll help the cameramen."

Mona smiled. "Fine," she said.

"Wait," Martin spoke up. "If I run the exact pattern each and every show—jump off the stage at the same time, high five the first twenty rows, hop up on the sound stage, etc.—won't people eventually catch on that I'm simply going through the motions? People go to more than one show, you know. The ones who follow me around the country..." His volume went up to prevent Mona from interrupting. "What's it going to look like with me waving and smiling the same way for every show?"

Mona tightened up. She had thought it was over. "We can run a questionnaire about how many shows are attended by each person. From there, we can determine if it's okay or not to repeat the performances."

"Hmm... I don't know."

"Or better yet. We can choreograph two or three different patterns to run during that sequence. Before the show, we can tell the cameramen, 'Sequence 2, Bob.' What do think of that?"

Martin wiped his forehead with the towel and closed his eyes. "You mean," he sighed, "In one sequence I'm gonna wave for ten seconds and another I'm gonna high-five thirty instead of forty people?"

"No, it doesn't have to be that detailed. You've got other things to worry about rather than how many people you are going to high five. That would be insane. I'm proposing that we let the cameramen know in advance what side of the floor seats you're going to run around; clockwise or counter-clockwise, when and where you're going to stop and greet the audience; stuff like that. Oh, I think it would be advisable that we let them know precisely where you're going to jump off the stage. Maybe we can place a little marker there."

Martin let out a naked disapproving sigh.

"Remember," Mona spoke patiently, "video sales are becoming a larger percentage of our overall sales. Because of that, we have to put more effort into them: production, the cover, editing, music. All that needs to be done."

"I think I know where this is going," Martin tipped on the edge of whining.

"Yeah. The entire show will need to be planned out and choreographed in advance, much more than it already is."

"So, what I have ahead of me is the task of choreo-graphing a show to look impromptu and impulsive."

Mona scooted her chair closer to Martin and locked on his eyes. "You're not alone in this. Most of it will wind up on my shoulders. This is a big business and we've got to treat it as such." She mussed his hair. "You've got autographs."

Martin Romaine hopped out of the chair and danced around on the balls of his feet like a boxer before the bell. He jogged about the room wiggling his fingers and stretching his wrists. "Where's my pen," he said to no one.

Mona tossed Martin a Sharpie and tried to catch his eyes. "Don't worry about it right now. You've got only one more show, then two weeks of vacation."

"Yeah," he said vacantly. Martin was in the zone. He landed on his feet, took a breath as a swimmer does before the dive and left the dressing room.

Mona ordered a fresh-faced blonde boy to fetch a change of clothes for her brother. A fresh towel, soap, shampoo, and conditioner were laid out. She opened her daily planner to see what appointments Martin had later that evening. A trip to the zoo with the Shriners and a late dinner with the owner of a local shipyard. When the boy returned with the clothes, she snarled, "You expect him to go to the zoo in wingtips and slacks?" He shot out of the room. Mona plopped down on the Laz-E-Boy and opened her spiral notebook to a drawing she made of her brother, the design for the cover of his next video: "Immense Outcomes." The sketch portrayed him standing erect like a Soviet-era Russian leader bracing against the wind, his jaw square with an otherworldly glow behind him. Should he be standing atop a mountain, or maybe driving a flag into giant rock-like letters spelling out his latest book? And where should his name be? Probably above him, in gold. Or burnished bronze? Rugged; definitely rugged. There was a hint of it in Colossal Power; the readers were allowed to see the struggle and rise of a man to the top of his game. The book had all the elements: A humble birth in a small middle American town, his early signs of greatness, the setbacks (the neighbor's refusal to allow Martin to date his daughter because of his economic background and dad's paralysis and most of all that reckless driving incident in England). It covers his threadbare existence as a young public speaker getting by on rotary club engagements, and his Homer-like travels through the Rustbelt getting into adventures and gaining followers.

She erased the suit so all that remained of the original sketch was his granite head. Her mind clicked. Many years back, at a state fair, the Clark County State Fair she believed it was, Martin booked forty-five minutes at a side stage next to a snow cone stand. To fit in with the surroundings, she put up their gas money for clothes that for once didn't suggest they came right out of Massachusetts: Georgia Boots, Levi's, flannel shirt and Caterpillar hat. Off the rack they were cardboard stiff, so Mona tied the clothes up in a ball, threw it in a mud puddle outside the motel and ran over it with the van a few times. She tossed it into the washer and drier then beat them against the brick wall in back. The bill of the hat was creased between the hotel room mattress and she personally clunked about in the boots for a day to break them in. The show's turnout wasn't tremendous, as none were those days. Between a dozen and twenty people witnessed any portion of his performance. Four people bought tapes and six signed onto the mailing list. She remembered well her brother up there on the stage. He had never, and hasn't since, looked that down-home. He eased back from his typical formal presentation style, which had already been honed to perfection. The ten-dollar words were omitted and replaced by an easy-does-it drawl, while he softened up his stab-slit eyes with a touch of the hangdog. He smiled more. The weightloss portion of the production was removed altogether. Martin became the compadre that nobody knew, in a hurry to share his secrets lest they go bad. He actually looked tough when he rolled up his sleeves. It wasn't done with milquetoast care but shoved up his arms mid sentence. And when he took off his hat to wipe the sweat from his brow—a masterstroke. No shower or shampoo that morning. An untended crop of hair going who knows where.

Mona sat up erect and grinned a toothy grin meant for nobody but her, the pencil cracking under her grip. She saw in front of her an entirely new direction for her brother—working class. It flashed before her in neon buzzing on and off. Martin Romaine had already cornered the upper-middle to lower-upper class demographic. Those people were brushing against the good things in life; they saw it every day as the boss strolled in on banker's hours or returning restful from one of their many vacation homes. There was no reason why they couldn't be that person instead of constantly having to drag themselves into the office every day at the same time or having to go in on a time share in Arizona with their creepy brother-in-law. That crowd was a lock. Next to conquer was the upper-lower through the middle class. Why should they be deprived of attaining their financial, mental, emotional and physical goals? Do they not have dreams of self-actualization and betterment? That demographic, perhaps more than any other, Mona was convinced, was most in need of her brother's strategies for success. It wouldn't be a huge financial sacrifice to invest in Martin Romaine's Super Success Package. Sure $795 is nothing to sneeze at, but the payoffs would be tremendous. Martin could convince anyone of that. Maybe discounts could be introduced. A sliding scale. Mona's mind raced. She scribbled down her ideas on the page opposite Martin's disembodied head.

*

I think I'm the only man ever to hold this position. What's said about my job (if anything is said) is true. It's woman's work. Keep all traces of a penis at home, for it shall hang there dead when forced to hear the menstruation excuse for using sick time. The women in the office had my number from day one. Man in human resources, play the period angle. Initially it worked. Whenever the monthly time was mentioned, my heart leaped into my throat and appendages withered to bloodless husks. Simply slide a piece of paper in front of me and watch the jellyfish sign it. They noted my discomfort and played it over and over. Three periods in one month? According to Lucy in supplies.

Then, at Mr. Emmons' insistence, I had to get tough. I devised the sick-hours policy, in which you call in over forty sick hours, you get those extra hours taken out of your vacation time. I announced this new policy, and instantly I was converted from pushover to tyrant, completely indifferent to special feminine needs. It landed me in sensitivity training, two days a week for two months. It taught me one important thing (not the sensitivity training, the entire menstruation business). Starting off soft and becoming hard is going to confuse and anger everyone around you. The best thing is to start hard and stay that way.

I'm dragging from a day at the office bean-counting vacation time, re-scheduling an entire department's work hours, and hearing tall tales of sickness. But still I sit at the kitchen table and read the damn Romaine book to learn more about the man's successes, which have naggingly been dancing through my head all day.

The introductory chapter is titled "A View from the Stage." And that's exactly what it's about; Romaine's vantage point at one of his own shows. No abstraction there. He describes the sea of people, all those eyes and ears upon him. Lights pop. The cheering. That goes on for a while so I begin skimming the paragraphs. He feels humbled in the presence of so many adoring people. A humanizing ego-check. Next he is on stage, before thousands upon thousands of admirers, reflecting upon this awe-inspiring spectacle that only a filled-to-capacity stadium can produce. The typical autobiography opener: A superstar at the zenith of his career taking a moment to stop, ponder and take stock. Flash, I imagine myself in his shoes, king of the mountain, looking back at this very moment—sitting here book in hand, thinking this thought. The beginning of something. I skip the rest of the introductory chapter and flip to chapter one, not very originally titled "Beginnings." It starts with his grandparents. I skip that as well and look for information about his mother and father; see how different they are from mine.

My eyes get heavy. I sit up and shake my head to keep awake. I'm set on finding a real person, someone who didn't spontaneously appear and occupy a vacancy for greatness. Otherwise how can he be of genuine help to me and people like myself? All right, his father cut hair, farmed a little and opened a couple convenience stores here and there. His mother was a schoolteacher. The family moved several times around the Midwest and upstate New York. Financial troubles. They settled down long enough in Ohio to have two kids: Martin and Mona... His folks are no great shakes just like mine—no psychology professors or poets or inventors of microchips found in televisions and radars. So if Martin Romaine did all this on his own, I have no excuse... Oh, I'm too tired. I lay the opened book face down on the coffee table and head for bed. It's never made so it doesn't take long for me to get comfy.

*

Martin returned to his dressing room, squeezing and twisting his writing hand as if a magical combination of tweaks, pulls and stretches could relieve the soreness created by two hours of autograph signing. Mona shut her sketchpad and observed her brother as he sat down and took a bite of his sandwich. She shook her head when he crossed his legs—working-class *real* men do not cross their legs; they're supposed to be spread way beyond a comfortable angle, at least shoulder width. Such a big task ahead. Where to begin?

Martin spoke up with a mouth full of sandwich, "How much time till the zoo?"

"About an hour."

"Good. I can plan the trip to Florida."

"Why don't I do that, you should re—"

"No. I need to keep busy." Martin snorted and took another bite.

"What have you been doing the last four hours?"

"Please. I can do those shows in my sleep. And signing autographs is hardly taxing. Why don't you fill in for me sometime?"

"I was just—"

"No, I'm going to plan the flight to Florida."

"I can do that stuff. You've got better—"

"I'm doing it!" He said carefully and with finality. "Now get out and leave me alone." The rising of his chest from heavy breathing was visible. Mona attempted to dissolve her brother's glower with a smile. He wouldn't budge.

"Fine," Mona said as she pulled herself out of the chair. "I can't wait until you go on vacation anyway, grouch. I hope you get the rest you need..."

Now for the first time in who knows how long, Martin was alone without simply being asleep. He sat waiting for the usual break in the silence. The crowds had all gone home. The seconds began to stretch. Periods of inactivity became wide-open nightmarish vistas for him, always, as he stood alone in a room. He breathed in the quiet and became weak, a shudder in his knees. The floor sank. Martin shook his head to free the cement drying around him and sped to the door. He opened it to make sure his sister had really gone. No Mona, just the distant swearing of the swing gang as they packed up the props, signs, lights and speakers.

Martin went for the phone. Where was it? He searched the room, looking under the laid-out clothing, behind boxes. He found the cord and followed it to the bathroom. Glancing up at the mirror, he noticed that his hair was wild like a mad scientist's (and in front of all those autograph seekers). After a run-through with his fingers, a strand floated down and rested on the corner of the sink.

Now where the hell was the address book? Did Mona take it when he booted her out? She took something. Why would she do that? To get back at him for being so disagreeable? Nerves popping like static, Martin began tearing up the dressing room with the clothing, empty plastic water bottles, flower bouquets from fans, cardboard boxes of merchandise to be approved falling where they may. He let out a less than menacing bear growl and waited for somebody to check in on him. Nobody did. On a scrap of paper Martin scribbled down, "Better security after shows." He went to the door, but as he touched the handle, thought he would rather keep looking than call Mona back in. The address book had everything he needed; the phone number to the airport, the rental car agency, the hotel, even the pool cleaner's number. And it was always kept with his pilot's license and flight log. He needed those too. He plopped down in the Laz-E-Boy to gather himself but the room began to wave in front of him like a magician's hand. No rest. He would have to find Mona.

Martin again peeked outside the dressing room, looking left, then right, then left again—the *smart* way to cross the road. Luckily, his destination led him away from the stage where all the action was, and to the smaller dressing room that the opening speakers shared. It was fifty feet or so down the hall, then a sharp left around the corner and past a maintenance closet. He padded along the hallway in his socks, knocked on the door and let himself in before anyone answered.

Three men stopped what they were doing—brushing teeth, reading the newspaper, and picking at the snack tray—and shot to attention. They angled for the first word to Martin, but he waved them off with a hello meant more for silencing than greeting. He cut directly to the immense body-builder turned car dealership owner/motivational speaker with a toothbrush in his hand and asked to join him outside.

Randolph Shuron followed Martin outside and gently closed the door behind him as if not to wake anybody. His efforts to appear non-threatening—speaking gently, the softened eyes—were ridiculous, as Randolph was power piled on top of power. Arms too big for any normally tailored shirt with a neck more like an odd rock formation jutting out of a mountain than a neck. People who spoke to him stood back, not necessarily out of fear, but rather should he fell they could get out of the way. His size smothered, an impassable wall. He reached out to shake Martin Romaine's hand. He was always shaking hands. If ten minutes passed without seeing him, Randolph would seize Martin's hand and shake it in renewed greeting. Men felt like infants as their hands were swallowed by his first-baseman's mitt of a paw.

Martin wriggled free of the handshake and sped through the flattering small talk about the show. "Randy," he said. "I need you find Mona and see if she knows where my address book is?"

Without hesitation or question, Randolph nodded. "Sure," he said with severe eye contact. Though Randolph was primed to go, Martin went into a lazy explanation. "I've got the zoo trip coming up and I need to get dressed. I don't have the time to go searching around for that thing."

Randolph nodded again. Still Martin continued jabbering. "First try searching the tour bus. It could be on the dresser or in my big black duffel bag...Yeah, check there first. Then, if you can't find it there, ask Mona." Martin sped through his words as if heavily rehearsed. "I need to make some appointments, you see. If Mona asks, just tell her that I asked you to get it for me. Got it?" He didn't wait for a nod or a word, and said, "Great, thanks."

Randolph broke from the huddle, spun around and trotted down the hall. Martin watched him go and sped back to his dressing room.

Martin was slipping on his sneakers when Randolph returned. The giant loomed over him, engulfing Martin in his shadow. Pretending the shoelaces were disobeying, Martin growled at his feet wrestling the strings. Randolph continued to stand above him, saying nothing. He was polite that way, never interrupting or imposing. But his size alone grew impatient and he began gently swaying from side to side.

The shoelace ploy was a failure, and Martin threw them down in hope that Randolph would get scared off like a bear from clanking pans. He tried another tactic: quickly thanking him and whisking him away with lightning inaudible words of parting. He sprang from the chair, shoes untied, and snatched the address book out of Randolph's immense hand. By the time Randolph gathered air to speak up, Martin's back was to him and halfway to the phone. "Hey Martin," he said in feigned afterthought.

Martin didn't turn around. "Yes, Randy?"

"I'd like to talk about the show."

Martin flipped through his address book searching for the number of the pool cleaner. He mumbled something that may or may nor not have been acknowledgement. "Zmuh..."

"The show," Randolph repeated, as if the force of his words would compel Martin to face him.

Martin found the number he was looking for, stuck his finger between the pages and turned three-quarters. His face went long, mouth slightly open in an expression of impatience never allowed on film. "Can we do it later?" he asked. "I gotta make plans, you know, the zoo."

"I want a few more minutes on stage." Randolph said.

Martin re-opened the book wrapped around his finger and looked down at it.

Randolph continued. "There's not enough time to make an impact." He clearly had been thinking about this for quite some time, rehearsing this very scenario, mulling it over in his mind, point after point; and finally with no prompting let the dam break, perhaps flooding Martin into submission with a downpour of reason. "The half hour I've got is a nice warm up, but just as I'm beginning to cook, and the audience is getting into it, it's over. How long have I been opening for you? How many shows has it been? And it's all..." Martin stared down at the pool cleaner's number in his address book. CRISPY-CLEAN POOL

CLEANERS. He couldn't stand a dirty pool. All the leaves and dead bugs floating around. Vile. Randolph continued. "My set has been a half hour from the get-go. I need to grow. I've reached a plateau and can't get my point across fully with the time I'm allotted. I've done all that I can with a half hour."

Martin gave Randolph the final one-quarter and faced him. This quieted Randolph, though there was more he had planned to say. He stopped and idled like a truck. He tipped toward continuing, but Martin's face erased all that.

"I hear you," Martin said soothingly. "We'll discuss this, I promise, but I have to work now." He placed a hand on Randolph's shoulder and moved him to the door with a calm, easy authority that all the towering bulk this ex Mr. Universe possessed was powerless against. Martin's attempt of puffing out and standing erect for comparable size however didn't work.

*

My very first Martin Romaine show. I brought along my copy of *The Colossal Power Rules All.* I've read it four times now. Well, the good parts. The stuff about his time in the Boy Scouts doesn't illuminate much. Filler, I suppose. Otherwise, I like what he has to say. It makes sense. In autobiographies, there is supposed to be some kind of turning point, a moment when everything in the narrator's life accumulates into a defining moment. The moment where he realizes early in life, "I'm going to be a dentist." "I must design rockets." "I will encourage people to live to their full potential." None of that in this book. No epiphany necessary. The DNA strings coalesced into a handsome man whose very words, whatever they may be, make people think they can become thinner, smarter, richer.

I'm pretty certain that I want all those things.

COCO wouldn't spend more on better seats. Section DD, Row F, Seat 2. Not even an aisle seat. I am almost the farthest distance from the stage you can get and still be in the stadium. There's an overhang above that envelops the gusts of wind, condenses it, and whips it right at me. My combover hair stirs in the air, lashing the poor lady beside me. She's kindly not saying anything. I use spit to smear it back down, tuck it behind my ear, anything, but it won't hold. I climb over the lady in seat 1—she hates me by now—and run down the stairs to one of the many merchandise stands. They're extraordinarily organized: the T-shirts are presented by size, videos sorted by release date. Barely keeping within the boundaries of politeness, people squeeze and muscle in to place their orders. They grip wadded bills in their fists, wanting to relieve themselves of it as if the money were repellant, despised and corrosive.

I look for the most sensible baseball hat available. I find one. It's teal. On it, Martin Romaine is taking off in flight like Mighty Mouse. There's no background; just Martin's raised left fist punching the sky with his opposite leg thrown behind. Curved over him in a semicircle are the words "RELEASE THE CAGED BEAST!" The letters are brick-shaped, old and cracking, and you know Martin Romaine is about to smash right through them.

I take my seat. White lights begin whirling around the circumference of the stadium. We're inside a huge blender. Cheers like TV static, up full blast. The lights slow down then begin spiraling down the bowl. Hard on the eyes. Accelerating frantically, they change to blue, then red, then gold narrowing in a ten foot UFO revving in idle, shaking to break free. Then it does and a volcanic spray bursts up (I feel its heat). The audience strains upwards and follows the shower of sparks as they fall. Boom! There's Martin. I know it's him by the Jumboscreen over the stage.

Martin bounces around the stage punching the air. I try to look at the man himself without the aid of the screen, but all I can make out is a brunette matchstick bobbing up and down. With all the focus I can muster, I keep my eyes off the Jumboscreen. It seems like cheating. For seventy-five dollars, I'm not about to watch TV. He hops off the stage and begins running up the isles. His hair keeps him recognizable even as he mixes with the crowd. My mind begins to fill in details from his autobiography. That high-stepping, jocular run toward the rear of the stadium comes right out of the book. He stops and waves. Though only a spot in the landscape, it feels like we're shaking hands. Waving and gesturing at us (me) as if saying, "Come on! It's me! Don't tell me you don't recognize me!" I smile; a little embarrassed at the effort he makes on our behalf. He's standing before me. What should I say? I'd tell him, "Good show," or "Great lights," or something stupid like that. One more sweep of the arm and he's off.

I take a moment to notice that everyone around me is watching the screen above the stage. Even a baby propped up in his mother's arms lets the pacifier drop out of his mouth as he stares at the 75-foot Martin Romaine.

He sprints back on stage, snatches the microphone from the stand, whips around to face us and launches into it. All in one grand sweeping motion. His delivery fervent and magnetic. Fast and breathless as if his entire body is blasting out those words, not just his lungs and lips. Is that really his voice, or is it filtered with reverb? A pouncing assault on the nerves. I breathe slowly to take it in, but it won't be diminished, and pieces cannot be picked and chosen at convenience. Take it all in or... no, just take it all in. I squeeze my eyes to sharpen the focus upon the matchstick. A big sound from an ant. The words flood me. I try to imagine them before they hit the microphone, as if spoken only to me.

Damn, I'm *charged*. How do I explain it? Let's just say I've been wearing the Romaine baseball cap constantly since the show three days ago. It's made me more self-aware, like a magnifying glass to the self. It's not about the baldness; I'm not trying to disguise it. All that disguising does is draw more attention to it and add a ton of weight to its significance. But that's what everybody at work is going to think: "Poor Joe. This is worse than the combover. He's stooped to using a baseball cap." That's what they'll say behind my back in their hostile pity. I know it.

But really the opposite is true. I am wearing this hat as a sort of talisman, a string tied around the finger reminder of things that need addressing, attention, and vigilance. The hair? Yes, the hair. But not just that. All sorts of things: My job, my love life, my third-trimester pregnant belly, my general outlook. People will accuse me of self-consciousness and they'll be correct... but in a good way. How does one improve oneself without self-consciousness, insight? I'm switching off autopilot and grabbing the controls. Yeah, it's just a hat, but that way I'm starting at the top.

Martin Romaine has given me a swift kick in the ass. I walk through the door and greet the receptionist with a hearty hello. She's barely conscious under that face paint. I notice it for the first time. I'm cognizant of other things as well. The building is dim, not from the lack of light, but from the people typing at their desks, carrying documents to and fro, or simply chatting amongst each other. A muddy light seems to ooze out of them, some more than others, and a fog hangs all around.

Instead of going to my office, I report straight to my supervisor, Billy Emmons (I've never felt comfortable calling him "Billy," though that's how he insist we address him). He manages the non-training, front office division of COCO.

Mr. Emmons doesn't have the kind of office that you can stand outside of gulping down breath or repeating for the last time your rehearsed plea for a raise. It's glass framed in chrome. No privacy for Mr. Emmons and I don't think he needs it. Even his desk provides no concealment; just thin polished oak splitting him in two at the waist. Behind him is more glass, an entire wall of it overlooking a gleaming busy city with the tip of a dead volcano off to the east.

Mr. Emmons' field of vision must be narrow. Unnoticed, I take a seat in the skinny chair before him. When I walk by his office he's always gazing upon indecipherable papers or a screen. A clean, unimpeachable man. The neatly trimmed beard gives his face more angle and a handsomeness which couldn't be achieved alone. One thing about him is that I can never tell when and if he's sincere. I like to think I'm pretty good at those things— seeing through a facade, the bullshit. With Mr. Emmons though, it's a mystery. He will ask you about your vacation, something personal, and seem to be silently pleading for you to keep your answer to within a sentence or two. The problem is he never lets on, and I feel that any reluctance I may have about his sincerity is merely a symptom of my distrusting nature.

A plane floats over the horizon, away from the volcano that will never again explode. Mr. Emmons stands and pulls his khakis down from his crotch. He grips my hand hard and sits back down.

We discuss Martin Romaine. I share my enthusiasm, which I notice for the first time around my supervisor is free of restraint. I tailor the story so it ends with a proposal to hire Romaine for a personal seminar with the company, not simply purchase a number of his audio works and books never to be seen as we had previously planned. I tell him I believe so strongly in the techniques' potential effectiveness upon our sales staff that I, Joe Median, am using them this very moment as I make this pitch. My delivery is so convincing; I blast through it with several examples of companies that have benefited from Romaine's services (Air Force contractors, football teams, pharmaceutical companies, even the President of Italy) that he agrees, albeit after a pause not for thought, but as a reminder of his decision-making power. I stand up and thank him. He shakes my hand again, sits down and scratches something on a pad of paper with a mechanical pencil.

"Hey, thanks Billy," I say. He looks at me and nods.

I have been given three weeks to hire Martin Romaine and prepare for the seminar. The door sighs shut after I walk out of the office. I look around, hoping somebody notices the victory on my face, and take the long route to my office.

Things are beginning to happen. New blood flows. Witnessing my half-dead co-workers slog in their toil gives me strength and resolve, actually energizing me. The men sag under the effort to maintain their stature. I pity them. These people used to be me. This is an office of chrome and glass and ebony-topped desks. Pencils with the company's logo on them. Stuffed animals on desks. Photos of the kids. Award plaques. Social bulletin boards. Comics snipped out of newspapers that flaccidly rail against office culture. Like A Band-Aid over a shotgun blast. A joke. I'll show them what can be done. I'll bring them Martin Romaine.

*

Martin's plane reached 67 knots and floated off the ground. The air buffered the wings and he pulled back on the throttle. He looked behind to make certain he was still aligned with the shrinking runway. It's good form. When the plane reached 900 feet, he called the tower and veered left and exited the flight pattern. He glanced over to the map on the passenger's seat. All was good; he was on his way to Florida.

He leveled off at 15,000 feet. Martin Romaine liked to fly high so he could only guess the details below, staring at the hazy landscape until his mind wandered. That and the steady hum of the engine put his brain exactly where he needed it. Outside was clear and a little chilly, good for the engine and perfect for flying. A couple puffy clouds hung in the sky as if lazily and unimaginatively painted there by somebody wanting to fill space.

The land below was big and wide and Martin gazed upon its expanse. He puffed up in the seat and glanced quickly at his reflection in the passenger seat window. Only the outline of his hair was visible, and though he couldn't make out the details, he gave the locks a good run through with his hand. It was just a habit, and he knew it. Fixing his attention back at the land below, his mind clicked. Words came. "God, it's huge. And people say there's nothing left to explore. Just look at this. Gaze upon the blurred vast beauty from up on high and fill in the rest. 'Everything's been done,' some say. Whiney unimaginative pinheads!... I can't say that... Just put this beauty and potential into words and let it take over. That's all it takes." Martin was lost in grandiosity, dizzy with the proud elation of life, staring straight ahead into a mystery he always felt on the verge of solving. He didn't feel (though any natural sense of equilibrium should have told him so), the plane losing altitude—not in a plunging sort of way, but a slow persistent descent of over two thousand feet below his original height, and now in violation of air traffic laws. Westbound flights flew at this altitude. Only happening to glance the attitude indicator on his way to another hair swipe did he notice it. Trees and hills and roads came into focus. He pulled back on the stick and gave the engine some throttle. The plane rose, and once again the land and water below returned to the perspective where he could continue his reverie. He set a good airspeed, carefully trimmed the rudders and checked his course so he wouldn't have to bother with it for quite some time.

Back on land, Mona was at work making the Romaine Enterprise's engine chug along. In her hands. All he had to do now was meditate upon the journey and allow God's creation to spark his imagination.

Chapter 3

Books

How To Do It Like the Successful People Do It.
Immediately upon release, Martin Romaine's first
work vaulted him to the status of Performance
Guru and it became an instant classic. Now re-
released with a new forward and an extra chapter,
re-discover this treasure or present it to loved
ones to read and cherish. Now available in leather
bound.
The Colossal Power Rules All! Currently on the
National Bestseller List, discover Mr. Romaine's
"personal journey to self grandeur." This book
illustrates how his power techniques were applied
to his own captivating life.
A Mountain of Worth: The interviews,
conversations and essays. This work will give the
reader special insight into the mind of Martin
Romaine in these candid interviews and
conversations with some of the most successful
people today who shape our lives. Not available in
stores.

T he customized plane Martin owned and was now flying to
Florida was a brief example of the immense rewards reaped
from his special insights. Confident and assured, he switched to
automatic pilot and looked to the skies. The sun was going down,

making the horizon a gentle flame. The cockpit began to cool. He felt compelled to interpret something from the sunset, to create a metaphor. It seemed to beg him. But everything he thought of or scribbled down was unacceptable, deflated of power. There's just nothing self-aggrandizing you can get out of a sunset. It doesn't inspire a sprint-to-your-goals attitude. Too meditative. Quiet reflection is for the end of the day, when the job's done. And the work is never done. Martin crossed off the fire and heat images he had written down and turned the sunset into a metaphor of regret; regret over a life of doing what you *should* have done over what you *must* have done.

He turned the cabin light on and flipped to a fresh page in his notebook. He wrote down the word "Vacation," with three question marks beside it. Underneath it, he scribbled the words, "What do you take your vacation from?" Below that he wrote, "Work?" and besides that, "Family?" and finally at the bottom added, "How to combine all three." He smiled and drew a big fat star and in bold letters wrote, "CHAPTER IDEA." Martin made a fist of victory, but there wasn't enough room to punch the air.

Mona was great. Minding the store and handling the everyday details of operation freed him to ponder the concepts. Like here in the plane: All he was obliged to do was find the inspiration and come up with ideas for chapters. Martin sat in the cockpit, at ease knowing his sister was below, her nose to the ground, keeping him clothed, fed and warm.

She had driven him to the airport that morning. He stared out the window thinking of the previous night's show, the next show, what to write next, what aspect of human development he would cover next. Next next next. As the car merged onto the freeway, Mona described her plans for the next few weeks. She had elected not to take the three-week gap between shows as a vacation, but rather get back to headquarters and fill the remaining opening slots for the rest of the tour. Martin pushed himself back into the leather upholstery, not really engaged, and absorbed the soothing mix of his sister's voice and the engine. Mona's half-hearted last-minute plea of hiring a private jet stirred him. It was the only time during the short trip to the airport that he spoke.

"I've got it taken care of," he had said in a calm voice that normally provoked nagging.

Not this time. They were both fully immersed in their specialized zones, their areas of expertise in which they held dominion—Mona at the wheel with a smiling Martin gazing out the window.

Martin's enthusiasm toward the new topic of vacations rivaled the hungry passion he felt on stage as the audience echoed his shouted slogans, "First you feel it, then you live it, and THEN YOU LOVE IT!" Those two experiences, the thrill of locking in on a brilliant idea and then thousands of people accepting its validity with screams and clapping and money couldn't be topped. That feeling had now dug in, and Martin knew good and well it's always been the prelude to a new all-consuming adventure.

The plane was off course two degrees to the southwest. It had been that way for over an hour, and it would be yet another hour before Martin realized that he was hundreds of miles off course, his plane low on fuel and requiring an unplanned stop. He continued riffing on the theme of vacations, imagining a program consisting of teams of couples, families, or singles with one of Romaine's vacation experts trained in Martin's brand of "vacation conditioning." Basic training for vacationers.

*

Driving back from the airport, Mona took out her sketchpad and opened it to the new rugged drawing of her brother. It grabbed her tightly and she spent more time looking at it than at the road. At stoplights, she stared at him until the cars behind her began honking. It was marvelous, no doubt about it. She brushed her fingers across the pencil marks like a nurse's hand on a baby, wondering. Rugged Martin. The concept was so good, so perfect for this juncture in his career, but it required more to bring it to fruition, a certain fleshing out that would require skills way beyond her ability.

*

I've got three weeks to get my shit together and hire Martin Romaine for a personal appearance at Conflict Control Systems. And I'm not about to appear before him in this cheapie suit of mine. The only way to show confidence is to wear it: on your face, in your hair, on your feet, and especially your body. The style of suit shows reveals a man as a peasant or a king.

I'm still wearing the Romaine ball cap. It's like a warm new brain sitting upon my own. I put it on as naturally as picking up my wallet off the bureau and sliding it into my back pocket and grabbing the car keys when leaving the house. It's got to go eventually, especially after I get the suit. But that's simply part of the growth process: You take what you need, the nourishment required to get beyond the next obstacle, then upgrade the supplies until the next stage, and on and on. I'll leave the hat behind when I no longer need it and never look back.

I now own all of Martin Romaine's books, and I shelled out a bit for a signed copy of his first one. A couple of his videos are in the mail.

It's all following his "Techniques of Power," in Chapter 1 of *How To Do It Like the Successful People Do It*. Step 1: Visualize the goal. That's done. I'm on Step 2: Do your homework inside and out. Here he mentions a separate product of his, the Super Success Package, in which you learn that there's much more involved within these steps, something he calls "Leaps within the Steps," where, as the goal is pursued, the person must take part and bear witness to the changes going on inside him. I am getting fitted for a suit today.

I skip the sale racks, as I feel purchasing something with the goal of saving money (nothing truly real) to be a compromise of my worth (something very real). If the best is what you expect, then the best is what you must get accustomed to.

The salesman, a guy with tender looking skin and very silky blonde hair gives me little time to browse before he starts making suggestions. I consider his ideas (he *is* the professional) and weigh them against my own tastes. After a few nods, I ask him to give me a few minutes to do further searching. I find a very blue suit, so blue it could be cobalt, and carry it to the desk for fitting. The salesman says, "Good choice," but tells me there's a suit a little lighter in color that's two-thirds the price of this one. "This is the one I want," I say with such conviction that he doesn't attempt to argue.

Proudly I stand in front of the mirrors as the Russian lady kneels before me adjusting the inseam. She tells me to relax into a "more natural position," but I stay the way I am, with my chest puffed out and head held high.

Martin speaks from my car's stereo as I head home. The words slide past me, though the power and conviction behind them drive me forward. I'm a little distracted with all that lies ahead. The next step is building a base of operations. It should be right where you live, in my case, the apartment. It will metamorphose into a dwelling that will serve as my fortress, my stronghold, and my refuge. As I visualize it, I also imagine Martin taking a break from car stereo to tell me, "You're on the right track, Joe."

My apartment is the flaccid dwelling of an indecisive soul, lifeless and overrun with trinkets of a sluggish past; weighing me down to the point where it takes all my energy just to push myself to the surface for air. My mind wants to jump out of my body, so I step into high gear.

It's all got to go. I begin with the walls. The paintings with their meaningless pastures, art prints by names everybody knows, even old pictures of me and my family, leave my walls forever. What shall take their place? Only work that touches me and fills my life with deep personal meaning. The phone rings a few times. I leave it unanswered. Do *not* get distracted.

Is something an accomplishment if it has yet to be achieved? According to Martin Romaine, yes. The process and the goal must be kept in perfect balance, given equal weight. It's true. I worked six hours straight and feel tremendous. Boxes are filled, old clothes bagged and the walls bare. I, the master, stand before it all, arms akimbo. My chest has not sunk from the moment I was fitted for my suit and there's no sign of it deflating.

The phone. I pick it up and there are messages. It's my Misty, asking about the show. Sitting down, I wonder if should I call her back right away. I'm holding the receiver, looking at it, wondering what to say. Before, I would instinctually and immediately return her messages, check in, find out what's what. There was never any design or forethought to it: dial the number, go into a thirty-second anecdote about work or whatnot, spend a few minutes passing the responsibility back and forth about what to do that evening or the next. All without a second thought, or a first thought. Is that the way we go about our lives, allowing the current to pull us along, this way and that? I don't recall ever sitting down and making a plan when it came to Misty. It was all impromptu. "Hey, let's go to the movies, why not Chinese food?" That was it. Just five minutes of planning would raise our connection to a higher level. Every moment a memory. It can be done. Relationships shouldn't be like ordering lunch. They should be magical, and, I think Martin said something like this— "If magic can be made, it can be sustained." So I sit back and outline a plan of what I want out of my love life with Misty, similar to the plan I made of designing my ideal apartment.

Going over the pie chart, after the five-point performance plan, the phone rings. I don't answer it; of course it's her. There's something inside that compels me to pick it up and say hello, but that goes directly against the plan. That's the old, unfocused me. "Whatever you do, do not sacrifice your goals for the immediate. It will only lead you astray."

The sun has gone down. The traffic outside steady with even intervals between cars. There was a time when I would have thought, "Where are they all going? They're all on their way to a party at the shore, snug in their sweaters, and I'm stuck here." It's not like that anymore. Maybe they are overlooking the ocean, eating steamed oysters from the grill, drinking margaritas and dancing to the strums of a single guitar. Who cares? I've got something better going on. The apartment is packed up. All that remains are the lamps so I can see as I draw up my plans.

*

Mona put up her own money for the commission of the painting. She didn't tell Martin about it. It was to be a surprise, a little treat. She assigned a code name: "Rugged Champion Study." Martin Romaine was hot, so raising interest was a breeze. She cast the line out and within three days, fifteen painter's portfolios sat on her desk in Romaine Enterprises headquarters. With Mona's pencil sketch of Martin's head as a starting point, they went at it with competitive zeal. They were told that each work would be paid for but only one would be used, the one portraying her idealized vision of the new Martin.

She consulted the artists on a daily basis, either through correspondence or in person, and she didn't prune her criticism. Frustrated that the painters were not properly conceptualizing her idea, she would snatch away the artist's brush and add a stroke or two before she could be restrained. One artist finally quit after Mona openly laughed at his rendering and called it amateurish and best suited for the inside of a dark cave. All the others, every painter who had applied, threatened to quit at one point or another. Hardly a stroke was made without her critique. It wasn't their work, she reasoned, it was hers and they were merely instruments of her will.

*

The apartment now represents my strategy for success. While the decor is aesthetically pleasing, it remains professional, unobtrusive. A thin palm tree with sharp leaves sits in the corner. One large, utilitarian, black and white portrait of the towering

Tetons is opposite my desk. Step inside and you can't help but think, "There's some serious business going on in here." I'm thrilled with the results. Like soil that will give birth to a mighty redwood, this is the foundation upon which my empire shall grow. My war room. Martin says to forget the old notion of what an empire is: "A large state or group of states under a single sovereign who is an emperor." A true empire is rather, "The fruits of accomplishment that acts to sustain its benefactor; no matter if it's a Fortune 500 company or a corner grocery store... or a wife and children." A symbiotic relationship that develops out of one man's self-realization. For me, with the work I have done remodeling my apartment, it's like the successful first date of that relationship. With some making out, I might add.

The toll-free booking number for Performance Power is available in the back of Martin Romaine's books. I dial it, and after a few rings I must choose one of the following options: 1: merchandise, 2: tickets for performances, 3: tour schedule, 4: listen to a brief clip from his latest audio book, and 5: bookings, followed by the star sign. I select 5. It rings a few more times and a spirited young woman answers me.

"Hello. Thank you for calling Performance Power," she says.

"Hi," I leave it at that, hoping to dispel the formality.

After a pause, she says, "How may I help you?" staying in character.

"Yes. I represent Conflict Control Systems and I would like to book Martin Romaine for a company seminar."

Immediately and automatically, she says, "I'm afraid Mr. Romaine's schedule has been booked solid for the next four years, can I—"

"Wait. Did you hear what company I'm with?" I snap into indignation as fast as she went into the pre-rehearsed quasi-apologetic canned response. The ease at which she dismisses my request and how my interruption failed to phase her peeves me.

"I realize your request, sir. I'm sorry about the inconvenience. We have several staff personally trained in Martin Romaine's techniques."

"Ma'am, in case you didn't know, Conflict Control Systems is a Fortune 500 company. We are the leaders of—"

"Sir, like I said, I am very sorry but Mr. Romaine's engagements are frequently booked months, and in many cases years, in advance. The status of the company or individual cannot make him cancel an engagement."

"But, surely—"

"Even if the President wanted counsel with Mr. Romaine, he would be hard pressed to break an appointment."

A pause. I contemplate staying on the line just to rile her. "And who are these important people that he cannot get away from?" I ask.

She remains cool and even. "Mr. Romaine's meetings are private and confidential, and are not available to the public. If you like, I can send you a tour schedule."

I shouldn't have given her that pause. "No thanks. I already have one."

"Why don't I get your address so I can send you some profiles of our many available speakers? Did you know that Randolph Shuron is now in contract with us?"

"Yeah. Go ahead and do that," I say unconsciously. "Where is Martin Romaine now?"

"He's taking some time off before resuming the next leg of his tour. Can I get your address?"

I give her COCO's numbers and hang up. My desk is immaculate with nothing substantial sitting on it but the Performance Power 800 number written on a yellow sheet of paper. I look around the apartment, my war room. The setting is right, but it's stale. No juice. A Blue Jay flies up to my window, hovers around, and thinking better of it, leaves. I look to the pile of Romaine books on the corner of my desk and it hits me. "A failure is a step to success." I had barely dipped my big toe into the pool and already I'm thinking failure. I slap myself hard across the face, I mean really slap myself. "Break free!" I plead with myself, thinking of some empowering Romaine slogans, but they fizzle and pop as they reach the surface. I'm still new to this. Better than simply committing to memory what he says, the phrases and oaths, his words must be absorbed and ingrained. "A man's life is not his surroundings. His life is the sum of the energy he expends. Good or Bad."

The apartment is impressive with its workman-like efficiency. However the operation's no good just idling. It's time to drop the hammer and let her roll. And what's a better test-drive than my girlfriend?

I sit up straight and reach for my relationship folder containing the outline of expectations I have of her and myself and our future together. It all seems to be in order, so I pick up the phone and give her some straight talk.

*

One of the guest speakers however, the enormously popular evening news broadcaster Larry Montgomery, cancelled his appearance at the next show. A tonsil infection. Mona's eyes narrowed in doubt. She's seen so many outstandingly successful people in any field you can name shrink to mouse size before Martin's inexorable drive and all the attention it receives. She could imagine Montgomery (a big-headed talking head) falling into that category. Otherwise, the sun was out and things chugged comfortably along. The show was weeks away, yet celebrities, athletes, performers and politicians whose popularity and skills were frequently on the wane were lined up for blocks to be a part of this. Each eight-hour show ("Festival" the official term) was easily booked. Mona went to the program and looked at the schedule of events.

Montgomery's cancellation left a vacant slot between the (upbeat) blues band and the retired Navy Admiral. Mona went up and down the list with her felt-tip pen and bumped the movie director down into that slot, requiring someone particularly lively to fill in the space he left open. Something physical... to pep them up. An acrobat troupe? No. Something that involves the audience on an aerobic level. An aerobics instructor! It was done a couple years ago and got the whole place hoppin'. A nice break, almost like a recess, where everybody gets worked-up and refueled. Mona picked up the phone. In five minutes, a semi-famous workout coach with five videos to his name and several celebrities in his resume was booked.

Mona used this change of plans as an excuse to check in on her brother. He wasn't in. Odd, as he seldom left the house when on vacation; but rather locked himself inside his Florida estate writing, reading or working out at his private gym, keeping busy busy busy. She hung up without leaving a message, and checked the status of the portrait, bumping the pressure to finish it up a notch.

The painters were now worked up in such an artistic competitive frenzy that they began employing underhanded practices like spying, rumor and even sabotage to keep in Mona's favor. A fine graying woman painter from Santa Fe came back from her egg-white omelet breakfast to find some kind of corrosive oozing down the canvas, leaving a smoking scab running from Martin's left shoulder to his knees. (Test results showed traces of H_2SO_4). She called Mona and had a good cry before demanding to know the identities of the other painters. It had to be one of them, she screamed. Mona diplomatically let her rant and eventually digress into heartbreaking tales of her son's accidental fatal fall from a bridge years ago. "This will not affect my opinion of your artistic merit or ability," she told the painter, and suggested that she get herself a massage and start over again. To raise the woman's torn spirit, Mona said the ruined work was definitely a front-runner and she sent her an overnight delivery of Martin's Super Success Package. After the half-hearted response of, "I guess so," to her pep talk, Mona thought of her brother and began giving quotes, snatches of paragraphs, and slogans overheard during the shows. It wasn't that difficult—the words just poured fourth on their own accord as she leapt from subject to subject. This is what Martin must have felt. A wide-open channel. Mona blasted rounds of inspiration into the phone while the painter at the other end sat at the kitchen table, fingers slowly dragging through her hair.

"Each darkness is merely a prelude to dawn."

"Are you up to the challenge? Somebody thinks you're not. But we know better."

"The only way I can get you to do anything is by pointing out what *you* want."

"The future is always here!"

Martin's words pummeled the woman out of her funk to where she had no choice but to get up, dust herself off and go forward. Mona left her with a verbal coach-like pat on the behind. Her last words were, "Now bound over those internal and external hurdles!"

Mona leaned back in her chair after hanging up. She was breathing heavily and was ravenous as if she hadn't eaten for days. Never before had she felt so close to her brother.

*

Martin Romaine told me through his writings to personally seek him out and hire him. He would no doubt be impressed by the determination, preparation, and execution of my plan. I will nourish myself on his written and audio works during the long trip ahead. A personal soundtrack. He will see that Conflict Control Systems under his guidance can rise even higher than its already impressive stature, and will be another feather in his cap. I picture it listed in his bio on the back flap of his next book: Artists, generals, senators, coaches and Conflict Control Systems.

So that's exactly what I do. I pack for a business trip— sensibly, professionally, and prepared for anything. Sharp and nimble. As I carry my luggage outside, even my car seems primed and ready like a thoroughbred waiting at the gates. I pack strategically: the suitcase goes in first with the overnight pack for hotel stays within reach and accessible. Everything fits.

It's time to say goodbye to my base for a while. The feeling must be the same as leaving your hometown to go off to war. You know everything's going to change; as you get bigger it gets smaller. My mailbox, buried within all the other tenant's mailboxes, seems tiny. Up to now, my entire life's worth could fit through that mail slot. I look around the front of the apartment building for a scene that I can take a mental picture of. It just seems important. I have a camera sitting on the front seat, but I don't use it; it wouldn't capture what I need. Nothing seems to suit me, so I turn the engine on, get back out of the car and wait for it. There. That guy I've never spoken to, always wearing the same blue sweat pants and a T-shirt with the word "Cabo" printed on it, steps out of his apartment and walks down the stairs. He picks up the paper, does a little stretch and walks back in. That's what I'll remember. It will have to do. A tiny fragment of my past to contrast with the exciting growth to come.

Misty, my treasure, my love, doesn't know I'm leaving. She's still trying to adjust to the new me. We made love the other night with such clenching thirst, both our hearts out, that I feel it's a good note to leave on. Lying in bed together I was gazing up, through the ceiling and beyond the atmosphere and into outer space with its comets and galaxies, I could sense her softly looking at me, also trying to see through things. She said she was happy that I now had goals. But I detected hesitation. You don't wish someone well but then try and get a read on him. Was Misty fearful that the old me was disappearing, and she along with it? Does she take this "Romaine thing" (her words) seriously? I turned to her and I said, "The gears are now in motion, and Misty, you're one of them. I love you now more than I thought I was capable of. Once you allow yourself to become swept along with me, there are no limits."

Martin says the memories you choose fuel the marathon (or potato sack race, it's your choice) of life. If you feed on sugary crap that satisfies you temporarily, you may sprint at the word "GO!", however the rot and decay is never far behind and soon you will find yourself flat on your face. Make your memories a recipe heavy in protein with the right amount carbohydrates and loaded with Vitamin B12 and you won't quit even as you hit the finish line. I have packed the hearty food from my past (Misty's loving gaze, my blue ribbon from sixth-grade spelling, my employee of the month plaque from two years ago) and downed a liter or two of training. Can I be stopped? I think not. Is there anybody out there that feels as good as I do?

*

Among the completed paintings, one stood like a snow-capped mountain above the rest. It had all the elements Mona wanted (and little wonder as she had her hands in it every step of the way) and not beyond her expectations (as that would have been impossible). "Stunning!" she said to the painter, a dreamy young man—almost a kid with those floppy curls and full lips—who spoke so fast he skipped syllables, whether it was discussing paint tints, asking directions to the store, or discussing his allergies. Mona, through sweet talk, threats, pouting and yelling channeled that energy in the right direction. Their partnership was so close that the young artist who went by the name of Knox fell in love with her, and he let her know it despite she being seventeen years his senior. Mona was flattered and she played along. And that too, Knox's ripe crush on her, was something she re-directed towards the work. He left pots of goldfish at her office, painted pictures of her instead of Martin, made fevered calls in the night pleading for her love, dinner, a trip to the zoo, anything. Mona thought the thin naturally tanned young man got off from being yelled at, so she reserved that for special occasions. He told her at one point that the painting had actual tears mixed in, tears dragged out by her indifference. And some of his blood too.

"Here is the *new* Martin," Mona announced to herself as she looked upon the portrait propped against her office wall. She simply adored that painting. It captivated her, made her consider scrapping all that existed of Romaine Enterprises before the painting's creation and starting from scratch. The ruggedness and confidence portrayed was palpable. Something more powerful than the Earth's measly sun beamed from behind Martin. His sleeves were rolled up, ready for anything. So much motion and power, he could crush giants beneath his feet. She told her smitten painter, "It's like you put what's inside my mind onto the canvass," and his heart soared. He nailed the, "serious grin," as she put it, covering every emotion (except fear) simultaneously. Mona could not deny it; this was a very special day for the Romaines. This painting of her brother represented not just all they had worked for, but opened a new galaxy of possibilities. It flowered before her in Morning Glory splendor and she closed her eyes, so happy, breathing in its perfume.

The runners up, adequate but completely washed out by the winner's blinding greatness, were purchased and sent to Performance Power's branch offices to be hung in reception areas and foyers. Her lovestruck painter was put on payroll and sent out west to set up a new studio. He gave Mona a pair of his sneakers and a shabby baby picture of him that she found sweet, and she kissed him goodbye, forever in the employ of Romaine Enterprises.

Martin had not yet contacted her and he was still unreachable at home. Very unusual. Red spiky balls of worry rolled in Mona's stomach, but she kept it to herself. If the news got out, dozens of their people would flood her office in panic, offering theories and advice. That would do her focus no good. Her brother must have been riding a crest of inspiration like herself, so she swallowed hard and pressed on.

*

Only a few hours out of town and already my voice must be heard. Ideas are boiling out of me. After all the plans have been set, the outline complete and the decisions made, there are a vast number of ways to start and stick to a plan. One: Set aside time each day for accomplishing your goals. Two: Reward yourself for goals accomplished. Three: Associate pleasure with goal-oriented activities. Four: Tell others of your goals before you set out to accomplish them. This is the one I'm about to apply. It places additional pressure from outside sources. If people close to you are aware of the objectives placed upon yourself, then you will be doubly motivated to achieve them. For if you don't, not only have you let yourself down, but the expectations of your loved-ones have been shattered, and they'll be reluctant to take anything you ever say seriously again. The individual lacks the presence of mind to always know what is right for him, so he must seek the help from his community. For instance, let's say I want to lose weight (which I certainly do. When I sit down, my belt buckle pinches my overhanging belly) and I believe that it will be OK just this once if I lapse from my diet and gobble down that box of cookies. Well, we all know that's the first step to failure. It starts with a simple creamy desert and lapses into a steady diet of Fettuccine Alfredo, hot dogs, and chocolate shakes (I like chocolate). Everyone you know will see what a weak-willed miserable wretch you are, unable to keep a promise to yourself or anyone else. So with this in mind, I decide to make a few calls.

I stop at a small patch of civilization just before the highway begins climbing the hills. There's a small diner with a logo of a bespectacled pig sitting down to a plate of pancakes and bacon. Next to the diner is a gas station and convenient store. Only a couple gas pumps in front and they're so dusty that you can't see the numbers on them. Cars speed by, either from the momentum from going downhill, or increasing velocity to climb it. I make my way to the bathroom at the side of the station and get snagged by an out of control blackberry bush. I free myself from its grasp and notice that the serpentine branches go on for a good twenty feet until they blend in with the forest behind the building. The wind from the highway traffic ripples their leaves.

A middle-aged Indian (Asian) with a formidable belly is sitting behind the counter half gazing at a tiny TV beside him. I look down at my own gut, which I'm always conscious of, and don't feel so bad. However when I consider it, he seems to get away with that paunch, it suits him, and my old self-consciousness returns. I pick up a bottle of water and stop at the enormous rack of pornography. Why such an extensive adult library? It's over forty miles from any populated area, and this road is little more than a hazy thoroughfare to the ocean. I flip through a magazine sitting at eye level. The girl-woman on the front cover looks angry, totally out of patience, and daring you to get an erection. I don't even come close, and search for someone a little younger and less disgusted by me. I spot a magazine at the top of the rack sporting a smiling girl with wide-open eyes, but I feel too bashful to reach for it.

There's a pay phone at the side of the building. Both Misty and my boss Billy Emmons are away, so I leave identical messages declaring my mission to personally seek out and hire Martin Romaine. My message to Misty is completely inappropriate in its formality, so I sweeten it up toward the end and get so caught up in sentiment (I miss her that much already) that I trail off into mumbles.

Now there's no turning back. Both my girlfriend and my boss have my intentions on record, magnetized and permanent. Pleased with myself, I climb back into the car. I give it all she's got to make it up that hill with speed, but she doesn't have much.

*

Nobody would ever dream of Martin blaming the landing on that crosswind, the one that suddenly shifted directions just as the plane was buoyed by the buffer wind ten feet over the tarmac. But that's what he did. It was the wind's fault! No pilot could see it coming or react quickly enough to counter it. What was he to do? He had his training, experience flying through choppy winds, and a natural seat-of-the-pants flying ability (at least that's what his instructor told him). The plane bounced along the runway, rising and dipping like a playful dolphin. It was impossible to think straight, as the recovery procedure insists that the pilot act against ingrained "natural responses:" wheel forward when you're diving, pull back when the plane points up into a skyward attitude. "Steer into the skid," they say. "Do not anticipate the gun's recoil as you squeeze the trigger." The wingtip sparked against the ground, shattering the red position light. This bounced the plane back in the air like it knew it wasn't ready to land, and because the airspeed wasn't great enough to keep it aloft, it plopped back on the runway and sprang into the air again. Martin's terror turned into annoyance at the plane's refusal to obey, like a stubborn cowlick no matter how many adhesives are applied. He was ready to smash the plane down, just to keep it put, but it settled itself onto the runway and went into a hobbled roll, drunkenly and without shame making its way down the landing strip. Martin's mind leaped to, "Is anybody watching?" He mussed his hair out of instinct. There are local pilots, he imagined, aghast at this crippled insect hobbling along the tarmac. Coffee in hand, they would walk slowly to the plane to get a closer look of this travesty, hiking up their jeans and ignoring him, immediately tending to the plane like an abused freckled child. They would scratch their heads and look under the wing; stunned that this ham-fisted "man" could treat a beautiful machine like an ape would a Stradivarius.

But there was no tower, and thank God no coffee-drinking men. Weeds had fought up through the cracks in the runway with dandelions making a wish whenever a twin prop took off, which was never. The ragged tongue of a windsock wagged lazily between wind directions. Martin pushed the throttle to a low RPM. The clicking cicadas in the sagging trees made him think the engine was sick. The plane loped off the main strip to a small paved outlet for parking, only two plane capacity. He left it idling, even at the threat of running completely out of fuel and wrecking the engine. The sound of the running motor buoyed Martin because, knowing when he kills it, there will be something altogether new to contend with. The silence.

The cicadas stopped their buzzing after the plane's engine was finally cut, but they quickly remembered that this place was theirs and went back at it. Martin cracked the window a hair, lest one fly into the cockpit and go for his throat. Sweet mossy air crept in. He sat for a few moments, then flipped to the back of his planbook and scribbled down, "Unplanned Adventure."

The landing strip both was and was not privately owned. It had for thirty-nine years been the property of a skeletally sinewy man with an iron skillet jaw whose sense of determined individuality and enterprise was stuff of local legend, so his name was permanently stamped on it. Dick Berg. Severity was his MO. He nearly threatened proposed customers into finding fault with his homemade cleaning supplies, weed killer, or "Men's Typewriter," The latter, he lectured ad nauseum, was designed for a man's unique camber. The traditional model forced a man to arc his wrists down slightly. Very fruity and unnatural. Fine for a woman; but a man requires a position his gender was already accustomed to. Think driving a nail into sheet rock with a long claw hammer. That's a man's way. So he cut a standard typewriter in half, placed the outside edges perpendicular to the table on stands with the keys facing outward. It was bridged together by a sliced-up muffler. The final modification was moving the space bar to the front facing the user to enable him to use continue using his thumbs for that purpose. A monolith of typing, a name he almost used, but the "Men's Typewriter" left little doubt for whom this was intended. That was Dick Berg.

His sales approach was no less forcelful. If you failed to immediately notice the wondrous application of his inventions, he hardly veiled his contempt for you, and raised an eyebrow in suspicion of your masculinity. Not a woman was approached, as Mr. Berg believed that since the men made (or at the very least, should make) the money, the only respectable thing to do was approach the breadwinner. And that challenge made sales inherently more difficult.

The nearly rusted-over sign facing Martin's plane said "Private Property," with several paragraphs beneath it, illegible except the format was reminiscent of a legal treatise. That's because it was. Dick Berg loved quoting the law in regards to his own rights or when a neighborly conflict arose (which was often). For minute property disputes, or if something of value only to him was missing from his land, he posted on the edge of his land overlooking the freeway for all to see, in huge red and blue letters, the names, birthdates, and addresses of the suspected parties along with the complaint in faux legalese. "I know the law," he said.

And he was extra protective of the airstrip. His baby. That thin bullet of land represented freedom to him. At any time he could load up the Piper and steal away for good, where a man can pursue what he pleases when he pleases. But he also knew it would be easy for somebody else to land in the middle of the night and take over the place, rob him of his rights. Thus it was off limits to everybody. Emergency landings were no exception, and a famous motivational speaker would have been no welcomer than anybody else. "You are on private property." "That is an arrestible offense." "I could legally shoot you." Those were his mantras, and they were concrete, except that Dick Berg had passed away fifteen years previous to Martin's unplanned landing.

The airstrip and surrounding land that Dick Berg guarded with constant vigilance and a home schooling of property laws went to no one after he died. And no one wanted it. His presence remained in the shacks he built and the warning signs he painted, ever existing like the swamp gas. Most of the land was canopied in Spanish Moss that had leaped from tree top to tree top, heating up the place like a greenhouse. The soil was not rich and all that thrived was shabby pine.

Martin opened the cockpit door and the humidity slapped him in the face. It was like breathing underwater. Everything outside was thick, with the sun almost gone. He felt the fat-bellied spider of night descend upon the canopy above and peer in, observing the size of his catch. Martin quickly climbed out of the plane and stretched the way he does before a long run on the treadmill, and just as fast he clamored back in, wanting none of the air out there to cling to him. He switched on the electrical system and cockpit dome light and turned to the map. The landmarks made little sense to him, as few of those symbols remained in his memory beyond his pilot's test. Even recalling the last definitive landmark before landing the plane was impossible. The trauma of bouncing down the runway had wiped that out for good.

Flip on the radio and call in for help? Being both out of fuel and lost would give his flying record a big black shit stain. Then there were the headlines: "Martin Romaine, the Can't-Do Kid." And of course Mona. She would never let him out of her sight again.

It was dark and there were too few choices. All that was left for Martin to do was go back to his notebooks and come up with a few inspirational phrases to spur a guy like him out of this situation, metaphorically speaking that is. He wrote down, "Feel Stuck? Lost? Gather your bearings and slash your way out!"

*

"So, Martin," Mona said to the painting leaning against the wall. "You want to know what's next?" She got close to fully engage him. He had everything: the confidence to lead you to a place beyond what others can see or envision, the broad shoulders to carry you, the face so focused, eliminating all doubt.

"Where have you gone, Martin?" she knelt on the floor before him.

She got closer and looked into the eyes, amazed how like her brother's they were. "I could have booked a flight for you. Why did you have to do it yourself? It was only a matter of time before something went wrong. They say don't fly when you're tired. And you were exhausted. After all those shows. All that running around, jumping off the stage, high-fives, meeting those people, signing autographs. Why couldn't you just stick with what you were good at—opening your mouth and speaking to their hearts, taking them to where they belong? I would have done the rest, gladly. And the funny thing is, I'll finally get to now that you're gone."

Mona spent a secluded vigil in her office. She cracked the door, snapped up the delivered meals and memos, and slammed it back shut.

Though not seen, Mona was certainly heard. Her secretary spent the duration of several workdays, from the moment she arrived to the time she went home, with Mona's phone green extension light lit up; dimmed only as she dialed the next number. What really worried her was when she heard Mona's voice from inside her office, either issuing demands or purely conversational, with the green light off. And she overheard her boss speak in that tone reserved only for her brother—with no green light. Could she be using another phone, a secret line she knew nothing about? Mona vacillated between the commanding sergeant when addressing "Martin," and syrupy sentiment when focusing on "Marty."

The secretary, wringing her hands as if to escape handcuffs, held fast. Mona was still the boss. She wrote down messages, sent calls to Mona's voice mail, and took dictation over the phone. The aesthetic and creative affairs of Romaine Enterprises were beyond her experience and training—she stuck to the business end—and the weird requests that Mona made (men's clothing, Martin's size but larger in the shoulders, for example) were the inexplicable creative powers acting at their height, she assumed. When tears were heard from the other room, the bird-faced employee of three years stuck her nose even further to the grindstone. She'd occasionally look up, longing to open that door, go in and wrap her arms around the weeping Mona on the floor, cat-like and pie-eyed.

*

Martin woke up, sticky and thick in the airless cockpit as the buzzing Cicadas outside mockingly reminded him that he was nowhere near home. He left the window open a couple inches but the air was so bloated it needed to be shoved through the crack like a half-ass beach ball. His back stung from sleeping in the cockpit seat and, stretching out, he glanced at the word "slash" written down the night before. He looked to the propeller and imagined himself shirtless hacking through the vines and fleshy jungle leaves. The gleam from his sweaty brow would attract rescue helicopters. He laughed, a twisted knot of ache that had yet to leave the womblike cockpit. Now it had to be done—his back demanded it.

It could have been the mucous-slick ground or his screaming back, or both, because on his first step out of the cockpit he crumpled to the ground. The wet mossy carpet soaked through to his ass and he swore for the first time in at least a year. "SHITDAMNFUCK!" He chained the airplane to the ring drilled into the ground, took his notebook and all forms of identification and began walking.

Everything under Martin was squishy. It made for slow going. He wished for a piece of dry ground, a fallen tree, anything to bounce off of. Leaves, sagging Cups of Gold and wet grass clung to him, also wanting to get away. Dick Berg would have put up a squawk about messing with his property and he would invariably threaten to sue though he believed neither in lawyers nor the law as it now stood. Yes, the man was indeed still alive in the sticky, disagreeable mire that Martin slogged through.

He composed slogans that this situation inspired and filed it all away in his memory bank of topics. It came naturally to him. Great material: the quagmire of life... what to do about it. Sure, it's easy to just sit in it, get acclimated. But you mustn't! Never! This is life! Trudge though it...

But Martin, tired and wet and hungry by now, stopped and shook his head. Trudge through life? What kind of message is that? He mentally crossed it off, but kept the earlier stuff.

He was free associating by now. He pulled out the notepad and dried his hands the best he could on his sweat-dampened shirt, and scribbled down, "If you find yourself without a goal, simply start moving. For when you're still you see all around, but when you move you're looking straight ahead." Martin was very pleased with himself (he even said so out loud, "I'm pleased with myself"). This fueled his march through the swamp, hacking and grabbing and slashing. He stopped and felt a breeze, so he must have been near the end of the hammock and close to a less-densely wooded area, hopefully leaving behind the reeking white stoppers at his feet. The foliage was so think that he had been skirting the edge of the jungle for quite some time. Martin noticed and laughed at the needless effort he had been exerting all the while. He laughed and instinctually pondered a metaphor for lateral movement but shook it off because he was getting hungry.

The plant life thinned considerably outside the tract. A stream down a ways snaked out of the forest and wound through a murky prairie. Beyond that, maybe a mile off, were power lines. He went towards them, footing more assured now that the ground was firmer. A minor triumph that Martin credited to resiliency.

Chapter 4

Bandanas:
The road to personal fulfillment is a long one.
Show everyone that you're in for the long haul
with this tough and practical bandana. Available
in black, red, and teal.

E verything up to this moment has been a preface to my life.
Too bad the preface spans thirty-nine years. This is Chapter
One of the Joe Story.

Martin Romaine's first book, *How To Do It Like the
Successful People Do It*, is my co-pilot. It sits shotgun beside me
as I drive, open to Chapter Two, "Raise Your Standards." See?
I'm already ahead. The title says it all—a commitment to serious
growth. This can range from the minutest details, like what you
eat or what you watch on TV, to the grandest of gestures, like
choosing with whom to share your life. Conversely, there are
things I must no longer tolerate. And God knows there's a lot of
them.

I was stunned to find I had already put the teachings of
this chapter into practice. I'm wearing it. The expensive suit I
would not compromise on. What's a better example of raising
one's standards than buying a new Italian suit one could hardly
afford? It's a symbol—which I have worn six of the seven days
I've owned it—of a heightened lifestyle that I have come to
expect.

I'm traveling southeast on an expansive eight-lane freeway and coming upon a major city. There's a sense of purpose to my driving: fast and smooth. I dodge and weave, overcoming the obstacles the other motorists offer. They vocalize their protests, impotent behind steamed glass, and give symbolic gestures instead of taking decisive action. Applying the raised standard practice to every facet of your life requires constant vigilance. It's a matter of pushing oneself to a newer higher level that shall one day become second nature. And it's scary at first, as in narrowly missing an offending truck by inches or going thirty miles per hour over the absurd speed limit. That's the price you pay for demanding more out of life. Martin said, "If you're scared, you're probably on the right track." And I aim to make myself as scared as possible.

I must drive the fastest. Some kid in an off-gold muscular truck openly challenges my dominion of the road. I speed along, accelerator mashed to the floor, knowing I must beat him. He refuses to look at over at his competition, me, like this is a non-issue. I try to meet his eyes, but all I get is profile. And then I remember my co-pilot. It informs me that this is not my battle, not my mission, and simply a sad display of lack of focus. I let go of the accelerator and the competing truck leaps forward to victory. Hiring Martin Romaine is my mission.

I think of the hotel, actually a modestly priced bare-boned motel—no phone, no cable TV—that I'll be staying in tonight. Is this what I deserve? Does it fit my new criteria? Surroundings of which to accustom myself? Or does it continue to reinforce the low standards I have held throughout my life? These are the questions I must always ask. Like panning for gold. Always. Constant. Relentless.

The sun is smeared behind me low in the horizon. My thoughts are locked into place. I skip the motel and instead get a room that costs twice as much but comes with terrycloth bathrobes.

*

Martin was right; the power lines beyond the prairie did parallel a road. When he reached it, he had to decide which way to go, left or right. It was noontime and the sun gave no indication of east or west, north or south. So he went right, as in the "right way," and began walking. There was a new book somewhere in all of this. Martin tasted it. Then came the metaphors.

"We are all on a road; some are centuries old, others we create."

"Whether the wind is at your back or in your face, it always helps you. The former is to push you along, while the latter cools your journey."

There was musky drinkable heat like back in the jungle, and no amount of speed, no matter how fast his pace, would cut through it. A half-hour of walking and seventeen inspirational sayings later, a car had yet to pass. Martin's body cranked while his mind churned, each massaging the other.

The proverb machine hummed. With his duffel bag slung over his shoulder, notebook in one hand and pen in the other, he didn't slacken his pace to scribble them down. The words hit the paper like bugs against a windshield.

"It takes strength to keep a pace, and a steady pace provides strength."

"We all at a point in our lives fear the constant nagging tick-tock of the clock. A tick reminds us of opportunities not taken; a tock speeds us towards unfulfilled goals. Tick! A second longer you must sit at your unfulfilling job. Tock! Dreams getting stale and out of reach. How do you fight the clock? You don't, you become the clock, measuring the time between one success and another. A metronome pacing the steps necessary for achieving your ideal mate, that dream job, your target weight."

Martin was that clock, hoofing it alongside dogwoods that offered no shade. It was high noon, the sun thick and close. This is what he strove for when flying. Instead of his mind filling in the details of an out of reach landscape twenty thousand feet below, ideas flew from him like sparks. It was being totally lost that did it; not merely being uncertain in an unfamiliar world.

Cluelessness, freedom from familiar grounds, notions about how the world was put together. This was the new muse. And she was singing.

But she didn't put food in his belly. And there hadn't been any for over 24 hours when Mona joined him in his hotel room for the hotel-prepared breakfast of everything and coffee. The staff, out of obligation to his fame, served him portions far surpassing his appetite. In fact, everything offered him was always too much, for to give an important person more than he or she needed was a smarter move than not giving enough. "Please," he said back in the days of futile modesty. "What am I to do with all this?" and demanded smaller, human portions. He could have said it a thousand times, it mattered not. His meals were at least three times the size of what he could put down, and the leftovers sat until they attained a uniform hardness, the eggs, the croissants, the hash browns, the fruit even. Always served with a flower. Weren't at least three quarters of his clients concerned about their weight? Was the food placed before him a reflection of his lifestyle? Yes to both. Despite this, he once again turned dilemma into a scenario that elegantly illustrated his teachings. "We Americans are confronted daily with more than we need. It is in front of us on the TV—succulent and juicy—demanding that we partake. Walk along the streets and there it is, in store windows, so big and plump. Why it would be rude, ungracious and downright un-American of us not to partake and, more importantly, finish it." But Martin showed that never finishing, as in business management, food, or maintaining a romantic relationship, is the cornerstone of success. "Never Finish!" Martin insisted. And that two-word line, drilled into the brains of true believers, helped America lose thousands of pounds of flesh. Want more money? Never finish! Win the heart of your dream girl? Never finish! That plate of Linguini with Alfredo Sauce? Altogether now—Never! Finish!

A passing truck swept away and silenced the hovering bugs. Martin stopped and watched it get smaller down the road. Suddenly there was traffic. He glided his palm over his hair scanning for renegade strands and stood erect, thumb out, way too dignified and upright for a hitchhiker. He had to fight off the new metaphors assembling in his head (metaphors that equated hitchhiking with seeking new opportunities, or better yet, having the courage to take a chance on something that will carry you far beyond your comfort zone).

A glint of sun froze upon a stopped car. It was new and idled calmly. Martin climbed in, said, "Thank you," and they were off. The new bugless silence didn't last. The driver, mustachioed and sweatered in blue, wanted a story. He offered smokes, a drink from a water bottle. Even a nip of something stronger, should the mood suit his passenger. Then to the questions. He asked without asking. And a handsome man with a haircut such as Martin's, who's to blame?

"What's a guy like you doing way out heah?" he driver spoke as if rolling something sweet in his mouth.

"Visiting." Martin looked ahead.

"Meeting somebody?"

"Car broke down." Martin glanced over to the smiling man in blue. "So, where are we going?"

"I'm Steve."

"Martin," Martin said, then gulped, and looked for a sign of recognition.

"Where you going?"

"The next town will be fine."

"That would be Cooperation City." Because of where he had picked up his new traveling companion, Steve went into the story of Dick Berg. He described the old man's legal crusades, the ferocity in which he countered any perceived slight, his off-limits compound, and that "Men's Typewriter" bought by no one. After a night of marinating in insect drones and jungle sweat, Martin found Steve's slow honey voice soothing. The countryside was no longer threatening now that Martin could view it from the safety of a new two-door sedan with leather seats. Nothing could have been finer. He settled in, too tired to be worried about what might have happened as a consequence for trespassing on a resourceful lunatic's land. What would he have done, being confronted by this bark-skinned man behind a couple barrels? Metaphors escaped him, and the thump-thumping bass synchronized with lasers were a thousand miles away.

Martin looked for a pause. "I'm glad he didn't spot me back there. What's his problem? Is he dangerous?"

"He's dead."

Steve's buoyancy left and he stopped smiling. He gravely mulled over Martin's question as if deciding which anecdote could best describe the character of a departed semi-tolerated relative in front of an expecting congregation. Looking at his watch and squinting, he said, "Well, I know folks avoided dealing with him one-on-one, but in a weird way they still liked having him around; if that makes any sense. I'm not sure if you can call it a love-hate thing, either. Perhaps more of an annoyance/amusement thing. Berg was always looking for an angle."

"An angle?"

"What I mean is, he bored into an issue like a tick until he found a confrontation, a contradiction, or something that may impinge on his 'rights.'"

Martin nodded. "I think I see."

"I know," Steve continued, looking at the road, "because I worked with him. Lord," he paused, reluctant to revisit those times. "It was *the* worst; must have taken ten years off my life, God bless it." He then looked to Martin to see if he was paying attention. He was. Then he continued. "As I said, he was big on his rights. Nobody could tell him anything, be it suggestions on what to do about the noise his car's engine was making to plain old advice about planting tomatoes. He took self-sufficiency to the limits. I was forced to deal with him. I'm a city inspector by trade. As an employee of the city, I had to inspect Mr. Dick Berg's property. When I was told about the assignment—I could tell right away when I saw that address on the dossier—I knew I was in for a nightmare, even if it was only over a fence. A *fence*. Berg's one of those people who thinks of their property an extension of their bodies and nobody's gonna tell him what to do with it, city ordinance of no city ordinance. I was sent to go inspect his new fence, make sure it was up to code. Property lines were not crossed. He was very careful about that. But the fence, over 150 feet of it, was eight feet high. Cooperation City's building code says you can't build a fence over six feet high. Well, when I told him about this, he went crazy, even called me Gestapo. He complained of harassment, said I was trespassing, and finally pressed charges against the city. He started a petition and got six people to sign it. Angry letters to the local paper. He put up giant signs on the side of the road his property connects to—about where I picked you up—portraying us as Mafioso. Then he hit the law books; copying and sending off these seventy-page documents filled with legal speak. By the time the court date rolled around, it made a pretty big splash in the town. Folks took sides. Some thought of him as a rugged individualist while others said he was wasting the taxpayer's money with his squabbles. He acted as his own counsel, prepared with volumes of notes, charts, and such and such. Well, the trial lasted maybe twenty-five minutes at best. It was thrown out and he had to lower that fence. It was to be six feet, no higher. Final. But, that was not to be the end. I had to—and honest to the Lord above I wanted no more of that business—I had to go out and check the damn thing to make sure he was compliant with the law. I measured the fence and it came out three inches too high. Six-foot three. He said he thought 'six foot,' meant 'within the six-foot range.' Mr. Berg was playing with me; wanted to see how far I would go. He know I was the kind of man to stick to my guns and make him take off those three inches, so the only reason he did that was to make me look like a bully. He had this smile on his face the whole time. Of course I pressed him, laid down the law, and of course he made a big public stink about it. The tables were turned, and I was viewed as the bureaucrat who wasted the town's taxes hassling an old man about a fence. It became public again, but never went to court, and for a good long time I became known as the "three inch man," or worse, the "three-incher."' Steve laughed a resigned laugh and shook his head.

Martin looked ahead and ran his hand through his hair, doing more damage than good. "I'm confused," he said. "So did people like him or hate him?"

"Yeah," Steve said. He made a grimace bespeaking the agony of taking a parent off life support. The answer, he felt, was to be the final word on a man's life. What did it matter? His audience was just a stranger he had picked up off the side of the road, elusive about his past, out of luck perhaps. Just a guy with stunning hair who needed a ride. And somehow this ride became Dick Berg's eulogy that was now being spoken, not by a wife or a child or even an old Army buddy, but someone he had considered a nemesis. Steve was too good a man not to acknowledge the weight of the responsibility, and chose his words carefully.

"I know," he bleated. "He was a terribly difficult man. But people must have sensed a powerful spirit behind under all that stubbornness, something extraordinary that could drive such determination. They seemed to admire, even envy, the force of his convictions. The ones who admired him the most viewed Dick Berg's tireless willpower as overshadowing his loony crusades. In some way everybody, myself included, fed off that willpower." Steve shook his head, feeling lighter and freer. "Well, if that's what it takes."

*

Under a ceiling so high the booths sat; a honed, sparkling representation of the company they represented, idealized and tarted up for public consumption. Alarming is the rate at which the conference area comes to life, the displays wheeled in, unpacked, unfolded and dazzling within half an hour. Some companies have entire departments devoted to planning these events. If they haven't already recruited recent graduates holding fresh B.A.'s in Event Planning, then the best trained, most attractive and charismatic employee is sent to represent the company.

The taxi, one autograph richer, left Randolph Shuron standing at the front of the hotel, an aptly named nine-story corner building suited to the keynote speaker's stature. The Paragon. On the marquee it said, in too many colors, "Welcome Speakers of Greatness! Featuring Randolph Shuron!" His gaze was yanked down to a thin, big-eyed boy named Todd holding a football. Randolph signed it though his football career didn't extend beyond high school. A wave of voices fell upon him. Bubbling out of the stew was a promoter, a reporter for the local news, several bodybuilder enthusiasts, and some kind of organizer.

He had to keep moving. Walking and talking. He checked in. Questions were answered and hands were shook. A Performance Power representative, a trim woman with a jet-black bob he had met backstage at a few of the shows, clawed her way through the gathered crowd and yanked him away for briefing. Her name, Suzi Stanford, fully accredited "AccomplishMentor," in the Romaine System

The booths now stood on their own power. And with two hours until the opening night Gala Banquet and keynote speech, the exhibitors either went to their rooms to make calls to headquarters or they sat in the hotel bar with loosened ties and something cold in hand, tongues wagging about a restaurant in Muncie, the weather in Flagstaff, or the crap hotel in Philly.

With her star intact, Suzi slid into a booth, exhaled and smiled for the both of them.

"Well, no time like the present to get crackin'." She took a sip of her drink. "Actually, you're doing the speaking, Mr. Shuron, so I guess perhaps you want to brief me."

Randolph shifted in his seat. "Okay, I have it all mapped out. First an anecdote or two, a couple jokey comments about my plane ride or something like that. From there to my struggling beginnings and triumphs with my automobile business, how

Martin's techniques and inspiration pushed me into new realms of possibilities, and I'll summarize the new package."

Ms. Sanford reached out to her drink, but didn't pick it up, as if waiting for something. "Hmm," she said.

"I'm sorry," Randolph said. "Do you want more detail?"

"No, that's not it." She took a sip, and kept her hand on the glass. "I just thought, we'll, you *were* Mr. Universe. Are you going to talk about that?"

Randolph shifted again. His seat behind the booth, like every seat in the world, was too small. "I though I'd try leaving that out this time. You know, a little variation."

"Hmm, I don't know," Suzi dropped the smile. "People recognize you as a former champion body builder. It seems strange that you wouldn't bring that up. I've seen you speak before, and you told some great stories about those days, like how you won a competition with a broken leg."

"I now have other pursuits. And I'm doing quite well at it. My new—"

The lighting in the bar was dim. Suzi leaned forward, still holding her drink against the rich rosewood table. "But your competition stories perfectly reflect Martin's teachings. The analogies are simple to follow as well as gripping to hear. Drawing parallels between such an exciting sport and Martin Romaine's techniques is a powerful formula."

Randolph looked down at his hands then back up at the Romaine representative who had completed her AccomplishMentoring program seven months ago. "Ms. Sanford, I've thought this through and honestly, when you really think about it, bringing up my glories from way back when would actually prove detrimental to what we're trying to teach."

Suzi looked at him flatly.

He continued. "I had accomplished all those sports feats way before Martin even started. It wouldn't take a—"

"Randolph. I hear you, I *really* do. But I'm not certain you realize that even the mere mention of both your names—

Randolph Shuron and Martin Romaine—in the same sentence is a knockout punch of possibility for the audience."

Everyone in the bar was drinking and talking, the show hours away. Randolph was silent. Ms. Sanford looked at him. He let out a long exaggerated breath and shook his head. "Martin had nothing to do with my bodybuilding victories," he said.

"Maybe that's true," Suzi said. "But don't break format now."

They left the bar and toured the convention center. A few stragglers were still setting up. Most booths were unmanned but told the story all on their own. Beyond the company names emblazoned on canvas (back-lit for the more established companies and publications), they had slogans written in cursive, abstractly describing their wares and arousing something elusive but undeniable in the passerby.

"The Mammoths are Born Again!"

"We put the 'Being' in Human Being!"

"Destroy your Limitations!"

"WE are the Performaniacs!"

Randolph was led to the booth where he personally would be signing up people for the Dream Acquisition Package as well as autographing his personal fitness guide using the Romaine Method, titled "The Complete Perfect Finish." It stood at the far end of a twenty-booth tunnel. Despite the dead-end placement, Suzi explained instead of being something you could just pass by, his presence would lure traffic and make *him* a goal to reach. She also told him that companies clamored for spots along the trail leading to him. His was "The Golden Path," she said, and her excitement over his presence once again began to rise. "A major coup!" she shouted, but didn't explain why. She shook his hand again and left him to prepare for the speech.

Randolph went to his room and called Romaine Enterprises headquarters. All they would tell him was Mona wasn't available and Martin was out of town. He then phoned his dealership headquarters. Sales were a bit sluggish, as they always were this time of year. He had put his trust in his staff and felt comfortable in letting them run the ship for a few days without interruption. They wished him well and apologized for nothing exciting to report. He lay back on the bed, curtains still drawn, and mentally went through his speech. The introduction, too much applause, a few witticisms, and into the meat. He tried to keep the pacing steady in his mind, as if he was actually in front of an active audience. The dealership, now in its eleventh year of business, owes much to Romaine. It was Martin that deconstructed Randolph's winning attitude and drive and outlined it perfectly. This was Randolph's method in front of the crowd: To reel them in with anecdotes of seemingly unconquerable challenges; something everybody, if not exactly relate to, could empathize with. A middle-aged man, possibly past his prime, that was looking to take an entire new direction. That's ninety percent of the crowd right there; the ones unfulfilled with the path they have thus far chosen, and frankly terrified to do anything about it. Terrified to take out that huge loan. Terrified to get out of that lifeless relationship. Terrified to change a way of thinking and set out to lose those thirty pounds. Then once he had them, POW! The success stories.

Randolph could help. He wanted to help. And Martin was instrumental in turning the average person's terror into something constructive, a plan of attack. Nothing new or foreign, but a basic idea that's so simple, so within our daily existence, that once it's heard, everyone goes, "Ahhhhhhhh." All within the Dream Acquisition Package, only $699. But you've got to make that step.

The stories of the car dealerships made perfect sense. Nobody is predisposed to building a city-wide chain of new and used car dealerships the way they are to becoming a sports hero. Size is irrelevant. Benching 400 pounds will get you nowhere. The 100-meter dash in record time means nothing. Pluck the average guy off the street, and if he takes a sincere and earnest effort while employing Martin Romaine's techniques, he can become a Randolph Shuron, successful entrepreneur. That's what he had always been trying to get across. Not weightlifting. Who can relate to that? A two-hundred eighty pound, six-foot eight mountain, freak of nature. Fun to watch, but impossible to emulate. If he could lose a hundred pounds and six inches right now, he certainly would.

Randolph wanted his speech to sparkle, to stick to the listeners and glow. This one was supposed to count. He lay on his hotel bed, staring up at the ceiling, and imagined the crowds of people beaming in newfound joy.

As his eyes flirted shut with sleep, Randolph smiled a winner's smile.

*

Martin Romaine was missing. Mona knew it and though she said nothing, a nervous tremor ran through Romaine Enterprises. She attempted to work through the shock that pummeled away at her machine-like, going about her daily routine, arranging visitations with senators and actors and authors, and all the while glossing over everyone's queries and concerns over her brother. The company rumbled with misgivings. It was ready to crack, and the news would soon reach everyone. Mona decided to hold a board meeting.

Everything was prepared. The outline had been laid out. Preliminary sketches were drawn. There was even a title for the next venture: "Mountain, Out Of My Way!" And at the top of the list was the painting. A painting by a young man she had told secrets to, mostly out of fear, who absorbed everything Mona wanted for her brother. Nobody, save Mona and the painter himself (he had signed a confidentiality waiver) was aware there even was a new project in the works. Mona strode through the headquarters' halls carrying the portrait wrapped in a twin-size bed sheet.

Romaine Enterprises Board of Directors, all nine of them, waited in the executive boardroom. They knew no more than anyone else on payroll, down to the lowliest mailroom clerk, about Martin's status.

Mona entered the boardroom followed by two male assistants carrying briefcases. Setting the covered painting on a stand, Mona said hi to slacken the mood. A young executive answered, "How's it going?" but was stared down by the others. Mona took her seat at the head of the solid monolithic slab of a conference table, and the suited assistants stood at rigid attention on either side of the door behind her as if thwarting assassination attempts. The staff broke into a competed vie for Mona's attention. They tried to force her sympathy by relating the pressure placed upon them due to Martin's MIA status. Simple representatives acting on behalf of their constituents.

"I've got the grand opening of a new Crowning Achievement center in Baltimore. They expect Martin to attend."

"The blah blah blah airplane manufacturing company wants a personal appearance."

"We need his approval on a new TV ad for his live video."

The desperation in the room made the words crawl and slither like an orgy of mice. Mona smiled them to silence. She stood and backed away from the table, closer to her suited assistants, and spoke with stilted formality.

"I want to thank you all for coming here. However I wish it could have been under better circumstances. Now why don't we all take a deep breath?" She paused a moment, and only the most sycophantic members made the effort along with her. "I understand all of your concerns. Really. But I'd like to give you something to think about. Think of this: Think of how concerned you are, and then think of how concerned Martin's sister is. Do you think for a second that your worries, your concerns, amount to a fraction of mine? I grew up with and spent nearly every day of my adult life alongside Martin Romaine. This is the longest period of time I've gone without speaking with him. That's a fact."

Someone broke in, "But—," and Mona silenced it immediately. "Now I want you to realize that I am holding nothing from you concerning Martin's whereabouts. I'm hoping, and I know that all of you are as well, that he is OK wherever he may be." Mona paused and looked around the room. "I want you now to listen very carefully to what I am about to say. You all want something from me today, just like we've expected something out of Martin all this time. Listen closely, and I will tell you what I have to offer. What I have to offer is this—"

Mona pulled the sheet from the portrait and stood back. The seriousness in her face melted as she gazed adoringly upon the painting. Marty stood firm and ready, stern yet understanding. He refused to look anyone in the eye, as his gaze was cast to the seas of nobler aspirations. The board saw Marty, a giant with ambitions beyond measure but also possessing a disarming familiarity. No one spoke.

The powers behind Romaine Enterprises sat at the long reflective ebony table. Marty was here. Everything would be fine.

"Ladies and gentlemen," Mona gathered herself. "I want you to meet Marty."

The board of directors nodded. They looked down to their notes, the outlines and details of their issues, their ongoing travails brought to a boil since the news of Martin's disappearance, and went back to Mona.

Mona continued. "This will be the new face of Romaine Enterprises. It will make or break us. We mustn't sit back and rest on our accomplishments, as that would go against the very teachings of the founder of this organization, Martin Romaine. 'He who is not satisfied will inevitably grow.' Martin was never satisfied. That's what kept this company strong. Marty is Martin Romaine's logical conclusion. Before I answer any questions, I want you all to take a minute and ponder Marty and what he will mean to Romaine Enterprises."

Mona left the boardroom with its members sitting silently before the painting of Marty, rugged and ready. She strolled throughout the building with the old oversized portraits of her brother, copies of *The Colossal Power Rules All* lying on coffee tables in reception areas, copper plaques etched with quotes hung on nearly every wall. "See yourself as if you were another person viewing the epic story of your life... is it a page turner?" The building—three stories of Martin Romaine. Upon her passing, employees snapped to attention. They greeted her, interjected superficial progress reports of their projects, and attempted small talk. No mention of Martin. Nothing was asked. No one had the nerve. Mona walked on, not slowing her pace as she parried the questions.

She moved from department to department, and eventually stopped at the wide vaulting foyer. The windows at the front went all the way up to the ceiling, and the doors, spanning half the size of the walls, were also made of glass. Despite their size, they were easy to handle, something her brother was extremely proud of. Enormous yet wieldy.

Martin dove unhesitantly into several mundane aspects of the business. He spent nearly a month overseeing the design and construction of the entryway doors, grabbing employees of all sizes to test the universal ease of opening and shutting them. "So, what do you think?" he demanded. Performance Power would remain the undisputed leader of human potential even if its front doors were ugly and cumbersome, but it was another one of his babies that had to be perfect. Just like the layout and assignments of the company's parking spaces he insisted on overseeing. Just like the White Elephant Christmas party a few years back he had to organize.

Mona stood in the middle of the foyer looking at the glass doors which turned out to be very difficult to clean (resulting in another Martin project), and shook her head. It was still early in the morning and the only other person there was the receptionist, half hidden behind a teak desk that was way too large for simply answering phones. She remained still, shooting furtive glances at her boss. Mona's back was to her. After a few minutes, the receptionist spoke up.

"Ms. Romaine. Are you waiting for someone?"

Mona spun around, "What?"

The woman shrank behind the huge desk but its size was lateral, the entire top half of her body still in plain view. She wore green, and this was her first time initiating conversation with Mona. Before it was simply, "Yes," or "No problem," or "I spent my vacation in Muncie Indiana." She braced herself and said, "I don't have you written down for any appointments, in case you're waiting for someone."

"Oh," Mona said.

"If anybody's expected, Ms. Romaine, I can go ahead and send them to your office."

Mona turned back around and faced the oversized doors. "There's no one. Thanks."

Growing slightly more comfortable, the receptionist faked a stretch. She remained behind the desk, protected. Mona folded her arms as if resigned to wait for hours. The phone rang a few times, and the receptionist quickly forwarded the calls. Nobody entered the foyer. Dead, like a holiday. The woman in green behind the desk spoke up again.

"Any news from Martin?" she said.

Mona didn't turn around. "What?" she said.

Beams of heat, concentrated and certain, struck the receptionist. "Uh, I was just asking," her words spilling out as Mona turned around, "about Martin?"

The words hung there lifeless. Mona looked at her blankly, mirroring the deadness in the air. But just for a moment. She walked to the desk. The receptionist didn't know whether to stand or not, and remained seated.

"What's your name," Mona asked.

"Shirley."

"Shirley. Actually, we are not going to call him Martin anymore. From now on, it's Marty," Mona said and smiled.

"Yes, Ms. Romaine."

Mona turned from Shirley the receptionist and went back to the towering easy-opening glass doors that Martin has spent so much company time on. She looked for a few seconds and turned to Shirley. "Hey, Shirley."

"Yes, ma'am?"

"Tell me. What do you think of these God-awful glass doors?"

Chapter 5

Tour Jacket:

We at Performance Power are thrilled to bring you the newest and most exciting piece in our wardrobe history— the limited edition collector's Tour Jacket! Join the Martin Romaine team as he speaks to the nation and beyond in this silky satin jacket with handcrafted stitching. On the front left pocket is the title of his latest book, "The Colossal Power Rules All," and listed on back is Martin Romaine's extensive tour schedule. This one is not to be missed; there's no telling how long this extraordinary garment will stay in stock!

Just before I left, Misty and I agreed that we would take active steps to improve our lives. And to show that we are completely on the same page on this, we blurted out instantaneously and without prompting, "GET INTO SHAPE!" It just makes sense to start there. The body is a vessel, and the finest wine will taste sour if drunk from a filthy dog dish. Actually, that's a Romaine quote from the second chapter of his first book, *How To Do It Like the Successful People Do It*. Our bodies that we have neglected for so long. Muscles hanging from our bones like fresh meat on a tree.

We sat at the kitchen table after dinner and drew up a workout routine that we could both be involved in and benefit from. It was agreed what was to take priority: Losing weight. Our plan is to start with low-impact exercise that focuses on the cardiovascular system. Raising the heart rate for the allotted time before the actual workout is the best for toning, which Misty and I want. Doing those things out of order means bulking up. Not for us, thank you.

I mean to get a great deal done in the few weeks that I have off. Of course there's Martin. He's the umbrella for my vacation goals. But personally, for me, the key word here is "change." And for it to be change, it must be noticeable. Noticeable to the people at work. Noticeable to Misty, and noticeable to myself. Martin said that deciding specifically what you want to change can be the toughest part, the biggest step of the journey. But for me, that's easy. I want to change everything! Mind and body and spirit and everything that comes between. And all that blossoms from raising your standards; something I've already done. I spend three times the amount I had planned on for the motel I'm staying in tonight. The television is bigger, there's a coffee machine in the room, and let's not forget the terrycloth bathrobes. My elevated living situation reflects my high expectations for myself.

Taking the "Vessel" example from Chapter Two, I begin with the body. With my workout plan as a guide, I crank out sit-ups on the floor.

Fifteen sweaty crunches and piranhas are gnawing at my guts. I had forgotten to stretch beforehand. I lay on the floor waiting for the pain to ebb. It smells so clean down here, as if the carpet was freshly vacuumed. A lemony scent. I wonder how many sit-ups Martin can do. Why doesn't he have a specific workout plan written out in his book? There's no mention, no example, of a sensible beginner's routine, just a footnote mentioning Randolph Shuron's fitness book and video for $49.95. I crank out ten more and my midsection burns like I was struck with a flaming tree trunk.

On the column beside "sit-ups" in my workout booklet I write "25." The number to beat. I decide to check in on Misty's progress.

After four rings, Misty answers the phone. She is so sweet, and I haven't even been away for a day. She's doesn't attempt to rush through the talk to get back to the movie on TV. I tell her of the more-expensive motel I'm staying in, and explain the decision to her and it's importance in the long run. Then we talk about exercise.

"It's Friday," she says, sounding tired.

"But didn't we agree on a plan?" I say.

"Yes. To exercise together."

"But I'm going to be gone for a couple weeks. How are we going to do that?"

"But we said—"

"Just because we're not physically together right now, it doesn't mean we're not together in goal."

"But it's Friday," she says.

And the conversation goes on like that, circling around the block. It would be easier if we were together right now, one hand washing the other. A kick in the pants. Poking and prodding. I tell her to tell me that I must exercise at least four times a week while away, and I made her ask me to tell her the same. That way, it can become a cycle of motivation, or an "Impulse Fractal," as Martin calls it. This is advanced stuff. Actuation that feeds upon its product.

I feel like I'm beginning to lose out to the television as Mona mumbles "uh-huh" in agreement with whatever I say. It is Friday, so I let it go. I make a last grab for her attention. We share words of love, and oaths to exercise tomorrow.

Only twenty-five sit-ups and already I feel my brain kickstart to life. Sitting there, I realize that the motel room can be converted into an improvised gymnasium. Any motel room. Martin's right again. Only a little imagination is required to accommodate a physical exercise, be it arms, legs, or back— wherever you may find yourself. I flop back onto the lemon-scented floor and hit the pushups. Since it's been high school and four presidents ago that I've attempted this exercise, I manage only six. I move to dips between a couple chairs. Good for the shoulders and lats. Within half an hour, I've got a routine for each major muscle group established. I copy it down in my Romaine "EncourageMental-Well Being Calendar" listed by sets and reps. I then go for a run.

I have never tasted blood before, and I'm certain what I taste in the back of my throat five blocks from the hotel, like a sparkler was shoved down there, is just that. My blood. I thud on for a couple more blocks; my feet slapping the asphalt like wet towels. The end of the next block is now my goal. My head empties, becoming a hot spent shotgun shell. Everything drains into my heart and my legs. I stop and vomit, too weak to fight it. Hashbrowns and orange juice splash onto the street. I try to make it end, or simply move out of the vision of passing cars, but I'm captive to my pain. It's got me shackled, forcing me to keep company with the results of my arrogance. Every vehicle, cars and trucks, they all see me. Some even slow down to watch, ironically, with revolt on their faces.

I'm unable to move from the beige puddle at (and on) my feet. It forms into a face, saying, "This is what you get, Joe. You thought you could defeat me," then laughs and mimics me throwing up. I gasp and shake, my throat a white flame. I take a step and almost collapse under my weight. Got to get away. My legs belong to someone else. I'm shivering with panic, like when you wake in the middle of the night with your arm asleep, dead of all feeling. I stagger a few feet from the puke puddle, and massage my legs in the hope that I can get blood moving and reform some connection.

I remain there, a bald guy in sweatpants, paunchy, next to his own vomit for the world to see. All is revealed, and there's nothing I can do about it. The passing cars continue to stare, but no longer do they see a guy getting sick on the side of the road. They just see me, and that's worse. Somebody screams, "Get a car, tubby!" My throat throbs to the beat of my heart. I cannot swallow.

Back at the hotel, I open the Romaine planner and write down the distance I ran. I guess it to be three quarters of a mile.

But when I go out later and measure it from my car's odometer, it's closer to one-quarter.

*

Mona returned and booted everyone out of the conference room. They shuffled out quickly, slipping in their wingtips and heels clamoring over each other in congratulations. "Great idea, Mona!" "Very exciting!" "Marty looks good! Is he taller than Martin?" She smiled and swept them along.

"Thank you, gentlemen. You can see that I'm far from done. Much work to do. I'll keep you abreast of the developments. And please—Marty doesn't leave the room."

And so the search began. She held private Marty tryouts and there were plenty of applicants: a kid just out of college with a B.A. in psychology, a former poker champion, some guy who did "special ops" for the Marines but wouldn't elaborate further, a retired Senator, a German professional golfer, a completely hairless cop, a few people wanting to make career changes, quite a few thespians, and a female chiropractor. They were given a single line by Thomas Carlyle to recite: "The greatest of faults, I should say, is to be conscious of none." But when *he* loped in she knew she had found her man. Anybody would do, she initially thought, but this guy was lean—real lean—and so hungry he was almost past caring. And that made Mona want him, instantly. He plopped down before her, dragged a hand through Martin-like hair, and said, "How about instead of introducing myself, you just call me Marty." That easy.

Mona spent half her working day in her office on the other side of the building two floors down, and the other in the conference room with her Marty. She went over the entire history of Martin Romaine as only she could remember it: his early accomplishments: Young Entrepreneurs of Ohio (where he came up with an idea of creating a mall skyscraper, 40 stories high), Regional Spelling Bee Champion, and for his sixth grade "career day," instead of visiting his father's barbershop, he consolidated all the kids that do yard work into one agency and made himself a tidy commission. Mona skipped the tales of Martin crashing his car when writing down an idea, or when he got lost driving to a graduation where he was the keynote speaker, off by 700 miles. She also wisely omitted Martin's famous forgetfulness: standing up the Vice President of the United States at a Houston restaurant. She relocated his Midwestern gap-toothed earnestness and charm a thousand miles west, and south some for a touch of down-home pragmatism, which the new gaunt Marty already had in spades, along with a strong survivalist streak. The nature of her career had made Mona so forward-thinking for so long that this trip down memory lane was a shock, and for the first time flew directly in the face of Martin's primary teachings: "Don't look back unless you want to go there," he always said. Though her brother's idiosyncrasies were withheld from Marty, they never had the opportunity to heap themselves upon her, higher and higher, as recalling them did now. Just a few: Talking and smiling at the same time. Over-trimming his eyebrows. Calling everyone "guy." Company fun runs. This however strengthened her resolve in getting Marty *just right*, and she wondered how Performance Power ever managed with Martin Romaine at the helm.

"Marty's presence has to be felt throughout the halls and offices of Romaine Enterprises headquarters before he can be felt in the hearts and minds of men and women throughout the country," Mona wrote in a memo, along with an 8x10 glossy of the Marty painting, to the employees. This edict prefaced the new western theme that was adopted and put into effect by a team of graphic designers and marketers. They were sent throughout the land to collect any item referencing to the old west (be it cowboy or Indian), the trucking industry, or the towering heights of the Rockies. Though Martin's upbringing was two time zones removed from Mona's new target audience, the headquarters were even further, and shipping the fenceposts from an actual corral in Arizona or a stuffed buffalo from Wyoming all the way to Massachusetts ate into the startup funds for a proposed "Power

Retreat" in Cape Cod. She assigned the publicity department the task of putting together a Marty portfolio (based on the spirit of the painting) to send out to their high profile clients. The opening lines of the introductory page, just as you open the Performance Power packet, reads, "Forget everything you think you know about Performance Power." And to reinforce it were log-letter fonts in the headings. "We're rolling up our sleeves here, getting down to business, and quite simply, you will not believe your eyes!" Flip the page, boom, there's the lean new Marty with a twinkle of the mischievous Martin in his eye. Then a roadside diner menu, where instead of biscuits and gravy and BLT's, are the table of contents. A crumpled United States map with burnt edges, silver sheriff badges marking regional branches.

Nobody was allowed to lay eyes upon Marty in training or enter the conference room where he resided. Meetings were set up and executed through conference calls. Mona's enthusiasm was infectious and she was back in charge. A more informal dress code was put into effect, then enforced. Absolutely no neckties allowed.

*

Interstate driving requires little concentration, a straight shot of paved smoothness, and I never touch the brakes or move the steering wheel more than two degrees in either direction. It's a good thing; my new workout has me aching with soreness and tighter than a clam. It took me several minutes just to climb in the car this morning. Bending my torso was out of the question with my hamstrings in quadruple knots. I climbed into the passenger seat like a pregnant woman with something new and living inside me protesting my dominion. My arms, unable to lift them for even a second (you should have seen me put on my pants), are resting on my knees, palms up, as I steer. The only way I can move the dead appendages is by jerking my body and hoping the momentum swings them close to the desired object. Freeway driving is all I'm capable of right now.

The rain starts and becomes horizontal, slapping the car and trying to bust it's way in. Like tracing that cartoon turtle in the papers, I follow the lights of the cars in front of me. There's a Romaine tape in the stereo but I'm hardly paying attention, just latching onto snippets and names that pop up. He is discussing the trials that Ghandi went through in his own lifetime and compares it to the father of four, trying to climb his way out of debt. In debt is one thing that Joe Median is not, so my mind drifts, carried along by the assuredness of Martin's voice. It's nice to have a co-pilot like this. Even if he has never experienced what I have or been in a human resource position, his principles are expansive enough to include all trades, all walks of life. The only doubt that enters his field of vision is the straw man used to illustrate a point, which is summarily chopped down and burned.

On the side of the road is a car with its emergency lights on. As I whip by a woman gets out. I immediately pull over to the side. Maybe it's Martin's ironclad voice that prompted it, but I like to think it was me. No hesitation. I like that. I have to back the car up some two hundred yards to reach her. The woman stands there, hand shielding her eyes, looking at me. She's soaked.

The woman's name is Sherry. There are two kids in the car, I can't tell their ages or genders from the rain-smeared windows. The car has a flat on the driver's side. I hop out and offer, almost demand, to fix it for her. I tell her I'm as soaked as she is by now, so the least she can do is make it worthwhile.

We have to move several suitcases and a couple boxes out of the trunk to get to the spare tire and jack. The kids in back twist around to take a look at me. One is a little blond girl of five or so. She smiles when I say hi. She has an older brother. Fourteen or fifteen. He sits there awkwardly not knowing what to do. The man of the car. Sherry yells to him from outside, "GET OUT AND HELP!"

Quickly I transfer the luggage from the trunk to the front passenger seat and the back where the boy, James, was sitting. He follows me, hands in pockets, while his mother spends more time harping on him to help than assisting me.

Cars whiz by, spraying darts of dirty water at me while I hunker down to work. James is ordered to help. He follows me around but won't look me in the eye. Sherry tells him to get his hands out of his pockets.

"I'm all right," I say, working the jack.

James spins from me but his mother cuts him off. She hisses something at him I can't hear.

"But he said—" James says.

"I don't care. I'm not going to have this nice man get soaked here all alone while you goof off," Sherry blocks his path.

"But—"

"Turn around!"

The kid looks at me. I have him hold the hubcap and lugnuts.

The car is sitting on a mild slope that dips suddenly into what looks like a bog fifteen feet off the road. I can't find the notch in the underbelly of the car where the tire jack snaps into. Sudden blasts of water, wind and dust from passing vehicles shoots under the vehicle and whips back at me. James is silent while he holds the hubcap like a bowl.

I wrench the jack into place and begin cranking. It's one big fight. The slope of the ground has to be compensated for, and my useless spaghetti arms are screaming. James is staring. So is the little girl. She's still in the car, peering out the window, about a foot from me. She smiles. It's too late to have her get out; the shift in weight would screw up everything. I have to take control.

"Honey," I say to her. "Will you promise not to move until I say so?"

She nods and keeps watching. A family is before me, dependant upon my brief mechanical skills. I imagine that I am the father; the person delegated to these tasks through aeons of civilization. This must be some kind of test.

The bolts are loosened but continue to hold the tire. The cranking gets easier. An eighteen wheeler booms by. I brace myself and will the car to stay put. It sways from the gust. Or maybe it's just me. I keep cranking. The car body lifts off the pavement.

"When are you going to take the nuts off?" James says.

This is murder on my arms. I groan to him, "I need to get—"

It slips, the jack shoots under the car like an escaped trout and the car flops to the ground. I consider catching it. It crunches down upon the flat tire, screaming metal on metal. I find myself lying on my back in the middle of the highway, having bound ten feet in a single leap. Cars are coming. My body doesn't work; I cannot stand, so I slither to safety. I reach Sherry's feet at the side of the road. The tire is still attached, now sitting on a very bent axle, and there's wailing coming from inside the slumped vehicle. The little girl is pounding her palms on the window, smearing the steamed glass. Her eyes blaze in pleading panic though all she has to do to escape is open the door. She's calling for mommy. James stands defensively, looking back and forth from the car to his mother, confused that none of this is his fault.

Sherry yells, "Oh my God!" and darts to the car to save her daughter. She clumsily opens the door and gathers the crying girl into her arms. Then she whips around and comes at me.

I'm on my back like a flipped-over turtle. I slip and shimmy on the slick pavement as I get to me feet. I slip some more; fearing Sherry won't stop when she reaches me. But she does, two inches from my face.

"WHAT THE FUCK WERE YOU DOING?"

"I was just—it was slippery."

"No, not that," she screams; her arms latched around the girl sobbing now out of momentum rather than terror. "Her!" and points her nose at the child hyperventilating before the next volley of tears. "Did you know she was in the car?"

Time stops. I now have two options: 1. Tell the truth. 2. Lie. Not too long ago for me, there wouldn't even be a decision, actually, yes there would be; the decision dictating, "Get out of this situation the fastest and easiest way you can." I could now say, "No, I didn't know the girl was in the car," and that would be the end of it. But such forces no longer govern me. I tell the truth. "Yes, I knew."

An enormous sense of equilibrium and synthesis envelops me, despite my aching muscles and tendons and despite the rain shooting sideways into my neck like wasps. I have unwittingly reached what Romaine calls, "The Brain Stage." I kinda skipped ahead to that part of the book one day when I was bored with the section I had been reading, the "Planning Stage." I didn't get far into it, but I think I have a good idea what it's about. It's about taking the path of greatest resistance, that way your willpower comes away lean and muscular.

"YOU KNEW SHE WAS IN THE CAR?" Sherry wallops me back into the world.

"Yes," I say.

"That's it?"

"I knew she was in there."

"What's your fucking problem?" She screams, and the girl begins crying again after hearing the f-word.

"Don't say that, mommy!"

I smile at the kid to get her to stop, and Sherry notices. "You're the last one who should be acting so damn casual right now," she says.

I can't help it; I am so pleased with the decision I have just made. Sticking to the plan despite the consequences. I also understand—for that moment I was under the car—that *I* was in charge. Why can't I still be? This inflates me with resolve. I patiently tell Sherry everything, the reasoning behind my actions. In my best judgement, felt the girl to be safe. The accident was an act of God, I say. The child is safe. I did them a favor and it didn't work as planned. Simple. We can take it from there.

"If you act like you know what you're talking about, most people will assume you really do. Then you will too." Thanks, Martin. The blood leaves Sherry's eyes and her daughter manages a smile when I ask her name. Noelle. James loses that

very different smile, a smile of watching someone else get the blame, as I herd them to the side of the road and safety.

This has been my quickest, most successful, conflict resolution yet. It takes longer for people at work to agree upon a brand of coffee than this.

Since I am somewhat responsible for their predicament, I accept falling short (I did my best with the resources at hand) of the task, I am now the warden of these three people. I begin unpacking their car. Sherry asks me what I'm doing and I tell her that they're coming with me.

"I can't leave you out here," I put my hands on her shoulders and look her in the eye. "There's room in my car. I'll take care of everything."

Sherry melts as much as you would expect a woman and her children in the rain with a bent axle to melt. "OK. Nobody was hurt. It was an accident," she says as if final words before drifting off to sleep. "Let's move on." We get the luggage packed into my car and plunge into the gray mists of the highway.

I'm still not certain what Sherry's ex-husband does for a living. What's a Venture Catalyst?

"Capitalist?" I ask.

"No, catalyst," she says.

I don't bother to have her explain, because I don't think she even knows.

They had split three years ago. She feels the children were suffering for it, so they picked up to be close to their father. Sherry leans in and whispers so the kids in back can't hear. "I'm concerned about James. When boys learn to be men all on their own they wind up a mess."

Rain pelts the window like war. We stop at a gas station so Sherry can call in a tow truck. The next town that has both a mechanic and a motel is forty miles away. I insist that I take care of it, arrange the tow truck, the mechanic, and the motel rooms. The only ones on the road are the ones that have to be, the long-haul truckers. There's nothing to prove by trudging through this wet mess and it's getting dark.

Sherry looks out her window and the kids quiet down, soon asleep and magically transported from all this. Father is probably on his boat floating in the bay, entertaining guests with Brie cheese and wine, business and pleasure indistinguishable. I see him as my boss, Mr. Emmons. Impenetrable and compulsively likeable.

James is looking at me through the rear-view mirror, and when he notices me noticing him he snaps his eyes back shut. He was the man of the house before I came along. I keep looking back but he doesn't open them.

The silence goes on a little too long for comfort, so I go into a pep talk and try some Romaine.

"Remember," I say. "These trials are just that. Pop quizzes for the really big tests later on in life."

Sherry looks over at me and says nothing.

"I know you must be upset, and being upset isn't necessarily bad. It's the byproduct of being set back from your goal. Up-Set... Set-Back. However, remember, it can also lead you astray if you do not keep it in check."

From the back seat, Noelle says, "Mommy, what is that man saying?"

But Sherry keeps listening.

"I too have had setbacks on this short trip of mine," I continue. "Actually, nothing but setbacks. But that's done nothing but help me re-focus on my mission."

"What is your mission?" Sherry says. "Where are you going in such horrible weather?"

"Oh, that doesn't matter, really. It's business," I say. "What's important is that I stick to my plan and follow the correct course of action that will lead me to my goal. That's important to keep in mind. For all of you." I turn to the kids. "Now here's a good exercise. Let's go around and say out loud a goal that we have."

Everyone's a bit dazed. Nobody talks. I initiate. "James. Tell me a goal."

"I don't know," he says and looks out the window.

"I'll give you a few moments to think of one," I say.

"I know what I want," Noelle breaks in. "I want a play oven."

"Okay, that's a start," I say. "But don't you want more?"

She looks at me and quietly says, "Yes."

"It doesn't sound like you really mean it."

"Well, it's not nice to be greedy and want too much."

"Noelle. There's a difference between being greedy and wanting things out of life. Everybody deserves things. They are just afraid of taking them, as if to desire them is bad. Now tell me what else you would like."

Noelle holds her stuffed rabbit to her chin and thinks. "I would like a new bike, and one of those—"

"You just want things?" I say.

"What?"

"You just listed stuff. You just want stuff?"

"Yes. I want toys and things."

"That's it? Just things?"

"What else is there?"

The rain keeps up, rhythmic and unrelenting. I look hard into the rear-view window at this darling little girl clutching her stuffed rabbit, the girl who wants stuff.

"Tell me what you want for yourself," I say.

"I told you. I want a—"

"No, not things"

"Uh, Mr. Median," Sherry attempts to interrupt.

I go on. "I'm talking about personal things, Noelle, not toys. Toys will not help you become a better person, or become smarter or nobler. Tell me what you want that will make you into the person you would like to become."

"I want to ride horses," Noelle says and smiles.

"No! That's not it either. Not what you want to become. What—"

"What are you doing?" Sherry shoots at me. "She's a little girl."

"She'll benefit from this," I say. "It will help. Now Noelle, tell me what you would like to fix about yourself."

"Okay. I would like to have longer hair, if mom will ever let me. I also want some more clothes."

"That's not what I mean at all."

"What, then?"

"Just listen—"

"Mr. Median!" Sherry says louder.

I speak over her. "Now listen, will you? What will make you a better person? Not things. Not physical attributes. Those will not help your feeling of self worth, or make you actualized."

"I don't get it," she begins softly crying.

Now both Sherry and her brother are on me. I wave them off like flies. I need to get this out of Noelle, both for her and myself. "STOP THINKING JUST ABOUT THINGS. THINK WHAT WOULD MAKE YOU, NOELLE, HAPPY. WHAT WOULD MAKE YOU THE BEST PERSON YOU COULD BE?"

Noelle is now sobbing, but she does answer my question. "I want mommy and daddy to be married again!" Then she's gone in tears.

"Oh, shit!" Sherry says, and swats me hard in the chest with the back of her hand. James yells, "Shithead," and kicks the back of my seat. My neck whiplashes, but I keep control of the car.

"What's your Goddamn problem?" Sherry screams at me. I feel the heat from her breath.

*

Bodybuilding metaphors came to Randolph a lot easier than car dealership metaphors did. When he looked out into the audience during his speech, he saw them begin to glaze over during what he thought to be a poignant story of successfully importing mid-priced Japanese automobiles and still being able to offer a lower price than his local competitors. Unconsciously, he lapsed back into a glorious tale of his first competition, glistening and out-posing all others, leaving the runner up in tears. Actually made him cry. Randolph was probably the most widely celebrated bodybuilder in the history of the sport. Children passed over fantasies of hitting grand slams or diving for the Hail Mary in favor of sleek, perfect trapezium muscles. There was something about the building and sculpting and perfecting of the body, and especially his prowess at displaying it, that stood him apart; insides that held up the stuff on the outside so damn well. A chest-thumping display of power through and through.

Suzi hounded Randolph not to break format, stick to the half-hour the glory days of Mr. Olympia, and he rebelled the only way he could, onstage. He would then gleefully trot off the stage and feign an apology, smirking at her toe tapping frustration. Daily he tried to contact Martin and discuss it with him. "Martin's away on vacation," they told him.

Was this the kind of treatment Randolph Shuron deserved? Hadn't he just gained his one-hundredth employee? All answerable to him. And him to no one. It was that way before, as a personal trainer. The boss. Even with his friends and family, he held court. His size and status warranted it. But now there was this Suzi woman, in her Cleopatra haircut and skirt suits, probably with nothing more than a BA in business administration (a BA of BA) under her belt, pecking away at his patience. "Randolph, you need to sign these glossies before we get to Boise!" Old shots of him posing in his Speedo's that he didn't remember taking. "Hey Randy!" (*nobody* called him Randy) "We need to talk about the time you spent on that anecdote about opening your first dealership."

And Martin, that prettyboy, for whom anything outside of blabbering for hours is a giant chore. And Mona, so busy she's unable to give anyone more than a fraction of her attention. He could just leave, go back to his business and his family, both proven winners, but there was something within Randolph's makeup, his wiring, that would not allow him to give up or quit. Everything he ever undertook he finished, if not completely dominated. Was this why Martin asked him to join these tours and little by little give him more stake in the company? Was Randolph a living example of Martin's teaching, even before Martin ever thought of them? Was there something in Martin's books or tapes or whatever that Randolph had overlooked? Was this as far as he could go? Randolph further immersed himself in the Romaine system for answers.

He re-cracked the Romaine books—the first time since being laid up in the hospital after dropping barbells on both feet. His wife brought the books to him, praying for his sake that he could soak up some of that bouncy Romaine energy as he sat depressed and immobile. Those chapters had done for him only what competition could do way back when—get his blood up and go go go, with everything outside the task at hand falling away. Even if there wasn't a goal, something clearly defined to seek, it put Randolph's mind in a state of constant alert. Fight-or-flight without the flight. After leaving the hospital, he prominently displayed *How To Do It Like the Successful People Do It* throughout his modest dealership. He gave copies of it as presents. Folks that purchased a car with all the added features (leather upholstery being one) received a copy. Always at his side, at the ready to provide that inspirational nourishment everyone needs now and then. He called it his, "coffee and steak all rolled into one." And when that old sportsman fury would spill out onto his employees with halftime-like screamed sermons, their hair blowing back from the storm of his voice, that book would catch the corner of his eye; a gentle hand resting upon his shoulder, knowing he had it in him to do it another way. The employees at the receiving end of those assaults gave that book a silent thank you.

Randolph never considered meeting Martin Romaine in person; as if the grinning, handsomely coifed gentleman on the cover was just a prop like bodice-rippers on romance novels. His floor manager said he saw Romaine on cable television, waving his arms and hopping around like a baby bird, tons of products to his name, the book being only one of them. He thought Randolph would like this guy's energy, even if Romaine didn't do a fantastic job filling out that sweatsuit and convincing everyone he was a fitness expert. More like a coach than a player. Everything else, though, Romaine had down.

It started with a phone call, then because of Randolph's star-power, a meeting. A quote of his made it onto a Performance Power newsletter. "Everyone owes it to themselves to be great. Martin Romaine is that reminder." A guest spot in one of his infomercials in which a staged conversation between the two lapsed into two hours, and later trimmed into a special promotional video. The prospect of joining the next tour only seemed natural.

Now Randolph wasn't necessarily looking for that old magic when cracking the book for the second time. He wanted a goddamn good reason for not reaching the heights he thought he should have reached by now in the public speaking business. Keynote speaker was okay, but it wasn't Mr. Universe. That book held secrets that he had always lived by and practiced but never found the need to describe. Now he needed it spelled out for him, cause it sure as hell wasn't happening on it's own.

The tour went well (as long as he stuck with tales of winning consecutive championship bodybuilding titles) and the harder he fought for change, the more resistance he got. Suzi was a tough girl. She stood up to him, and Randolph began to grudgingly respect her for it, even if at times he imagined chucking her out of the moving tour bus. His size and fame had no effect upon her. She had been the captain of her college softball team. In high school she was the debating champion of the entire state of Delaware. Now Suzi Sanford had arranged a photo shoot of Randolph Shuron, *the* Randolph Shuron, lifting a fake oversized barbell over his head with the words "strength" painted on one side and "wisdom" on the other. She ideally wanted a doctored shot of Martin deadlifting Randolph, but Randolph's blank stare quickly nixed it.

"I think Randolph needs to be concerned about Randolph's needs," he said one day over breakfast, hoping the borderline tendencies that third-person speech hinted at would cue her to a person becoming unhinged. But she just ran with it

"Well, I think that Randolph should realize how folks out there view Randolph before he starts making rash decisions," Suzi said.

"Randolph feels himself getting awfully mad," he glowered.

*

The rooms overlook the freeway. The rain is just as it was, sideways and punishing. Time means nothing in conditions like this. Everything hangs suspended. Efforts wasted. No one talks as we bolt straight for our rooms.

After the bathroom, I hit the sit-ups. The knives are still turning in my stomach and I manage only six grunting half crunches. It's raining too hard for running. I chock up trying to fix the tire as exercise. A fire burns my chest during the pushups. Only three are possible. Deep knee bends are out of the question. No stretching, either. Randolph Shuron's tips in the book seem like they're written for professional athletes. Marathon runners and linebackers. There's a picture of him in shorts, straight-legged and bent over with his palms flat against the floor. I try it, grunting against the thirty some-odd years of wound coil my muscles have become. My body comes alive only to protest my efforts with stabs of pain. I do what I can (touching my kneecaps) and stand still, listening for anything from next door.

It is silent. The family is safe. I have spirited them from harm's way like lambs huddled together in a burning barn. If I owned a pipe I would smoke it right now. Instead, I get out my notes, pick up the phone and try to get a bead on Martin Romaine.

I phone headquarters up north. From the clipped replies I receive, it must be the same receptionist I spoke to earlier or somebody that was trained right alongside her. Again I ask for a booking with Romaine, and again they try to assign some underling, "trained in the teachings of the Romaine Method," in his place. Totally unacceptable, and I tell her as such. She pauses, summoning up another canned response. "Is he at a workshop now?" I ask.

"No. He taking a small break from his tour."

"Then is he available, in the office? Can I arrange a meeting or speak with him?"

She pauses again. "No, he's not in the office. And he makes all meetings through another party."

"Well, then. Can I leave a message for him?"

"Yes, I can connect you to his personal secretary, but you should expect a delay in response as he is on vacation," she says.

"Vacation?"

"Yes."

In his book, I flip to a picture of a huge rambling estate somewhere outside Miami. His, "refuge for meditation and revitalization." Excelsior it's called. A place that reflects his philosophy completely. That's where he is now, I just know it.

The word, "action," is the centerpiece of the next topic covered in Martin Romaine's book. He explains that action and action alone is what separates those who look upon their lives with pride and those who reflect upon their shortcomings with shame. The first line of the chapter says, "Through the very act of buying this book, opening it and reading up to this point, you have decided that you are going to be the former." Not only must you raise the standards, as mentioned previously; they must be put into practice. That is done through action. It's all so simple. Continuing in the opening paragraph, he states, "If you decide to put the book down after you have read this line and never open it again; if you never think of or hear the name Martin Romaine again in your life; even if you've forgotten everything I've said up to this point, I can sleep soundly at night knowing that I've imparted onto you the number one key to success: ACTION! In fact, I'm so confident that this is the number one ingredient, I want you to close the book now, put it away and not pick it up for exactly a week. In that time, I want you to act on something you really want. Go for it! Now close the book! CLOSE IT!"

It's funny. Just as I had anticipated the raised standards topic of the previous chapter by purchasing that expensive suit, so have I anticipated this chapter by taking action. It's almost like I'm writing this book. Nevertheless, I do close it, and take his final words as a prompt to push myself even further. I know what I need to do.

I hear low muffled voices from the room next door. It's Sherry and James. The tone suggests a mild disagreement. I move closer to the wall but cannot make out the details. Just the steep rising and sudden end in pitch followed quickly by the same. I sit back on the bed to make a call to Misty, but close my eyes instead, planning my next course of action.

Like a cold splash to the face I awaken. The screams from next door tear through the walls. It's Sherry and James, mostly James. I get up. Action. That chapter was all about action. So I act.

These are not co-workers. These are real people, a family. But aren't co-workers just an extended family? What's the difference? "Welcome aboard! Welcome to the family," they say. I pull my pants up and make for next door.

My knocks upon the door are lost amongst the yelling. I pound on it. "Open the door," I shout like I'm the boss. They keep at it. A young couple walks by and does a lousy job pretending not to notice. They pick up the pace and keep walking. I imagine that they think I'm the father, the man of the family locked out of a major family crisis, impotent and pleading for forgiveness. I bang on the door and demand to be let in, loud enough for the couple now fifty feet down the hall to turn around and take another look.

Who's in charge? I am. I yell for Sherry to open up. There's a brief pause and they go back at it. Then I call out to

James. "Come on, James, be a man!" He doesn't even give me a pause. I look around and rattle the door handle. I call out for both the mother and her son. Then I try Noelle.

"Noelle, honey," I call out. I repeat myself half a dozen times until she timidly answers.

"Yes," she says.

"Could you please open the door?"

She pauses, then says, "I don't know if I should."

I kneel down by the door to get closer. "I could make your mom and brother stop fighting."

"I don't know."

"Wouldn't you like them to stop?" I say.

"Yes."

"Well, if you open up, I can help."

Then the bomb drops. "But you're not my daddy."

But it doesn't hit me. "I know," I say. "But I'm a friend."

The couple walks by again, and this time they slow down as they pass. I'm crouching by the door, saying, "Come on now, honey, open up." I wonder if they think I'm talking baby talk with my wife.

I say, "Noelle. If you want your family to get along, you better open up the door right now."

She opens it.

James is sitting on the bed, elbows on knees, holding his head. Sherry is at the small hotel table, drilling into him. It's about him not wanting to move, especially to be closer to dad. She sees me and stands up. "What?" she says.

"I'm here to mediate," I say.

"Who the fuck are you, anyway?" James pipes up.

I am right there at work again, except this time I'm taking the initiative. In typical conflict resolution, at least in the workplace, the employee (in this case, me) bears full responsibility for bringing the problem to the attention of the relevant parties. That's what the brochures say. However now I'm breaking protocol, pushing it way beyond its defined status. I elevate it. How many times have I seen people at work, bright and well educated, behaving no better than kids in the schoolyard? It can erupt from a debate over one *vs.* two-ply toilet paper in the bathrooms into a searing, ugly debacle, undermining the well being of the entire workplace. Maybe it's working at a conflict resolution company, or maybe it's my nature that illuminates and calls my attention to employee discord, no matter how subtle. I notice it in the subtleties of their small talk. Instead of "How was your weekend?" it's "How was *your* weekend?" It festers and spreads like mold, and yes, protocol states that I cannot head conflicts off at the pass lest they obviously prove harmful to workplace morale and productivity. But why must I wait? Shouldn't I be allowed to intervene in contentious affairs before they grow to possible irreparable proportions? Isn't it wise to change the oil before the engine begins knocking?

So like Martin says, I take action.

It's extraordinary how bubble-like it is when you're performing at peak level. Nothing can touch you in that bubble, no matter the protests, complaints, or attempts to stop you. You're at an elevated state of consciousness and a certain rational level of thinking is completely abandoned. The training, talent, and experience are all essential, but they too seem to drop away. The groove is on.

I think I hear protests, curse words aimed at me. But it's cotton and I'm a bullet tearing through it. Flashes of, "Fuck you," "Drop dead," and a few phrases about, "father"-this and "you're not my husband"-that. I don't know. I'm at the helm. The lion tamer doesn't see the lion's eyelashes or toenails as he wields the whip. He sees the entire beast, the blending of the cage around it, past present and future.

I play them like a Stradivarius, a fugue where each is a separate melody that I deftly blend together. They go to hell and back, and in fifteen minutes they are crying and hugging each other like it was forever.

In what can best be described as a post-orgasmic afterglow, I leave their room. That same couple is outside. They jump and pretend that they are passing by, confused about which direction to go. I feel like I'm floating above them, looking down, and laugh so they can hear. "Pitiful humans," I say, and laugh again.

I return to my room walking so tall, so straight, a posture so foreign that it hurts. But I don't care. I hit the floor and do at least 100 pushups, then flip over and crank out over 200 sit-ups. There's no pain afterwards, and I feel like I can do more.

I gather all my things: my clothes, my personal planner, everything, and leave the hotel without saying goodbye. I get in my car and head to Florida. Excelsior.

Chapter 6

The Almighty Cube:
You will simply be astounded at this offering: The Romaine Cube! Imagine fifty videos in one package. That's right! Fifty! For the first time, every video Martin Romaine has ever produced all available together! It includes everything from his most famous presentations: "Marriage Mania!" "It's Your Business!" and "Keep Your Child from being Childish!" And many many more! You'll have it all! Choose from quarterly, biannually, or monthly payment options.

He told me not to open the book for a week and I don't. No need to. The last word it said was "action." It blasted me forward like a cannon.

I went through in five hours what most people do in a lifetime—got educated, had a fulfilling career, and most of all, raised a happy family. I found some people, protected them, and taught them how to co-exist together. They were hurting, wanting and bewildered, wondering what to do with themselves, and I taught them to not look outside of themselves for help, but to reach deep down inside, and to each other, for their strength.

Now they will find that husband and father of theirs, sit him down, and tell him their demands. Just like I'm going to do with Martin Romaine.

I am in top form. I call Misty and open my heart to her with love. She says she's amazed and delighted at my new confidence, and asks if I have been drinking. Ha ha! What a girl! She has been running and going to the gym, following our workout plan to the letter. The first day out, she says, she was able to make it about two miles without stopping. Two miles, and she'd never run before. She said it wasn't so tough, while I made it all of three blocks before losing my breakfast. No throwing up like me. I'm happy for her, happy that she's made an important step in improving herself, thus improving our relationship. By making ourselves better people, there are no limits to what we can accomplish. At this, I feel confident in proposing my new plan for us. After hiring Romaine to speak at Conflict Control Systems, my original design was to fully immerse myself in our new lives together, working on self-fulfillment until it became second nature and a matter of course. But I can't wait. She senses my excitement and prods me to share.

"What is it, honey?" she asks.

"Oh, I don't know," I say. "Things are going really well for me."

"Sure seems that way."

"Yeah, I'm real happy about it, but I'm also really happy that you've decided to join me."

"Good," she says, waiting for more.

I go on. "Well, at first, I was kinda worried. I thought that maybe you weren't really interested in making all these changes. You know, changes to improve *us*. I thought that maybe I was in this all by myself."

"We're in this together, sweetie."

"I was concerned that we were going to take different paths, or you were content the way we were. The same goals, the same fitness, or lack of, the same professionally—"

"Is there something you want to say?" she asks. I feel her smile through the phone.

"How do you know I want to ask you something?"

"A woman knows these things, Joe."

"I was going to wait."

"Why?"

"I just wanted to be with you when I asked. I wanted it to be special."

"Oh, honey. You don't have to do that."

The clouds outside part, just enough to let the sun peek in. It floods the valley like a tidal wave, washing away the gray.

"Okay dammit!" I say. "What does it matter how far we're apart for me to ask? If the time's right, the time's right."

"Yes." She follows.

"Okay," I let out a breath. "Misty?"

"Yes dear?"

"We've known each other for so long. Time is meaningless when we're together. I know you like I know myself, because you're a part of me. I know what we were, and more importantly, I know what we're about to become. And I want it to be together. We've made vows of self-improvement, and I want to take it farther, to its natural conclusion. Misty?"

"Yes," she whispers.

"I want us to be a power couple. What do you say?"

She doesn't answer. Oh, God! These are the things you ask face to face, not over the phone, through the wires, in different time zones.

"Honey?" I say. There's a slight cough at the other end, so I know that she's there. Then a tiny scraping sound. Just for a second, like she was scratching herself with the phone.

"That's what you wanted to ask?" she finally says.

"Yes. I know it's kinda early to be planing this, what with us just beginning our workout and I haven't found Martin Romaine yet."

"But—"

"Just let me explain. I've got such high hopes for us. It'll be wonderful. So, how about it? Maybe I'm jumping way too far ahead. No. No, I'm not. I know what I want. I want to be half of a power couple. With you. I'm ready for that commitment. So come on. Do you wanna be a partner in a power couple? Just you and me?"

Misty's quiet again. Now it's like a long tunnel, with something way at the other end, powerful and building up momentum. But the train doesn't come. "Yes," she says. "That would be great."

"Great!" I yell. "I say we celebrate by going out for a great big run!"

*

The board, all nine members, had grown so accustomed to accommodating Mona's demands that approaching her with concerns of their own was completely foreign. Their input was mainly budgetary or whether a major market was being overlooked. They played a cautionary role. "It's too soon to introduce the companion video." "I don't think we need to release more than three different sweatshirt designs." So, when they felt the public was ripe and ready to meet Marty, they had become the aggressors. Knowing well enough that the entire board approaching her intervention style with their demands would throw Mona on the defensive, they elected one of their own to confront her. Christy Sanchez. Poor Christy, they said it was purely co-incidence that she was the only woman on the board. Was she the board member closest to and most trusted by Mona? No, nobody could claim that role. Christy's smile broke through any fear her co-members expected her to have, and once elected she stood up, pressed down the front of her new crisp jeans that had replaced her skirt suit, and said, "I'm on my way." The time Mona spent in her own office, as her receptionist informed Christy, had become rare, as Mona was now in what she termed, "Intensive Training," with Marty in the conference room. Off limits to everyone. It was this extended waiting for Mona to appear that took it's toll on Christy's fortitude, as if the widows have long been boarded up in anticipation of the hurricane and she sat in the quiet basement, hands folded.

Wearing jeans doesn't make you laid back, as she learned, and only serves to bind and pinch when sitting about, day after day, in front of your boss's office waiting for her to appear. Christy dreamed of her cotton blend skirt that moved lightly around her legs like the wind. She got to know the personal receptionist well, sharing tales of their elliptical relationships with their boss.

That Friday, just as everyone was leaving the building for the weekend, Mona showed up. She walked quickly to her office door, as if trying to avoid notice, head down looking at the carpet with arms full of documents and pamphlets. She mumbled something to the receptionist and went in. Christy followed her in, knocking on the opened door. As Mona set the load down upon her desk, the receptionist's voice came from her phone. "You've got a visitor." And there was Christie wearing the jeans that had just begun to break in and an older Martin Romaine button-down oxford. No briefcase, no papers; just an unarmed stop-by.

Mona stood there, not knowing what to do with her hands, "Christy! Hello. You still have one of those old shirts, I see."

Christy smiled. "How's Marty?"

"Fine. He's coming along nicely."

They had never spoken to each other alone, apart from the other board members hidden behind the long colorless conference table, preoccupied with memos, charts, or Martin. Christy noticed an athletic intensity in Mona. She had clearly lost weight from all the hours spent on the new project, and the heavy lifting of her notes made the veins in her arms pop.

Christy tried to summon a mental picture of Martin; hoping his face or his grin or his hair could give her some confidence. But it was like Martin had never existed. Not a hint of him—a lock of hair, a quote, nothing—was there. Like a wonderful talent you couldn't explain and never bothered to question, dancing or playing the piano or solving an impossible math equation, was gone. And you can't re-learn something that came so naturally.

"So you're happy with Marty?" she said.

"Oh, yes," Mona said cautiously.

"When does the rest of the world get to see him?"

Mona put a hand on her desk so she could be near her work. "He's not ready, Christy."

"We've been going over some numbers, Mona. A number of shows have been cancelled. So far a quarter of this leg of the tour is shot. This is a business, and no business can survive like this. Hibernating," Christie said.

"I figured I was going to get some pressure soon," Mona said and smiled. Christy tried to interrupt, but Mona spoke over her. "We can't release an incomplete product to the public. Martin may have in the past been a little vague about his goals before hitting the road, and it worked for him, but this is something else. It's big. Marty will change this company in a huge way. It's not like a decision of whom we're going to quote on our book jackets or a new color for our hats. This mustn't be rushed."

"How much longer is it going to take?"

"As long as it takes to be perfect."

They both stood there. Mona looked at the notes sitting on her desk and straightened the pile with her fingertips. Christy said, "There's more to a business than getting the perfect product out there. It's a matter of timing, too. Tough if you're already established, and ten times as tough if you're the industry leader. Halting production will leave a space for someone else out there to fill, and you know there's dozens of them out there waiting for the opportunity."

Mona cemented herself into place, saying nothing. She stood, hand planted on her notes. Lying in the corner of her office were poster reproductions of the Marty portrait awaiting her OK. "All right," she breathed. "I thought the press packets to our major supporters would help, but—"

"It only goes so far," Christy said.

"That's what I was about to say."

"The people need to meet Marty."

Mona turned away; she couldn't bear her brother's wide-grinning gaze on Christy's shirt, and everything about him that bothered her—the clumsiness, the forgetfulness, all those stupid wasted hours on doors and office parties—smacked her hard.

"Let me tell you," she spoke up, "and you can run along and tell the rest of the board what I have cut out for me. Maybe you'll be able to see beyond the numbers and demographics to what *real* work I have. Remember the big deal we used to make about a new book coming out? The fanfare? The publicity? Pictures? Interviews? Planning tours? Laying everything on the line for one little book? Well, Marty is so big, it will make a new book in the works look like the decision of what flavor potato chips to stock in the vending machine. I want to share with you exactly the mission I have before me. What I want is a person so self-assured, so certain of the effectiveness of his methods that it hardly needs to be told. A walking, talking version of that poster over there. I'm *not* going to plop someone up there on stage that the customers can simply compare themselves with and possibly aspire to, hence the new look. That's what it's been about all along: a conventionally handsome and intimidatingly confident Alpha male bludgeoning you over the head with his success. That makes the audience feel worse. That, Christy, is my goal in all of this. I could go on and on, but there you have it."

So *this* is the Mona the others had warned her about, willfully backing herself into a corner to justify lashing out. Practically encouraging it. Christy stepped back once, and said, "This is what you want me to tell the board?"

Mona looked at the old Martin tour shirt. It read, "Let Martin Romaine Take You UP! UP! UP!" She sat down behind her desk, placing both hands on the fat pile of notes. "No, I want you to form a subcommittee to discuss the exact time, place and method in reporting what I told you to them." She shook her head. "Oh, and don't forget to include visual aids, like pie charts."

"I'll tell them whatever you want, but they still need something for the customers, if not Marty himself, then the anticipation of Marty. Something."

"All right. Have the art department design a Marty brochure. Mention an upcoming tour, merchandise, and how this will make them rethink everything they thought they knew about Performance Power. Send it to everyone on our mailing list. Will that do?"

"Yes," Christy said, the sweat soaking into her jeans. As she exited the office, Mona called out, "I want to look at it when they're done. And get rid of that shirt!"

*

A straight shot to Martin's home. No rest. Though I was instructed not to open the book for a week, I flip to the color photos of his radiant beachside manor. The house, closer in scale to a compound, has two full pages dedicated to it with three professionally done pictures. The first is taken from the street as if just arriving. The driveway loops in front of the covered entranceway like a hotel and back around a small jungle grotto sprouting out of nowhere, providing an illusion of privacy. Off to the left side are three parked limousines, two black and one white, glinting in the sun like coins. The second shot of the house is from the sea, it shows the vastness of the compound, buildings low and wide. The main building, the centerpiece that draws your attention, is typical Florida coral except it has a mission-type bell tower on top. Then there's the aerial photo. The grounds look like a child dropped a bunch of pink and yellow blocks by the sea and left them that way. There doesn't seem to be much order to the sprawl, but even at this vantagepoint the master building draws you in. From above, it's shaped like Australia. The caption under this shot reads:

When it came time to design my home, I tried to image what Ponce de Leon was envisioning during his quest for the Fountain of Youth. He made vague descriptions of a tropical setting untouched by age and the world around it. I confess that at times I consider myself a spiritual descendant of the explorer, as my ongoing pursuit for fulfillment and living to one's full potential seems to mirror his yearning for a place that halts the aging process. For to live fully is to stay young! When guests, from actors to generals to CEO's of corporations, come to stay at my home, they confess to being in a place outside of time where typical laws of nature do not seem to apply. I have to agree! But it's not limited to the rich and famous. Once a year, I hold special private three-day training seminars here. Turn to Appendix C (Training and Workshops) for more information.

I don't turn there, but close the book. That's where he's staying. That house. Shouldn't be difficult to find, next to a body of water, probably an inlet or bay. I know exactly what I'll do: I will walk up to the front door and ring the bell. When it opens I'll clasp his hand and shake it. He will have been at his desk overlooking the glassy sea, rubbing his chin for inspiration (and it comes as easy as blinking). He'll be wearing the tropical equivalent of a smoking jacket and slippers, most likely, a billowy shirt with the top two buttons unbuttoned, linen slacks and bare feet. The salty cool air will roll off the ocean and into an open window, stirring the potted exotic plants and thin canopy bedding that hasn't yet been made. There will be a tall glass of orange juice and a poppy seed muffin in front of him that he picks at. A stack of letters by fans and a possibly a movie star just dropping a line. Life is light and free, and each breath he takes seems to make him lighter, as if it isn't oxygen at all going into his lungs, but some sweet perfumed buoyant elixir.

The air I breathe isn't so sweet. It scrapes and rolls along the highway pavement, bounces under semi trucks and shoots into my windows. It slaps my face awake, gritty like rolled around in an oyster. But the closer I head to Florida, the lighter the wind becomes. Is this the way the aged feel as they begin their final days here? A sense of life extended endlessly forward, where the stillness makes now seem like forever.

This is what Romaine means in Chapter 5 when he says, "You can be striving harder, with more single-minded ferocity, than you ever have in your life, but still feel a warm feeling of tranquility." That's the zone, or the bubble, or the flow or whatever you want to call it when you are doing that one thing that propels you forward, making you into the embodiment of your ideal. It's called the, "Region of Placid Action," and it's been around for ages, according to him, in the teachings of Swamis and their exalted meditations, the Dervishes in their otherworldly states, and finally Jesus upon the Cross, when he discovered the true meaning of his sacrifice after his initial doubts. Martin Romaine said he was very proud to place a definition on this vague but profound term, and has placed a copyright on it.

Everything is pointing forward: my life with Misty, my career, and my mission. This is my mission: finding Martin Romaine and hiring him to personally train my company. I'll return to that glass building at COCO, mountain shining in the distance, with the contract in my hand. Companies that hire him to speak, just for the day, increase their sales up to15%, and those that place their managers in Romaine week-long retreat training seminars increase their sales sometimes up to 35%! Perhaps a little piece of that will come my way.

I drive through the night, so lost in my thoughts that I suddenly catch myself and realize I hadn't been paying attention to the road, or that I was even driving, for quite some time. Mounds of burning bodies, writhing and dancing, could have flanked the highway and I wouldn't have noticed. I don't want to stop, rest, eat or anything, lest Romaine suddenly leave home for a conference or to meet a senator or visit a college, his vacation over.

It's late at night, and still it's hot. Cracking the window helps a little. The wind blows the lapels of my Italian suit—my uniform—and they rise like wings. I have no desire to ever remove it, my armor of blue steel, with me a soft smooth turtle. It will be cleaned so it can shine before Martin like heaven's glory. Soon a closetful of suits just like this one. The wind blows yet everything is still. Florida, 'gaters slide along, eyes above the water, swamps holding secrets, eternal bodies spread on beaches, breasts strain skyward for freedom, buckets of rain, palm trees promise heaven, where young and old stay that way forever.

But it *is* hot. I'm here. Miami. The humidity hit the moment I crossed the Florida border, and even with the windows rolled down the soupy heat couldn't be cut.

Sweat oozes out, soaking the armpits and collar of my suit a darker blue. The air is drinkable.

I stop at South Beach for a view of the ocean. The car seat is slick from perspiration. Rising, I peel the slacks from my legs and ass. The suit is now two-tone, the dry half gun-metal blue, with the wet portion a shiny cobalt. There's a breeze coming off the beach. It tastes of salt and smells of coconut suntan oil.

If I'm not the best-dressed man on the beach today, I'm without question the *most* dressed. No one (not even the titanically overweight or cripplingly aged) is wearing long pants, much less a suit. I make it to the beach, which is packed with glowing bronzed people from another world, laying facedown, playing Frisbee, drinking bottled water, laughing with friends. As I walk among them I feel that the city is already mine. They are my guests, my children. I make a rare appearance from my high-rise office (can't be bothered to change out of my suit, too busy), for a quick hello. They are at my feet, here for and because of me. I can see them clamoring to get up out of respect, but I insist that they just sit back down and enjoy themselves, and they oblige.

It would be nice to sit on the beach and watch the waves, toes dug in the sand, but my rear-end is still sopping from sweat. The suit needs to be cleaned.

I must move rapidly enough for the air to cool me, but not so fast as to build up a sweat. The suit is shiny clean again, and the well-defined creases cut the air. Despite the laundress's protests, I insisted upon extra starch.

"But sir," she said. "Are you sure—"

"Extra starch."

"But for a suit like this—"

"I know what I want, thank you."

"Sir?"

"Yes," I breathed out.

"With all this starch, you won't even be able to sit down."

"Well, I'm very busy, and I don't expect to be doing much sitting."

I walk stiff-legged just south of South Beach, hoping I'll come across the Romaine Estate, Excelsior. The homes here are titanic, turquoise and peach, but nothing near the scope and breadth of a compound as pictured in his book. It's mid-day, the sun is at its zenith, and I'm cooking. The blue chrome of my shoulders reflects the sun onto my cheeks and neck, and I feel my scalp (what the remaining threads of hair don't cover) begin to sizzle.

It's too hot to take, so I push the sleeves up to my elbows and roll the pants legs up to my knees. The material crunches like fall leaves. The sweatlogged dress socks collapse leaving my bone-white calves exposed.

These beachfront homes, despite their extravagance, sit in unprotected plots. Excelsior must be in a gated community somewhere else.

One of the few brunette Caucasian women I've noticed since arriving in Miami is behind the counter at the Office of

Tourist Affairs, a pink stucco hut feebly striving for Art Deco with its pronounced doorframe and glass bricks. Hairline cracks sprouting from the ground spreads along the walls. The woman is in her thirties and wears a white short sleeve sweater. She pokes lazily at a computer keyboard and doesn't look up. I browse the tiny office with its one isle of tourist merchandise, inspecting the shot glasses with the words "Sunshine State," or "Florida Fun," stenciled on them. Clocks with pictures of oranges where numbers should be. I had better get Misty a gift.

The woman, looking half-asleep and itchy under her sweater, had never heard of Martin Romaine. I ask if she's certain, and she shakes her head. Is he an actor, or something? she asks. Not being an actor, nor a musician, or at the very least, a clothing designer—she shows zero interest. The man is seen everywhere, and I find it very difficult to believe she doesn't know who Martin Romaine, spokesman to the world, is. I quiz her.

"*The Colossal Power Rules All*?"

She shakes her head.

"You see him every night on TV, advertising his programs?"

Still nothing.

"He's alongside senators—"

A shrug and an armpit scratch.

"—actors—"

That gets her attention.

"—and other really famous people?"

"No," she says with finality. "I have never heard of him."

It's difficult to accept. How can he not be known? I walk around the store and pick out some trinkets for Misty: a small address book with the picture of a lone lifeguard station on the beach, a snow globe of another beach scene with glitter instead of snow, and a baby alligator imbedded in Lucite in what I suspect to be a paperweight. As she rings up my purchases, I try her again. I describe Martin's eyes—inviting yet intense, then his

hands— smooth conductor's flourishes, and finally his hair—
like a cascading golden tidal wave, frozen in time.

This she recognizes. She lights up. Sure she knows him;
she went out with a guy a while back who tore Romaine's picture
out of a magazine and ordered the stylist to give him an identical
cut. It didn't turn as well, she says.

There's an area just outside the city where, if you want to
become a resident, a committee must vote you in. The homes and
estates are perched on private beaches. Folks inhabiting this
community all have names: CEO's, musicians, athletes, actors,
even "Egyptian princes," according to the cashier. But then
there's a spot further along for the truly prominent. The plots are
larger and the homes are not within sight of each other. No such
thing as neighbors in the traditional sense. Like national parks
unto themselves, each with a sweeping view of the sun as it rises
out of the boiling ocean and into their lives. That's probably
where Romaine lives, according to the solitary brunette woman
behind the counter, now dreaming that she's there, in one of
those homes, drink in hand alongside some magical person from
TV, radio, or print.

"Where?" I ask.

"There," she says, and points south.

Like most cities, once you leave the metropolis proper and
ragged outskirts, it starts to get nice: manicured lawns, healthy,
clean vehicles, friendly and inviting shops you couldn't pawn
your wedding ring to, children in yards. Then it gets nicer. The
houses become fewer, either older or more modern, secluded
behind tall fences or strategically buried in complicated
landscape. Fewer people are to be seen, and the layout is no
longer grid-like. Here we have windy, narrow roads.

At this point, it typically thins out into rural communities,
quaint if lucky, but most typically a bit spooky and best to be
avoided. The difference between those cities and ones that are
vacation destinations like here is instead of the property value
going down, it skyrockets. It is coveted land, the stuff of lottery

winning fantasies. The homes are far from the street, behind gates that open electronically, with humanity seldom seen on the expansive lawns or collecting the mail. I don't see a single soul during my drive through, and slowing down to squint for movement in distant windows yields nothing.

What makes this a contender for the American Riviera is the territory that lies beyond even the gated communities, vaulting over the imaginings of the common man. Worlds unto themselves, inhabited by the mythic. Creators and giants outside, yet very much a part of, society. History without them would be incomplete; names that are ingrained in everyone's consciousness like DNA. These are folks whose very existence is tenuous, delivered to us only through technology, seldom live, and when they do venture out among us, their very public presence makes news.

If the previous upper-crust gated estates appeared haphazardly scattered throughout their neighborhoods among snaking roads with British-sounding names, these lands completely defy territorial boundaries. Fences, gates, and strategically placed arborvitums are not needed here, as these dwellings, expansive and sprawled as they are, are buried deep within jungles, perched halfway over the water, at the other side of a forest. I attempt to keep relatively close to the ocean, but the road often climbs up and back around to more traditional neighborhoods. I have no choice but to follow a road next to a river, and I'm obviously heading away from the ocean. It winds until I reach a gate with two stone-carved pillars. The one on the right has a camera on top, it's iris shining as it follows me. I make an eight-point turn to swing the car around and push on to the east, back to the water.

I hit a road that appears to parallel the ocean heading south, though my view of the crystalline waters comes and goes as I go over slight hills or disappear in the woods. The trees thin out and the Florida of our dreams begins to form: the gravity-defying towering arched palm trees, the ocean a polished jewel, and beaches spotted with sea grass until fading into the soggy choked brush. This is all broken up with swampy inlets or bays that almost form small islands. Romaine territory. I slow down and turn off into any tiny path or driveway or exit I can find, no matter how overgrown or unpaved. Some lead into miniature stagnant lakes just 50 feet off the road. Others into uninhabited dwellings of balsalike flimsiness. Some die out, eaten by the vines that have taken over. Others end at houses not far from the road but hidden just the same. They have at least three American cars, with one that hasn't run for years, sitting out front. A woman looks at me from her kitchen window as I back out of her driveway.

To my left is ocean and sand, and to the right is quick dense jungle that may be covering hills. Difficult to tell, it's so thick. I drive into it. The road narrows. Vines and palm leaves slap and slide along the car like a carwash. The road keeps winding. On and on.

The road curves left, and it keeps turning, feeling like I have gone 720°. The greenery thins out and the road widens. Then, BOOM! The Romaine Compound. Excelsior! I recognize it from the book. It's off in the distance, beyond more dense jungle, in a partially cleared section of land along a mild cliff, possibly the only one in Florida, overlooking the ocean. Peach and orange and yellowish-colored geometric shapes surrounded by palms. The road goes one way, to Excelsior, and it disappears suddenly in the jungle.

The Romaine estate with its grotto in the circular driveway appears just like out of the book. The surrounding greenery makes the peach colors pop, or it could be the gold trim around the immense front door and windows. Only two limousines are parked out front, the white ones, sleeping like cats on their bellies.

As if arriving at a hotel waiting for the valet (I've never had valet parking), I park under the covered driveway. I sit with the engine still running in case two bald wide-shouldered guards wearing tropical vacation wear jump out of nowhere and I have to make a getaway. Nobody appears. I gulp down breath, hammer out the wrinkles in my suit, and step out of the car. I stand there, trying to think of Martin, his hand on my shoulder leading me to meet himself. But then I imagine a very different Martin Romaine, black circles under his eyes, underlit, standing in his doorway glowering at me. "Why are you here?" he croaks. I run back to the car and open his book to a random page near the back. I glance at a quote in the margins of the section, "Requesting a Raise from your Boss," which says, "No one can make you feel inferior without your consent."

Ten minutes of knocking and ringing and there's still no answer. I walk to the side and peer through the windows. Nothing, it's dark. Far away the waves hit the beach, sounding like the freeway down the road from my apartment, always present. The limousines are dirty and the tires look a little low. I try the bell again, lock my car and walk around the house.

The salt air bites my eyes. It's a multi split-level home; a large porch juts from the top story. Stairs wind down a densely flowered slope that merges seamlessly into a courtyard with a pool fashioned to resemble a lagoon. A u-shaped bungalow surrounds it, save for the view of the ocean down below. When I reach the pool, I discover that the stairs continue downward. The plant life thins out, and the lowest part of the house is a modern rectangular addition jutting away from the rest of the house. This is the room I had imagined Martin Romaine in, sitting at his desk, looking up from his writings to the sea for that extra boost of motivation, then going back at it, fueled by nature's majesty. I peek inside. It's similar to what I had envisioned when I first read about the place. The relationship of the room to the sea seems to have come right out of my imagination. It's removed enough to offer a wide vista of the ocean, but not too far off for a quick jaunt to the warm waters should the mood hit. I didn't imagine the windows occupying the entire oceanfront wall though, but rather expected something a bit more colonial with modest exposure. Nevertheless, it's a fine modern compliment to the natural surroundings. I try the door and it's unlocked.

*

Cooperation City lined a river and didn't stray far from it, stretching around a bend and bleeding up into the hills. The kind of city that, once you leave the highway, you drive down into; down, down, down, until you reach the river at the bottom. Two small bridges cross it, and up you go again into the residential area that climbs the hills, scattering until all that remains is the occasional home buried in forest that belongs to one of those weirdos that you only see late at night in a convenience store buying a jar of peanut butter and a can of WD-40. All that keeps the mosquitoes from taking over this town like falling angry clouds is the river that slides along with a temperature two degrees below what they like.

Steve the driver said, "Cooperation City, and why not?" He dropped Martin off at a service station with a convenient store. Like a father dropping off his daughter at a slumber party, he watched Martin enter before driving off.

"Oh Jeez, what are you doing here?" came a voice from behind the counter which in turn was behind two-inch thick Plexiglas. "Mar-tin Romaine!" The cashier stood up, but didn't leave his station behind the register. He wore a light blue T-shirt so thin chest hairs were visible with something heavy weighing down the single breast pocket. Possibly his wallet. About sixty, with dark, sinister eyebrows totally unrelated to the crackly gray hair on top the consistency of Chinese noodles. He squinted through the Plexiglas for a clearer view. "Ha! Ha!" Martin slid up close so the old man would keep it down and not draw attention. Force of habit as the station was empty except for them. The attendant, with the additional weight of a faded nametag with a B and an L pinned to his shirt, thrust his hands into his rear pockets, then hunched over and pulled out a copy of *How To Do It Like the Successful People Do It* from beneath the counter. He pressed it against the Plexiglas for Martin to see. "Isn't that something?" he said. He didn't ask the author of this book, a celebrity of certain magnitude, now standing before him in his store what he was doing in Cooperation City. Billy, as he introduced himself, was as casual as a phone call.

"I hope you found it helpful," Martin said, as he always said to people who cornered him.

"Well, that's the thing," Billy said. He let the book fall with a dead dog plop beside the cash register. "I *don't* think it did." His voice was muffled behind the Plexiglas barrier you couldn't blast through with armor-piercing bullets. Martin's coif, undamaged by the deficiency of gels, sprays and mists, may have made Billy feel a little self-conscious, because he in vain attempted to tame his own crinkled curls with his oil-stained hand. It didn't work and defiantly sprang back up. "How do I do what you said we could all do?" he said.

"Sorry?" Martin sensed a lecture and he was right.

"You see, I saw your commercial on TV, and it sounded like just what I needed. I felt like I was stuck, living in Cooperation City all my life, never really getting out or doing anything besides working here or re-building engines or fishing. Sure, none of the people in your ad were anything like me—they seemed like they already had it made. But I liked what you said, and what you said: 'At any time, if you wish, you can be re-born into something new,' it really got me thinking, like, 'hey, he's right. The only reason I'm stuck in this life is because I choose to be.' So I sent for your book and started reading it and I liked it. It was the kick in the butt—like how you feel after drinking a pot of black coffee—that did it for me. So I would read a chapter or two from this book, then jump up, ready to take on the world. I even figured out what I wanted to do—organize alligator sightseeing tours for tourists. Or get work in a Formula 1 pit crew. Either one of those things would be really nice. Reading a chapter would, as I said, get me fired up, but all I was able to do was picture myself either leading folks around the swamps as they took pictures of alligators, or running out to the track and quickly change tires. So then I thought, 'OK, I'm getting ahead of myself. I've only read the first few chapters.' And every time it was the same—a big sugar rush. And there's the problem—it didn't tell me what I really needed to know: How do I do what you said we could all do? And in the back of the book was a list of all these other things you offer: videos, more books. And I thought *this* book was kinda expensive. I can't afford or take the time off to go to Hawaii for two weeks for one of your seminars."

Martin said, "Think of what I offer as an investment. An investment—"

"An investment in yourself... I recognize that line from your book," Billy said.

"Yeah. You would be giving up quite a bit of money and time, but in the long run I guarantee the payoffs would be worth it."

Billy shook his head. "I was hoping to get a how-to guide, like how to re-build a carburetor, except substitute the carburetor with your life."

The station had two cars for rent, usually as loaners while somebody's vehicle was in the shop. The sedan wasn't running, so all that was left was a blue van with the speedometer needle stuck at 120 MPH. It could actually reach only a shade over fifty. Martin bought it from him straight out. He told Billy that he would send him the Super Success Package, but Billy only shrugged and said thanks. Martin then asked if he had known Dick Berg. He couldn't shake the image of that piney-armed old timer shaking his fist at the world.

"Yeah. I knew Dick. He'd come in and pick up some spark plugs or other parts for his car. We talked shop a few times. He knew his stuff, all right. He used to work on satellites or something like that for a living. Government work. This town's been pretty quiet since his passing."

Martin also purchased the healthiest thing he could find— dried apples (loaded with sodium). The speedometer read 120 as the van climbed up the main road onto the highway offramp. He thought of Dick Berg, in coveralls and up to his armpits in machine parts, a greasy legal tract in his hand. There he was, walking among the land that he alone tended and made work. Then he remembered Billy from the service station. A how-to guide. Martin never really thought of "how." How? He only talked about Why. Why your life isn't good enough. Why you seem unable to get off your ass. Why you should have a positive, go-for-the-throat attitude. It was his weakness with "how" that resulted in Mona making all the company decisions and forced an emergency landing on Dick Berg's personal airstrip. He reached the onramp, and instead of heading south towards Miami, he drove back to Dick Berg's property (it wasn't a home to Mr. Berg, it was "property"). He felt as exuberant as Billy probably did after reading one of his chapters.

*

Martin's disappearance somehow reached the public, and Mona discovered this when the receptionist forwarded a call from a nationally syndicated newspaper columnist. The gentleman announced himself by name, Herbert Cady, no deceit or trickery involved in getting through to Mona. Famous folks from all over the world went through the woman up front.

"Missing?" Mona tightened. "Where'd you hear this?"

"A source," Mr. Cady said.

Mona used this opportunity to gather herself and close the notebooks on her table, as if the interrogator on the other end could peer through the telephone and into her office.

"Mona Romaine, is your brother either missing or lost?"

Mona sat back in her desk chair. "I don't know where you heard this, sir, but I certainly don't appreciate your intrusion. If he were, do you think I would take time from trying to find him to talk to you?"

"This *is* news, Miss Romaine," Herbert responded. "You don't seem terribly fazed by this."

Mona laughed a pissed-off laugh at his smug directness. "No, it's not news."

"Your brother is a well-known man. He's got ties with the President, for one. Folks are concerned. They want to know."

Mona laughed again.

Herbert Cady went on. "Then where is he?"

"On vacation."

"Can he be reached?"

"No."

"Why not."

"He's working."

"I thought you said he was on vacation."

"He's got a different idea of what a vacation is than you and me. He didn't get to be where he is by playing Canasta and drinking Pina Coladas."

Herbert kept at it. "When was the last time you spoke with him?"

Mona paused. "That's none of your business."

"So you haven't spoke with him for a while—"

"I didn't say that—

"There's news, from reliable sources, that he's missing. And you don't seem to care. I find that very difficult, you being his sister, to believe."

Mona twisted up the volume. "Well believe it. The only "lost" he is is "lost" in thought, and the only "missing" he is is "missing" being out on the road if front of people."

"Can I quote you on that?" Herbert said.

"Mr. Cady, if I were in your shoes, I'd fuck off."

"Miss Romaine..."

Mona hung up and went back to her notes. However, she had lost her place, flipping pages and slapping them down to get back to where she was. She stood up and pounded her fist down upon the desk. These kinds of interruptions are unacceptable. A complete waste of time...just like the way it used to be. Earlier that day, it was a community college requesting an appearance by Marty. A community college! And yesterday she had to take a call from Korea asking what she thought about a 50-50 cotton poly fiber blend for the new baseball caps. She would definitely have a talk with the receptionist about screening the calls.

Chapter 7

The desk does *not* belong here. It's just a few feet from the king size oaken bed, nowhere near the bay windows as I had imagined it, so the first thing I do is set about to move it. My muscles are limber and no longer protesting, and already I feel the payoff from my workout regimen. Sliding the shiny black desk across the hardwood floor is quite easy. I've come a long way to get here. I want it to be perfect, just as I had envisioned. It's what Martin would want.

I leave everything else in the room the way it is. It's impossible to tell the last time it's been inhabited. No indication of life within these walls. No dust trails as I run my finger along the windowsills. The bed is made and the nightstand beside it holds a couple strategically placed old hardbound books. One is on botany and the other is in German. I open the first one and its spine crackles. The room seems like a showroom designed for a magazine spread covering celebrity homes. I'm disappointed. I thought I would find a clue to Martin's persona, a physical manifestation (as in a college sweatshirt laying over a chair or half-drunk bottle of wine, a gift from the President) that could help me grasp this man.

Two pads of paper lay on the desk. One is thick-milled business stationery with the Romaine logo, a brick M-shaped tower with "Colossal Power" in tiny letters, across the top. The other pad is plain white unlined. I take a sheet from the latter and write down the major points of my proposal to Martin. It's good practice for reinforcing your attack strategy when the pressure is on.

I move my luggage into the room and wait. The rest of the house I do not venture into, and don't care to; wandering amongst the kitchens, guestrooms, libraries, and gymnasiums would only spread him out in my mind into a chunky marmalade, impalpable. The phone rings, and I stand very still looking at it as if Martin will suddenly walk in toweling off from a dip in the ocean.

I sit at the desk, hands clasped behind my head and gaze outside. I'm at the tip of the cone, everything opening up before me. The ocean with its flaky white waves is a starry funeral shroud. It belongs to Martin. He has devised a self-perpetuating machine that builds upon itself, success compounding success and spreading its arms wide.

The closet, however, I do not consider off limits. It's the walk-in kind, of course, with an oaken rectangular island, ten feet long, sitting squarely in the middle. On one side of the island (more of a barge of drawers) are the shoes. Each pair gets its own drawer with a small glass window for easy viewing. Seven rows high and five columns wide. This ranges from Italian loafers to wingtips to running sneakers. On the other side of the barge are the dress accoutrements: two cabinet doors that open to many smaller sliding drawers inside. They contain the tie tacks, cuff links, money clips, watches. Over twenty watches. Lining the walls of the room, in two levels, are his clothes. Suits on top and separates on the bottom. It is organized like a men's clothing store showcasing unworn handmade garments. I take the time to count the suits. It somehow seems important. One hundred and seventy six. The assortment has no color scheme that I can tell, but I squint and blur my vision to see if a pattern appears before me. Some kind of code. More clues to the success story that is Martin Romaine. Could they be sorted by designer? Or year they were tailored? Or the fabric? Or maybe the country in which they were made? Is there a suit in there that was made by the same guy who designed mine, El Rubiani?

I pick out a white bathrobe that seems more fur than terrycloth it's so fluffy. This gives me the ease and comfort I so sorely desire. Besides, I need to let my suit breathe. I can't escape the fear of my El Rubiani irreparably warping out of shape if I stay seated in it. The salesman said, "It's a standing suit, alright." I thought he meant outstanding, but maybe that's not what he meant.

How can a desk chair be so comfortable? It's nothing but a modern wooden ribcage, but it envelops me like tortoise shell. I'm able to sit there, just relax, at complete ease. I have recreated my mental image of Martin at home—simultaneously at work and on vacation. My feet are up. I snap up the phone and place it to my ear. It cools my ear. Everything outside is silent, like the ocean and the palm trees and the birds in the sky freeze to say "cheese" along with me. It's not Martin Romaine, but Joe Median in the picture. Should I phone Misty? Is she a part of that picture?

The picture starts moving, and I'm speaking with her. I make it clear right off the bat that I can't talk long; I've got meetings lined up all day. Someone's even waiting in my library right now. Who was it again? Looking into the little black book, oh yes, the CEO of the #1 contractor of spy planes for the United States Air Force. But I miss her, and really look forward to getting the chance to break away, go someplace nice, just the two of us.

Despite all I have, I tell her, she is still my proudest achievement.

I place the phone back in the cradle and gaze out to the ocean. The phone rings. I look at it. It's really ringing. I wait for it to ring twice, an old habit, and answer it.

"Hello, Martin?" asks a real voice. She asks quickly, like the opportunity will immediately vanish if not jumped upon.

I say nothing

"Martin? I can't hear you." I sense a tremble in her voice. "Where have you been?"

"Yes?" I say.

"Martin?"

"Yes," I whisper, and move an inch away from the phone, like a rope will fly out of the receiver and lasso me.

"Where have you been? Martin? This *is* Martin? We've been up here—"

"Yes," is all I can say, and I hang up.

The phone instantly rings again. It rings and rings for over ten minutes, then stops. What did Martin do to this woman, I wonder? She's not a wife. He doesn't have one. A girlfriend? A relative? His sister? A secretary? Whoever it is, it's someone who cares. Who knows? I'm getting hungry.

I see Martin looking out from the cover of his book, those chestnut locks amassing in a perfect unstoppable army. Windblown grass after a hurricane. All symmetrical, very alive, real. Too perfect for human hands, and too natural for machine or tool. Then I go back to mine. Something must be done.

I am a mere shrub to his forest. Action must be taken. Volume is the key. I head to the adjoining bathroom and reach for the hair products of which there are dozens: gels, cremes, conditioners, spritzes, mouses, relaxers. I take a gel (at least it looks like gel), a heavily frosted white bottle that has no writing on it except the number 6. Using that and the hairdryer, I am able to build up my thin combed-over threads into something close to yarn. It seems to speak to me, just as the hairdryer rattles off. It says, "Nice Try. Keep at it."

I iron my suit. The phone rings a few times throughout the day, but my mind is too preoccupied to answer it. The canned peaches I had taken from the kitchen sits in the corner of the room. My planner is open. Sit-ups and deep knee bends are getting easier. Gotta keep up with Misty. I see her running farther every day. Hope she doesn't run into another man with all that new energy of hers. I take jogs along the shore. Not much. I want to be there when Martin returns. Missed opportunities is the number one reason for failure. But Martin doesn't like that word, "failure," he explains early in his book. It suggests finality, where it's actually the prelude to success. He prefers to use the term, "Get another crack at it."

Each sunrise warms me awake. The phone calls thin out. My planner is perfect. Every day for the upcoming year is accounted for. I know what steps to take professionally and personally for maximum growth. However I begin to feel a cause for concern. The fires need to be kept alive, especially during times of re-grouping and re-assessment. I answer the next call.

He asks for Martin and I say, "Yeah, it's me."

It's Richard Greener, the CEO of the 2nd largest automobile manufacturer in the United States. He hadn't spoken to Martin for a couple years. I tell him I had just gone out for a run and quickly go into a few lively anecdotes. Met the commissioner of baseball, the President from two terms ago. We yuck it up over one of his limos breaking down on me. He says he's laying off 35,000 employees. Then we get down to brass tacks.

"Martin, I know it's been a while," he says. "But I would like to have you come out and meet me as soon as possible." He sounds like a gritty Army general, whatever they sound like, asking and demanding at the same time.

"Well, what's going on?" I ask.

"It's big. I'd like to have you here, in person, to discuss it. We could talk at my winery or over dinner or something. Stay in the guest bungalow."

"Hmmmmm," is all I say.

He pauses, then goes on. "You're gonna make me tell you what it is right now, aren't you, you bastard!"

"Yes, Richard."

"You know me, Martin. I don't like discussing big matters over the phone."

"I've got this tour I've got to get back to. Perhaps I'll be coming to your town soon. Let me check the schedule—"

"All right, stop screwing around," he barks then takes an audible breath. "Is there anybody in the room with you?"

"No."

His company, the 2nd largest car manufacturer in the United States (I feel the need to remind myself), is getting bought out by an overseas buyer, a competitor. He says the only thing standing between the deal being done is himself. He has two choices: 1. Agree to the buyout, offer no protest and keep his job, or 2. Fight it, go to court and try to protect the thousands of additional jobs that will probably be lost, and most likely lose his own. He says if he takes the legal route, he'll be able to buy time for the major shareholders to rally a defense. This would however result in enormous legal fees and probably stall productivity to devastating effects... I begin to lose him amongst the legal and financial jargon, but his desperation brings me back. Greener is tortured, like a child choosing which parent to live with for the rest of his life. His steely voice develops a crack that spreads the more he speaks, and I expect it to break wide open and him to fall in. He unloads it all, not waiting for acknowledgement. He finishes with, "God, I'm in Hell. I'd rather have cancer of the nuts!"

...It's a slam-dunk! I would expect this to be a lot harder. These are the decisions that affect the world, reverberate throughout history? The answer comes as naturally as opening my eyes in the morning and putting my feet on the floor. I however let the time stretch to appear giving this weighty matter the thought and deep consideration it deserves. At least until his breathing quiets down.

"OK, Richard," I tell him. "I see the dilemma you're in. But let me ask you this. Do you want me to give you tips on how to get through this difficult decision, or do you want me to tell you what I think you should do?"

The crack in his voice widens. "What a nightmare, Martin. I can't sleep. I blow up at everyone. My kids won't talk to me. Who knows why."

"Let's focus, Richard."

"Yes, focus," he says.

"Now, what do you—"

"Just tell me what I should do," he breathes out, defeated.

"OK, Richard. You listening?"

"Yes."

"Sell it."

"But—"

"No! There's only one thing that's important—the company. It must live. Selling it is the only way for it to survive. Think of it as a child, a very big important child. It doesn't matter who its parents are, just as long as it's cared for. Let it live and breathe."

"But—"

"Stop with the buts. Buts are giving you a coronary, keeping you from enjoying your life. Buts are blinding you from your baby's well-being."

Minutes pass in silence. I pick through the desk drawers, fiddling with Martin Romaine's stapler and pens.

"You're right," he says weakly.

"Richard, no hesitation."

"All right, dammit. Yes!"

The cracks seal up. The General is back.

The sun's final rays fan across the waltzing ocean waves. Birds like white darts fly by. Mr. Greener demands that I visit him out west, and soon. We will dine upon creatures from the sea and great beasts from the field. There will be a private chef. Together we shall sit in a private box seat somewhere for some kind of event. Key to the city. He's drained of his burden and aglow. He says so, "aglow." His words. He tells me to expect a new limousine soon. It's too much, I tell him, but he doesn't hear me. He's the General. Finally, before he says goodbye, he tells me that he loves me in a masculine way I never thought possible. These people certainly are different, and I am among them, risen, in a realm so complete it's not the loss of ego that describes it, it's the very opposite—complete ego.

I am now ready. I leave the room the way I had found it. The terrycloth robes are folded, the watches returned, the underwear back in their drawers. It's time to visit Romaine headquarters.

*

Knox, the touched artist behind the Marty painting—now reproduced hundreds of times in every format possible: brochures, leaflets, posters, cropped and placed on business cards, T-shirts, billboards, and business envelopes—had not ceased showering Mona with declarations of devotion. His love letters a steady stream of unending affection despite the weeks that had passed since being transferred to Romaine Enterprises West Coast Branch. It was genuine and true. Mona reciprocated as much as a woman who was leading a major corporation and spending hours each day locked up in a conference room with a replacement for her brother could be expected. Paintings of *her* arrived, along with scented letters. (Men write scented letters? Knox did. Rosemary and lavender, provides a calm focus.)

The day Christie, once again roped in as acting liaison from the board of directors, made the ultimatum that Marty better hit the shelves soon lest there be dire consequences, Mona realized that she was really on her own. Did Christie and the board represent all Romaine employees? Was that why Mona constantly had to remind folks from marketing or the newsletter, the "Magnum Monthly," to cease using the word "Martin" in all upcoming products? Even folks who trivially mentioned her brother in passing were stared down with pugilistic intensity. Not a problem for Knox out west, as he had never met, nor have much use for, Martin Romaine. To him, folks naturally endowed with surging amounts of ability and drive have no use for Martin and his ilk. A mere matter of redundancy. He was the sole person Mona knew who had interests outside of Martin or Marty. So, when the door closed behind Christie, Mona went to the sticky note with Knox's phone number. She had it for weeks, and the sticky portion of the note was no longer sticky.

Knox threatened to fly out and visit, but never did. He was smart enough to realise that, though it works in the movies, arriving unannounced flowers in hand in the middle of a board meeting with important partners and clients wouldn't fly with Mona. So when her invitation for him to visit initially seemed like a flippant tease, he said to her, "Please don't say this unless you really mean it, cause I'm not strong enough to handle the rejection if you don't." She laughed, and he was walking through those easy-open glass doors at Romaine Headquarters the next day.

Strolling the headquarter grounds hand in hand beside a duck pond, she told Knox that he had as much to do with Marty's creation as she did. She felt a certain special bond with him. And if his heart had soared before, it now blasted off to the outer edges of the solar system. She greatly appreciated him not constantly questioning her about Marty. When would he be ready? What will Marty have to offer that Martin cannot? The answers to these and other Marty-related questions lay entwined within the souls of Mona and Knox; attempting to explain it vocally was preposterous.

"Why can't they just leave me alone and let me get on with the work?" Mona stopped and turned to him.

Knox wasn't certain whether this was rhetorical or not, so he just softly gazed upon her.

"That's what's so great about having you around. You're the only one who understands Marty like I do, so there's no need to discuss him."

"Yes, I do feel the same," Knox said. "So—"

"And the more people ask about Marty, the less confident I am that they will ever understand."

"I do feel that Marty is—"

"Please, do not say his name," Mona spun around and kissed Knox quiet. They stopped at a bench on the other side of the duck pond. They now had a full view of Romaine Enterprises Headquarters, beyond the water and parking lot, sitting solitary like a neatly wrapped birthday present.

Knox spoke up, describing the work he had been doing at the West Coast branch office. The interior, he said, was in keeping with the theme of western expansion. However, he wanted to modernize it a bit—horse and saddle replaced by plane, automobile, and train. Prairie vistas are now stadiums. Tiny cellular phones and pocket computers are the revolvers and knives and whips of today. The traveling speaker is the lone gun for hire, aiding the native settlers in conquering the modern savage terrain.

"Mmm," Mona said absently, as if waking herself from a dream. "Yeah, it's great that my concerns about Marty can be shared with you, even though they not even be mentioned." She placed her hand on his knee and leaned over for a soft kiss on the cheek. She laughed. "Ah! Soon enough those schmucks on the board will see what we've envisioned all along. They'll say, 'I'm so sorry for having doubted you, Mona.' And after that, the whole country, and maybe the world, will get to share in what we created."

"Mona," Knox said.

"Please," she said and squeezed his hand. "Let's not talk. Let's just sit and be together."

So Knox was at Mona's call when the pressure rose, like when members of the board took turns arriving unannounced at her office. He was given his own office adjacent to the art department where he enjoyed local celebrity for being the creator of Mona's muse. He worked at his desk manipulating the original Marty design in dozens of ways according to Mona's specifications: "Make his neck a bit thicker. Go easy on the intensity of his gaze. Try another pose; he looks like a gigolo!" The in-house graphic designers and artists were delighted to have someone at their boss's request take the reign of their department, because the only orders she had given them were vague at best, "Plaster Marty on everything you see! Don't just replace Martin's face with Marty's. It goes way beyond that. And remember, get rid off all previous images of Martin." Knox repeated her orders—complete saturation—because all the time the two spent together gazing at each other across restaurant tables, walking hand-in-hand in the park, lying under white cotton sheets, on breezy country drives, his work was never touched upon. It was debriefing time for Mona whatever they were doing and wherever they went:

A bite of chocolate mousse: "I think if I keep at it, and get his tone of speech right, he'll be ready in a month."

Thirty seconds after orgasm: "It's nice to get away from Marty just for a little while. Do cowboy boots come across as too bumpkin? And I can't decide on the hair: a tad longer and wild, or clipped short..."

At the end of the workday, she would run up and jump into his arms like a crushed high-schooler who knows no other manner of greeting. Who cares if everyone saw? A watermelon slice could be stuffed into her mouth and she couldn't be smiling any wider. Theirs was a working passion, with Marty the love child.

It was crunch time, and the board was insisting upon the goods lest they take matters into their own hands. To make up for lost time and lost revenue, they were threatening to mine the entire backlog of Martin Romaine speeches, products, videos, and interviews and assemble them into a "greatest hits," package; a retrospective of his life's work. And everyone knows that's the royal kiss off for any creative-minded vocation. Their argument, that nobody was buying, was "Everyone, from the casual fan to the die-hard Romaine follower, will be able to have a compact, concentrated overview of his major work and ideas, with some added never-released extras as a bonus."

"I can't let this happen," Mona sobbed into Knox's neck.

Then he did it. After two weeks of watching Mona lose weight and color from breathless motion, he said, "Maybe he's ready."

Mona held on to him. "Have they been talking to you?"

"I think it may be time to let go, Mona."

She stepped back from Knox as if noticing a boil on his forehead. She narrowed her eyes in a way he had never seen before, and understandably, as this was her on-the-attack boardroom face, in no way resembling the floating afterglow he had been the first person in seven years to witness. "Knox, you're talking exactly like one of them."

"I'm just saying—"

"What?"

Knox breathed in through his nose. "I know a little something about the creative process. I *did* paint Marty, and trust me, nobody ever thinks the work is complete." He stepped to Mona. "You've got to trust yourself, and trust what you've made. It's hard, I know."

"He's not ready."

"Maybe I can help; perhaps I can take a—"

"No!"

They stood there silent. It didn't look like they were going dancing and out to her favorite chophouse owned by the Russian as planned. Knox considered throwing her down on the floor and taking her right there now that their blood was up. Not like a couple nights ago when they got back to her house, full of Margaritas. That was a planned, stylized brutishness that surprised no one (but was still fun). He had spun her around and, bam! right against the bookshelf. This would have been the real deal. "Shut up, you!" he would bark at her, biting into her neck. "Let Marty go, and get over it!" But this was her office, and she knew the layout best—the letter opener on the desk, a mechanical pencil in her pocket. So what he thought was the middle road—between what was going though his head as she yelled at him, and doing nothing—was actually the worst choice of all three.

"Mona," he said, interrupting her.

"What?"

His lower lip went fat with a cutesy surrendering pout. "Let's do what we did the other night."

"Huh?"

"You know, a couple nights ago," One of Mona's eyes went narrower than the other, a shade of recognition. So he blurted it out. "The bookshelf..."

Mona opened her mouth, then closed it, then screamed, "You fucking shithead!" and leapt for his crotch, smashing him against the desk. Ice picks shot white fire into the back of his legs. She laughed as he cried out. What she gave may have been considered a kiss, mouth gaping wide to gulp down his head. She disengaged. "You may know about art, my sweet," she said gently touching his face. "But you don't know a thing about commerce." She clawed his head back toward her.

Knox was sent back to the West Coast office. The absence would fuel their love, she said. Besides, passion spread between love and business compromised everything. And when Knox let slip out that sometimes he wished Marty was out of the way, well, that made it much easier for her.

Considering the frequency in which he kept in contact, it was like Knox had never left. As if he had moved his office down the hall...a few thousand miles. He continued to supervise the ad campaigns for Marty's debut: "Forward to Basics." Mona's time was divided between the disembodied voice of Knox over the phone and Marty who she kept sequestered in the conference room.

Knox reverted back to the persistent amorous longing that predated his stay with Mona, only this time with more arrows in his quiver: this was now LOVE. And with quotes romantic tied to those arrows, he sent them soaring across the USA, a bit distracting for Mona who now was spending upwards of fourteen hours a day hammering away at her project.

Marty was too spazzy for a two-fisted straight shooter smothered in the trappings of old west culture. Not what Mona had in mind, and she let Marty know this each time he acted up, pleading and begging and demanding that he was ready to hit road, shake some hands, get the job done. She would sit back clucking, "This won't do. You call *this* casual wisdom?" causing him to stamp the floor in renewed fury.

Mona waited patiently for the stamping, which had sent an old canoe paddle propped on the wall crashing to the ground, to cease.

"Each time you do this, Marty, I feel like we get farther from our goal," she said.

He stopped and stood there, arms crossed tightly across his chest breathing with concentration.

"Better," Mona said. "But you seem so tense."

Marty didn't move.

"Come on," Mona grinned. "Try a swagger."

He let his arms flop down and buried his fists deep into his jeans pockets.

"Hey, that's good," Mona smiled.

With it's saddles, beat up guitars, juke boxes, Indian headdresses, bronze buffalo statues and portraits of statuesque Freightliners, the room looked like a cross between the Roy Rodgers museum and a truck stop. The ebony-topped conference room table was stacked high with new merchandise ready for production. Marty plopped weather-beaten on the corner of the table.

"I like that," Mona said.

Marty gave a cracked stare.

"Don't look at me like that." Mona said. "Before you know it, there's going to be photographers taking hundreds of shots of you. I hope you're prepared."

Marty sat propped up by the table, portrait still. His eyes followed Mona around the room as she strode about discussing the fantastic plans she had for them. She kept looking back at the Knox's portrait, making comparisons. The room with its artifacts of past generations thousands of miles removed, grossly lit under fluorescent lights, was tombstone mute. A rusted-out bear trap. An oversized novelty Indian head nickel. A chrome truckstop stool.

"You're *not* ready!" Mona blurted. "You're not stepping foot out of this room until I say so!"

*

Look at those glass doors! They reach so high and open with such ease. The foyer is spacious yet sparsely laid out with only a few thin-framed chairs opposite the receptionist's desk, which is a lean compliment to the interior. As I enter, the receptionist, a woman with hair a flat slate of singular black walks out of the room. On her desk is a pad of stationery, unmarked, with the stencil, "Marty," on it. That's it, no address, no slogan, just the word Marty in a log font with stubs of cut away branches. More rustic than I'd expect. It's a registered trademark. I stand there for a moment waiting for her return, but not content to dally I wander through another set of glass doors, not as impressive to behold, and they take more effort to move.

The hallways are dim. Voices and sheets of light pour from under office doors. Renovation is clearly underway. Blank patches on walls where pictures had once hung. Roughly hewn benches out of place in the modern surroundings. A lamp made of spotted cowhide. A neon sign, meant to simulate a beer ad, says "Marty does it Right" just removed from its cardboard box. I walk through the halls, a phantom in echoing corridors. My briefcase is at my side, everything's in order. The outlined proposal with my business card stapled on the right-hand corner is on top. The fleshed-out plan lies beneath it. Brochures about my company. A binder with our history and achievements.

Extra business cards. My suit looks good. It's creased and sharp. I'm a blade, slicing its way to the top. Not a person in sight, and the voices are so distant I begin to believe that they are simply waking dreams rattling through my head. A horse saddle sits on the floor surrounded by packing popcorn from the box it was shipped in. A few feet away, a couple rusty rifles sit on an otherwise empty desk. I finally see a framed picture. A photograph of a eighteen wheeler, shot from below so it's towering, blinding in chrome. It sits on the floor leaning against the wall.

The hallway narrows into the elevator waiting area and I take it to fifth floor, the top. There I see only one set of doors, thick and open and light spilling out.

He is leaning back in a chair with his back towards me, and I know it's him. His hands are clasped behind his head with heavy boots propped on the windowsill, gazing outside onto a wide field with thin leafless trees. Beyond the field, almost against the horizon, is the freeway. It's busy.

Without turning around he says, "Hi there," and raises his hand and lets it flop down, slapping his leg. I say hello back and he twists his neck to see me. "Oh, I thought it was somebody else," he says. "Have a seat!" He kicks a chair out from under the long, black obelisk-like conference table. I take it and sit at the table next to him. "How about these boots? He says and shuffles them on the windowsill. I'm breaking them in. And how about that view? Look at all those people going from here to there; hot-footin' it for some special reason. Hmm. Don't get me started. What can I do for you?"

Boom, right into my rehearsed pitch. The words fly out of me. I let them belong to someone else as if I'm sitting at the far end of the conference table watching myself sit straight up in the chair, asserting a healthy level of eye-contact, articulate and confident. He continues gazing out the window, and I think he's listening. Or perhaps he's looking at his new boots. Do they have steel toes? He's wearing perfectly worn-in jeans with a flannel shirt that's buttoned all the way to the neck. He interrupts.

"You at a job interview?"

"Sir?"

"You looking for a job?"

"Uh, no. I'm—"

"You want me to work for you? Is that it?"

"I suppose I want to hire—"

"Then Joe," his feet fall to the floor with a thump. "If you're gonna hire me, why are *you* doing all the work?" He then stands up. This is not the Martin Romaine I remember from the pictures. This man towers, like a perfect capital V but much leaner, and his skin hums with a glow. His presence is like a projected movie on a screen before me, and I'm in the front row straining my next to gaze upon him.

"Tell me how you got here, Joe." His voice seems to come from all around.

I breathe out, "Mr. Romaine, I don't—"

He turns to me and places a hand on my shoulder. "First thing, Joe. No Mr. Romaine. In fact, no Martin. You will call me Marty. Please go on."

I tell him everything, and unlike *confession* preparing for punishment, I tell him what I want, how I had been following his teachings in order to hire him to go speak to my company. I tell him I believe so much in the system that I'm using it right now.

Marty smiles, just a flash, and it dissolves into an iron stare. "You did your homework, Mr. Median. You worked your ass off, if you pardon the expression. Got the techniques down pretty well, and remarkably fast."

The air is glass still. A bronze Indian sits hunched in his horse at the other end of the conference table.

"May I make an assumption, Joe?" Marty snaps me back to attention. "Despite the time you've spent practicing and honing the stuff in those books, you still don't have much to show for it. Yes?" His back is towards me, hands folded behind him like a patient math professor.

"Yes, well—"

"And where before you had a low opinion of yourself, your abilities, your past and whatnot, you now feel that you have the tools and the confidence to accomplish just about anything. Right?"

"That's the idea, Mr. Romaine," I spit out before I can catch it.

"Marty," he reminds me gently. "It *was* the idea. Frankly, I'm impressed with the initiative you've shown in getting my attention, as well as your willingness to adopt new ideas. But like I say, you gotta keep moving, take it to the next level, reach higher, push the envelope, the whole shebang. I've been thinking about a whole new system, Joe, something that will really work, and you, if you will, would be perfect for the accelerated program."

He is grinning, one leg propped up on a chair. Is that hair real? It's beyond perfect, and not in an artificial way, prefabricated and scripted, but nature's beauty condensed and luminous. He interrupts himself. "God, I love things that are close to the earth," he says reflectively, fingering the spear of the drooping bronze Indian warrior. "Everyday things and everyday people. That's what I'm all about." Then he compliments me on my Romaine hat and says there's a new one coming out, much more rugged looking. It would look good on me. "And that suit," he continues. "A man after my own heart. Well, my old heart." As big and engaging as the jumbo screen all those weeks ago, he now consumes my entire field of vision. The traffic, the warrior chief headdress, everything in the room, evaporates, and it's just him. Marty. I keep my senses alert, the circuit open to catch everything he has to share. And he's gonna share all right, because he spins around again, as if declaring the President's just been shot, grim-faced, sallow, and slams his open palm on the table. Marty takes the back of my chair and rotates it so I'm facing him framed in the window. In the sun's glare he's not much more than an outline. He leans back against the window, folds his arms and crosses his legs.

"I bet you're wondering what my revolutionary new plan is," he says and winks.

I smile at him, silently, so not to break his rhythm. He winks again and smiles back, and stays that way.

"Oh heck!" he breaks away and slaps his knee. "That's the old Martin; holding out for dramatic effect. I'm a straight shooter. You bet! Joe, do you feel you're at the level where you can act successfully, but still have to *wait* for that success?"

"Yes," I tell him, though he didn't expect me to interject. He looks at me and goes on.

"You've worked your tail off following those techniques to the letter. What do you have to show for it?"

This he expected me to answer. "I feel better, I'm in better shape. I'm—"

"Of course you do; the old system is sound. It gets results, all right."

"But you're making it sound like—"

He laughs. "It's a *good* system," he says. "You work, you get results. I wanna make it simpler, Joe. Now can you think of a way for that to happen? Seems like I've already got it all down to the bare essentials, eh? I bet you're saying, 'Now what the heck is he talking about, makin' it simpler? It's as simple as can be. Cause-effect.' Stripped to the bone as it is—" but Marty jolts and catches himself. "DAMN! I'm doin' it again. Building it to the big pitch. So old hat." He stops and takes a long look at the shiny black leather saddle sitting beside a cardboard box with the words "T-shirts, Forward to Basics," written on it.

He turns to me and breathes out. "This is my new plan: all results—no work." At this, he smiles again.

Marty says he wants to test out his new program out on me. I'm the prototype upon which future endeavors will be modeled, and the way I perform will ultimately determine the overall success of the program. I say yes, and now it gets hazy. "Great!" he whoops, slapping his knee. He runs over, grabs and shakes my hand and says, "Nice to be working with you! I can just tell that this tour will dwarf all previous ones in levels of attendance and overall sales." Then he has me perform a "symbolic gesture," as he puts it. A display of commitment. Open the door," he says, and points to the closed Brazilian Redwood doors leading to the hallway. He puts his two hands together as if in prayer, not breathing. "Remember, Joe," he says. "You alone determine the outcome of all this."

Like a fighter with his trainer seconds before the first round, everything else is blocked out. I gaze upon the brushed steel doorknob. I imagine that the handle is scorching from a fire on the other side. I feel the pressure bubbling up from within this Indian-decorated conference room, and once I twist that handle, an explosion will erupt us out the doors—a mass of memos, pens, woodcarvings, conference chairs and feather headdresses our vapor trail.

*

Martin reached the spot where he was picked up hitchhiking, the bugs waiting for the return of that rich, succulent Midwest boy. He kept driving until the presence of Dick Berg made itself felt. Billboards big enough to adequately advertise FREEDOM, LIBERTY, and JUSTICE appeared like giants signaling you to their kingdom:

> **The Draft is Slavery!**
> **Taxes are Theft!**
> **Legalize Freedom!**
> **Taxation is Wage Slavery!**
> **Serfs Only Had to Pay 10%!**

Martin waited for the KEEP OFF/PRIVATE PROPERTY/FORGET THE DOG, BEWARE OF OWNER/PROTECTED BY SMITH & WESSON signs to signal the entrance into his land. Some had survived the years since Mr. Berg's demise; rusted out with only a few visible letters remaining, but with no less impact than back when he was alive and cleaning his guns. A chain with no lock was thrown around the driveway gate. It had rusted together, and Martin had to give it a few solid Kung Fu kicks to break it loose. He left the van behind, because after twenty feet the praying mantis trees and the gumbo-limbo and the hungry Spanish Moss had narrowed the driveway down to standing room only. He fought off the metaphors because that would be missing the point of this adventure altogether. He had scribbled down plenty already when swiping his way through the marshy jungle that morning.

Nature hadn't completely overtaken Dick Berg's house standing way, way off the road, however the stretched creepers high above canopied it from the sun. There was still plenty of room for the cars, trucks, boats, and motorcycles that had been auctioned off after his death. Nobody wanted the house and land, and it was easy to see why. This place would forever be Dick Berg's. The door was unlocked. Martin looked inside the steamy human aquarium that he had decided was to become his new headquarters.

*

We decide to first hit my company, Conflict Control Solutions. The flight over is a cram session where Marty chants and repeats his objectives. His phrases are economical, tight and insistent.

"No work...All gain."

"The time you spend on improvement is time you could be reaping."

"Let it come to you."

I stand before COCO a living testament of the benefits from Marty's teachings. They hardly believe it's me up there, smiling and shouting with fist-pumps and slogans. If Marty did this with old Joe Median, hopeless personnel manager, imagine what can it do to them. Misty is sidestage, and I see her, starstruck and gripped by my ballet of words. She's in a crisply tailored lavender business suit, her hair sturdy, with a smile that's here to stay. I had surprised her yesterday by showing up at her apartment unannounced, taking her up in my arms and burying my face in her neck. We went for a run and she showed me her upper-body workout. Her back and triceps look like young healthy trees. I whisked away her to a restaurant that cost a solid weeks salary to pay for. And this morning I bought her that suit, the female equivalent of mine. When Marty first saw us together, in our suits, I'll never forget what he said. "So you two wanna be a power couple, huh?" We nodded simultaneously. "Forget it," he quickly followed. We were shattered. What? Didn't we have what it takes? But he couldn't keep the charade up for long, and broke into that picket fence Marty grin. "Forget wanting to be a power couple... just be a power couple. Poof! There you go. You're now a power couple. Wasn't that easy?"

Like training for the Olympics, getting up before the sun rises, eating just the right foods, all to prove your worth for a few seconds. This was my 50 meter dash. I perform before COCO with such unconscious precision, I almost feel robbed over the lack of real energy it takes.

We nail it. They're so impressed that my boss, Bill Emmons, shaking my hand in congratulations is swept aside by our CEO, Phil Hutchinson. The sharp-nosed, dark-haired *big man* hardly ever makes appearances, and now he has his arm around my shoulders. He leads me aside and tells me that Marty and myself have it all figured out, and he wants to be a part of it. If we agree to plug Conflict Control Solutions as the first to endorse the new system, I could be a liaison between the company and Marty, with COCO as a launching pad to dozens of other companies, creating unimaginable connections. He pats my rear in parting, nods, and says, "When we get done, we'll have more business than we can handle," with a certain worry in his voice.

I have a list in hand of all COCO's business connections: publishers, banks, temporary job placement agencies, retailers, distributors, shipping companies. It's astounding how Hutchinson's endorsement gets me into the front door of so many businesses. Between his stamp of approval and being under the Romaine banner, we have the key to the country.

*

Twenty-two hours, the longest Mona had ever gone without seeing Marty. She felt he needed that time alone to contemplate all that she had taught him. Let him acclimate with his surroundings, assume the quiet nobility of the Native American, follow the cowboy commandments of never going back on his word and helping people in distress and the unwavering persistence of the eighteen wheel truck driver. He had the entire wing of the third floor to himself though he was confined to the conference room. Mona grew uneasy with the idea of Marty spending all that time alone, like laying under the sun too long, and as she emerged from her office, more than half of the board of directors were outside sipping coffees, chatting, or looking down at papers in their hands. They flashed upon Mona, but immediately looked away. The secretary was gone, with Christy sitting at her desk, head down at folded hands. She looked up, and before Mona could lash out at them for ganging up on her, Christy told her that Knox had quit. She stood up and Mona took a step back, her arms full of the usual assortment of binders and papers she hauled throughout the compound. She gripped them tight. The board members strained to keep from making a sound while Christy spoke. She was wearing a new Marty sweatshirt. On it, Marty's face smiling with the quote, "In the Wide Open Spaces, Everyone Succeeds!"

"He left a message late last night, after everyone went home. He said that we don't need him anymore, and that was it. I tried reaching him this morning but his secretary told us that Knox caught a cab for the airport."

Mona politely excused herself from the group and went to the conference room. If any board member was brave enough to sneak up to the closed doors and listen in (nobody was), they wouldn't have heard muffled crying or heartbroken sobs; they would have heard her going back to work on Marty. Drilling and quizzing and prepping. When the news reached the employees of Romaine Enterprises that Mona booked a flight out west to gather Knox's work (by contract, the company's property), they shut themselves into their offices to avoid bumping into her on her way out. And they stayed that way for days. Only the clicking of keyboards or mumbling on phones could be heard from their offices.

Mona returned two days later, pushing through the headquarters' tall glass doors. The receptionist jumped up and blocked her path to hand her the birthday card that was sent around the building. Mona took it, said thanks, and without opening it went straight to the conference room. In the elevator, she thought about how the men in her life always got into trouble when they were left alone. This now doubles the time Marty was left to his own devices. A man gets some pretty strange ideas while in seclusion. She had gone through Knox's studio looking for anything bearing Marty's image and was blown back by the paint and paint thinner fumes. There was a color he had invented, called "Mona Blue," which was actually the color he used for Marty's eyes. All work prior to his employment with Performance Power was stacked in the corner. Everything else was dedicated to Marty. Every pose imaginable had been documented; most of them unusable for her purposes: Marty in a perfectly supine position, Marty throwing a javelin, Marty in Rodin's "The Thinker" pose, even a collage of over a dozen Marty facial expressions (no one would ever want to see Marty in terror). No use for Marty raking leaves. There was a portrait, Marty's arms and legs spread revealing his bone and musculature like Da Vinci's Man.

Her flight beat the paintings and sketches and artist's notebooks she had sent back to headquarters by postage, and wiping her sleep-filled eyes with the hand holding the unopened birthday card before the conference room doors, she knew Marty was gone.

"Why didn't you tell us," members of the board mach-punched her shoulder, "that Marty was done? You're always so full of surprises!" They would have lifted her onto their shoulders and carried her throughout the building if her lover hadn't just picked up and split unannounced. Their faces straightened in this regard, echoing the sentiments and birthday wishes in the card she had yet to open. But as if smiles were forced upon them and futile to resist, they lapsed back into merriment. "How exciting! When's his first show?" They broke off from her one by one and as they left they admonished, "No more surprises like that in the future. You had us scared!"

Mona instantly found herself at a loss for anything to do; the momentum that she had built up over the last few months wouldn't let her sleep, and it wasn't until she received news back after Marty's first show that she allowed herself to leave the corporate offices and take a bubble bath at home, hoping it would work. She said to herself, though it wasn't her decision, that she had finally let go. It was over, and the success or failure of her work will be borne out over time. Though the urge at times was enormous, she resisted contacting Marty or his entourage lest she reveal uncertainty or distrust. She had thrown the switch. The wheels were in motion. Leave it be. My work is done. Sticking my hand back in will only gum up the works.

*

Randolph ransacked the books for something to dissolve the glue he seemed to be stuck in. But he couldn't find much. Martin's crisp quotes egged him on, and like a frothy wave at sea that lifts and carries you—and just as it seems like it's about to poop out—another one comes along. The books were good like that, re-fueling for a big surge, but for a single key, there was zilch.

So he surmised he could either double his efforts, re-asserting the practices put forth in the Romaine System (write down all the emotions you experienced over the last week, categorize them into "ineffective" or "effective", and evaluate the actions that led to them. Then take action to increase the number in your "effective" list), or he could walk. He considered the latter, dropping all this public speaking shit and going home to his business. He initially believed that travelling the country would be a great way to redefine himself in the eyes of America as a successful entrepreneur (which he was) with the added bonus of free advertising for mid-priced imports. Instead, he became a Romaine mercenary, flexing his past before the wide-eyed audience, daring them to prove The System wrong.

Nobody told Randolph that Martin was long gone, and it wasn't until Marty's fifth show; a solo effort stripped down to two hours, that Randolph received the new press packet. So, Martin and Mona had been too busy developing this new "Marty" character to return his calls. A statement in bold letters: Randolph has no decision-making power in Romaine Enterprises. The owners could toss aside and re-write the rules as they pleased while Randolph had to stick with the Mr. Universe script. He squinted at the press pack—this bony guy decked in blue jeans, expensive hiking boots, and open smile. He knew Martin pretty well, and initially couldn't buy the image of him as a no-nonsense, get-under-the-hood and do-it-yourself kind of guy. Too New England. But it was damn convincing. This couldn't be Martin... He waited for word from either Martin ("Marty" if that's what he wanted to call himself) or Mona or even one of their secretaries. A week went by and nothing, like being sent to into orbit with Ground Control forgetting all about him. He dug out Marty's tour itinerary from the press pack, tracked down the entourage, and menaced a woman on the other end to get Martin/Marty.

Randolph was greeted with a stapled-on Georgia twang. "This isn't Martin, sir," Marty said.

"Yes, it is, Martin."

Randolph heard a sniffle, like the person on the other end just woke up. "Nope, not Martin. You're talking to Marty. Now who is this?"

"This is Randolph."

"Oh...hi. Can I call you Randy?" Marty cleared his throat.

"No."

Randolph looked for something to punch. He had to remind Marty he had been on tour for over two months.

"Yes. Yes!" Marty shouted. "Of course! *Your* tour. How's it goin' out there? What would you—"

Randolph pounced. "A change in format."

"Huh?"

"That's right. From now on, I will no longer make a single mention of bodybuilding while on stage. It's tired and it's got nothing to do with what The System's all about. I'm going to talk about my business and that's final."

Randolph mentally held on in anticipation, bracing for the slick dismissal that Martin does so well.

"Talk about what you want to talk about," Marty said. He waited for Randolph to answer, and when Randolph didn't, he continued. "This is America. Say what you want. Those people are there to listen to you. If you can pull it off, break format until the cows come home."

"Really?" is all Randolph could say, swaying from the blow that didn't come.

"Yes, really," Marty said, accent getting thicker. "I don't know what Martin told you, but Marty says, 'say what you want.' If you don't think what you're doing is working, then it's no use in thinking someday it magically will. Yeah?"

"Yeah."

"All right! Anything else, Randolph?"

"Uh, no." Randolph said.

"Okay. Well, I gotta get outa here! All right? Hey, but do me a favor?"

Randolph reached for something to grab. "Yes?" he said.

"I know I told you to talk about what you want to talk about. But just one little thing. Stuff is changing around here. Try to lay off pitching the older Romaine products."

"Then what do I do?"

"I don't know. Hell, talk about yourself!"

What Randolph had expected to be a tugging current instead was a dust devil that swept him up and left him hanging upside-down from a tree. He scratched his head and lay down on the undersized bed in his hotel room, his feet hanging off the end. Behind him hanging from the wall was a portrait of a turn of the century fisherman, the one with the rubber hat that droops down at the sides for the rain to pour off. He was looking wistfully at the ocean.

Why no more mention of the products? And that accent...

Instead of celebrating his newly granted freedom, Randolph stared up at the ceiling, eyes wide open. Martin's, or Marty's, mysterious and inexplicable switch in attitude seemed like another way of keeping him at bay, a series of bizarre maneuvers to further ward off his advances in the company.

There was no way to gauge the audience's reaction to the omitted bodybuilding tales. The lights smoked them out and the PA reflected back only his voice. He got laughs and applause as he had in his previous performances. So, on his first time out under a different format, it seemed to work.

And—he could be so petty for a guy that outweighed her by two hundred pounds—he didn't tell Suzi about the conversation he had with Marty before stepping out on stage. Then, halfway through his new presentation, Randolph glanced side stage and it must have been by chance alone, certainly, that the sole stage light that caught her was a red gel, transforming her from a peppy lip liner brunette into a toe-tapping incubus. He had the go-ahead from Marty, but nonetheless was chilled by Suzi's taught piercing wrath. It messed up his timing and he lost his place and he finally staggered to a lame end with a knock-knock joke.

"Knock knock?"

"Who's there?"

"Tank."

"Tank who?"

"Tank YOU! Good Night!"

Randolph exited the stage opposite where Suzi fumed in parental disappointment, and he broke into a sprint. He buried himself in the thick expanse of autograph seekers out in the lobby.

The autograph line stretched past the merchandise tables and the corn dog and coffee stands, nearly reaching the restrooms. Randolph whipped out his signature and personalized notes to the folks in line, shook hands and took pictures arm-in-arm with strangers, unconcerned about the constant questions about how much he can now bench press or his thoughts about performance-enhancing drugs. A nice thick padding of people between him and Suzi. He felt so damn good sitting at the autograph table, still tall enough to be face to face with most of the people standing there before him.

Chapter 8

Keychains
These custom keychains come with popular Martin
Romaine quotations:

> *"I Will Not Wait."*
> *"The Best Me I Can Be."*
> *"Only Greatness is Acceptable."*
> *"When in Doubt, Win."*
> *"See It and Be It."*

This is going to be a supremely rewarding experience! Martin said to himself. Complete self-reliance. Or is it self-sufficiency? The house had in the fifteen years of vacancy collected a half-foot of dust and moss that softened into a spongy, springy carpet. It was now like the inside of a sub tropical cave, aquamarine and smelling like fish food (kids had found it too creepy to get drunk in). Everything, which wasn't much, that folks found worthy to haul away was hauled away. The rest—books, file cabinets and chairs—blended in perfectly with the wet slick walls. If the house were floating in space with no gravity, there would be no way to tell floor from ceiling. Martin scraped the fungus and moss from what appeared to be a picture hanging over the fireplace. Beneath the sludge was a portrait of a soldier, possibly Mr. Berg, two cylindrical tanks tied to his back with hoses leading to a skeletal rifle in his hands. A long arc of flame shot out of the end, frying a tall palm tree. The soldier grimaced, or perhaps it was a smile, revealing some very long teeth. In what was probably Berg's master bedroom, standing besides the bed/army cot/slab of algae on four legs, was a green creature standing alert. It looked like it had just swum up from the bottom of a swamp. Martin looked closer at the upright stiff thing standing waist high, and scraped away at the green goo with one of his credit cards. Beneath was very dark-brown matted fur, and around its neck a collar with an identification tag, a military dog tag. It said, Simon. Rotweiller. Atheist. Martin cleared his throat and decided not to set up camp in this room.

He had never camped in his life, but he knew it all starts with shelter. The elements to face inside the house rivaled the ones outside (bugs, mud, cold), except the rain couldn't get it. That alone was the deciding factor in staying indoors.

Taken all together—between the seminars, books, live appearances, television interviews, and one-on-one meetings with presidents—Martin Romaine had come up with a total of 668 steps forming dozens of lists. The steps for making a decision. The top ten empowering emotions. Seven traits of hugely successful people. Five steps to take when preparing to lose weight. Your 10 top influences. Seven people you admire most. Three things you imagine for yourself in five years time. Fourteen days to what you want to be. Six steps to mental mastery. The twenty keys to a more romantic marriage. He sat on the corner of the bed, feeling himself sink into the green mattress, attempting to assemble in his mind a new list of steps that would get him through this, and come up with a hierarchy of necessities for this test. There was shelter. Then food. Everything beyond those two were luxuries: entertainment, companionship, love, comfort. He wrote these with his finger in the algae on the bed. But then he stood up. This was his old pattern; write down lists, organize them in degrees of priority until they lose all meaning. *This* was going to be different. No list was going to tell him what to do. Early man killing and then dragging Mastodon carcasses back into the caves didn't follow steps. There was only one thing—survival.

He had never caught his own food either. Outside of going fishing a few times as a lad with his grandparents in Michigan in a lake stocked full of Rainbow trout, everything he ever ate was store or restaurant purchased. He'd plop the line into the water and even though he could see the slick wedges finning about underneath, nibbling wisely on the salmon egg deftly missing the hook, none would give themselves up. "Oh, why is grandpa catching all the fish?" he asked his grandmother. So she, taking a break from chain-smoking menthols, told young Martin to pour coffee from the plaid-colored thermos. With her leathern hands that could handle hawks talons unprotected, she re-latched a fish onto his hook and slid the catch back into the water. "Looks like you've got something there," she said and winked at grandpa. Martin reeled in the line and without feeling for life, grabbed it by the tail and whacked its head against the side of the boat. He said, "Look, I got one! And it's guts are already gone," holding up the already cleaned fish to his grandparents. So Martin grew up without having to handle the messy innards, which makes everything tick. And his dried fruit (also without the innards) that he purchased from Billy's convenience store back in town had run out by his second hour of survival camp.

The next morning, stretching his back with a Downward Dog, he realized that the change he saw for himself would essentially hinge upon one thing: Catch, prepare and consume his own food. Everything else would blossom out of that, and the flame-throwing Dick Berg in the portrait over the mantelpiece grinned in agreement.

If there was a fishing pole remaining in Dick Berg's shabby estate, it had grown over with so much moss and algae that it now blended in with the vines or Strangler plants that populated the place. Martin did find about three feet of line used by the resourceful Dick to bundle up a decade's worth of Life magazines. He bent a hook out of a TV antenna and tied it to the end of a shower curtain rod. Martin rolled up his pants legs and set for the stream he had passed yesterday when exiting the swamp.

He figured a shaded area somewhere along the stream would be the best place to throw the line in, a cool spot that fish prefer. With the last wad of dried fruit and some American spit, he dropped the line in. Fishing metaphors, with their themes of waiting patiently, quiet time spent in silent isolation, things lurking beneath the surface, etc. fought for the title of King of the Mountain of Martin's mind. He attempted to shake them free by imagining cleaning the fish he would soon catch. How did it go? Crack it over the head, then take out the hook? Or was it the other way. Or did it matter? *Like fishing, there are several steps to accomplishing your goal: One, Prepare with the correct equipment. Two,...* No! Stop it! After catching the fish, clean it. When do you cut the head off? Sometimes the head is left on. Martin had been served fifty-dollar pan-seared fish with the head on, but he didn't care for picking at something with a face. The head would have to go. Could it, or the guts, be used for bait later? Cannibalism. *Waste none of your resources. The Indians used every part of the buffalo they hunted, as you must utilize all the strengths of your sales team.* Knock it off! Now you start the slit from the asshole and move up to the gills. Martin was certain of it, and he grimaced away any metaphor for that business.

The line tugged, but with little struggle. Martin yanked. The end of the line swam towards Martin confused and poked its toad head above the water. The bumpy lump that looked like the back of an eighty-five year-old waitresses' hand shook to free itself of the antenna hook that poked out of its cheek. Martin grabbed the chubby critter by its rubbery round belly. Eat a toad? Its eyes went wide as Martin pulled out the homemade hook. It wiggled out of his hands and plopped back into the water.

Nothing else bit, and nothing was going to; the frog made off with most of the dried fruit on the hook. Martin realized the only real way he was going to survive this was to act as Dick Berg would act, and that, according to Steve who picked him up hitchhiking, was to be as doggedly fierce as possible. Act independently, no matter the inconvenience. Have a house on the roadside made of rattlesnake hide. He walked back to the house as Mr. Berg would walk, a shambling iron lope, chewing on jerky or Days O' Work that wasn't there. The house, underneath the blue-green algae, was the model of complete self-sufficiency. Berg didn't have a sister who picked out what sweater for him to wear that day, nor was he beholden to make anybody but *himself* feel good.

Dick did it all.

Martin discovered a moldy notebook in the bottom of a file cabinet. The leaves were sticky thin and green like snot rags, but words could be made out. Written on tape on the spine was "Daily Doings." It was a journal of every activity Mr. Berg did throughout the day, from re-building a carburetor to gathering eggs and preparing breakfast to patching the roof. There were no comments otherwise. No adjectives. Simply a list of what he did, usually ending the day by building furniture or, surprisingly, teaching himself Portuguese. References were made, it appeared, to other journals. "See 'Electronics,' for freezer schematics," when his fridge broke down. There was a separate journal out there somewhere with his notes and thoughts about his various legal dealings. And maybe a notebook on how to properly catch a fish. The exact times of Dick Berg's daily activities weren't recorded, but it was clear that each waking minute of his day was spent sustaining his existence, like running on a hamster wheel that was responsible for food, shelter, and warmth. Everything. His mission was to be entirely self-sufficient, and he worked constantly at it. The admiration that Martin had for Dick's independence suddenly ballooned into intimidation. And what made the intimidation complete was how foreign Dick's life was from his own—a brown bear envious of a hummingbird's ability to hang still in the air. Martin knew that he only needed to accomplish one feat to gain admittance into Dick Berg's world. Catch his own food.

After two weeks of living off nothing more than jungle leaves and mosses, and one jar of browned peach preserves found under Dick Berg's bed, the frog now sounded scrumptious. He'd eaten them before, though not in the froggy, hop-hop, familiar way, and had paid handsomely for the privilege. Afterwards he had flaunted eating the heavily garlic-sauced meat to his friends and associates like it was a wild adventure, like hunting Rhino or jumping out of a plane before careening into a mountain, an orphan child tucked ender his arm. Martin set out for the same fishing spot as before, pole in hand, with the resolve that if he caught a frog before a fish, then that would be his dinner. He thought Dick must have a recipe for cooked frog somewhere buried in the house, but maybe using it wouldn't be the Dick Berg way. Using another man's recipe, you know, a little fruity.

*

We're on the top level of a two-story tour bus. Marty is speaking. His style is both engaging and lazy. He is spread expansively on a thick leather swivel chair, legs wide, hands folded behind his head. "God Damn," he slaps his knee. "I look back sometimes at the old stuff and just wanna retch— 'System of Success...' Blecch! Systems, procedures, techniques, strategies... what a load. I say chuck it! That's right. Dump all those books. Those videos. Bomb the seminars. Burn the notebooks with the useless boring algorithms and scatter the ashes to the winds. I suspect you're thinking to yourself, Joe, 'Now what the heck is Marty talking about? I spent all that time memorizing and obsessively ingraining those well-worn strategies, and now I gotta forget 'em?' Yes, Joe, you do. What do we really want? I'll tell you. Maximum success, minimum effort. That's my lesson, pure and simple. Get that job. Have that husband. You won't watch the weight disappear, cause it'll already be gone."

From Hutchinson's connections, we are able to reach several companies and corporations, and branching out from there to travel agencies, clothing manufacturers, credit card companies. Ours is no longer just a service for the big shot Furtune 500 companies or senators or NBA championship teams. Everybody gets some. They're intrigued by the accessible and approachable Marty. Everyone, from management on down to the kids in the mailroom, assaults us with questions after the lectures. Marty happily accommodates, and he constantly stresses the following concept: "Forget the path. Be at your destination now."

We go from tour bus to private jet to limo and back to tour bus snaking and cris-crossing the country. The companies we hit are left breathless, shaken and changed. Each one falls in with Marty's plan... though he hates the word "plan." I set him up and he knocks 'em down. Everything that I've ever wanted is right here before me, and what's funny is that the more I want (recognition, cars, homes) the easier and easier it is to have. And, as Marty envisions, soon it will be a matter of just thinking about it and it will appear.

And Marty's following grows. Engagements are quickly added to accommodate the demand for more appearances. One thing I especially admire about him is his refusal to do individual seminars with important names. He says that meeting with just one person is a waste of time; he wouldn't tell an Oscar Award winning director, Governor, or whomever anything different than he would a middle manager for office supplies in Boise. He wants to reach as many people as possible. A nice gesture of modesty, even if I wouldn't mind meeting a few sports legends or perhaps a Congressman.

I should also mention that Marty is impressed with my development. Misty and I are suited up and standing tall wherever we go. We have bought houses and cars sight unseen and still untouched. I keep my job with COCO in an advisory role, doing less, earning more. We're sexy and strong. People look at us and they see *the* power couple, a mobile unit that projects an image of unquestioned prosperity. They want to be like us; they tell us so. Marty stands behind me, pleased as I greet the swarms of autograph and advice seekers. His arms are folded while wearing an earthy smile.

"You're a natural, Joe," he tells me before a show. "A natural! It'll take everyone else weeks to catch up to you, if ever." He brushes the invisible dirt from his well-worn jeans and lopes around the room. Leaning back against a cabinet like a horse he's trusted since a child, he continues. "I like what I see, Joe, and there's no end in sight. Keep going! Life's too short to be patient." Marty then stands straight, tall and lean, and from my vantagepoint, he blasts through the ceiling towering into the clouds. He looks down and asks Misty if he and I can have a few minutes alone.

After she leaves, Marty turns to me. "Things are indeed looking good for you, my friend. Now see the results you get from *my* system?"

"Yes indeed, I do," I tell him.

"And there's more where that came from, you bet! However I see it as being somewhat lopsided, Joe." Marty looks at me seriously like a wining Manager that goes to the mound and tells his pitcher to wrap things up. "I see you putting all your eggs in one basket, everything's going towards your professional life. Remember, if it's one thing I'm trying to get across, it's that whatever you want you can have right now, and certainly not limited to just one thing. I think you see where I'm going. Your professional life is stellar, monumental. But don't let it end there. Get me? Now what do you think I'm getting' at?" He says and looks away.

"Misty?"

"Yep."

"I should leave her, get somebody better?"

Marty laughs, "No. But she's not your ideal as of yet, eh?"

"She's getting there, working—"

"There you go. The two very words I'm trying to cancel out: 'There' and 'work.' I hate 'em. Let's just ditch the word 'work' altogether." He squats before me as if warming himself by a campfire. I still feel like an elf at his feet. "Keep her, by all means. She's a wonderful girl. Just have her match your ideal right away. You know science and the medical field have made amazing strides lately at perfecting the human form. The bodies that previously took women years to develop—what with diets, exercise, and denial—can now be obtained with a few quick and simple procedures. I just want what's good for you, Joe."

Boom! Misty is my ideal mate. With the vast amounts of work that has been done on her: the tucking, the inserting, the tightening, the cutting, she won't have to lift a finger to maintain her newfound beauty. Even the effort she would have otherwise taken to apply her makeup has been eliminated—it's now tattooed on her face. Another living monument to my realized desires.

We hit the road hard and fast, followed by a modest legion of fans. These people travel alone, with their families or in organized groups to see and hear Marty. "We're getting through to them," he tells me. Nevertheless, he still seems unsettled, as if stopping for a moment's rest would begin the calcification and decay. A shark must always be moving. Marty never sits up straight in a chair or stands without leaning against a dresser or doorframe, but you know there's power that's coiled and ready to spring. "But I'm not certain if we're getting our true message across," he continues. "You'd think that after one or two seminars, they'd be putting the teachings into practice." I detect a hint of annoyance in Marty at the efforts people put forth and the attention they give him, the unwavering gaze, the waiting in line for a handshake, even longer for an autograph, and the days and weeks spent following the tour throughout the country. "Don't they get it?" he scratches his head, "They exert too much. Not just over me... but over everything."

But Marty isn't entirely correct. As we begin the second leg of our tour, I notice a change. People show up to the seminars as before, but not as repeat customers. Real live testimonials of the fruits gained from Marty's lessons. It's obvious at first glance that they too have begun holding themselves to higher standards. They paint a figure of freshly gained prosperity. Where before they rattled about in their ten year-old cars, they are now behind the wheel of new, or slightly used, mid-to-high end automobiles. Husbands and wives look brighter and healthier, attired in the latest styles. They trumpet us with praise. Marty however is going so fast he takes little notice. He insists that he must reach everyone. But he also needs me.

I get more time on stage. It's integral to the program, he says, that he has a living, speaking success story, someone who shares their background standing before them. A perfect warm-up act. And I do this with such ease—just being myself. I hook them with the tale of my transformation from luckless nonentity to vigorous go-getter, and leave them hanging on the line for Marty to pull in.

*

Like winning the lottery and seeing that last kid off to college all rolled up into one, Mona sat in her office. She had created a self-sustaining entity and the less she inquired about it, the more successful it became. The numbers said it all. They were way up in the black, all graphs pointed up. She stamped the checks and handed all companies requesting a Marty appearance onto the folks in booking. Guest speakers became superfluous; the tour no longer required testimonies of the rich and famous. The Marty juggernaut was its own success story. And it was an added surprise when the sudden extra surge in attendance and revenue coincided with the addition of this new guy, Joe Median, to the payroll. "Who is Joe?" she asked, and was handed a dossier of this thirty-nine year old slightly chubby fellow who worked as a human resource manager for Conflict Control Systems. She looked at his picture—Mr. Median on stage with his arms spread wide, leaning slightly back, and very toothy as if in the middle of a punchline. Mona wondered how her philosophy behind the Marty phenomena (which she informally titled "Down-Home Run") tied in with this Joe character, but she wrote it off as the magic of Marty at work. The show steadily became stripped down. No more fireworks. Costume changes gone. The doves set free.

Performance Power, a subsidiary of Romaine Enterprises, was getting renewed attention from the media. The new tour was touted as a "Return to form, a more straightforward presentation like the old days, free of the hype," when in actuality, even as Martin and Mona toured alone in that van, the shows always had a certain degree of dazzle. All they could afford as supporting acts back then was a sword swallower, cheap fireworks, or the regional manager of Pizza Hut. They used whatever they could, anything that fire and zoning laws would let them get away with.

The staff at headquarters eased off the constant monitoring of the tour, which had proved to be the most reliable revenue maker in Romaine history. Waiting like wolves, the board of directors had initially been, to report any disasters back to Mona. And when none came, they got together and threw her a surprise party celebrating the "Success of Successes." There was Marty's face on the cake, the frosting nearly capturing that enigmatic homespun wisdom. When Mona finished off her short speech with, "...it looks like our little Marty made good," and the staff threw away their paper plates and headed back to their offices, there was warm certainty in everyone's hearts that all troubles were behind them. All they needed to do now was occasionally check the oil and the tire pressure and the rest would take care of itself. But after Mona took that last bite of cake, she decided to finally check up on him.

Marty's assistant didn't recognize Mona's voice when she called. She pinched off Mona's request to speak to him mid sentence, but Mona struck back. "Tell him it's Mona. MO-NA."

As she waited, she visualized Marty trotting into the room and scooping up the phone.

"Mona!"

"Hello, Marty."

"Hello Mona!" Mentioning the addressee's name on first contact was an affective tool of gaining immediate intimacy.

"I hope you don't mind me calling," Mona said, feeling him out.

"Ah, why should I mind?"

Now that Marty was on the other line, Mona didn't know what to say. All prior contact was dedicated to observation—taking special notice his hair, that certain way he was taught to slouch, etc. She'd quiz him with questions like, "What if a person keeps trying at something—I don't know, politics, let's say—and fails year after year, what do they do?" and closely monitor his facial expressions, his hands, his stance, and especially whether he was pained at the proposition over not having a simple pat answer. As he gradually adapted to and confronted these scenarios with an easy humor and grace, Mona got more personal. "What are *you're* weaknesses? How much of a person's past, in percentages, is important to their development? How open to criticism are you?" she prodded. His actual vocal responses were not heeded. It was all in the presentation. Fey, wishy-washy or unsure responses were zeroed in on and mentally shot out of the sky. And if Marty was convincing enough in his one-foot-on-the-bumper assuredness, then the audience would go along with him no matter what came out of his mouth.

Now out of habit on the phone, Mona zeroed in on his tone. It was right on; perfect in cadence, pitch, warmth, and with a trust that demanded the same in return. He must have learned that himself.

"The tour seems to be going great," she said, trying to pull something out of him.

"Yeah, it sure seems that way."

"Having fun?"

"You bet!"

"Attendance is up from last year."

"Good to hear," Marty said, no surprise in his voice, "Good to hear."

"You're looking great up there on stage. I saw a little footage of you. Beyond my expectations. And that new guy—"

"Yes, Joe. He's perfect."

"At first I was surprised by your choice in him, but it makes complete sense now."

"The audience really responds to him," Marty said.

Mona pictured Marty at the other end, the phone tucked between his ear and shoulder, comfortable enough to be asleep, leaning back in a chair, booted feet crossed and resting on a table. She knew now what she wanted.

"Your growth is really something," Mona said.

"Why thank you. Isn't that the plan?"

"You're making some interesting decisions."

"Yeah? Of course that goes with the territory; rugged individualism demands risky ventures. Plunging into the fog of the unknown, optimism leading the way."

"I'm just surprised. The Joe decision. Quite extraordinary, that one."

Marty chuckled. "Oh, that one just came along."

"Along with your decision to leave."

Mona could see Marty sit up in his chair with an armed casualness.

"The domain of the individualist is a vast one. What did you expect?" he said.

Two thousand miles of phone static between them. Mona sat in her office all day with nothing to do but keep her eyes on the numbers, watching them rise, sink a little like an escaped balloon pushed briefly down by the wind, and go back up. Sometimes to an important client or just a little kid asking nicely she'd send out an 8x10 glossy of Marty, the autograph forged. And then it was wondering what to do with all the new spare time, maybe take up a hobby. Sharpshooting? Learn Middle Eastern cuisine?

Marty kept going. "A cowboy to ride the range, a gear-jammin' trucker. That's me. You know the only way for it to be was for me to hit the road on my own. Sounds like a song... 'Hit the road...on my own...' Mona, you did a fine job. I hope you've rewarded yourself."

"I'm not sure if I know how," she said.

"Well, if you lack direction, perhaps you need to come to one of my conferences!" Mona could feel the wink through the phone.

*

Misty is pregnant. It's tough to control yourself where you're within the presence of your ideal mate. "It's a natural progression." Marty says, beaming. "If you do everything right, your child will never have to lift a finger. In fact, I would consider it a failure if the child ever lost a drop of sweat due to unneeded effort. For 'Ease is too Much Effort!' Shit. I gotta remember that."

The faster I go, the slower everything around me becomes. The dressing rooms aren't immediately cleaned. Meal preparation seems to takes longer than I remember. I attribute it to the inability of others to meet my raised expectations. Or perhaps these things are expected to take longer at finer and more exclusive establishments. "Eat!" Marty demands of everyone, especially me. "It's yours, take it!" And take it I do. The wine flows, exquisite food heaped high. In one particular restaurant specializing in pan-Asian cuisine (over thirty-five different forms of sea life available on the menu, a dozen mollusks) perched on the top of a 75-floor building overlooking the twinkling city lights, I unbutton the top button of my pants and excuse myself for the bathroom. Behind me I hear Marty say, "Soon you won't even have to get up to do that!" followed by a burst of laughter from our dozen guests.

I rush into the stall to do my business, and there I see one of Marty's more popular quotes, "We will not wait," written in thick solid red ink behind the toilet. I'm thrilled to see that our message has become so far reaching, embedded in the public's consciousness. Beyond the seminars and scribbled on the bathroom stall wall in a four-star restaurant half a mile in the air. I look closer at the lettering. It's slightly faded, as if been there for a while. The walls could use a new coat of paint and the toilet doesn't display the luster typically associated with such upscale establishments. Bathroom odors mingle with hastily applied pine scent. And when I exit the stall, it's like I am suddenly transported to a fastfood franchise, the kind of place you stumble into cross-legged after taking the freeway offramp. Just enough to pass health codes. The sink has dirt rings, soap dispensers empty with crusty residue around the nozzle and replaced by a worn-down bar of yellow soap. In my former days, this would be the typical state of my own bathroom, but here? I walk back into the crystalline splendor of the dining room with its deep wood tones and gigantic fish tanks and take my seat. The bathroom quickly begins to fade like all the fears you had as a child, foreign and unrecognizable. Course after course is set down before us and the drinks keep coming. Marty leans back and talks and talks. With ease he segues from meeting a newly assassinated foreign political figure to trekking through the arctic. Then, in silent unanimous decision, we're on our feet and ready for the next stop, our hotel lounge. The Maitre d' helps me with my coat, and like a repressed memory bubbling up, I get a flash of the bathroom. I lean to him and say, "The bathroom..." He eases me into the second sleeve and says, "We've been rather understaffed in that department." I follow the group. The Maitre d' sees us out and when we leave, says to me, "It's been surprisingly difficult. Maybe it's the seventy-five story climb that scares them off."

Misty's pregnancy coupled with the non-stop touring schedule has inspired me to add my contribution to the Marty canon. "Preparing your Unborn Child for Success." My writing skills are limited, and I haven't done any real research since I wrote a twenty-five page paper in college about the Industrial Revolution (mostly plagiarized). I begin outlining and experimenting at the same time. My theory is: Why wait until you have developed self-awareness when you can literally have your cognitive processes fashioned for success from the very start? I begin with the heading, "The Primeval Foundation," and start off on a light note. "The only way to develop the ultimate sense of success is to attain it from a previous life...so unless you're Hindu, you've got a distinct disadvantage."

It only seems *logical* to start off by making certain everything within earshot of the womb portrays a solid positive message of achievement. I bombard the fetus around the clock with live readings of Martin Romaine's written works, new slogans and theories by Marty, lessons I've learned along the way. And Misty chips in with insightful comparisons between her old, lazy self, and her new idealized self and how it's enriched her life. I get close to her tummy and share with the embryo my dreams and goals, both for the child as well as for myself. We play recordings of chamber music, symphonies and fugues by the great composers.

In the middle of a calculus derivative recitation (which I don't even begin to understand), Misty looks down at me. "Joe."

I finish the equation. "Yes, Honey?"

"There's been something I've been thinking about, concerning the child."

"What's that?"

Her forehead is crinkled out of worry. "I'm a tad concerned that our child will eventually find out about our old way of life and what kind of effect it will have upon him."

I lean over to her ear, quietly reminding her of the rules we had developed, *"Keep everything in a positive tone. Do not let your unborn child be privy to unpleasantness, be it family strife, social conflict, popular media, etc. If a serious matter is to be discussed, keep the tone jovial, for the underdeveloped social brain will interpret it as conflict and cause undue malaise."* She nods in understanding. We keep a smile on our faces..

I continue. "I've thought about it too, honey. And it's a simple solution."

"Simple? It's impossible, Joe. The past is permanent. I don't know what to do," she says smiling.

I perk up, gleeful. "Why, it's not so hard. All you got to do is remove all traces or mementos of our past selves."

"That's—"

"Dearest, what's so difficult and not good about it? (I don't catch the 'difficult', but change 'bad' to 'not good' in time). Not only will it be beneficial to Junior over there—Hi, Junior—but it will aid us enormously."

"Everything, Sweetie?"

"Yes, Everything. We'll make a game out of it. The person who finds and does away with the most souvenirs of our past: old pay stubs, cheap old clothing, books, trinkets from vacations, whatever, will be treated to a day spa. Can you think of any that come to mind, sugar?"

"Hmm... How about pictures?" She calls out like an impatient child.

"Yes! That's a very good one. Anything else?"

"Furniture, I suppose. Cars. It could be just about anything purchased before a few months ago."

I'm not eager to mention this one, but since we have smiles on our faces, it should diminish the impact. "Misty, the parents."

She loses her smile, and her posture sags a touch from the upright star pupil of before. "The parents," she says.

"They should be number one on the list, hon." I kneel before her and touch her belly. "Think about it. They're seventy-five to eighty percent responsible for forming us into the adults that we were. Our old selves are the products of them while our new selves are the products of us—and Marty—but mostly us."

"But our parents? Never again?"

"It's the only thing we can do. You know that they will treat us as they always have and not even begin to grasp what we have become. The same old folks with their same old low expectations. And if that doesn't convince you—keep smiling, dear—think of the negative impact they would have upon our child. One minute the kid would be with us, constantly challenged and pushed to greater heights, and the next he would be around the folks, doing what they're always did, poisoning him with compromise."

Misty looks down, but continues the smile. God Bless her, what a trooper.

Our venues begin to blur into one another. We are ferried along highways, skies and railways until we reach the same places: the booths, concession stands, stage and light show waiting for us. Only the attendees appear to change. The old telltale character-istics of our clientele—last-minute hope bordering upon desperation—are gone. And they're not sycophants who hang onto every uttered syllable, humble and reserved before Marty, but rather they stand before us front and center with a definite purpose: get the info and get out. No time to waste on musical warm-ups or guest lecturers. During pauses in Marty's presentation they are down at their notepads or screens, scrib-bling and typing. Business plans or proposals, I suspect. And how good they look! They're mid to low-priced business attire have been replaced by seasonal top-shelf lines. Hair is perfect. Rings and watches and bracelets sparkle in the crowd like a jewel sea.

The crowds keep growing, and this paradoxically forces the tour away from major metropolitan areas. There are few man-made structures that will accommodate all our attendees, so we rent out farmlands. The folks camp out overnight in tents pitched beside their high-priced German, Italian, and British luxury automobiles, meals prepared on propane stoves.

All the while, our living arrangements and travel itiner-aries become even more cloistered and secluded. We are hamsters transported through a Habitrail. A series of boxes. The plane box. The bus box. Hotel boxes. Backstage and dressing room boxes. I feel that we are in a giant office building, arriving at different floors seeing the same things: foyers, bathrooms, dressing rooms, stages... all the same but at different altitudes. Misty and I naturally are inseparable. Our pre-natal child training has become routine and no longer requires a self-conscious act of monitoring and pre-determining the positive or negative impact of our actions. For the people who meet us for the first time, they think we are courting lovers, sweet and new. "What a lovely relationship they have. So supportive and positive. He bends over backwards to meet her every need." It's true, I don't want Misty to undergo even the minutest notion of strife, so I have hired two people to wait on her while I'm working. One for the necessities: food, clothing, lavender and salted baths, one for enrichment: to read to her and the child, massage and acupressure, and to produce a comfortable environment that promotes peace of mind.

Marty takes me aside, gushing over the value of our partnership. He says our current success would have been impossible without my dedication and complete mastery of relating to the average workaday guy, unfulfilled both professionally and romantically. He tags along as I go downstairs into the hotel restaurant for meals, and we frequently break into impromptu strategic planning sessions. We're like college frat brothers amused by the slightest thing the other does, securing our self-image by having it constantly on display before the other. He tells me we're changing the world.

I lead the audience in the chant, "If you're sweatin', you'll be regrettin'!" and tell them if they repeat it to themselves with as much enthusiasm as they can muster before every endeavor they undertake, they will invariably cut investments down to nil while still reaping enormous dividends. It's from a new system that Marty has titled, "Not An Ounce of Strain." I hammer into them the importance of recognizing the needless efforts they have made which, instead of bearing fruits, has only over time robbed them of their vitality. This leaves them raw and ready for Marty. It's an elegant system, even though it's an enormous challenge varying the tales of unfulfillment night after night to the ever-expanding masses of people.

A number of Marty's fans have banded together to form a union of sorts. They occupy the front rows, are the first ones in line for autographs (This one woman with a large, muscular neck has come to me six nights in a row asking for my signature), and they act as impromptu body guards, waiting for us as we leave the venue hours after the show has ended. I've heard an acronym tossed around—FOM, "Friends of Marty." It's a fan club, which Marty doesn't approve of (he says it's too other-based) and they frequently approach us for promotional gifts: signed tour jackets, rare Marty portraits, luncheons with Marty or myself. Members (whom we have grown to know on a first-name basis) occasionally disappear for a two-week training seminar. And when they return somebody else goes. Multiple FOM members are always present at our shows, so nothing gets by.

FOM has one program that I particularly support. They gather funds to sponsor an underprivileged family that displays a strong willingness to succeed and benefit from Marty's teachings. They follow the tour for two weeks and get the opportunity to join us on stage. Who knows where they find them? One week it's a family of Navaho Indians from Arizona, the other a family of five, every member employed at their local Wal Mart. And that's when I see them, in the front row looking up at me as I hit the stage, the desperate souls I plucked off the side of the road that fierce rainy day. Sherri, James, and Noelle. They look as struck over seeing me as I them. Noelle's eyes light up, and I can read her lips. "Mommy; it's that man!" Sherri is smiling pleasantly, and even James reacts to my speech. He lets out a laugh in spite of himself when I deliver a punchline.

We meet backstage. Sherri tells me she didn't think I was the Joe that FOM was talking about.

Despite my unannounced departure from the hotel, she explains, they managed in reaching the children's father. Sherri said my sudden and inexplicable disappearance after our intervention was part of the big picture: "Another test along the way." Alan initially was thrilled to have "the unit together" and he took them all out to dinner at a French restaurant. He insisted that they stay in his expansive stylishly furnished home. The next day, however, and with no more than a half-hour warning, said he was leaving for Belgium and didn't know when he would be back. He left them in his 8,500 square-foot house—a TV and bathroom for each family member, but no cash and no access to cash. The refrigerator was stocked with unidentifiable food: tzatziki, some kind of curry, eggs half the size of chicken eggs, green swampy juice. They fried up a cut of Japanese beef that had a $250 price tag. The food, whatever they could stomach, lasted only a week. Sherri spent the remainder of her funds stocking up on bulk rice, cereal, bread, peanut butter and noodles from a restaurant distributor fifteen miles out of town. And when that ran out she had to get a job. She worked the counter at a sandwich shop in the part of town that people who had the money to buy the homes she was staying in strolled about on weekends. Some of her customers, waiting for their custom-built sandwiches named after Italian cities and holding bags containing shoes it would take her six solid days to earn, were her ex-husbands neighbors. So she took her wages back to that big house, only able to afford food and toilet paper. The luxuries she had to let go: the cable, the cleaning lady once a week, even the telephone voice messaging service. When the Croat gardener was sent away, the yard went to hell and earned complaints from the neighborhood association. That made the family reluctant to leave the house, peeking out from behind the curtains before trips to the store. Sherri said she would have sold off a couple of the television sets, but they were built into the walls when the place was constructed. She was also willing to hawk some of the artwork, but had no idea where to take the paintings and awkwardly-shaped oversized sculptures. Besides, most of it couldn't fit through the door. It drove her nuts: she and the children had immoderately pricey Norwegian chairs to sit on with WIDE-screen televisions to watch, but no cable and no reception (except for staticy PBS), bottles of unpronounceable spices from all over the globe with only frozen hot dogs to sprinkle them on. Bordeaux, but no milk. A lush, modern house, but no air conditioning. Exotic tropical plants outside growing wild. The story ended with Alan returning from overseas, appalled at the state of his house and property. He couldn't leave her home alone for one second. This is the kind of thing that drove them apart in the first place. How could she let this happen? How do you re-build a family with this level of gross carelessness? He screamed at her that his standing the community was probably shot. Was he harboring boat people?

This time he stuck around for two days, and once again with little warning announced that he needed to get away, take a break and clear up his head.

She applied for the FOM tour contest, describing the conditions she was suffering through, and she won.

"So close," Marty says leaning in the doorway. He nods and stretches up tall, the way he always does when delivering a point.

"You were that close," he says displaying the distance between his index finger and thumb. He peers through that space at Sherri. "You had it all right there, and you blew it."

I introduce everyone, and even Misty arrives flanked by her entertainment assistant. Marty gets down on one knee in front of little Noelle and shakes her hand like she's a true-life princess. Then he stands up in front of James, sizing him up and gripping his hand tight, nothing need to be said.

He walks to the door and turns around. "All of it, right in front of you. I can't think of a more perfect example of what I'm trying to teach. Listen up, Joe, cause this is the next step in what I call, "Ideal Development." Let's say it everyone: 'I-deal Development.' God, Sherri; I wish you saw me before you got into that situation, because if you did you'd still be in that house, except this time with the gardener, the cable, good food, all that stuff."

Sherri says, "But I worked."

"Oh, working's got nothing to do with it. Am I right, Joe?"

I nod.

"It's got to do with something else entirely," Marty stops and bends over to flick the invisible dust off his shoe. He straightens back up with a small grunt. "What would you say if I told you, now stay with me people, that you can have all that stuff—not just the house, but the house keeper, the fine wine, everything... even some nice clothes to throw on top of it all— without working?"

Before anyone can answer, he pipes back up. "Sure, you'd say that's crazy. 'What's that nut talking about? Why he's been sniffin' too much of that boot polish.'" He chuckles briefly, then gets serious. "But it's true. Sherri, I've got a proposition. I'd like to help you, teach you my techniques in getting and keeping what you want, but I also need something from you. You see, Joe has been a fine example of the effectiveness of my teachings—look at where he started and see where he is now. By God, I believe he could teach me quite a few things... But I need a family for this one. If you'll let me, I'll enroll you in my newest and greatest instructional package, the "Effortless Success" package, for free, and you can simply give testimonials to it. We'll closely monitor your progress and use the findings to illustrate and further perfect the techniques."

The plans are drawn up. Marty chats with the children, asks them what they want and promises that they will get it. He makes the rounds around the room before excusing himself. As he reaches the door, Sherri asks exactly what it was she did wrong.

Marty turns around and smiles. "Well, first off. You worked too hard. But more importantly, attitude can produce more than effort can. More on that later." He leaves the room with a wave.

*

Randolph's forearm felt like it went through a wasp-hive it stung so bad. A four-hour autograph signing. But he didn't mind. Pain to him was a good thing if you came away victorious. Like a hickey after making out. He saw Suzi approaching and smugly stretched taller, giving him a one foot four inch advantage.

"Before you say anything, I spoke with Martin," Randolph said, not looking at her.

"Marty, you mean." Suzi waited until he looked down at her. He did, and she got him with that glare.

"Oh. I forgot," he puffed out, but Suzi was already walking.

So Randolph continued with the new format, describing his adventures in the automobile business. Then audiences began shrinking. Supporting acts were let go and a few dates in smaller towns were cancelled altogether. Randolph compensated by making his stage presence more threatening, stalking the stage like a wrestler awaiting his opponent, bouncing on the balls of his feet. He fabricated stories to add dazzle (lifting the end of a compact car off the ground to display to a customer just how compact it was/ auctioning off his bodybuilding trophies to finance his first dealership). He would leave the stage panting and pass Suzi's leveled gaze without acknowledgement. Straight to Martin's books he went, flipping through for something to jump up at him. Each dwindling audience was the same: an obvious decline in enthusiasm no matter his volume, posturing, animation or vein-popping neck muscles. And at the end of the last show, he saw Suzi standing sidestage accompanied by lackluster applause. She wore that same uniform expression, like waiting in the lobby for an oil change, that Randolph translated into peeved mockery. He swung in on her as he passed, spitting, "Fine! You'll get sports stories!" and clomped off.

Sitting at his hotel room desk in the terrycloth bathrobe that fit snug like an undershirt, Randolph understood that a menacing ex-Mr. Universe turned automobile dealership owner stood as much chance being an effective public speaker to middle-aged female real-estate agents aspiring to earn their gold jackets as a figure skater to a bunch of firemen. There was a crack as he ka-plunked his elbows down on the desk, chin resting in hands.

Folks weren't buying as many mid-priced imported automobiles as before. That's all his people back at the office could tell him. Sales were down, way down, they explained when he phoned to tell them he was quitting the tour. What could possibly compel people to abandon the good sense of purchasing an affordable vehicle with excellent gas mileage for luxury sedans? Because that's what they were doing. And after the customers, it was his top salesmen that were abandoning him, leaving to go head their own dealerships. Forget the Jap imports. It was Caddy's, BMW's and Jag's on up to the Italians.

"HOW COULD YOU LET THIS HAPPEN?" Randolph boomed into the phone, scanning the Thanksgiving-colored room for something to destroy.

"We can't force them to buy cars," the voice at the other end said.

"Sure you fucking can," Randolph's voice collapsed.

The employees had to be paid, and it wasn't coming in from cars. Randolph bit his lip and hung up the phone. His only relief came from not telling Suzi that he was about to quit the tour.

Now that he was funneling his tour earnings back into his business, and the show's turnouts were dwindling, Randolph's sense of adventure on stage disappeared. Suzi didn't have to tell him to go back to the glorious bodybuilding days of yore. He did it on his own. She said nothing when he stepped offstage, grimacing under boiling eyes, after his "return to form." With not a trace of condescension she smiled at him, and that somehow made it worse. Maybe, in Randolph's mind, she knew he was backing down not from defeat, but rather out of desperation. Bodybuilding tales all dried up, it was sad to see Randolph Shuron reach back to his high school football days describing how he single-handedly held the opposing team at the two yard line all four downs, thus advancing to the state semifinals. As he sweated under the lights, he began to wonder if those stories ever happened at all, or if he was telling someone else's magnificent past: Suzi's? Or Martins?

Sports tales or no sports tales, the audiences kept on shrinking. He could neither sweet talk nor threaten them back. His tank-like intimidation (when he had the heart to summon it) stirred few into action, so he turned to Mona back at headquarters. She answered the phone distracted to a degree he thought only Martin was capable of. The sound of endless paper shuffling could be heard, and she had to ask him twice throughout the conversation who he was. "Randolph! Yes! I assume you're knocking 'em dead down there, eh?"

"Have you seen the numbers, Mona," Randolph blasted in.

"Oh yes! Aren't they terrific? I never thought he'd be embraced like this so soon!" This got Mona tingling with vigor, and she zeroed in like a shrink that finally got something interesting out of her patient. She launched into detail after fawning detail about her Marty, and especially what an effective "real-deal" he was.

"No," Randolph interrupted, attempting to project his bulk through the telephone. "I'm talking about *my* numbers. The crowds are ten percent the size they were two months ago."

"Oh. I didn't think about that," Mona said quizzically. "That's funny."

"I'm doing everything I'm supposed to be doing, and nothing's keeping their attention."

"Have you had the chance to meet Marty?" Mona said.

"We spoke over the phone, yes."

"Well, what did you think? Isn't he something?"

Randolph gripped the receiver tight. In times when his words floated and popped like farts in the bathtub, he needed something to keep his hands busy. And if nothing were around, he'd grip just above the knee and lock down, keeping his fury a closed circuit.

"Uh," he said. "We didn't talk that much. My tour."

"Well, didn't he offer any advice?" Mona asked.

"Yes, a little. But it didn't quite work for me."

"Hmmm. I suppose you're using the old Martin approach?"

"Yes."

"That must be it." Mona paused between sentences so nothing was lost. "Trust Marty, Randolph. The old Martin way is deeply ingrained in you. But it's not too late... In short, do what

Marty would do. I'll send some materials. Pamphlets and videos. Study them carefully. They'll help."

Randolph's breathing could be heard on the line. "What happened to Martin?" He said.

"Martin is gone," Mona's voice went steely thin, holding something back

"Gone?"

"Yes. I can't think of any other way to put it."

Again, more breathing from Randolph's end. Mona spoke up. "I know you were a good friend to him, but—"

Randolph interrupted. "Gone?"

"As gone as someone could be," Mona chirped. "But don't worry. Marty seems to have it well in hand. Remember— do as Marty would do, but think of Martin. I do, and I always will." Her voice began to crack so she hung up.

Randolph could dead-lift the rear wheels of a mid-sized sedan off the ground, but the mental strength Mona showed over the literal loss of her brother astonished him. She's who she has to be—tough.

Everything around Randolph was getting smaller, more compacted, while he retained the same enormity. His breathing now constantly audible. Even on stage, between sentences. "Our values are the winds, huh huhhh, by which our actions are blown." The air was thin. And the pamphlets that Mona sent were closer in size to brochures. An 8x10 glossy of the original Marty portrait. And another one, a photo of Marty mimicking it perfectly—or was it the other way around? There was an undeniable resemblance to Martin, but the more he watched the videos of Marty's live performances on stage—his loping entrance to his skipping and skidding stops—the less he saw of his old mentor. He was like the President's dopey brother who constantly makes the news with his tripped-up antics but was nevertheless the people's favorite. A regular Joe reluctantly dragged into the x-ray public eye and not knowing better than telling it just as he saw it. An uncle stepping out from the garage wiping grease from his hands. *Honest* grease. Martin, fresh from a Tai Chi lesson carrying a bottle of spring water, would not be found in the same room as Marty, who's definition of formality is probably an ironed shirt. Soon the only resemblance Randolph found between the two was the hair. That, my friend, was a winning formula, transcending all cultural and socio-political boundaries.

Randolph could handle the shift in aesthetics, but Marty's workless philosophies were much harder to swallow. The contrast between the two was certainly to blame for his sudden decrease in popularity and, wisely, he realized if he ever wanted to see cars roll off his lot again he better adopt Marty's new winning formula, and fast.

Acquiring Marty's brand of ultra laid-back pragmatism was a sweating strain for Randolph. How does a six-foot eight-inch jock with two percent body fat, ex Mr. Universe, Mr. Olympia, Mr. World, etc. owner of several once successful automobile dealership do it? He spent hours in from of the television watching Marty's totally alien brand of easy advice. Hopefully through osmosis it would sink in, or at least bulldoze through a lifetime of *earned* achievement. And there was that partner of Marty's, that tubby guy who performs those skits with his family. Joe? Where did he come from? That guy went beyond being a model for bad behavior and entered the domain of pure irritability: galaxies from the world Randolph knew. He did however boost Marty's counter examples by pole-vaulted leaps. The initial wincing and groans from the audience over Joe's inability to grunt his way out of his hapless predicament turned to "aaahhhh's" of pity. Their empathy rose from familiarity, recollections of their own past...

Fuck that! Not Randolph's past! And Joe's impotent and visionless decisions seemed obvious to him, way too obvious for *his* pity. So instead of that, he felt nothing but hostility, opposite of what was expected. Opposite like the way he had exhausted himself in the effort of appearing casual. As practice, Randolph crumpled from his Trojan erect stride into a head-bobbing lope. This killed his back. While most people ache from straining muscles they otherwise neglect, Randolph ached from not using his. He was unlike normal men. In these uncertain times, bound by an ill-fitting Northwest logger outfit, Randolph Shuron wondered what left he had to offer.

In the jeans that wouldn't break in and an itchy wool shirt, Randolph stood before his audience. He had abandoned his original script, and after days of squeezing his brain over what Marty would say in his place, came up with nothing. Maybe that was the point: to reinforce a lack of effort needed to attain success, no effort should be put forth in teaching it. Randolph's head was in a knot. Should he simply strut around the stage, arrogantly displaying the riches and fame that came (supposedly) so easily? He began walking, but it wasn't a confident, self-possessed stroll, but rather quick feverish strides. If it hadn't been for the kid in the front row—a fourteen year-old boy with an Adam's Apple so prominent it cast a shadow across his throat, wearing an oversized football jersey—gazing up at him unblinking, Randolph probably would have kept on pacing the stage. The blonde freckled angular boy, rapt in hero worshipping admiration, looked like a skeleton floating in a tent. Randolph squinted at him through the stage lights.

"IF YOU WANT MY OPINION," he tossed a holler to the audience as if trying to reach the rear seats, "I SAY DON'T BOTHER!"

The audience collectively sat up in their seats. Randolph stood there, erect in his stiff jeans. He looked back to the skinny kid in the front row and kept going.

"If success isn't self-evident, don't your time. I can go on and on, as I've done in the past, preaching about hard work and sacrifice, but tonight I'd rather tell you how it really is. Look how big I am. I'm huge, and it's all *muscle*! That's a fact, and that fact made me into the superstar I am today. If you don't have something like this from the get go, try something else, cause you're kidding yourself. Sorry. If you're not predisposed to greatness like me, don't expect to go pro. If you weren't born a chess champion, you're not going to be a chess champion. Be smart, people!" With that, Randolph ran offstage and to his dressing room. Applause followed, the sheer volume and exhilaration of which he hadn't heard since he first began giving lectures a long time ago. He stumbled through the dressing room and into the bathroom where he threw up into the toilet.

*

The folks now in attendance no longer even remotely resemble the crowds from just a few months ago. Everybody is of the highest rank. Designer suits and evening wear, one-of-a kind couture. Gleaming watches and earrings. Tanned and fit. Fresh from overseas or the country club. Gorgeous. They settle for nothing but the finest, and actual fights break out over the seating arrangements. Security tells us that nobody will take seats in the back. Men in tuxedos in shoving matches, women in swirling clouds of taffeta pulling each other's hair, all for the prestige of the front row. The violence isn't widespread, but health and fire codes become an issue as the chic guests cram the floor like a rush hour train.

One distinct peculiarity about these people. Their shoes, though Italian or alligator hide, are almost all dusty and worn. I hadn't been out of doors on a normal city street in over three months. The only time I see sunlight is when I go from the tour bus to the hotel, and even then I'm surrounded by security. So I assume it's just rainy outside. It's autumn, or somewhere thereabouts.

Have we lost our original clientele, the folks frustrated with their dead-end jobs, their loveless marriages, their uncontrollable kids? The people who need us the most, have they been pushed aside, marginalized, usurped by a leisure class grabbing onto the latest fad? Maybe not. I see a glimmer from their past as if the heels, tailor-made slacks or bareback dresses aren't completely comfortable. They're walking around in new skin, letting it run the show. But goddamn if they don't look good, in fact much better that I do. At times I feel slightly awkward around them, childlike even. Success stories. Every one. Briefcase in hand, flanked by their dream woman or man, glancing at fat rocky watches, phone to ear. On the go.

So what the hell am I in all this? I go to the dressing room bathroom and look into the mirror. It's been awhile. I fully expect to see Marty, but I don't. It's me. Not the new me. Not the old me. Something else. Closer to the old me. Not even pre- old me. A worse old me, it seems. Older, fatter, balder, gray rings around red sleepless eyes. My flesh half-full balloons of meat. I had long since hung up my El Rubiani suit for the construction worker-after a twelve-hour day attire that has become the Marty uniform. I leave the dressing room and exit the stadium.

Mounds of garbage and piles of boxes line the sidewalks like the ignored remnants of a yard sale even with the "free" sign put up. Refuse pours out onto the streets. Shadowy expensive automobiles with tinted windows cleave a single lane through the rubbish.

Marty calls from behind. He's leaning out of the security entrance.

"Joe, where you going?" he shouts.

"Out," I say.

"We've got a show."

"What's the matter with this place?"

Marty doesn't leave the doorway. "It stinks. That's the matter with it. Come back in."

A silver car, shiny and low to the ground, hums by. "Nice ride!" Marty says.

"It's a dump!" I yell back.

"Don't you know stadiums are always located in the shitty part of town? It doesn't matter if the team wins or loses, the fans trash the first friggin' thing they see. Best to keep the rioters out of the nice neighborhoods."

"But the car."

"Another success story coming to testify, I presume. Come on!"

"Every car is like that, Marty."

"Drug dealers. I'm certainly not coming out there, so get in here, Joe!" He is holding his nose.

I walk back. "I don't get it. All those cars."

Marty shuts the door behind me. "Lots of drug dealers, I suppose."

Back in the dressing room. "I've really let myself go, Marty."

Marty's trying out some fingerings on a baseball, a present from a hall-of-fame pitcher. "Nah, you're fine. Just workin' hard. Proud of you. Everybody's very proud of you. You're perfect, Joe. Nobody can do it quite like you can. And with Sherri and her family joining in, it'll be stellar. Stellar!"

"I need to take better care of myself," I say.

He's not looking at me. "Ah, don't worry about that right now. It'll come. Remember, let your *attitude* do the work." He does a wind-up but doesn't release, then stops and underhand tosses it onto a chair. Marty keeps moving, bouncing up and down on his toes like he's got to pee. "I'm joining you with Sherri and her bunch real soon. Perfect. Perfect! You already know each other. Wonderful. A beautiful team!" He trots out of the room, mumbling as he goes.

I meet with Misty. She is flanked by her servants and radiant like Goddess of the Nile filtered through a Vaseline-smeared lens. Effervescent. Aglow.

"How do I look?" I ask her.

"You look fine," she says picking a radish off a plate. Lying on the bed in her robe she's a curled rose pedal.

"Come on, hon, be honest. I look like crap."

"Why are you so worried? It doesn't matter what you look like physically; your success makes you big and beautiful."

The servants leave. I kneel down next to her and place my hand on her hard rounded stomach. It's smooth like a pearl. "He's going to be something, Misty," I whisper to her.

She nods.

"Is everything working out OK?"

"Feeling fine. A bit tired at times. He kicks once in a while."

"Good... How about attitude-wise? Everything going smoothly?" I stand up.

"I suppose so." She says delicately plucking a baby carrot off the tray.

"Suppose? That doesn't sound too encouraging. What kind of answer is that?"

"It's how I feel," she says.

"What's the baby supposed to make of this? 'I suppose'?"

"I don't know."

"There you go again. 'I don't know'."

Misty continues picking at her veggie platter. "What's your point, Joe? And why do you keep repeating everything I say?"

"So you can hear what you sound like." I try to get eye contact. "I hope you do, because the baby certainly can. The positive atmosphere would help, or so I thought. The music, the reading, the supportive, friendly people. But they're just a small contribution to the child's welfare."

"I'm taking great care of the baby!"

"Are you?"

She levels her eyes at me. "Joe, you're beginning to upset me."

"That's what I'm talking about. You've got to monitor your attitude better. Please. Just think of the child." I once again kneel down beside her. "Please, honey. You're a beautiful woman. *Let it in.* I'll help. Like an athlete needs a personal trainer to instruct and guide for ideal performance, so does the mind. And what drives the mind, but attitude? Don't give up now, honey."

"You try being pregnant," she says, chomping on a hunk of cauliflower.

"Come on, put a positive spin on it," I tell her.

Chapter 9

Combs

Mr. Romaine himself crafted the design of these handsome combs. Imprinted with the words, "Start at the Top." Can you think of a better way to begin the day?

Daily Planner

Need reminding of your daily goals? Let Martin Romaine plan your day, week, or year with this outstanding "accomplishmemento."

We go weeks without coming anywhere near a metropolitan area. Outdoor venues, performed on a travelling stage that's set up and broken down by dozens of crewmembers and roadies, draw huge crowds. We shoot some videos. News coverages. Guests and more guests, all special. I am teamed with Sherri, James, and Noelle as the example of a family that would be ideal candidates for Marty's program: each member on their own course, hardly together and only barely rocked by the wake of the others. To the father (played by me), these people have become peripheral to the central and prime tenant of his life—obligation. Their basic needs are met, so it could be said to work. Christmas is recognized. Occasional dinners out while the kids stay at home. Not the type of family that films porn in the basement, shoots heroin between their toes, or wakes in a sweat in the middle of the night with knives at each other's throats.

Those types wouldn't benefit from our planning strategies of "Familial Synchronization," but would be better off in a more hands-on environment. We represent the family that did everything right, but nevertheless feels deprived of a heart full of rewards.

Marty puts us through three weeks of boot camp-like training. The time I spend with my new stage family eats into the moments I usually spend with Misty and the child. So I go from running a family of four where I have intimacy issues with the wife, strained father-daughter relationships, and raising a drug-free teen, to suddenly slamming the brakes and spinning the wheel where I'm an expectant father, bright and planning for the future.

The pregnancy is my burden as well, so I don't let up on Misty. My comments are kept positive and sincere. I can imagine the strain with that big, shifting sack of flour tied to her. So I take over. I feed her mind pastoral thoughts of calm and peaceful notions of whimsy. I try to involve her, get her to participate, so she's not a passive spectator but a vigilant and active participant, mind sharp. These are some of the exercises I introduce:

- Try to outdo the person in putting the most positive spin on a situation. I secretly let her win because I don't want her to feel discouraged over losing.
- Watch a movie and give it a happy ending. Jake LaMotta gets out of jail and becomes a child welfare advocate. They find out what "Rosebud" is.
- Put a positive spin on physical discomfort. "Boy, this laying flat on my back is certainly helping my spinal alignment."
- Constant smiling. It's a proven fact that if a happy brain can make the face smile, then a smiling face can make the brain happy.

I understand her plight and overlook the initial lack of dedication. If we keep at it though, these behaviors will become second nature. And that's what counts, the payoff. A sigh of exasperation and exhaustion is followed with a smile. Abdominal pains met with laughter. This and the language tapes: French, German, Spanish, and Mandarin Chinese played to her tummy. Recited calculus equations. Poetry. Bach, Mahler, and Charlie Parker on the stereo. The baby will be born giving us lessons.

Misty drifts off to sleep mumbling a French word she doesn't even know the meaning of. Fromage. I want to be just as much a part of the child's upbringing as the mother. I press my hands to her belly, trying to feel a pulse within; and hoping that it's strong.

*

Mona felt like a psychologist who invented the cure for depression. Not a pill, but rather a few words (copyrighted) spread to the ears of all sufferers. And no need for return visits or checkups. Cured.

But Mona was a shrink who was beginning to miss opening the door for her patients as they arrived, their barely concealed shame over ambiguous ailments, holding out a hand for those who needed it. Sitting them down, and through warm empathy and understanding, they open up. Through well-earned trust, slight noticeable improvements.

After her phone conversation with Marty, Mona no longer waited for the financial and demographic reports of the tour to arrive on her desk for perusal. She now monitored it all like an over-involved college football fan following the stats from as many sources as possible. Her office became an air traffic tower of tour information. Spreadsheets, photographs, itineraries, video captures, expense reports, recipes from restaurants, eyewitness accounts; all of it went straight to Mona. And it didn't take an MBA (which Mona wasn't) to see that the tour was extremely successful. Attendance records were shattered. New T-shirts and merchandise couldn't be designed and manufactured fast enough. After developing a severe case of Carpal-Tunnel from signing stacks of 8x10 glossies, Mona bought a stamp bearing her signature.

Marty's first written work, "Not an Ounce of Strain," a thin 25-page document of his new teachings, hit Mona's desk. A note from Marty was attached, "How about a 1st pressing of 10K? ASAP, please." Mona picked it up, weighed it in her hand, and thought, "How do I market something that barely outsizes a pamphlet?" She flipped to the first page. It read:

> Imagine living two hundred years ago. You're a farmer. You get up before the sun rises and work throughout the day, well after the setting of the sun. What do you do when arrive home after the fieldwork is done? Why, you work some more! Homes need to be maintained. Families tended to. Your livelihood is directly proportional to your physical effort. And the only help you can expect to receive is from your spouse, your kids when they're old enough, and maybe a horse or two. Your muscle makes the world move.
>
> Then comes the Industrial Revolution. What does it mean for you? Why, less physical work. Suddenly there's steam and machines than can produce a thousand times more than your puny back ever could. You can now work less and get more.
>
> Skip ahead in time. Advancements in technology. Most of the work you now do is with your brain. Very little physical effort is required of you to lead a happy, successful life. Then comes computers, vast banks of hard drives that hold more knowledge and computational power than the smartest person in the world could ever come close to. All the smartest people in the world!

There is no longer a reason to learn your times tables. You don't even need to know how to spell! After those two great advances in human progress, where does that lead us? Something else to do both the physical and the mental work. Sounds great, but are we better off? Maybe, maybe not. I look around and see people working their butts off to achieve financial independence. And so very often, tragically, it doesn't happen. People die alone, with nobody and nothing to mark their existence here on Earth. We have these amazing tools to do anything we want, but we're still slaving for somebody else, still in debt, still fat, the family unhappy and not communicating.

Let me share with you something completely revolutionary but nevertheless common sense. Remember what I said about advances in science and technology making human effort obsolete? Then why the heck are we still working, still straining our brain to come up with a way to make it big? I say, "Stop it!" That's right. Now this will take a great leap up faith. So, before you read on, I want you to take the following to heart. Here it is:

I NO LONGER NEED TO WORK
FOR WHAT I WANT

Once you learn and fully ingrain this simple sentence—so it underlies your every thought and action—you can go on. If you can't, return this book. Get a refund. Spend the money on a movie. But if you can accept this simple underlying principle, the world will open up for you. From there, I will share with you the following:

- Quitting and making it big

- Sweatless weight loss
- Your ideal everything
- How to make effortlessness work for you

Wow! Mona picked up the phone and called the publishing division of Performance Power. "Not an Ounce of Strain" was going straight to the press. She placed the thin stack in front of her and thought of a way to market it. It was definitely going to be the shortest book they have ever released. How to charge more than $5 for it, make it worth their while? It was Marty's first work. It contained his mission statement, his proclamation, the dawning of a new era in Romaine Enterprises. Leather-bound, gold lettering and padded with tons of pictures. Promote the hell out of it, Mona thought, and they could jack the price up and see a decent return. It was a go.

You couldn't walk ten feet without spotting a copy of the 1st edition pressing of "Not an Ounce of Strain" in Romaine Headquarters. One on each desk. Promotional posters hung on the walls. Freshly printed company stationary with the title across the top. A store display, holding sixty copies, sat in the front foyer beside the receptionist's desk. Perhaps that's what led her to quit and pursue a more rewarding vocation: starting her own line of husky ladies lingerie. In her exit interview, the receptionist said that it was time to call her own shots. She even told the office manager conducting the interview, Kimberly, a tiny woman with outdated blonde hair, that she should consider the same: perhaps they could go into business together. This was no way to live, sitting at a desk like this asserting the miniscule power you're handed. Be your own boss! See it and be it! The interviewer nodded, and quickly learned how the receptionist's departure would cause a lot more hassle than imagined. A replacement couldn't be found. Nobody responded to the ads. Job placement agencies were no good. Job fairs were a bust. Kimberly tried them all. She was forced to have folks from shipping, the front office and even herself sit up front and greet guests. And it wasn't until she found one woman, who made it explicit that she was only taking the job as "seed money" for her upcoming venture: a company that conducted guided tours of the Seven Wonders of the Natural World, and demanded four times the proposed wage, that Kimberly confronted Mona.

"Four times the proposed wage?"

"I can't find anyone, Mona. It's been weeks, and this is the only person interested."

"Job fairs?"

Stacks of tour and expense reports occupied the chairs in Mona's office, so Kimberly remained standing. "I went to two of them. Initially, people were excited to see Romaine Enterprises recruiting and they came running up. But when I told them about the receptionist job, they seemed almost insulted that we, of anyone out there, would expect someone to take it. I told them of the benefits, the competitive wages, everything, and zip, no takers."

"Fine. Offer her twice the initial offer."

It was proposed and it was flat-out rejected. She wound up with three and three-quarters times the initial wages and insisted on starting no sooner than Wednesday the following week. They now had a new receptionist, Juliana, who grabbed any ear available and went into detail about the wondrous awe of the Paricutin Volcano or the shimmering splendor of Victoria Falls.

By the time Juliana had arrived on Wednesday, angular and over-professional in a custom-tailored dusty blue business suit, Kimberly was gulping antacids to settle the ulcer that was now eating away at her stomach. Employees that hadn't just recently quit for greener pastures were demanding higher salaries, better benefits, more vacation time, company cars, and larger offices. They had their *big* plans, more accommodating to their ambitions, and made it clear that they were here only on a temporary basis while their capital grew. They also went into lengthy, unprompted descriptions of their upcoming vocations. Whomever was present got the treatment: secretaries, janitors, folks on the other end of the telephone line (probably a client), even the Italian guy who worked the lunch bus in the parking lot was subjected to dozens of grandiose proposals. He listened to folks that wanted to be senators, CEO's of timber companies, entrepreneurs, athletes, musicians, international playboys, racecar drivers, movie directors. Mona was forced to give in to their demands because an over-worked Kimberly had attended every job fair available and found very few people interested in those once coveted positions. It was all happening so fast. Nobodies from the mailroom, quiet kids who once humbly handed her the mail in the morning, were now running fashion houses in Paris. Her personal secretary's crime novel set in the Australian Outback was climbing the bestseller list. Romaine Enterprises was forced to jack up the prices of their merchandise as well as shut down the entire art department (everybody was quitting anyway to begin their Disney rival animation companies) in order to cover the increased costs of the employees.

"Success owes less to ability than to zeal." That was a quote Mona had drilled into Marty repeatedly during his training, and now she heard it again. This time, it was from the UPS guy. He was outside her office, going into pie-chart-like detail of his gold medal aspirations for 200-meter hurdles in the next Olympics to a woman from accounts receivable. Mona opened her 1st edition copy of "Not an Ounce of Strain," that she had not read past the introductory chapter. She flipped through it and found that very quote. There it was, in a section titled, "Number One for All and All for Number One!" She read more. It was good. Economical and straight-shooting. No anecdotes and no fluff, as if giving instructions for starting a lawnmower.

Mona watched the news, and the same thing that was happening to her company was also going on throughout the country. Employees were quitting and getting rich. CEO's were popping up everywhere. Over the last three weeks movie stars per capita had quintupled. Good fortune for everyone. A triumphant raise in standards was sweeping the land. Everyone wanted the best, and they were getting it, effortlessly. Mona turned off the TV and folded up the newspapers, getting back to business. The numbers said it all. The rocket-like sales curves had hit their peek and were flattening out. Book sales in particular were the most telling, inversely proportional to the demand for Marty's new work. Sales of all other articles of merchandise—from ball caps to backpacks to combs—had almost completely dried up, seemingly in cities that Marty's slimmed-down mercenary-like tour had passed through. According to accounting, the only things making money were Marty and Marty's new book, and that was not enough to keep the company going.

Two more people quit Romaine Enterprises between the time Mona booked a private jet and flying to meet Marty on tour the next day. She had packed for action: always on hand her thick leather organizer, the very one that her brother Martin had personally endorsed a couple years ago. Notes, illustrations, diagrams and accounting ledgers were stuffed into her suitcase along with two business suits. The original portrait of Marty sat downstairs in the company vault along with historical mementos of the Romaine legacy: amateurish handwritten banners from her and Martin's very first shows all the way to plaques of thank you from the President of the United States. There was even the old cast from Martin's broken leg, the result of an over enthusiastic punch in the air that caught him off balance and he toppled off the stage. Mona had sold her car to cover the medical bills. Martin, someday, was going to build a museum out of all this stuff. He threatened to do it himself, just as he had wasted all that time working on those idiotic easy-opening glass doors in the foyer. "I need a hobby," he said. The keys to the basement now belonged to Mona and Mona only, and if she could she would seal it up for good, keeping all Martin (as well as Knox) memorabilia, locked away.

Martin was no more, and Mona knew she could have stopped it. She wasn't going to let the same thing happen to Marty.

Looking at the neatly aligned blocks of land from high in the sky, she thought of the vaulted basement. It hadn't entered her mind until now, now that the biggest reminder of Martin and Knox lay just ahead.

*

We finally entered a metropolis, and I wouldn't have known if it weren't for the radio reporting the traffic outside. It's one of those northeastern cities, filled with colleges and rarely mentioned in popular press—neither excesses nor legends to distinguish it from any other. No reputation outside of simply being, "pleasant." Perfect for the people that live there, but barely an "Oh," or "I heard that was a nice place," from folks who may meet its inhabitants. But it *is* a city. Skyscrapers that barely outnumber the toes on your feet. An art museum with a few artists you've heard of. And a single professional sports team.

Feigning a stomachache, I excuse myself from breakfast. A mother-like guilt seizes me as I put on my coat. I imagine Marty's face crushed from disappointment, as if I'm about to violate some promise never taken, and I have yet to step outside.

There are no taxis to be found in the streets that are oddly filthy for a progressive Northeastern city. A cat relieves itself on the sidewalk right in front of me. I look through a payphone phonebook and call a cab. No answer, just ringing. The line of the next taxi company I try is disconnected. Another has an answering machine that gets cut off in the middle and leaves two seconds to leave a message. One rings and rings. It's a Friday. After thirty rings, someone answers. It's a man's voice; sounding as if he had just woken up. I ask him to pick me up and he says, "I guess so. It'll be a while. I need to pick up a few things. A half an hour."

Heaps of garbage lines the streets and it smells like a sewer. The sidewalk is an obstacle course with it's discarded couches, wound-up stacks of newspapers that are coming undone, even plates of dirty food and silverware. It's resembles the last town I saw; the only significant clearing is the middle of the road to make way for traffic. An abandoned gas station with its doors wide open. A flower shop with visible, dead flowers inside. There's a hugely popular national chain convenient store with a help wanted sign. "Great Wages! Countless opportunities for advancement!" It too, is closed. This is where I tell the cabbie to meet me.

Signs stand unlit in front of boarded up shops. This goes on until the four-lane road disappears under a highway overpass. There's one open establishment—a car dealership. It's on the opposite side of the street half a mile down the road. The only one. A Bentley dealership, on the outskirts of town, open for business. I should tell Marty. He's often mentioned the superior class and handling of Bentleys.

There's traffic. Beautiful automobiles zip along in a mutual understanding that there's no time to waste dilly-dallying on the road. Dream cars, and everybody owns one. They're harried as if they had just thrown on their suits late for a luncheon. Even the kids in the back of their parents' car look like they're on their way to a final exam. Three young teens glide past me on bikes, smooth and relaxed, pedaling only when needed. One of the luxury cars breaks from the traffic stream and stops beside me. It's a flat black Jaguar, smooth and rounded like a bar of soap. A tinted window electronically slides down and a dark-skinned, almost Incan looking fellow whose hair is combed back but nonetheless thinning so you can see the scalp asks casually where I want to go. I tell him the cab's on the way. He says he is the cab.

"Get in," he says

"Is this a luxury service? How much is this going to cost?"

"It's the normal fare," he tells me, getting out and going around the car to open the passenger door. "But with luxury style! This *is* a Jag."

"I just need a ride downtown; nothing fancy," I explain as he waits by the opened door smoothing his suit jacket.

"Hey, you called for a cab, and here's a cab." He pats the roof.

We pass the Bentley dealership. There's a fair amount of people milling about. They're in suits, shiny designer warm-up's and light linen outfits talking with salesmen, gliding their hands along the glassy caramel surfaces and stepping into one of baroque machines. A mammoth gilded banner strewn across the parking lot announces, "Imagine Yourself Without a Bentley!"

Then the driver says, "I'm getting one of those." He hocks up a phlegmy lugie and sends it out the window. "Yeah, those Bentleys are pure class. But I'm just getting used to this one. Getting gas, though..."

"Is that what you had to do before picking me up?"

He looks at me. "Yeah, you know how it is."

"I've been away for a while," I say. "So what is it? Shortage?"

"No... yes, of sorts." He rubs his eyes. The laminated nametag dangling from the rear-view mirror says Alejandro.

"Then what?"

"You kiddin?" He looks at me suspiciously.

"No, like I said..."

"You better not be screwin' with me... Nobody wants to do it."

"Do it?"

"Run a gas station."

The highway is the same as the streets, elegant automobiles in a hurry. And the garbage. Plastic shopping bags and paper cups bounce down the road nearly hitting vehicles before whooshing away at the last second. We enter the city proper. Not much life. It's mid morning. I ask the driver to take me downtown. I compliment him on his car.

"Thanks. I'm gonna have a fleet of them," he says.

"Yeah?"

"Uh huh. My own business. Upscale cabs. The only game in town. Screw limos! That's for punks on prom! All Jag's, or Bentleys. Not my ideal career choice, but it'll do for now."

"Then why you doing it?"

"Somebody else in town already beat me to the other thing I wanted to do: own and run a Lear Jet rental service. So for now, I'm gonna open the first luxury automobile taxi service. I don't feel like I'm settling too much, and maybe when the demand for Lear Jet rental goes up, which I'm sure it will the way things are going, then I'll move right in."

I get out at the downtown promenade. Alejandro says even though he's got really important things to do, he'll come and pick me up whenever I want. I tell him to come back in two hours.

The stink nearly knocks me back into the cab. The city smells like an open grave. Is this the result from me being away from metropolitan areas for so long, confined to filtered dressing room air? Even the sweat from the worked up audience whipped into abandon had become more bearable with nicer, and more frequent, tastes in cologne and perfume. The trash is worse here than by the hotel. Not a hint of organization. There's pizza boxes, empty oil cans, half-eaten chicken drumsticks, wadded-up paper, a blown-out computer monitor, newspaper sailing down the streets, tires. People briskly weave through the rubbish as if it were other pedestrians. They move fast, determined. Behind me I hear a dull thumping crash. It's a bloated cardboard box dropped from a window, a plume of receipts and papers settling to the ground after it. A woman from eight stories above, the one I suspect responsible for nearly killing me with her company's documents, is looking down. She disappears for a moment then comes back, pulls out and overturns a wastepaper basket, letting the contents sprinkle down after the burst cardboard box on the street below. She stops, looks in the container, and gives it a final shake.

The commuters are exquisitely attired. There's two variants: tailored suits and the high-end "rugged urban wear" that Marty's been wearing and endorsing. They don the latest Italian suits, shiny as polished armor, click-clacking along in wingtips and heels. Their hair matches their wardrobe—processed and dyed, conditioned and gelled to give it that healthy look. The latter group wears trousers and skirts that could nearly double as fatigues or logger dungarees. Shirts are tucked-in yet comfortable, invariably plaid or checkered. Their hair likewise matches the mood of the ensemble: a bit longer and unkempt than what would be acceptable in a typical urban professional setting.

They race along either on foot, bicycle or automobile, stopping for nothing. I see two snappy gentlemen bisect at a corner and begin a shouted conversation. They maintain the same brisk pace and swat sideways high-fives as they meet, and continue talking, bellowing louder and louder until out of sight. Actually, everyone's voice is raised in pre-kickoff expectation. Their voices drown out the engines of the passing cars that glide briskly by in respect for each other's time.

So many handsome people. I begin to feel uncomfortable, and hungry. For me, those two things go hand-in-hand. All I see are businesses, glass and metal. No restaurants. I include coffee shops in my search. They too are missing. Nothing service-oriented: No shoeshine, no laundries and no food. I continue to walk until I'm well out of the downtown area and into a spot that appears more urban, less business. The same crowds dwell here, including a younger group who mimic the attire of their elders but with conspicuous twists on the variation: the suits are hipper and edgier with odder cuts and more confrontational colors. Gargantuan boots that could crush small animals. The Marty inspired kids don urban camping clothes that appear slept-in, and some have a pronounced military look to them, as if on leave.

Finding a place to eat in this part of town is just as difficult; the store fronts slowly morph into high-end clothing shops, art galleries, and business-supply stores. No coffee and no snacks. Feet sore, I finally find a restaurant. I can't determine whether the name of the place is in French, German, or Chinese. "CEOTHIE?" It does however have six stars under the name. Not four or five, six. And oddly, beside the stars, it says, "New plates and silverware for every customer!"

The Maitre d' frowns at me. I figure the lunch hour hasn't yet begun. He wordlessly seats me, and I ask him about the plates and silverware policy.

"That's right, every meal," he says handing me a menu.

The items on the menu are spendy, almost up there in price as the gourmet establishments that Marty and I frequent, if I may say so. The interior, though, is a dump. It reminds me of the Chinese take out joints you see underneath the elevated subways. There's plastic plants that nevertheless still look dead, a fake fireplace that's turned on and wobbly, a poster of Heimlich Maneuver instructions visible behind the counter, yellow stains on the walls and ceilings, and visible wear spots in the carpet. I take it to be one of the word-of-mouth places that excels so magnificently that they intentionally flaunt conventions of class and sophistication. I could see the Queen of England being escorted inside and gushing over its charm. The Maitre d' returns and asks me about my beverage. I order wine and ask him again about the flatware.

He snorts sarcastically, "That's why you have to pay so much," and returns to the kitchen.

The food is good, not extraordinary, and nothing that would attract heads of state. It's slightly risky with the spices and the cream isn't overpowering. Still, I would be hesitant to bring Marty here. I sit back, look at my belly, as big as ever, and let out a breath. My waiter returns, looks at me rubbing my belly, and I'm certain I see him shake his head. I ask him once again about the dishes.

"Sir," he attempts to say patiently. "Are you from out of town? It's standard practice in restaurants. It comes with the meal." He looks at me. "You must be, from the looks of things."

"You throw away—?"

"Yes!" he says. People turn around and look at us. Not everyone, but enough.

"Watch," he says and takes my plate, saucer, wineglass, and the utensils sitting in front of me. He walks behind the cashier's desk, and with his foot nudges out a wastepaper basket.

He drops them in with a clank. I hear them chip and shatter. He calls out to me, "And you don't have to pay extra."

Paying at the counter, I look down into the trash basket with the broken dishes, leftover rice, and half a duck skeleton. I tell him I'm sorry, I am indeed from out of town. He doesn't bother to ask me where I'm from, and when I ask why they do this, he says, "You want to wash them?" I say no, but couldn't he get somebody to do it? He groans softly and says, "Sure the same person who wants to polish my shoes," and he brings up a dingy wingtip, scarred and frayed on the outside. I walk out and hear him say before the door closes, "Fat ass. Probably from Europe."

Making my way back to the business district, I take a close look at people's shoes. They are either in the same state as my waiter's, filthy and unkempt, or brand new out of the box. All high-end styles. This I find unnerving. Everywhere it's like this. Sprinkled amongst the ripped-apart pallets, car parts, mail and splintered furniture that litter the sidewalks are shoes. Removed and discarded.

Across the intersection a car stalls, a cobalt blue BMW. The person behind the wheel, a woman with high, hard brunette hair, a bandage over her nose and a silk scarf thrown around her neck, grinds the ignition. It lunges once and stops. I see her swat the steering wheel and get out. She opens the back door and pulls out a thin briefcase. Leaving the stalled car in the middle of the intersection, doors still open, she walks across the street toward me. I think she's going to ask me for a hand, but she pulls a telephone out of her coat, taps the numbers and speaks. As she passes, I hear, "Oh, forget about it. I can't stop for anything. Life's too short to be patient."

Everywhere I see the product of Marty: the hair, the clothes, the laid-back intensity. Even the walk, his purposeful loping stride. I duck under the awning a company titled, "Come On, Take It!" and looking in the windows I see a bunch of computers on desks blinking with nobody sitting at them. Only a young guy in a black T-shirt, poking at his hair, trying to get it just right. There seems to be a hissing in the air, and I don't know if it's me, but everyone is whispering "success." Successsssss. It's there all right, or maybe it always has been and I just noticed it. I close my eyes and take deep breaths, imagining soft glowing air rolling in and out of my lungs, just like Martin described in his first book. My heart slows, and a brief calm envelops me. I keep my eyes shut, opposite of a child avoiding sleep and his dreams. If I remain this way, they won't notice that it's me, Joe Median. I stay put until the cab returns.

     Heading back to the hotel, Alejandro the cabbie goes back to describing his plans for the future and how his Lear jet rental service will soon conquer the entire eastern seaboard. Then westward. I stare at the beautiful automobiles zipping alongside us, and others sitting abandoned at the side of the road. Alejandro's going on, this time describing his perfect wife. Every aspect of her, be it her hair, legs, education level, sense of humor, whatever, outshines Misty and hence makes me feel worse. He describes a multi-thousand dollar watch that sends out warning beeps two minutes before the stock market closes and three beeps when he reaches the maximum heart rate for a man his age. It also aids digestion, he says, but he doesn't explain how. He's lecturing me as if he were Marty and I'm the poor desperate slob that plopped down three-day's pay for a seminar. The hints about my weight, comments about my shifting attention span that assumes a lack of focus. I appear to be the very person who needs this kind of pep talk. I don't answer (it's his car) and I sink into the smooth firm leather upholstery. Alejandro's volume goes up as he describes his unhappy brother that stamps papers all day long in some clerical job out west. And on and on.

It's two hours before the show and there's Marty, sitting on a merchandise booth signing autographs. His voice sings out above the crowd.

     He's lecturing what appears to be a college couple. Even with their thrift store attire, the two are unsoiled and beaming as if dirt could just glide off their porcelain skin. They stand before him; heads leaned back with slight knowing smiles. "But just remember this," Marty says. "Remember, for every clump of dirt, there's a thousand diamonds." He nods and they smile. Marty waves me over. "And here's *my* diamond—Joe!"

The autograph line is long. They step up, eager to share their success stories: one woman lost one hundred and seventy-five pounds but is still a leviathan. She leans against the table to balance herself, winded from talking, and gives Marty a clop on the shoulder when he tells her how sexy she looks. He asks her how she lost all the weight. She answers liposuction, and Marty springs to his feet giving her a big hug, however she shakes her head and says she doesn't deserve congratulations because she hasn't reached her target of losing an additional one hundred fifty; the skin must be given time to adjust to her new body lest it hang to the floor dragging behind her. Marty says he understands; sometimes the limits of science can slow down our progress.

"Well, how do you feel now?" he asks.

"Oh, wonderful. I have so much more energy!"

Marty's face narrows to quasi-seriousness. "And aren't you glad you didn't waste months of your life on diets, torturing yourself as you endlessly trotted on the treadmill watching your friends eat that delicious ice cream?"

"Oh yes," she says. "I want to thank you both, Joe and Marty, for the wonderful example you have set for me. What a team you guys are!"

She ambles away, and Marty shouts out to her, "Come see me again when you get that next liposuction, you sexy thing!"

Marty claps my back and returns to the fans who look like they were born into success, and no stretch of the imagination will allow you to picture them droning away in an office or plopping on the couch the minute they get back from work and two minutes later being fast asleep. Energetic and natural and at ease. And suddenly I feel very out of place, as if I am that kid brother with a bowl-cut who walks into his cheerleader sister's slumber party. Nonetheless they approach me, quick to grab my hand (even giving me hugs), saying without me they never would have begun to envision improving their lives. Gorgeous women kiss my cheek, V-shaped men with square jaws and button noses wring my hand. Marty winks at me.

After the last fan leaves, Marty sits on the merchandise table. He's leaning back supporting himself with his arms. "Ah merchandise," he says. "You can write down what I've got to say on a receipt for a cup of coffee. But people want it repeated and repeated, over and over, each time from a different angle, with a million examples. Hell, it pays the bills, don't it?"

"I saw something. Marty," I say.

"Saw something?"

"Outside, I—"

"You went outside? Where'd you go?" he glances over at me, still leaning back.

"Uh, I went downtown, the city center. Checked things out."

"So you've got enough time for some leisurely sightseeing?" This is the first time I hear sarcasm come out of Marty, and it seems new to him, like he's trying it out. "I sure wish I had time to paint the town red, just go off by myself and see the sights."

"Marty, I—"

"How nice of you to let me shoulder the burden while you go gallivanting. This isn't a vacation tour, Joe." He sits up, hands on his knees.

"I saw some things, Marty."

"Mm Hmm."

"The downtown looked like it had been bombed and the only people left were the ones who profited from it. It stank, grease and garbage everywhere."

"Okay, Joe. It's just a stop on a tour. Nobody said you have to raise your kids here." Marty picked up and flipped through one of his thinner books, "*How to Make Ravishing Love to your Spouse after Fifty Years of Marriage.*"

"We caused that, Marty," I say.

"Sorry?"

"People were walking along quoting you, us. Right out of our lectures."

Marty tossed the book back onto the table and stood up to face me, hand on my shoulder. "Well, Joe. Did they seem happy?"

He's standing so close, at least a head taller than me, that I have to look up to meet his eyes. "I don't know," I say. "They looked good, determined and on the go. Right out—."

"Don't think I'm being condescending, Joe," Marty says as he smiles pleasantly down at me. "I'm just trying to form a picture of what you saw." He sounds like my old boss, Mr. Emmons, smiling stupidly but making me feel even more idiotic; a father listening to his child blubbering about the bully that pushed him in the mud. "Did these people seem prosperous?" he asks.

"Well, I suppose so... I'm talking about the actual city... A mess... Living in their own filth."

"Were *they* a mess? Their clothes? Stuff like that. Did they not bathe?"

"They were fine. Their surroundings. Garbage and broken-down cars. I think it came from us. Dumping their trash wherever."

Marty cracks his knuckles. "I see," he says. "I see your concern, and unfortunately, it's completely unfounded. And please don't think I'm upset that you went out. It caught me by surprise at first, but now I realize it was a good thing, checking out the effect we've had. And you know what? I'm pleased with what you saw. I didn't tell anyone to go out and become slobs. Otherwise, they're doing exactly as I envisioned, living an uncompromised existence. Wonderful to see. Wonderful. Successful and happy."

"But the smell..."

"Oh, Joe!" he's says smiling. "It takes time for our surroundings to adjust to a major step in human progress. Some things lag behind, but not forever. It'll be fine."

"The mess."

"I can imagine." Marty straightens some audio books that didn't need straightening. "Did anyone recognize you, Joe."

"Actually, no."

"Hmmm. Well, how'd they treat you?" he smiles.

"Like I just hopped off the boat."

"OK," he said. "Now Joe, though it's generally against my principles, I say be patient. Hell, if I could talk to the cities the way I talk to our audiences, everything would be fine. I'd shout, 'C'mon, Cincinnati! What are you waiting for?' But I can't. Just hang on, Joe. You'll see."

Marty walks off to his dressing room, waves to me without turning around and shouts, "You'll see, Joe! Just don't go outside for a while!"

*

The one thing Martin couldn't shake as he trudged along in search of the fishing spot was his desire to be heard. He improvised a speech based upon his new Bergesque leanings. A speech about the benefits of shutting up.

"As you people can tell, I've got the gift of gab," short pause for laughter. "And gab I did. I thought I was different from those gossipy co-workers or relatives on the phone that never let you get a word in edgewise. You know the types. Blah blah blah, 'You wanna know (hiccup) what's the matter with the world?'... blah...blah...'I've just *got* to tell you about what Uncle Ned did at the wedding'... blllllaaaaaaah... It's as if one moment of silence would cancel their entire existence. And I thought I was different because...well, talking *is* my job. It's what I get paid for, for crying out loud!" Another pause for laughs. "After all, you guys aren't shelling out your hard-earned dollars to watch me to do ballet. And you don't want me to, believe me... But was I really all that different from Cousin Blab or Gabby Bill, spewing words a mile a minute to just hear myself speak? No way! Why, I'm a teacher. I instruct. I advise... This is my right. But then I began to look closer at what I really said and, let me tell you it was a heck of a shock when I... FOUND... NOTHING. It's like I was giving instructions on how to screw in a lightbulb without ever mentioning the actually lightbulb or the socket. Everything I said was so abstract that it took ten times as long to make my point, if one ever were made. And from this, it was clear that the more I said, the less was actually taught. This extends to all areas of life. Talk is a major interference to progress. Talking doesn't move you forward, it reinforces the past. You can't talk and listen at the same time. You can't listen, you can't learn. You don't learn, you're stuck. There's a definite benefit to shutting up. Maybe that should be my motto: 'Shut up and get to work!'"

Martin made it to his former fishing spot, and now he was praying for a frog to bite. Outside of the measly dried fruit chips he bought in town and the swampy plant life ripped from the ground outside the house, the last time he had a real meal was the hotel breakfast two and a half weeks ago. Oh God, was it good! Fluffy omelets with Feta cheese and olives! Orange juice. Buttermilk biscuits. Seasoned homefries. French roast coffee. And peppered bacon, which he didn't even touch. He was too full and tended to shy away from the fatty stuff anyway. Not good for the muscle tone.

Nothing touched the line. The water was still. Dick Berg meant for this to be a challenge, much harder than simply casting the line and pulling out dinner, even if the dinner had warts. If it was meant to be that easy, you might as well pull up to the drive-through and place your order. Some other way? Hunting the food? Martin had shot a .22 rifle as a kid, plinking away at empty soup cans at his friends' grandfather's land outside of town. His aim was OK, but it wasn't until right now that he imagined looking down the barrel at a white-tail deer with its neck stretched nibbling at clover (was there deer in the Southeast swampland?). He thought of the furriest, most adorable frolicking animal possible suddenly looking over to him, and with impossibly big glistening eyes pleading, "How could you? Look how wholesome I am." It's not something he typically imagined, but Martin was so hungry, his stomach gnashing at itself in a kind of self-cannibalism, he hollered out loud to his imaginary doe, "Tough luck, Fuzzy Tail!" and imagined the creature's head blowing apart like a catsup-filled water balloon. Tossing the fishing pole into the swampy water, he went back to the house, this time determined to eat the first edible moving thing he could find.

*

Randolph sent every dime he made back to the dealership, which now employed a fifth of the original staff. The rest of them had left to become rich and maybe famous if the mood struck. He had no desire to scribble out his signature for people who believed that he was still a success, but Suzi nudged him into sitting at the autograph table with his Sharpie, reminding him it was a part of his contract. The rest was eggshells for her. She saw in him something burning, while offstage he conversed with fans in monosyllabic monotones.

Like a tongue constantly jabbing a canker sore, they lined up before him, a few of them carrying his supplemental workout book published by Romaine Press. In their power suits or designer jeans and sweaters, they looked like both sides of a movie pitch: the demigod producer and the hungry screenplay writer, both wanting something.

Randolph was a few minutes late from brushing his teeth and changing out of his sweat-stained Pendleton. Suzi dared to remind him that his signing was limited to only half an hour, as they had a scheduled appointment with the owner of a local lumber mill. He said nothing and sat down, armed only with a Sharpie and a small stack of 8x10 glossies from ten years ago, back when his hair was less gray. He wanted more up-to-date ones taken, but did they listen? Randolph mentally shook his head and grabbed the pen. The line descended upon him, and maybe he was a little more attuned to the questions and comments today, but they were much less obtuse than the usual, "I'm a big fan, What's the most memorable moment of your career, or What advice would you give to a kid just starting out in blah blah blah?" These questions were purely informational. They wanted the skinny, barely taking the time to introduce themselves or shake his bear claw hand before drilling him for info. Like picking up the phone, hitting zero, and asking for that phone number. In and out, no time for dilly-dally. Randolph kept his smile, rubbing his feet together under the folding table, and thought how much he would rather be back at the front lines selling cars. The questions kept coming.

"What is the acceptable overseas shipping charge for one hundred BMW's?"

"I want to use a famous golfer's name on a product. I'm not at liberty to tell you who it is. What is the minimum percentage of gross sales that I should offer him?"

"Upon opening dealerships, is it feasible to open more than one, say, a dozen initially, or simply open a big one as a base, then satellite from there?"

"Can I use your image for a pickle company I am founding?"

Only a few people had anything under their arms to sign, and the ones who did immediately dropped the freshly autographed copies of his book into cellophane envelopes, walking off and appraising the worth of their new acquisition. Randolph's commodification was complete. Folks waiting in line looked down at their watches, then letting out a puffed-cheek breath, glowered at the people in front of them. By the time they reached Randolph, their patience had worn down to DMV proportions.

Randolph was ready to chew through his arm to get out, and do ten thousand push-ups in his hotel room, if necessary, to forget it all. He spotted Suzi standing beside the entrance of the men's bathroom. She glanced down at her watch and signaled to him to wrap it up. A dozen people still waited in line. They resembled powerful lawyers itching to speak with their clients. Suzi had that impatient, parental look to her, glowering at Randolph to hurry up. It was that same look of disgruntled disbelief she gave when Randolph first broke format. He ignored her but kept catching glimpses, her arms now folded in pinched displeasure. A woman reached the front of the line. She fit perfectly the description of a "little old lady" except instead of wearing a shawl she carried a briefcase better suited for a power broker. Her arms were thin and spare flesh hung under her jaw.

"My son was a big fan of yours, Mr. Shuron," she rasped. "His bedroom walls were covered with pictures of you."

"Great," Randolph said, and glanced over at Suzi standing beside the blocky humanoid symbol of the men's lavatory. He must have gone over the allotted half-hour because she now shook her head in unmistakable condemnation. The woman creaked a step closer to Randolph.

"Yes, my son was always talking about you," she said, slowly setting down her briefcase. She asked for an autographed 8x10 glossy made out to him.

As Randolph scribbled out his signature, "To Pete, Best..." the little woman said, "So, what have you done since your bodybuilding days?"

Randolph banged his fists down upon the table, causing the remaining glossies to jump. He leaned close to the woman, inches from her face, and screamed, "NOTHING! I'VE DONE NOTHING IN TWENTY-TWO YEARS! I HAVEN'T STARTED A BUSINESS! I HAVEN'T WRITTEN TWO BOOKS! I HAVEN'T TOURED THE COUNTRY SEVERAL TIMES SPEAKING TO THOUSANDS OF PEOPLE..." But she didn't get to hear the rest of what he didn't do, because her heart stopped. She bit down twice for air, making a squeak like a pinched balloon, and fell sideways over her briefcase.

Some of the folks in line who looked like lawyers were lawyers. They took sides, immediately offering their services to Randolph or hovering over the dead woman protecting their catch from invading herds. Suzi looked at the woman then at Randolph standing and breathing with his chest rising in waves. He looked back, icily identifying her in that smoky gray suit of hers. There was no recognition in his eyes, and that scared Suzi, so she turned and walked.

When the thin yet certainly strong local sheriff Alan Scott arrived, the self-appointed lawyers for Randolph competed in ordering him not to say a word until consulted. The opposing lawyers simply said, "assault," and pointed at the instantly recognized Randolph Shuron. Sheriff Scott politely asked Randolph to come with him, and Randolph, saying nothing, walked out handcuffed to the patrol car.

The sheriff drove and began talking. Randolph wasn't listening and definitely not responding, but there was a presence to the sheriff's voice that wouldn't be ignored, a certain Marty-like swagger and that made Randolph want to leap for his throat.

"You know what, Mr. Shuron?" the sheriff said, the tanned creases in the back of his neck oscillating like little mouths. "You're the first famous person I've ever met face to face. And you work for Marty. I never really cared much for Martin Romaine; always thought that stuff was silly; him jumping all over the place like he's on drugs waving his yachts and houses in your face. But that was before Marty. Now *him* I like. Cuts through the BS. I actually was going to see you when I heard you were coming to town." The sheriff turned around to make certain Randolph was listening. "But then I caught a video of Marty. He got his message across loud and clear. He said, I remember, 'If you gotta see me twice, then I've failed.'" He turned around again and said apologetically, "So, you see why I didn't come and check out your show." They crossed the freeway into the brief business district, which consisted of a main street with antique shops, diners, sporting goods stores and taverns. Folks along the sidewalk looked at the huge figure in the patrol car's back seat as if their local sheriff had thrown handcuffs on a bear. "But you gotta admit, one week I'm watching a Marty video—and I really liked it, I did—and the next I've got the famous Randolph Shuron in the back of my patrol car! That's gotta mean something. I'm sure you know this, but Marty said, 'If you don't know what move to make, you just don't have a clue, take any opportunity that comes along.' And I'd think you'd agree, Mr. Shuron, this is an opportunity!"

Randolph felt like he was on parade. Folks shielded their eyes from the sun as they squinted out the gargantuan stranger riding in the back of Sheriff Scott's car, and the sheriff, being the local small town sheriff that he was, a friendly sort, gave them his customary wave. This was typical, but was certainly unnecessary was stopping to chat it up with the town's real estate agent, Pete Lockwood, jaws flapping over extending the playground at the park. Pete heard nothing about a park because of the muscle-bound superstar sitting cuffed in the back seat. "Is that?" he nodded towards Randolph. "Yep," said the sheriff. "Well, I better go."

With the town consisting of little more than a main drag and a couple thousand people, there really is no long route to the police station, however the sheriff was making a concerted effort. "I hope you don't mind, but I've got a few errands to run. I take it you're in no hurry," he said. First, he stopped at an auto supply store where he brought the owner out to the car under the premise of determining what size windshield wipers he needed. Then he picked up a chicken sandwich and a diet 7-Up from the drive through. They repeated Lockwood's question, "Is that Randolph Shuron?" "Uh huh," the sheriff answered. "But I gotta go."

The police station was a two-story brick box. Brittle Nevada hedges sat under the windows. Another patrol car, the rest of the town's force, was parked in front. One of the self-appointed lawyers that Randolph didn't recognize from the venue was waiting. He told Randolph that he "convinced" the other lawyers to back off—Randolph was his. The lawyer, Conrad Beals, winked when he said "convinced," but didn't go into it. Sheriff Scott, like a kid who wasn't letting his prom date out of his sight, told him to get lost and Beals countered with "attorney-client privileges." As Randolph disappeared around the corner on the way to the cell, Mr. Beals' voice echoed out, "Don't worry, Mr. Shuron. You didn't touch her!"

"I know," said Randolph as they passed a 6x8 foot map of Nevada tacked on the wall. It was the first thing he had said since the old woman crumpled lifeless to the ground. His throat felt sandy and cracked like emerging from a ten-year oath of silence. Unlocking the cell, Sheriff Scott said to Randolph, almost regrettably, "I'm surprised you'd blow your top like that, working for Marty and all. It certainly isn't what he teaches." Though he stood only an inch shorter than Randolph, he was only as wide as one of the captive's bullish thighs, quadriceps like hams. "Maybe you ought to think about that," he said, and KA-CHANG! went the cell door.

*

I take Marty's advice and don't go outside. The distraction's not worth it. I make a silent solemn vow not to venture from hotels, dressing rooms, planes, limos, stadiums and outdoor amphi-theaters. Curtains are drawn before I arrive at my hotel. I plan my sleeping schedule around travels so I don't inadvertently peek outside and witness the sad state of the world. It's a good idea; but it still breaks my heart to see the towns and communities lag so far behind humanity. I wish I could talk with cities as if they were people, shout words that would inspire a downtown to look forward, think great thoughts, and act upon them. But I can't, and refuse to watch it limp along in its last days.

I rehearse my role of husband and father to Sherri, James, and Noelle, honing each skit into a perfect three minutes of familial strife. My frustrations over seeing less and less of Misty bleed over into them as if they were my own family. But how can I tell whether they are or not, as I've never had one before? Yesterday Noelle caught a splinter in her hand backstage and ran to me, yelling, "Daddy, it hurts!" and I backed away from her and the handful of blood and skidded out of the room in search of Misty. Behind me, the little girl with squished-up face groaned, "Oh! Daddy thinks I'm disgusting!"

I'm so overwhelmed with job responsibilities that all I have are a few moments to drop by Misty's suite to dispense parental advice. "Remember that Arias played to the child will develop the right side of the brain while fugues will focus more on the left," I tell her. "Try not to frown, because the child can sense it. Smile and remember that each parting is merely a segue to a fulfilled desire." I snatch kisses, lay in bed with her at night rubbing her swollen belly as if preparing the genie for emergence. There's no time for exercise, and my physique begins to mirror hers.

Marty is thrilled with Misty's pregnancy, proud like an expectant grandfather. He brags to guests, leaders of business, football coaches, everybody about the "awesome miracle on its way." He uses the word "awesome" in regards to the child and the upcoming birth. Not a word to be trifled with, he says. It's a word he reserves for only, well, awesome occasions. "Something that inspires awe," he says, "must not be used lightly, but for this event I holler it without reservation... AWE-SOME!"

I go before the audience each night pretending that Sherri is my wife and James and Noelle are my kids. These skits are preludes to the topics Marty will be covering. During the first act, the wife and I are bickering because our "family time" is compromised by the hours I spend at work. Then we all freeze, standing still like a paused movie. The lights dim and Marty strolls out followed by a single spotlight. He weaves between, around and in front of us as he launches into the subject: "Managing Time for the Important Ones in Your Life." This is a massively successful approach, and the amount of skits or "Solution Scenarios," as they're called, have increased from three to six a show. These scenarios are:

- Communicating with and raising your kids in an economically deprived neighborhood.
- Managing the appropriate amount of time for work and family.
- How to resolve family conflicts constructively.

- Dealing effectively with the death of a spouse or loved one.
- Managing family expenditures wisely.
- Cultivating and maintaining the passion in a marriage.

The last skit was easier to pull off than I anticipated. Initially, the idea of portraying sexual arousal towards a person I hardly knew, let alone wasn't attracted to, in front of thousands of eyes was unbearable. However Marty noted this and advised, "Terrified? Great! Use it to your advantage!" And that's what I did, and still do. Before tens of thousands of people, Sherri and I awkwardly circle each other, too mortified to touch. Marty steps out from the shadows, shakes his head prompting audience relief, and shouts, "Get a room you two." The place explodes as we stand frozen in boxer shorts and cheap lingerie. The lights dim and we rush around in the dark for the "after," scenario. This dramatizes what Marty had gone over for the last fifteen minutes. The lights go back on, and we are in new positions. I run into the house clutching flowers. She's waiting in the bedroom wearing something sexy while the kids are at grandma's. I flash her two tickets to Bermuda. The lights fade to black as we passionately embrace.

Misty is walking on the treadmill, Mahler's 1st symphony is on the stereo, and I am sitting in a chair next to her reading Shakespeare sonnets out loud. This has been our child preparation routine since conception (which is explained at length in the working draft of my book), but has unfortunately dropped off in duration due to my packed schedule. I seldom get more than twenty minutes alone with her and the kid, so, whenever I can break away, I call and tell her to get prepared for what I call an "Embryonic Workout," and later a "Fetus Training." This has been an independent project of mine, something I have worked on without Marty's knowledge, with the credit going solely to me.

Marty walks in. He always announces himself by asking a question before he sees you, walking around a corner or entering a room, and I seldom hear the first half of it. He's in mid sentence and stops, looks at Misty sweating it out on the treadmill, and then at me.

"What's going on?" He says.

"Spending time with Misty and the kid," I tell him, the book lying open on my lap. Misty is pumping away at the treadmill, head down in concentration.

"No. What are you *doing*?" He says, eyes leaving mine, scanning the room.

"Huh?"

"Tell me what you're doing," Marty says.

I stand up. He tells me not to, but I do anyway. "We're spending time together; me and the family."

"The family he says." Marty stops peering around the room and locks in on me. "It looks like you're doing something else."

"I'm reading and she's working out," I say.

We raise our voices above Mahler. Misty, breathing hard and dripping sweat, looks up and smiles at us, then goes back down.

Marty lets out a sigh. "And you're doing this for the baby?"

"Uh, yes."

"Working for the baby?"

"Preparing for the baby's future. That's what we're doing, Marty."

Marty lets out an even more pronounced sigh. "Working for the future. The person whose supposed to be my partner, behind my back, working away. The baby's future..."

I lay the book open face down though I don't anticipate reading anymore today. "Yeah, Marty. So what?"

Marty takes a step forward. "Why don't you call it what it is, Joe?"

"What?"

"Come on say it," Marty says with a patronizing smile.

"Say what?"

"WORK! Say work, Joe! Nah, forget it. You already have. Do you think everything I've said, we've said, to those people is bullshit? Oh, 'I'll talk a good game to all those suckers, pitch this snake oil, but I know better.' Is that it? I'm dead serious about what I say Joe. I'm not on tour to see the country, a sightseeing trip of America's stadiums and hotels. This stuff is real to me. And you've witnessed it in action, Joe. Out there, on the streets, in their hearts."

"I'm thinking about my kid's future. I'm going to be a father, Marty."

Marty opens his mouth, stops, and takes a step back as if he sees a dripping cyst on my forehead. He flips off the radio. "I want Misty to hear this," he says. She stops pedaling and looks up. Marty, erect with hands on his waist, puts one foot on the coffee table. "Our teachings are not good enough for Joe! Yeah, fine for the poor folks out there who don't know any better, but for Joe, nah, he's too smart. How do you take what you do seriously?" he whips around to face me. "I mean you stand in front of all those people testifying to the power of effortlessness, but you go around and do just the opposite, plugging away, sweating, laboring like before..."

I recognize it; Marty is in presentation mode. Turned on, instinctive, fueled. It can go on for hours, and he has it in him to last days on one topic. Pontificating, creating an anecdote to prove a point, digressing only to come back and nail the thesis. I've seen him on automatic pilot before, with a lecture lasting through the night. Everyone will be leaning back in their chairs at the dinner table while he's front and center, sitting up straight like the star pupil with a full bladder. And he does get emotional at times; vague people with vague old-fashioned codes of conduct really get to him. They affront him personally. Like I have done now.

Even if he is getting me mixed up with his intellectual opposites, I don't want it to go on for hours. I lose the thread of his point and zero in on the tone, which I don't find in the least acceptable in front of Misty and the child. I interrupt.

"Just tell me what the problem is, Marty. I'm tired."

"Fine, I'll let you know what it is," Marty says and rolls up his sleeves. "You're doing things the old Martin way, not the new Marty way. And with a child coming into the world; that's what makes it truly disappointing."

I manage to get out only, "ALL RIGHT!" before I rhino charge him. Because he's off balance from his Marlboro pose he flies out into the hallway. I swing the door shut and lock it. "Joe," Marty says from the other side, "Where'd *that* come from?"

There's a moment of silence, then Marty shouts, "You know, Misty, you can get all those results without the work!"

Nothing more is said. I'm very sorry my kid had to see that.

Chapter 10

#1 Foam Hands
Just for fun. Show them what's on your mind.

Balsa Wood Flier
This easy to assemble glider is engraved with the words, "Flying High and Never Coming Down." A great stocking-stuffer and kid-safe.

Calendar
A quote a day. Each day you are given a message by Martin Romaine to practice and take to heart. The holidays are given specific quotes relevant to that occasion. Valentine's Day: "A mate is nothing more than the result of your intimacy investment."

M ona couldn't decide upon the best way to approach Marty. How would he react to her sudden appearance? Upon seeing her, would he scream and collapse into a puddle of goo? Would he run up and embrace her? How about attempt to stab her with his autograph pen? She had decided to use the approach that she had always used with Martin—catch him right after a show, still buzzing, needing sleep but nowhere near able to. Defenses at their weakest.

She had arrived in time to catch his performance. She purchased a cheap ticket in the upper deck of the immense outdoor stadium, and found herself virtually alone up there with everybody taking their seats down on the floor. Five minutes before showtime the nosebleeds had yet to fill, so Mona moved up several rows. Fewer attendees than expected. And a vastly different crowd. Gone were the conservatively attired hopefuls; the ones who had up to this point in their lives sleepwalked through their jobs, or their families, or both. The bread and butter now replaced with Brie. Two variations here: the slick chrome uptown types, ultra self-conscious of their crisp new attire, or the nouveaux-outdoor folks, mirroring Marty's laid-back ruggedness. Both crammed tight against the stage, jockeying for the prime spots. Everyone hungry.

The lights went down and then they went back up. No music, just a man's unembellished voice—no reverb, flange, and no echo—"Please welcome Marty!" This was nothing like the spectacle-filled jubilees of the past. Not a sparkle of a firework. Marty slowly walked out, hand shielding the stage lights as if it were his first time before a crowd. He waved off the cheering. They obliged and he went straight into it.

"Sorry to silence you like that. You didn't fork over all that money to hear yourselves cheer for ten minutes. And I know you didn't pay for lasers and bells and whistles. Nor did you pay for some famous opening speaker, some guy who had been successful long before he had ever heard of or met me. And while we're at it; I'll bet my shirt that you didn't spend your hard earned money for this introduction!"

The crown erupted in applause. Marty waved his hands and continued.

"But there's good reason for it. It actually illustrates what the Marty system is all about. Number one: Know when to point out the distractions in life—my introduction, for instance. Think of all endeavors like a steak. It can be anything: a job, your relationship, even the entertainment you seek. It doesn't matter. So you've got the steak there before you. You cut off a piece and pop it in your mouth. But what's this? There's fat! You've just tripled your efforts with that itty-bitty piece of fat just to get it down. Chew! Chew Chew! Gulp! It's more work! And you know how I feel about that. So, CUT THE FAT!

"Number Two: Everybody's sweating about spending their "hard earned money." They say your money is the reflection of your efforts (a fallacy I will cover later on tonight), so naturally you don't want your efforts wasted. This cycle enslaves us all. Our parents instill it in us at a very young age when they insist that we go out and get that paper delivery job. Learn the value of a dollar. Waste not. Now think how much easier it would be to spend the money if the money weren't hard earned. Think of all that would be cut away, like the fat, if this were the case. Say goodbye to the anxiety, the fear, the compromise, and especially the sweat. People have lived this way throughout history. It's nothing new, and I'm going to show you how to take the "Hard Earned" out of your money."

Marty took a breath, ready to launch into number three but he stopped, thought better of it, and shrugged. "Number three...ah, forget number three! Let's get started!" He ran off the stage and the crowd went nuts.

When the lights went back up, a man and a woman were standing on the stage. This was the new act that Mona had only heard of through second-hand descriptions and snapshots of previous performances. They were underlit, and would have looked sinister if they weren't so frumpy. They stood in a mock living room with a television, a green/brown couch beside a small table with a lamp and a picture of a rainbow hanging on the wall. The man of the house, the new guy on the Romaine payroll, Joe, had just arrived back home after a day at the office. He removed his jacket, revealing a doughy spare tire straining against his light blue workshirt. His eyes empty sockets. Mona heard a groan in the audience. The "wife" on stage, a good compliment to her corpulent counterpart, not necessarily in body type but rather in destitution, leered at her exhausted husband. Their eyes matched.

From the domestic bickering and needling, it was clear that the topic of this presentation was the management of time between business and family—neither of which was fulfilling.

The time he spent away from his middle-management-with-little-chance-of-significant-advancement-career he spent achingly dwelling on it. And he could barely summon the energy to defend a job he cared so little for.

"But this is for all of us. That's why I'm working," Joe farted out.

A sigh of recognition came from the crowd.

Joe's stage wife didn't answer. She shook her head as he plopped onto the couch. He was too spent to address his wife's demands, spent after being spent all day at work. Spent as his two kids came down stairs and knew better than to waste their time telling him their problems. They went through truncated routines of dinner and the bills. The crowd winced as he bit into a powdered doughnut hidden in his briefcase. Then, as this scene was about to stretch into infinity, the family froze. Marty jogged back onto the stage, sped up like very old film footage in comparison to the previous glacial slowness of the others. New lights beamed down upon him, making him Spring-fresh while the stale family behind him remained ghostly underlit. He looked at the audience as if waiting for an opinion, turned to the family suspended in time, and went back to his audience. They waited. Marty shrugged.

"Speaks for itself, doesn't it?" he said. The audience grunted in agreement. "But, it's easy to dismiss problems that seem so transparent, so obvious," Martin countered. "But imagine being right in the middle of it, like finding yourself under water not knowing which way to the surface. You think you're hundreds of feet down, when in actuality, if you simply turn around, there it is. A way out. Fresh air."

Marty paused again. He thumb-pointed over his shoulder at Joe and the family. "So you want to know how to avoid his fate? This is lesson one, folks. The best way of getting out of trapping situations like his is to never get into them in the first place. Stuck in the middle of somewhere? Stop putting yourself in the middle of things!"

Then came the "after," scenario. The lights no longer shone from below, highlighting the family's ill proportions. They appeared thinner, wealthier, happier. The kids gone. The husband didn't arrive home from work; his work was at home, if you could call it work. He gave a few commands on the phone, hung up, and the wife skipped in, beaming, with two airplane tickets in her hand. They froze again, but this time the lights didn't go down. Marty came jogging on stage.

"As you can see, they're doing quite well. They followed lesson number one: Avoiding getting into the middle of things. What in fact did they avoid? See any children there? That's right, no children. That's what they avoided getting into the middle of, and look at the benefits. But maybe you're saying to yourself, 'What if I already have kids? Am I out of luck?' Nope, not at all. If it's too late to benefit from lesson one, then you should pay special attention to the following topic: How to make your obligations work for you."

Mona sat through the remainder of the show. It was roughly the length of a movie. Not the "festival" that it once was. It proceeded according to this pattern: Marty illustrating a modern dilemma, Joe or Joe's family acting it out, Marty interrupting to point out a valuable lesson, and finally the actors portraying alternatives. Looking at the handsome, smart crowd, Mona knew the show served as a reminder of a life they once led or could possibly slip into if they didn't watch out. Preventative motivation. Like driving school where they show the film "Blood on the Asphalt." Lousy drivers who fail to heed the laws of the road get tossed through windshields. Baby carriages are ground under careless tires. Direct, uncompromising, and very very informative. She noted Marty's infectious enthusiasm upon the audience as well as their collective loathing over the distressing scenarios on stage. But what really stood out were the empty seats. And this meant one thing: No repeat customers.

Even under the severe stage lights Marty hadn't broken a sweat. He trotted off stage with the applause behind him. Mona was waiting in his dressing room.

"Nice work!" she said.

"Yeah," Marty said nonplussed picking at his hair. "You caught the show?"

"Yes."

Marty kicked off his shoes and took an almost running dive onto the couch. He leaned his head back and peered at Mona though his eye slits, grinning. This was nothing like the dressing room from the days of Martin. It resembled a hotel room that a late night traveler stopped in for a few hours sleep, not bothering to bring in clothing, toiletries or a briefcase. Leaving it as he found it. Martin on the other hand would have instantly transformed it into a laboratory with his new T-shirt concepts, pages of notes, five changes of clothes and half-eaten sandwiches. All that occupied this room besides Marty's reclining body was a cardboard box filled with a dozen bottles of natural spring water.

"Yes, things are going quite well," he said.

"Attendance is down, Marty."

"That means it's successful." His eyeslits were so narrow Mona couldn't tell if they were even open.

"To whom?"

"To the clients, of course." Marty now closed his eyes, still resting on the couch. His smile grew wider.

"Marty." Mona said. "It isn't for us—"

"Sure it is. It proves—"

"I now see where I screwed up," Mona said casually.

"Huh?"

"You're shooting the whole load in one show!"

"I'm giving them what they need."

"Martin spread it out over dozens of speaking engagements, seminars, books, and videos. You're giving it away practically for free."

"Yeah, Martin," Marty sighed.

Mona continued. "Think about what's going to happen if you keep at it this way. The attendance constantly shrinking due to you and this new book of yours."

Marty's eyes popped open. "You read it? I really hoped that you would. It's not crammed with all that filler like Martin's books. He's always repeating himself, stringing you along with no payoff."

"If you keep going, nobody's going to be reading it."

"Oh, I've got plans," Marty said dreamily. He pushed himself back deeper into the couch, parrying Mona's insistence with paraphrased selections of his live show and book. Mona knew what to do when he went into a self-propelled loop like this, immune from external stimuli and especially her. She walked behind him and clamped down on his shoulders. After a solid working of the joints and muscles, his pontifications became mumbles and finally silence. She led him to a chair where he sat up straight with a glazed stare. It will take a hell of a lot of work to get this tour back to where it's gaining clients instead of losing them, Mona thought while gazing into his caramel-colored hair. First, supporting acts would be re-hired. Stretch the show out, way out. Make the audience work for the big payoff, if there is one. She had anticipated Marty requiring some guidance but not a complete overhaul.

The "father" from the skits, Joe, still in his sausage-tight blue work shirt, walked in. For all the royal screwing up that Marty did, Mona concluded that Joe was the one thing that he got right. Up close she could see it.

*

From what I had read about her in Martin Romaine's autobiography, Mona had, from the very start of his career, accompanied him on the road. And now here she is, two weeks before we kick off the Pan-Asian tour. He's sitting, back straight with his eyes closed; unstirring and restful in a way I've never seen him. Statue still. Mona is behind him, broad shouldered and strong working her hands down his back, eyes locked onto his neck. She looks up and smiles, and brings her index finger to her lips. I move to her and she leans over and whispers, "Hi. It's a little thing I do called, 'Winding up.' Hello, Joe. I'm Mona."

Marty opens his eyes and practically sleepwalks to the couch, splashing onto it spread-eagled. He looks at Mona and lifts his arm, I presume, in greeting to me and lets it fall.

Mona smiles again. "I just saw your performance; you're perfect, Joe." After her introduction, which isn't an introduction at all, she launches into new tour plans. I look at Mona, this woman who shares Martin's thin upper lip and unblemished, albeit lighter skin. I try to reason it that this woman has played a huge role in the development of Romaine Enterprises, but I can't conquer this tinge of resentment over Mona who, after all our success, immediately tells us that we need supporting acts, who we can and cannot book in time, and what changes should be make for the upcoming months overseas. She explains the various modifications that will have to be made for a culturally different audience. She's got a thick day planner opened, looking at Marty, then me, then back to Marty. Marty is glancing at her through thick milky eyes. It's like his energy had transferred to her. She doesn't share his informality and listener-friendly easy-goingness. The nonexistent pauses between her points fail to let us "chew" on them, as Marty would say. But the drive and enthusiasm, however, is identical. She's so in love with the work, as Marty is, that it's infectious. Her zeal has a touch of desperation behind it, like she's trying to hold on to something, keep it from slipping away.

Mona is ever-present, backstage and at every meeting, papers and schedules and plans in her arms. Though she hasn't yet put her foot down on any of the decisions we have made, she's very involved and often asks Marty's plans for the future. He replies that he just wants to see this tour until the end, whenever that will be, and write a new book with the possible title, *The Unlifted Finger*. She even stops me, curious about my take on Marty.

From vague questions like "What do you think of Marty?" to more pointed ones: "Does his enthusiasm ever frighten you?" to the outright bewildering: "Does his hair need to be lightened?" or "How about his personality? Too Hayseed?" They spend a lot of time together behind closed doors. It's tough that decisions are being made without me, but Misty reminds me that this *is* their operation, their baby.

Marty has me flooded with work and he takes every opportunity to point out the superiority of his new teachings over the old, or "crap-ass," Martin way that endorsed "self-slavery." He'll send me rich, chocolatey cupcakes throughout the day, shiny silken suits tailored for my build, watches with altimeters and compasses built in, and even hands me a fax of the new home in Hawaii I now own. Not wishing to upset him, I'm more secretive about the fetus training and book in progress. Misty, weeks away from delivery, is growing weary of the exhausting regimen.

"I'm tired of working all the time!" she screams.

"Come on honey," I tell her, holding her hand. "Not much longer and you'll get a rest. Then we can hire a nanny (trained by me, of course) to take care of him."

"But I'm sick of it!"

"Please honey, not in front of the kid."

She stands there, hands supporting her lower back. "I'm so tired."

"You've got to keep smiling," I say, grinning as an example.

"And I don't want to smile!" she winces.

I stand my ground, trying to plant my smile on her face. I stress the importance of constant vigilance to ensure the success of our child. She sighs and says she sometimes envies the people in the audience who seem to attain everything without trying, just like Marty says. Misty is dead on her feet, and that makes it easier for me to badger her back into a good mood. "Only another month."

Whenever I see Marty, be it backstage, walking the hotel halls, etc., Mona scribbling down notes trails him. Marty announces an off-the-cuff mission statement and she will write it down and develop it. She'll break away from him and start in on me, drilling me with questions about Marty while I eat breakfast or return from an autograph signing. She asks me how his mood has progressed over the last few months and how his delivery on stage has changed since we've begun the tour. Is he a good guy to work for? How's his attire? Any changes in the way the audience have responded to him? Would you recommend him as a possible employer to a friend or relative? She jots down my answers in that thick organizer of hers, thanks me, and is off again in search of Marty.

*

"The first step in a journey is always the hardest."

Martin used to know where that line came from. It was somebody Chinese, of that he was fairly certain. Chang Kai Check? Bruce Lee? Or was it Martin's mother teaching him to swim? She sort of had Chinese eyes. The humidity broke and as it dumped globs of rain, Martin spent the day inside flipping through Dick Berg's technical books. Ham radio user manuals and 25 year-old refrigerator guidebooks disintegrating in his hands taught him nothing about catching food. Moisture seeped into the house.

He was so weak from hunger that the only person of whose place in the world he was certain of anymore was his sister, Mona. Hers was calling the shots at Romaine Enterprises. Martin grunted and went outside and stalked the grounds of Dick Berg's property looking for something to catch and eat. Once he took that first step maybe he could teach that know-it-all Mona thing or two.

It was a few years ago. Martin was backstage between acts pulling off his sweater to change into his "vacation wear" khaki shorts, button-down Bill Blass shirt, and Teva sandals.

With the sweater over his head, he slammed into the 8x10'
replica of his first book, spun into a prop guy and stumbled back
through the curtains and onto the stage. His hair, his beautiful
hair, emerged from the sweater like a coughed up hairball. He
grinned like it was planned that way. Because of this, Mona hired
what she called "a designer," but McMurray (that was his first
name) never drew a sketch or touched a sewing machine in his
life. He simply knew what looked good on whom. His official
title: "Style Sculptor." He had chosen the outfits for a certain
singer's (considered a household name in fifteen percent of
households) background singers for his last tour. Martin
reluctantly accepted McMurray's input and was soon free from all
clothing decisions. Mona had final say, stepping in before the
shorts that were too short or shirts that looked too liquid reached
Martin. The outfits were laid out in neat stacks between acts.
Each ensemble was assigned a small chalkboard sign stating its
purpose. "Business Formal." "Karate Chopping Block."
"Sweatsuit." "New England prep." Mona took it light years
further when, looking to maximize the efficiency and avoid any
other disasters that seemed imminent the way her brother
feverishly ran about backstage, she expanded McMurray's role.
He was now Martin's dresser between sets. Martin screamed,
"No!" at the proposal, and locked himself in his hotel room with
a bottle of wine. He drank three glasses before emerging. Mona
explained insurance liabilities and lost revenue should he hurt
himself between sets. He could be free to focus upon the show
between sets without the last-minute anxiety over whether he
pulled his pants on inside-out or not. "And let's not forget," she
summed up, "McMurray is a professional. He knows how a man
should look. Especially you." Martin started off with McMurray
handing him his sweatsuit, then allowed him to tie his tie, and
onto sliding on his loafers. Mona ordered McMurray to be totally
silent during changing time lest he interrupt her brother's flow.
Martin was allowed to stay within his head, so the transition from
getting a Windsor knot to having shorts removed and slacks
pulled up and buckled went virtually unnoticed.

"The little luxuries you get accustomed to," Martin said out loud as he stumbled his way to the landing strip. He scanned the ground for a honey-baked ham or pot roast that someone may have carelessly left behind. Fat southern bugs looped about like lazy rollercoasters, dropping in for a bite of Marty, but he was too slow to catch them. He didn't consider their nutritional value, thinking of the critters more like tiny machines engineered to annoy than actual living things. The air was so thick it could be tasted. It's little wonder nobody wanted this land, a cyan/brown aquarium with the stink of a soiled mattress. The ground below him the consistency of pudding that had just begun to form skin on its surface. Yum, pudding.

Martin knew that if he could somehow find a way to feed himself, then he would gain admission into the world of Dick Berg with all the trappings that went with being a "sovereign man." Maybe he'd get to fire that flame-thrower that Berg cherished so much. Maybe instead of bursting though his namesake banner at the beginning of shows in his silky running shorts, he'd torch through it, emerging from the ashes wearing a camouflage headband.

The Piper Cub sat at the runway chained down by its axle. Martin climbed into the cabin. It was the first time he had the opportunity to get a reflection of himself since his unscheduled landing. His face was almost unrecognizably gaunt. The beard worked well, and the dirt smudge on his forehead gave his complexion a rugged authenticity that no tanning booth could ever accomplish. The hair was spiked like a demon's claw. He mashed it down and turned away like a murderer that couldn't bear to face his victim.

"Use what you've got." Dick Berg would say something like that. He siphoned a couple pints of fuel from the plane into a dented coffee can and left. There wasn't much else that a downed plane could offer.

*

Every major American metropolis has been visited at least four times by now. We've dipped into some of the larger Canadian cities as well: Vancouver, Montreal, Quebec, though I wouldn't have known it if I didn't have to tip room service in foreign currency. Misty is huge in the belly but still very active. I see Sherri and the kids more than I get to see her. Marty and I are constantly having impromptu brainstorming sessions. "Non-Stopportunities," he calls them. He'll be waiting for me outside of my hotel room or dressing room door, grab my arm, and it's another five hours in the lobby or conference room with ever full coffee cups in front of us. Sleep is fitful, and often I wake in the middle of the night wondering who's lying there beside me. I spring up and peer into Misty's soft sleeping face to make certain that it's her.

Everyone is someone else's project. Misty is my project. Marty, under constant scrutiny, is Mona's project, and I am Marty's project. He's got me so busy with planning and rehearsing the family strife skits that I can barely pull together half an hour a day with Misty and the child. After rehearsal with Sherri and the kids I'll run back to the hotel hopefully for a few moments of family time, and Marty will be waiting either in the hallway outside the room or inside pontificating about the merits of not waiting for success, with Misty chomping on cheesecake, laughing away. Laughter's a good thing for a developing fetus, so I let the junk food slide.

"Oh, I was just amusing Misty with my tale of the fellow who worked so hard for his successes that he developed an aneurysm, never able to enjoy it. Kinda funny when you think about it," he'll say. Then he will grab me, and again we're planning for next show, making tweaks here and there. Mostly stuff about timing. He wants segues between the skits and his presentations to be seamless. And he always has food with him, from bags of chips to leftover crown roast from the night before, always encouraging me to "treat myself like a sultan." My prenatal conditioning experiments are put on hold and I think he wants it that way. The only time I have alone with Misty is when I stumble into the suite and collapse onto the bed at night. If Marty thinks I would be too exhausted to practice Martin Romaine's old techniques—exercise, going over my accounts, self-actualization meditations—he's right. I'm a fudge-filled log unable to pull off my pants before falling asleep.

Mona rushes through the hellos before quizzing me about Marty. I'd like to think her hyper vigilance is the combination of an adoring sister and a savvy businessperson, but her attention to each minutiae of, for instance, his sitting posture or the way he pronounces the word "treasure" (is it "tresh-ure" or "trayhs-ure?"), seems excessive. She's frantic like a person who has trained a gorilla to change a baby's diapers and it's the gorilla's first day on the job. Mona asks me, "Do you think people like Marty *too* much?" "Is he he's too enthusiastic?" and before I can answer, she'll say, "Where's Marty now?" and take off without another word. It doesn't appear that she's enjoying her job.

The kids, Noelle and James, have grown increasingly disobedient. The girl is a spoiled princess prone to screeching outbursts if she doesn't get her way, and James threw a chair at me, screaming that I was "the worst father he ever had." Marty hasn't covered what to do about children's violence toward their parents. And things with Sherri aren't too peachy. Our delivery on stage, according to her, has become mechanical, impersonal.

"It seems like you're too busy to give us the time we need," she says.

"But I'm trying to make the show perfect," I say.

"Can't you see that we're merely going through the motions?"

"I'm so tired..."

She sits at the make-up mirror detailing her eyes. "There's no passion up on stage."

"I'm sorry. If only there was more time."

"You need to reevaluate what's important, Joe."

"I know," I say.

"Either way, changes need to be made," she says into the mirror.

I sprint across the filthy street, leaping over discarded suitcases, mannequins with shredded expensive clothing and an engine block, back to meet Misty.

Marty's there, lecturing again. I stop outside the room and listen. His words are easy and casual, probably like he is, leaning against the wall. It's like the stadium has shrunk yet retains its density, shrinking and shrinking until his audience becomes one. Not a wasted syllable and never has he sounded more deliberate. "I want to ensure that you don't work another minute of your life," he says. "You're this close..." he goes on. "I need someone to take over for me when I can't do this anymore..."

So that's the reason for the Gestapo training, no rest, no peace? Marty keeps talking, but the words just float about. Taking over. Me? Logical, being the recipient of months and months of Marty's knowledge. Like asking the father of the bride for permission to marry his daughter, he's first approaching Misty. I see myself on stage now, in his place, his words for Misty becoming the words from my mouth into the ears of the world. What he/myself are saying I don't even know, but they're working their magic. They're all looking at me. Then words jump to the front: "Supreme Galvinizer. Limitlessness. Child of infinite influence?" They are Marty's words. I shake my mind free and wait for a pause and go inside.

Yes, Marty is leaning against the wall. He pushes himself off like getting out bed and slaps my back in teammate brotherhood. "Ready for work?" he winks. Misty is smiling up at me, and Marty smiles at her. He grabs me and leads me outside, saying, "Big plans. BIG Plans!"

Audience numbers continue to decline, and the only one it seems to effect is Mona. She either skulks wraithlike about the hallways of stadiums or runs through the hotel lobbies, grabbing me by the collar demanding to know where Marty is. No longer does she stop to consider my opinion of the show or Marty's performance.

And when she does find him, she drags him into the nearest room, slams the door, and turns the TV volume up full blast. The last time I see this, they're inside the room no more than twenty seconds. I hear Mona pleading with him. "Marty! Marty! Please!" and he bursts out, the lights from the TV flashing behind like lightning. Mona then darkens the door, glowering, and slams it shut.

I'm with Sherri and the kids rehearsing the "Win Back Your Family" skit when Mona approaches. Black skidmarks of sleeplessness line her eyes. They look unreal. She grabs me and pulls me into the dressing room.

"Joe," she says. "I'm looking for Marty. Where's Marty?" Her arms are filled with documents and that organizer she's never seen without. Not an inch of her suit without a wrinkle.

I tell her I don't know; I never know until he finds me.

"I really need to find him," she says, and tries smoothing a sheet of paper against her leg. "He's got something planned and is not telling me."

I don't say anything.

"Do you know what it is?" she looks up at me.

"No," I lie. "I thought you guys always worked together."

"We used to. I need to see him."

"The falloff in our attendance?"

Mona allows herself a little break from her burden, setting the pile of documents down on the table. She keeps the frayed organizer tight under her arm like a running back. "Yes, that's part of it."

I go into little half-ass theories: it's the middle of summer, it'll pick up, we should book different opening acts, but she shakes her head waving off my suggestions like pesky gnats.

"No. No, Joe," she cuts me off. "Marty's teachings are working too well, and it's coming back to bite us."

"I would expect this to be considered a success."

"No Joe, it's not. Imagine we're a cold medicine company that cured the cold. Actually cured it. With one pill, no more cold. So much for repeat customers. Or a car that lasts forever?

Or a diet that works? We're shooting ourselves in both feet. This may be the end if something isn't done. So, you really need to tell me, for the sake of my career, your career, and the careers of hundreds of Romaine Enterprises employees: if you know anything about Marty's plans you've got to tell me."

I keep quiet.

"Joe, do you know something?"

"No."

Mona looks at me, and like evacuating a burning building hastily gathers the reams of paper and leaves. Walking out, she turns and takes another look at me as if she'll suddenly catch something.

Misty and I share brief moments at night lying in bed looking up at the ceiling, just like the old days. She says her nerves are shot from the severe fetal workout regimen and especially from constantly monitoring her emotions. I tell her that it won't last much longer, just hold on; not just for the kid's sake, but the book I'm planning will make a stunning addition to the Performance Press library. Sacrifices must be made.

"But Marty talks about abolishing sacrifices," she says not looking at me.

"Yes, soon we will be able to."

"I want to do it now."

"Please hold on..."

"Why can't we just live the way you and Marty are constantly preaching?"

"You two *have* been talking a lot..."

"He doesn't say anything to me he doesn't already tell thousands of total strangers," Misty says and rolls over.

We have eight days of shows in a row, two shows per day. The only people I get to see and converse with are Sherri and the kids on stage as we act like a modern unhappy family unable to find the time, recourses, or the emotions to support each other and, after Marty makes his appearance, quickly demonstrating how all these aliments can be relieved. He winks at me on stage, and after a performance, whispers, "You're really getting it, Joe. You're bringing such authenticity to the role." It's true what he says; it comes so naturally that it's no longer work. I turn my attention to the audience. They are totally engrossed in the skits, grimacing as I make all the wrong choices and then brightening with relief as we freeze and Marty comes sashaying onto the stage. After the shows we head out into the foyer to sign books, the line of people snaking and disappearing into itself. They walk away tightly gripping their signed copies of the new book "Not an Ounce of Strain." It's thin and handsome, only forty pages. I haven't had the time to read it. After the signing, folks mill about examining their new purchases and milk last-minute advice from Marty. I leave him chatting with a handsome upper middle-aged couple with a young well-mannered boy, quite young for a couple their age. I hear the kid say. "Boy he's gross. I don't want to be like him." Then Marty says, "You sure don't, kid."

It's Mona again, waiting in the foyer across the street at the hotel. She's alone except for one immaculately dressed silver-haired gentleman behind the desk. The ever-present pile of documents sits on a table next to her. She click-clacks over in her heels and shoves me onto the couch.

"Why didn't you tell me?" She says.

"What?"

"About his plans when I asked you?"

"What plans?"

"Don't bullshit me, tubby. The satellite." She stands above me, cornering me in the couch.

I try to disguise the breath I let out and tell her I don't know anything about a satellite.

"You better not be wasting my time, Joe," she says. Mona had hunted Marty down and forced him to tell her his big secret. He said it was to be a surprise, a masterpiece he could call his own. He had sold three of his homes to purchase his own satellite from Russia. With it, he would telecast a live performance, complete with translated subtitles, all over the globe reaching an audience it would normally take years to contact via conventional touring. Mona interrupts herself and asks again if I knew anything about this, and grows somewhat relaxed at my complete ignorance of the whole affair. I figure this tale Marty told her is just that, a tale, because it's much easier to swallow that letting me, Joe Median, take the reins of Performance Power.

"This is what he told you?" I ask.

"Yes?"

"Well, I like the idea. Very ambitious, and a real time saver." I lean back in the couch.

Mona lets out an exasperated grunt, and the guy behind the desk looks over. "Is there a limit to what you don't know? Have you taken a look around you? At the streets? There's a stink everywhere. Have you taken the time to notice that we have to shell out fifty dollars to get somebody to make us a sandwich? Even our crew is leaving; the lighting guy took off to start up a new ski lodge in Switzerland. We've tripled everyone else's salaries just to keep them on. And they now want a percentage of the company. No one will take out the trash. Most of the buildings and houses in the area have been abandoned for better ones. If you want a car to work, you gotta buy it new, cause nobody's gonna fix yours for you. Then, if Marty goes through with the telecast, it'll be this way all over the world. Where have you been the last year?"

"It'll take some time for the world to catch—"

"That's what Marty keeps telling me, but in the meantime, who's gong to do something about the trash, deliver the mail or fill our cavities? And think about this, Joe. Maybe the world will adjust to this sudden, 'leap of evolution,' as Marty calls it, and maybe it won't. But think of this. Hear me now. No matter what happens, it will be the beginning of the end for our livelihoods, for Performance Power. Fewer people are attending these shows because Marty is so effective. And what if his message reaches billions of people? You might as well write off the Asian tour. You wanted to see Europe? The Eiffel Tower.

Well forget that as well, cause nobody's gonna show up. They won't need to."

It's difficult seeing Mona like this, and I'm almost beginning to believe her. "I don't think you need to worry, Mona."

"This is real, Joe. Don't you like your job?"

"Yes."

"Then you've gotta agree that this is a bad idea."

"But the people are going to hear him anyway," I say.

"Yes, I know. But we will be touring for at least two years, building more capital and making plans for the future of the company. Marty wants to blow the wad. Joe, wouldn't you like to see the Great Wall? Wouldn't it be nice to get to see Spain with the family?"

I tell her that I will speak to Marty. As Mona has basically been shut out, I'm the only hope, she says.

*

It was Marty's fault that Randolph sat stewing in a Nevada jail cell, forced to modify his "Hotel Workout Regime," due to inadequate facilities. This was the sole thought in Randolph's head. Anxiety over his car dealerships tanking were replaced by the mocking grin of that redneck Marty. The lawyer Conrad Beals visited him daily. "I'm trying to move you to a bigger city, at least Reno, but this sheriff wants you all to himself. He's already writing a book about this and is waiting for the interviews to come rolling in," he said in disgust. "But don't you worry; I'll take care of you."

Conrad explained that there's no way they can charge him for murder for yelling at a woman. "Even manslaughter seems a stretch," he mumbled to himself. "Ah, we'll get national attention for this one. That'll be good. Everyone will see what a sham this is. Yes sir!"

Conrad Beals didn't know whether to bring creature comforts such as a television, a microwave, art prints, a suit and so forth to show Randolph in a better light, or to "dingy up" the cell to show the squalor they were keeping him in. He scratched his head about how the public should perceive the situation. Nevertheless, both he and Sheriff put their disagreements aside— agreeing there was plenty of Randolph Shuron to go around—and went out for haircuts together in anticipation of the news crews that would soon be descending upon this tiny berg.

The crews didn't arrive and there was not a trace of the scandal mentioned on national television. Beals, fearing they were overlooking an explosive event, fired off calls to the major newspapers. "But this is Shuron! Randolph Shuron! He's behind bars for murdering an old woman! Doesn't that mean anything?" he pleaded. They told him they would send someone out if the story developed, but you know how travelling is nowadays; it's gotta be nuclear in order to justify paying those traveling expenses. The sheriff and the lawyer long since had their statements, several drafts in the making, prepared for the media feeding frenzy. But they couldn't get a bite. Not for lack of effort did they fail in getting national attention for Randolph. In the end, all they were able to raise was a third page four-inch story in the North Nevada Centurion. **Shuron's Shouting Slaughters Senior.**

Conrad Beals dropped his client and went on to bigger game in Los Angeles.

"How am I going to defend myself?" Randolph Shuron said from his cell that no camera documented the shabby condition of. Inside was one torn-up mattress, a drum of weight gainer's formula to help supplement the protein in his diet, a notebook with strategies for reviving his business that were steadily being usurped by Marty revenge fantasies, and a cheap red sweat suit for exercising. He touched upon the idea of releasing a new book on how to keep fit while in solitary confinement.

"I don't deserve this case," is all Mr. Beals would say. Randolph wondered if that line came from Marty. Or, if it wasn't a direct quote, then maybe he inspired it; a way to gracefully get out of an obligation that was beneath him. Like dumping a loser boyfriend.

"The woman has no surviving family members," Beals explained "The 'son,' she was getting your autograph for died years ago in a motorcycle accident. The state will prosecute. You'll get bail. No worries there."

Sheriff Scott held more hope that Randolph's fame would eventually pan out. He immersed himself in the slender volume of Marty teachings, "Not an Ounce of Strain," and asked Randolph for the address of Romaine headquarters so he could order a signed copy. Awaiting its arrival, the sheriff would visit the cell for discussions of all things Marty. "I knew Martin Romaine," Randolph said. "And I really respected him. But I don't know this Marty guy."

"Oh, come now," the Sheriff Scott countered. "How can you say that about the guy you work for?"

"I'm not working for anyone now."

"What?"

"Marty is the opposite if everything I believe in," Randolph said and wrote something in his notebook.

"I guess that's why you're in here," the sheriff said.

"He's to blame for this," Randolph didn't look up.

"I don't think so. You do the opposite of what Marty says, and you're in jail on charges of murder, and I'm out here, empowered and on the brink of advancing my career astronomically." Sheriff Scott sounded like he too was lifting lines from Marty.

Randolph tossed aside the notebook and threw himself down on the cool cell floor, squeezing out push-up after push-up until all sound and thought melted away like a forgotten love, or better yet, unwanted fat.

Chapter 11

Ball Caps

"Caged Beast" Show them what you're all about when you wear one of the most powerful clothing items available, the "Free the Caged Beast Within" baseball hat. See, and now wear, Martin Romaine in action as he breaks down all the barriers.

"The Heat." Performance Power is proud to bring you the companion piece to the sweatshirt. Show them what team you're on—the "PP" team.

I return to the hotel suite dragging from yet another real fight with my pretend family. Sherri wants me to cut the junk food from my diet while the kids refuse to clean their dressing rooms. I open the door and Misty is gone. Instantly my mind leaps to her in labor under blinding hospital lights, huffing and counting like they tell women in labor to do. I call the nearest hospital. It rings thirty times before someone picks up. Misty's not there. I try two others. Nothing. I call in a couple prop people from down the hall and shove a handful of bills at them to get them to help me look for her. Entering the foyer, I see Mona. She has set up camp so she can catch Marty should he pass by.

"Did you talk with Marty?" she says.

I tell her about Misty, and Mona plops onto the couch. "Oh, God," she says. Instant defeat washes over her. She looks down, then toward the door, and takes a long concentrated breath.

"She's in labor," I say.

"I was wrong," Mona whispers.

My throat crackles with heat. "Let's find her."

She looks up and says weakly, "You won't find her."

I turn around to leave. With effort, she speaks up. "Joe!"

I stop and she says, "She's with Marty."

My heart falls to my feet and I'm anchored. She moves her eyes down to my chest. "It's not a satellite," she says.

"What?"

"Worse than a satellite."

Child of infinite influence. My head flies from my body. It soars through the foyer and speeds down the city streets with its tumbling plastic bags and abandoned cars. I see Misty and Marty together in a hotel room. He's leaning on his heels against the wall. They're smiling in a knowing, conspiratorial way.

Mona cannot look me in the eyes. "Joe," she says. "Did you have any idea?"

I'm still there, looking in on Misty and Marty. Marty and Misty. I hear the word "limitlessness," again. "No," I say.

"Nothing?" she asks.

I shake my disembodied head. "What do you mean worse?"

"He's taken your child, too."

Child of Infinite Influence

"My baby," is all I say.

My heart's a goldfish flopping outside its bowl. Mona stands up. She reaches into her frayed organizer and delicately pulls out a white business envelope. She opens it and takes out a folded yellow lined sheet of paper, handling it like sacred parchment, and lays it flat on a side table. Mona stands back from a pencilled sketch of Marty's head, which captures his relaxed defiance I know so well. She begins to talk.

We're back in my room. Mona's speaking. I gulp down air to put out the tire fire in my gut, and names—Marty, Martin, and worse, Misty—flare it back up. I'm bitch-slapped by the truth.

Smack! My wife's gone.

Smack! What about my child?

Smack! I'm a (convincing) example of how not to live.

Smack! I'll have to go back to my old life at Conflict Control Systems.

Smack! If the real Martin is gone, then who the hell is this Marty person?

I sit there, boneless. Mona's talking, but my mind clicks between two panels: Marty and Misty taking synchronous assured strides down anonymous halls of power, and Billy Emmons' office at COCO. He's not shaking his head in foreseen disappointment, but might as well be. "Sorry it didn't work out," he says. "We'll, you better get back at it; we've got four people coming in for the assistant stockroom supply manager position that you need to interview." Minus one Misty, one kid, and one future.

I exhale, forcing the air out and hoping it never returns. The word, "Marty," though pushes it back in. "We have to stop him." Mona says. Who is she talking to? It's not me. "Goddamn it, Martin." I hear. Everything is thick, still, incapable of movement. A husky deadness. Then, as if rising from beneath the ocean's blackest depths, only a haze at first, parting schools of silvery fish as it climbs, comes a quote from Martin. It's from his very first book, *How To Do It Like the Successful People Do It*. It says, "Clobber the crap out of defeat! If it meets you, spit in its face! If you meet it, tear its throat out!" It starts at my feet, tingling, and the rest of my body awakens and surges into action.

Mona is at the desk, fingers buried in her hair. She's rifling though papers and documents, some old and worn enough to be transparent.

A white spot leaning against the hotel bed headboard focuses into an envelope. It's angled like a mini shelter. I make it to my feet. The envelope has written on it, "JOE MEDIAN." Inside is a sheet of Marty stationery with the log font. It's not in Misty's handwriting as I hoped. It reads.

Joe,

By the time you read this you probably know what's happening. I'm certain that you're furious beyond words. Though I don't believe in wasting energy in outright fury, I can certainly understand it in your case. When you cool down, I would like you to carefully consider what I'm about to say. Just like Mona has told you the truth about me by now, the same can be said about you. You are someone else's creation. Not mine, as I would have hoped. You belong to Martin Romaine. Perhaps that's why the partnership was doomed. But we do believe the same thing: Your child will be something special. So, to fulfill my promise to the world, this has to be done. It's not what Mona planned, but I can see beyond her. Such a future awaits your child! Everything accomplishable! I just couldn't stand to sit by and watch you poison Misty's and especially the child's mind with Martin's horribly enslaving teachings. It had to be done. It's what's best. I'm sorry. We did great things, Joe, but you see that this is something else altogether.
Well, I'm not one for speeches. You know about myself and economy! Wish us the best.
Marty

The note is snatched from my hands. Mona grips it as if it will come to life and scurry away. She reads with black-circled eyes and nods her head, taking it in, then looks up at me. She steps forward and squints. "Martin!" she laughs and eyes me tentatively as if I may bite. "This is the best you can do!" She whoops like Marty does at the end of one of his shows. Her smile is sick.

"So this is what you've been up to," she says looking at me like speaking to a television.

"What?"

"Joe Median. I get it!" she laughs shaking her head. "Martin, you ass!"

I feel split open and scooped out. My skin is rice paper, propped up by stale hot air. Mona gets closer as if trying to decipher, if only she stares long enough, a hidden message embedded within my face. She speaks up, still squinting, "Martin?" There's something inside me, and I can feel it boiling in my stomach the more she speaks at, or through, me. I can't gulp the breath to speak, so I reach up and claw at the source of my nausea, that mouth of Mona's. I press hard and feel teeth against my palm. I can only get out, "What the fuck is—" before the tip of her heel drives into my shin. I keep my hand where it is, but she swipes it away. "Martin!" she screams.

My gut burns like my first jog by the freeway way back when. "Shut up," I burp out.

Blood is smeared across Mona's lips with a strong red drop at the corner or her mouth. She charges and has me pinned down upon the hotel bed, arms locked around me in a first-day-of-school-fear grip. She says, "Martin," and I groan out, "Please."

We lay there, myself mummy still and Mona staring. I tell her the only time I've ever seen Martin was at that one show, in the stadium hundreds of feet away. Her grip loosens, strength evaporated. She had reached out thief-like for that sack of money with the dollar sign on it, and poof! upon touch it disappears in smoke. She is suspended in that space of momentarily having something and it's sudden and irreversible loss. Mona rolls off me. Against the headboard where Marty left the envelope we lean, a married couple of forty years before the television. We're looking at it, but it's not on.

Martin. My suit. The exercise. My job. My hair. I think of these things and my heart comes back swinging. "Who is Marty?" I say.

"I told you, somebody I invented. A guy I hired," she says looking ahead as if the TV's on and cannot be missed.

I say nothing.

"What do you know about Martin?" she turns to me. "Where is he?"

I stay quiet.

"You've got to know, Joe," she says.

I feel like I'm sinking. There's more silence. How long, I don't know.

Mona grabs my shoulders and turns me to her, forcing eye contact. "Look, I know it's a shock. But we have to act."

"Yeah," I say.

Mona takes charge. She mentions Martin some more, as well as Marty. I never hear Misty's name, but I do hear, like the whoosh of passing cars, talk of my child. She shakes me and says it's time to go, the force of her conviction alone propels me. Clothing is stuffed into bags. Mona shoves me out of the room. Following her down the hallway, I see open doors into rooms that haven't been cleaned for weeks. Sheets piled up in corners, small wastebaskets overflowing with garbage. And let's not forget the smell. Once confined to the outside, it's barged its way in and here to stay like squatters. And this is a four-star hotel. Being lost and disembodied has oddly clued me to the surroundings. Our tour bus driver, Lance, born in a Brussels slum, gets off the elevator as we enter. He is wearing a tuxedo with catsup stains above the cummerbund and a top hat jauntily propped on his head. I had never seen a real top hat before. He smiles at us. The same check-in person behind the counter—seemingly the only one still employed here—is behind the counter yelling into the phone, "I don't care the price! Buy three of them!" Just as we leave the foyer, Sherri and the kids appear. She's in her bathrobe for the "Win Back Your Family" sketch exactly as I had left her. She blocks my path.

"Where are you going?" she demands, arms folded, the kids behind her; James puffed out looking on with poor Noelle clutching that Goddamned stuffed rabbit. "And why are you spending so much time with this woman all of a sudden?" Sherri continues. "What kind of husband and father are you? What about the obligations we made? To the show. To each other? Look at yourself, Joe. How did we end like up like this? We really need to talk."

Mona hustles me along. Sherri calls after me. I faintly hear Noelle ask, "Where's he going, mommy?"

I'm thrown into the back of a dusty limo and Mona jumps behind the wheel. A tight hand now grips my heart, allowing it to beat at its whim. We move. I can't bear to look outside, so I sink down into the upholstery. The sun through the windows is scalding. Everything is under the eye of something else. I go back to the mental picture I had taken all those months ago, the day I left on this journey. The neighbor in his sweats, venturing outside his apartment only long enough to get the paper reporting news he had no effect upon. Had Martin put it there, like dropping a slide into a projector? Does that neighbor exist? Am I him? All these people I've met? The limo slices down the road. It's quiet except for the cardboard boxes flattening under the wheels. I'm sprawled across the back seat like strung-out rock star. Mona calls out from the front, demanding I tell her where Martin is.

"I've never met him," I say.

Her back is to me, but I can feel her neck tighten like a guitar string. "Please, Joe."

I repeat myself and the string snaps. "THINK, YOU FUCKING TUB OF GUTS!"

"But—"

Mona's head oscillates in fury. I expect it to spin owl-like to face me, fangs bared. But her voice softens. "Just tell me if you know."

"I don't know. I need Misty," I say.

"I believe you, Joe," she says quietly and seems oddly pleased. "Let's find Marty."

It's good that she's no longer yelling. I didn't even know what was on my fiancé's mind, the woman I had lived with, confided in and loved for the past six years. So how am I gonna know where Mona's renegade public speaker is?

Like recovering from both chemotherapy and a month-long booze bender, I can't move. I'm hunched below the windows avoiding the outside as if the bags of garbage we are plowing into are actually people, freshly dazed from a Marty seminar, splitting open like overripe pumpkins.

"We need some serious muscle," Mona says as she drives, pedal to the floor. Randolph Shuron had been out there "in the field" doing seminars, picking up scraps of members mostly in the Mountain time zone. Mona steers with one hand and paws through her planner with the other, ripping out sheets until she finds Randolph's tour schedule. I can't picture him doing anything besides posing while oiled up in his Speedos, but maybe there's something about a person possessing the will to carve his body into a perfect sculpture of muscle that his mind isn't far behind.

We charter a plane, and because the price of a shoeshine now costs as much as a condominium, the cost of hiring a pilot (who takes time out from his brand new restaurant chain) makes a serious dent on my credit limit. He won't shut up about his new exciting venture, the "calling in life that he had deprived himself of due to societal-imposed responsibilities," and nearly forgets why we hired him. He asks if we want to franchise out a couple of his restaurants called "Potatoes" which serves nothing but potato-based dishes. And coincidentally, the plane we charter is owned by Alejandro, the cabbie/entrepreneur that drove me to town weeks ago. A framed picture of him hangs in the office behind the stunningly beautiful desk clerk. The plane, fresh from the factory and flown only once, is poised like a greyhound at the gates. This too is available for purchase, offers the clerk narrow-eyed and sumptuous. She explains that for being a Leer jet, this one is somewhat on the low end.

In the sky Mona surveys the land below as if she'll suddenly spot her Marty tending a smoky flame and forming the word "HELP!" out of rocks. Not once does she take a look at our lush living arrangement, complete with a bowl of fruit and freshly cut flowers. The white leather upholstery under me is like sweet butter. She keeps her eyes out the window, even after we rise above the clouds. I sink into the chair as if on a beach, and let myself smile just a little bit when I spot a bottle of champagne chilling beside the pilot cabin door. But then I imagine Marty (feet up, more relaxed than me) and Misty in a 747 customized with Louis the XIV furniture. They're clinking thin-stemmed champagne glasses and laughing.

Randolph has an appearance in twenty minutes and the redheaded promoter is squeezing invisible tennis balls in nervous fury. His otherwise mild face twisted up in anger looks unnatural, painful. And this terrifies me. No Randolph and he wants answers. "What are you guys going to do about it?" he demands. "Big famous dumbass jock can't bother to make it out to our nothing town, eh? I never wanted that bonehead anyway. They just dumped him on me when I asked for Marty—" he blasts. Mona freezes up and leaves the room. I tell him if Randolph doesn't show up then I will take his place. If he wasn't filled with such panicky rage he would have laughed, but straight-faced says, "You're no Randolph Shuron, and certainly no Marty... but they *have* heard of you..."

I go on stage and I bomb. The usual routine, a sure-fire success in the past, is now hopelessly inadequate. Playing the pitiful loser barely able to keep afloat in any aspect of life—be it romantically, professionally or otherwise—means little when there's no one to present the alternative, and the full weight of the mistakes in my life plows into me like a swinging gorilla. The audience feels it too. They wait for a remedy to my presentation, some kind of answer, and when it doesn't happen, first their faces open in incredulity then in aggravation. The promoter is side stage, face buried in hands. He's waiting for me, face matching his hair. "What was that?" he demands. But I spin around, remembering Marty's high-stepping strut. The audience gasps and I take it for a good sign, but it takes more than a puffed-out chest and toothy grin to make it work. A lot more. It's true what the flamehead promoter said—I'm no Marty. I'm no Randolph Shuron either. I can't even portray a convincing "after" portrait of myself. I'm the eternal before picture, profiled with my gut hanging down. Then the boos come, and fighting through them with shouted sentences like, "The word 'can't' has the word 'can' in it," throws fuel on it. The ones who don't walk out stay to jeer. I'm not a representative of what they are—they're way beyond that—I'm something they have been and want to bury for good.

Breathing hot smoke in my face backstage, the promoter threatens to sue Performance Power for breach of contract and screams that he will send the word throughout the land what incompetent shysters we are. His people run up in a panic, saying that dozens of unhappy attendees are demanding a full refund this very instant. Mona and I run for the exit, the wild-eyed promoter trailing us, his people behind him, and a rumble of unhappy conference goers on the other side of the curtain coming to a boil.

We backtrack through Randolph's tour schedule, our funds flowing to our pilot. He says we must consider the folks who now refuse to re-fuel the plane, and the close-to-non existent mechanics to periodically look over the engine. So of course his fees are high. He has no interest in being paid in Super Success Packages and limited weekend training getaways in the Bahamas. "Hey, I saw one of Marty's shows, paid $35 for the cheap seats, and he showed me all there is to know. I gotta hand it to him," he says. "He gets his points across quickly. Besides, I don't have the time for more seminars; I've got some self-actualization to actualize." Taxis and cab drivers are a thing of the past, and rental cars are no more, so we are reduced to the two following scenarios: purchasing a new luxury sedan we'll only use to get to the conference center and back to airport, or being lucky enough to get for free a brand new, otherwise modestly-priced automobile that nobody wants. They're literally being given away or traded for lunch. We track down other promoters stood up by Randolph and they're all twitching with bile, letting us know that us, "and that big fat fuck of ours," have ruined them. Radio Shack owners and runner-up Miss Americas don't fill seats. Offers to make it up and re-arrange someone else in the future are refused. All of them, each promoter we meet, are no longer promoters. They are now pursuing grander, more notable pursuits: senators, actors, CEO's. They cool down from their teeth-clenching anger long enough to tell us their plans. "You know," one said. "I've watched football for nearly thirty years. I know the meaning of teamwork, the best strategic plays to execute. I'm way better than 95 percent of the ones already out there, so I've decided to become a professional football coach." But they give us the same treatment—threats of lawsuits, spreading the bad word, etc. as we turn around and leave for the airport.

We let the pilot and plane go. He notes our desperation, but once we mention we're not able to pay him his requested price, he starts packing. He soars off to his new life, which he mentions we we're more than welcome to invest in should we desire; too big an opportunity to miss. Potatoes.

We buy a new German car, hearse black, with seventy-five miles on the odometer and leather seats that came from a cow massaged from the moment of birth. Cars on the highway are seldom; folks get around nowadays by jet plane. Flocks of them buzzing across the sky. Everything that can be abandoned is abandoned along the roadside: semi trailers, furniture, cardboard boxes, bed boxsprings, stuffed animals, books. Most offramps have nothing to offer. Gas stations are fully automated; you slide your credit card into the machine, and the pump is freed and ready for use. There's no one for hundreds of miles. Towns that had populations of less than 100,000 are now empty.

Maybe if anybody still bothered to report the news, we could have found out sooner that Randolph was in jail. The last promoter to see him, long since caring about the whole affair, tells us we had better screen the people we hire, and pointed us to where Shuron was being held.

The deputy down at the station, yawning loudly over the phone, agrees to get the sheriff only after we notify him of our connection with Marty. "Both the sheriff and myself are big fans of his, and it was especially hard for us to have to jail Mr. Shuron," he says. We arrive at the police station downtown. The only person incarcerated is Randolph. Sheriff Alan Scott, arching his thin angular frame, is waiting for us. "Well," he says cordially, "It sure is a pleasure, Miss Romaine. I must say that I've certainly benefited from Marty's work." He explains that now, under Marty's inspiration, he is following the lead of the nation's most famous criminal attorneys and law-enforcement officials. To advance his career he will be arresting only high-profile suspects. He doesn't budge until he shares with us his hopes of moving to a bigger city and possibly consulting for televised criminal investigations. "But Goddamn it," he slaps his leg, making his deputy look up from shining his shoe. "As it turns out, stuff like this ain't no longer news. I thought Shuron was a pretty big fish. But I can't get an inch headline. I felt certain that I'd get a little exposure before someone came along to bail him out." He states the bail and asks if he can get his picture beside the famous Mona Romaine. "It'll be good for the book I'm working on," he says. He also asks to take one with me. I stand there as he stretches himself even taller. He rests one hand on his hip and another on my shoulder, smiling beyond comfort, mimicking perfectly the 8x10 press release glossy of Marty and striking the same pose.

Randolph, Mona and I get a hotel room; one that lives up to the luxurious standards of which we had become accustomed. The only standard available. Only four or five star hotels remain, the rest gutted and boarded up or used as warehouses. Randolph is stunned and on the verge of tears when he sees the state of world he has reentered. The garbage lining the sides of the road. Nobody outside. He explains that the sheriff who, growing more and more ambitious and trying too bleed him for advice about attaining success, was the only person he had any contact with. He had grown impatient and eventually critical of Randolph's teachings of hard work, practice, planning and wise yet fruitful investments. "This isn't what *Marty* teaches!" the sheriff spat. And because of his seeming "betrayal" of Marty, the sheriff said he would see to it personally that he suffer under the full force of the law.

"How the hell did Martin become Marty," Randolph finally says. Mona stands back and speaks in a brisk, clipped and seemingly rehearsed way. The shadows on his face shift as Mona goes into detail about finding a substitute for her lost brother. She held tryouts until the perfect one came along. Her only criteria were: laid-back and independent; she would do the rest. And she found him. Shambling in and plopping down in the chair before her desk. A hand sweeping through his Martin-like caramel hair. Completely self-possessed yet with an eagerness to please. His answers to her questions were met with a toothy grin, a pause long enough to have you yearning for the answer to come, and delivered with casual offhand sagacity.

Randolph listens, and through no effort of his own, the shadows alter his expression into heart-stopping menace. Mona won't look at him, and the words keep coming, enough to finally nudge her into a plea for his help. She stops, and after several ticks of my six time zone watch, he stands up and looks at me. He speaks, but not to me. "When I first spoke with Marty," he says. "I thought 'OK, Martin's trying a different approach, but it was this Joe person that I didn't understand; he doesn't seem like the kind of guy that Martin would want representing him." He looks at me like I'm a lab specimen and takes a step closer. He's so large I can't see around him. "I guess we better find this Marty," he shrugs and smiles. Then Mona walks over.

Those two have very different approaches at getting results. Way beyond good cop bad cop. Their assaulting demands raining down upon me, shouting over each other, can hardly be called "working together." Their breath scorches. I see myself in Martin's book the moment I cracked it open. There's his hair. An unplowed field of chestnut hay. The kiddie pictures of him and Mona, she seven years old shouting, "Come on! Cough him up!"

Then the little girl sweetens up and coyly pouts. "Come on, honey. You can tell me." I'm floating. Randolph carries me into the bathroom. "THINK!" he booms at me. Crash! I splash into the cold, black ocean. I see the moonlit Romaine estate that edges the sea. The chapters surge forward. Small crowded hotel banquet rooms. He's got a definite knack for it. I spit out water. Martin says, "Raise your standards." I see my beautiful Del Rubio suit hanging there waiting for me. Chapters flip along, each one outlining different steps. "List what you value. Increase the worth of all around you. Imagine. Define. Research. Act. Increase it some more." Repeat. Randolph is ebullient, and like a tap dancing Grizzly the hurt he could put on you would be totally accidental. "You want what's best for you, don't you?" I see Martin looking up at me, in the stadium, lights throbbing and beats pulsing. He waves and he's off. The sea is now swamp, but I'm yanked out of the tub and thrown naked on the bed. Randolph says, "We'll whip you into shape, but it'll take work. God, look at you!" Mona is stroking my forehead, and she's Misty, happy to join me on the road. "Great," she says. "We'll get to see the world!" I see before and after images of her; one digging deep into a pint of ice cream, and another in power suit, trim and tight. She's groaning over the severe baby-training regimen I put her on. I'm in the air, heading south, but I'm lost. Randoph reaches a giant hand around the plane and shakes it. A new book. No cover, just pages. The first is that mental snapshot I took of my apartment's parking lot, the neighbor picking up his paper looking at me. I'm wearing Martin's clothing, writing notes, answering calls. The sea air pours into his room. The water on my body is now sweat, huge leaves slapping me as I run. Randolph's in one ear, and Mona's in the other. They're yelling at each other. "No no no no! Don't shake so hard!" I'm with Sherri's family and they depend on me, and though I'm not the greatest father, I'm working feverishly to keep it together. Back from the grueling office to work just as hard on the wife and kids. Time for everyone, especially myself. I get back from work, fresh from Mr. Emmons, but it's not my apartment, or backstage, but a house, paint peeling and surrounded by the same wet leaves and mosses and I have to break in to enter. Randolph is holding Mona back; her teeth are bared in hunger. "I'll get it from him," she hisses and slobbers. But I feel good. I'm back home. I say, "Dick Berg."

*

Martin searched for something dry enough to throw airplane fuel on. The fireplace with its overgrown moss was indistinguishable from the rest of the house. The flough clogged with innumerable species of plantlife. He decided that would be his second task after the food issue, cleaning the chimney. Once everything he set his eyes upon stopped taking the shape of his favorite delicacy, like the guy whose buddy in the lifeboat forming into a drumstick, working on such tasks would be as easy as a "how do you do."

He picked up green hairy sticks like a kid in a warzone gathering limbs blown off by landmines. With enough fuel, they'd burn, even if they were moist enough to twist into balloon animals.

The brown thing that scuttled around the side of the house, the only thing that moved, seemed the least lifelike of anything in the past three weeks on this property. Martin said, "Otter!" even though it wasn't an otter, and he peered around the corner at the pink-tailed ass of a rat. It carried itself with a strange kind of dignity. Martin winged stick after stick at it, and it ran out stupidly into the open, looking back incredulously at his attacker. "Dick let me stay here," it seemed to say. But it got fat and lazy on the farm, and a twirling green branch pegged it in the back of the head. Martin stood watching as it rolled onto it's back, tongue sticking out, twitching and hissing like the worst villain of a mysterious past who got just a little more than he deserved. It looked up at Martin.

Though it had been decades since Martin had cleaned a fish, he assumed rats were handled the same way. Eat what you can and waste nothing that can be of use. Just like the Indians. What can you make out of rat guts? After years of neglect and pilfering and unforgiving southeast nature, there was nothing in the house sharp enough to do any cutting. The flame-thrower picture was behind Plexiglas. Martin pulled out his platinum Visa card, but that didn't come close to breaking the rodent's bloated rubbery skin. He trudged through the swamps with his kill and the fuel, back to the Piper.

Martin got a good foothold and sawed the animal's belly against the propeller's edge. He could feel it widen in his hand like a wet tennis ball. He winced with effort, then PLOOSH! it gave, impaled on the propeller tip, with guts and a thin sac of five puffing cashew-sized babies hanging by a thin red string. The rest he would have to do by hand, quickly. Ripping sinew from bone and peeling clumps of hair, all the imagination in the world couldn't turn that pink-eyed devil and it's spawn into a t-bone.

"I bet you've never done anything like this!" Martin hollered to the wind as he cracked the hind legs back into a Broadway split to remove the fur. He didn't want to head back to the house lest he lose his nerve and realize what he was about to put into his mouth, so he finished the job beside the plane. As he cleaned the thing with his fingers, pulling away stuff that didn't resemble meat, his face was locked into the crooked jaw of determination of the flame-throwing Berg, a mask shielding him from all unpleasantness. If he kept that face everything would be fine, *from here on in.*

He gathered more soggy stumps and built a fire on the runway. The meat was lanced by another stick and it helped that it no longer looked like what it was. It began to glisten and pop over the unnatural orange and green flame. Smoke from the tree moss curled around it. Martin held it there until the meat turned golden like a Florida weightlifter's biceps.

Martin searched for something he could compare the taste to. His mind jumped to the exclusive establishments he'd been invited to by congressmen or CEO's; restaurants headed by cooks with names so foreign it would be embarrassing to even try and repeat them. Nothing as simple as a Jersey Diner or a Toledo Denny's. Duck with Aspic? Steak Tartar? A Vietnamese soup he knew nothing about and simply ordered from the menu by number? Or week-old old salmon sautéed in an ill-prepared Long Island Ice Tea? It was too exotic tasting, and he was too damn hungry, to call it wretch-inducing. He just savored the act of chewing (though he didn't make a career out of it) and felt his strength return almost instantly.

The makeshift "salad" he prepared, however, didn't go well with his meal. The poison ivy instantly caused Marin's esophagus to inflame. He could think of nothing to say, no magic words, to prevent his air passages from slamming shut and sending him into wheezing unconsciousness. He lay there emaciated beside the plane; the name Marin Romaine dissolving in the thick Southern sky; and his last thoughts were of himself.

*

No such thing as a simple anecdote in Marty's endless pontifications, impartings, preachings, or otherwise plain talk. They all had a purpose: to teach, inform, and reveal. Each one had a delicate arc and a firm impact. How he could make the choice between chocolate truffle cake or peach cobbler pie for desert an impromptu lesson in successful micromanagement was a thing to behold. I hung on to find out where him borrowing my shoehorn would lead. I guessed it would be something like a lesson in self-sufficiency (a favorite topic of his), but it marvelously and imperceptibly wove itself into a speech concerning big industry shifting their workforce to third-world nations being beneficial to all. Perhaps "Dick Berg" was an amalgam of two different topics I somehow threw onto one name. "Don't allow yourself to become an anonymous Tom, *Dick*, or Harry!" with "Realizing that you should be your own boss is merely the tip of the ice*berg*." It couldn't have come from Martin, and the reason I know this is because the names he made a habit of dropping in his books and seminars were instantly recognizable: movie stars, senators, captains of industry, heads of state, Nobel Prize winners.

Mona pours through her brother's past correspondences, looking for a Richard Berg, a Rich Berg, a Dick Berg, a Rick and Ricky Berg, and to make certain she's covering it all, looks up Dick Berger. Horrible name. Has there ever been anyone of note—a philosopher, king, or freedom fighter—that went by the name Dick Berg? Randolph entertains the name "Dick Berg" being an abstract idea (I'm surprised that someone of such sculpted enormity can be so insightful) but he's unable or unwilling to elaborate upon it as if he suddenly realizes what he proposed is quite loopy, especially for him. "Maybe it means something," is all he says. We search the public records and get one name, only one person by the name of Dick Berg in the history of recorded events to ever make the news. In a tiny newspaper nineteen years ago, the Cooperation Bee, is a grizzled man of bamboo bones standing in front of a fence. The byline says, "Dick Berg, No Fence Sitter." It's the story of a man refusing to lower his fence three inches to meet the six-foot maximum height. It was initially eight feet and, apparently intentionally, he didn't shorten it enough. He stands there in his Levi's with rolled-up cuffs like defending a castle.

"That's him," Mona says with resignation and turns away.

I ask her why Marty would be interested in small potatoes like this. An illegal fence?

"Read the quote," Mona said.

"'This is *my* home. This is *my* life. Nobody's gonna live it for me, and I wouldn't let anybody try if they did,'" I read aloud. Those were the last words of the article. The finality had a certain journalistic impact even if I didn't exactly know to what end. I tell Mona, "I'm not sure what that means. It sounds like something Marty would say, but—"

"Look at the picture," she says averting her eyes as if just identifying a deceased family member.

With all his weight on one leg, leaning against the fence but nevertheless planted solid on the ground, I see Marty. His chin high, challenging. That old laid-back intensity.

We peel out in our mid-price sedan that nobody wants and head east. Two thousand miles gives me ample time to imagine Misty and Marty smiling and baking in the sun beside Mr. Berg's outdoor pool overlooking the steamy gulf below. Randolph complains of the cramped conditions. His dealership used to sell these cars, but he had never ridden in one. Mona's behind the wheel, staring ahead and seldom speaking. And when she does talk, it's a vacillation between slapping herself in the head for making Marty too ambitious, or blaming the "scarlet seductress," my Misty, for leading him astray. I feel a tug to defend the woman carrying my child, but Mona's pointed focus is probably the only thing containing her rage. And maybe my child has been born, an oversized Performance Power ball cap on his fuzzy baby head, Marty tossing him gently in the air. I try not to think of the kid calling him daddy, but thinking about not thinking about something is the same as thinking about it. Randolph's fitness advice doesn't help. "What you need to do to get rid of that gut," he lectures me, "is by starting with crunches. Then move on to bicycle peddling on your back. Then keep your spine flat on the floor, curl your legs and have them resting to your side. Great way to isolate the obliques." It's good advice, but when I think of it I'd rather just get the liposuction.

The long stretches of highway with the tiny isolated homes in the distance look no different than they did before. Unconcerned and unattached. Maybe a few more abandoned cars, but it's not as noticeable as the changes that have taken place in the centers of civilization, the metropolitan areas. Heaped-up garbage and cast-aside scuffed loafers. I keep my eyes averted. Folks who had failed to magically transform into presidents of major corporations or celebrities based solely upon their wishes I imagine banding together into an unholy union of the unfulfilled, wielding chains like whips and baying like dogs. Looking for blame. But there's no evidence of this happening because like Marty had promised, everybody is getting what he or she wants. So why am I thinking this? Maybe it's because Marty's not around to re-calibrate my thinking to the positive.

Randolph and I get along well. He sees me as a project, something he can test his physical conditioning regimen on. "When this is over," he stops for a serious moment, "I'll personally see to it that you have a stomach you can cut diamonds with."

We don't verbalize it, but all three of us want to wrap our fingers around Marty's neck and squeeze until it turns black and falls off. We may as well be strangers on a bus; one heading to the dentist to get his plaque chipped away, another to visit a cousin, and the last to see a hockey game. Mona won't let anyone else drive. She even insists on paying for our non-nutritional vending machine meals. Randolph winces as he bites into another "Country Oats" granola bar, the only thing that fits his diet. "I'm not getting the protein I need," he says.

We pass the population sign for Cooperation City. 2,304 people. Mona tssks, "Jesus. The back of beyond. Is this where Misty was born?"

"What?"

Mona goes slack-jawed and dull. "So's she can bring Marty home to Pa?"

"Marty took her," I say.

"Breedin' the yung-un's..."

"Mona, we're from the Northwest."

"Same thing."

"Well, I think you need a shrink," I say and look over to Randolph who probably wants to jump out of the car. "So easily replacing your brother like you did."

She shuts up.

The town of Cooperation City, sunken away from the highway and snug against a river, appears to have missed out on the Marty phenomenon. Either that, or the place was previously such a backwater hole that a fishing supply store and a tavern with the first two letters missing to make it a "VERN," is their idea of the fast track. If it isn't, and somehow they resisted Marty's logic-proof and irrefutable declarations of certain success, then I admire them for it.

Mona gulps air and goes into how Marty doesn't represent Martin. Or is it the other way around? Martin's gone, his plane probably plunged into the Gulf of Mexico. She found a replacement.

"He resembled Martin," Mona says, ignoring the mid-morning town as it gasses up for the day. It's like she is before a second-grade teacher, confessing to cheating on a spelling exam. "And he was green and hungry. I thought he'd work."

Randolph sits up and leans over to Mona. "Who *is* Marty?"

"Let's ask Dick Berg."

Marty and Misty and the baby (I imagine him being named Roger for some reason) would make a good family. The father a stable provider, never revealing his doubts about the world or himself in front of the wife and kid. No complaints, no regrets, completely accepting of the responsibilities he has toward his family. Not like I would be, I assume. Misty had, under my insistence, aimed for something greater and learned that it wasn't terribly difficult to achieve. She had the boob job, the tummy tuck, absorbed enough art and culture to navigate society, but most of all allowed it to really sink in (all the way to her heart) that becoming a better person was more than an abstract notion but inevitable. Can I say the same for myself? By the very fact that I'm thinking this, probably not.

The first person we ask, a woman with a baby stroller full of groceries, points us to Dick Berg's property. It's ten miles away. "You'll know when you see it," she says.

We get back on the highway and I turn to Randolph. "Randolph?" I say.

"Yes."

"What are you supposed to do about self doubt?"

"Jeez," he says rubbing his eyes. "Bury it."

"But it can't be that simple."

"Joe, if it's one thing about achieving success, you've got to keep things simple. Doubts, philosophical quandaries, and even a certain degree of insight need to be suspended."

"I'm not sure if I can—"

"I'm not saying that they can be eliminated altogether, Joe. They're always there. Defeat always breeds uncertainty. After lost competitions, though they've been few, I've had doubts about my ability. It's as natural as stubbing your toe and feeling pain. 'I'm not good enough. I lost. Somebody's better than me.' You'd need a lobotomy to get rid of those thoughts."

"Then what do you do about them?"

"They're just tests man. Tests."

The sign at the entrance of Dick Berg's driveway, though the paint is flaking and weathered, clearly reads: "This is PRIVATE PROPERTY. The owner is LEGALLY ENTITLED to use DEADLY FORCE to protect it. AND HE WILL." Thick viney webs woven by monster spiders blocks most of the entrance, the inside a cave-like darkness that I don't care to enter. The car won't fit. Mona climbs out, rips a fistful of the ropy plants aside and goes in. Randolph and I follow, trying not to touch anything as if whatever makes contact will form some kind of unspeakable marriage and your offspring would be, uh, I'd rather not think about it.

It clears to a "house" that had long ago melded with the mildewed landscape. There are two other structures, not much more than huge slick blocks with barely visible window and door outlines. A tool shed and maybe a garage. The house sags under the dampness. If this is where Misty has been dwelling since they've left, she's not the woman I thought she was.

"Get over here!" Mona hollers from the front of the house. Randolph steps gingerly as if the earth will suddenly swallow him up. Paper beats rock.

The house is empty. There's still hope for my Misty! I know it's really shallow to judge someone by their living conditions—we're all human beings with feelings—but to see her sitting there in a burnt-out Laz-E-Boy, menthol cigarette hanging from her fingertips and screaming for Marty to run to the store for diapers would be too much to take.

Randolph enters, quickly scans the room and says hastily, "OK. There's nobody here." He looks at me, for the first time, for support.

I see how Mona got to be the co-president of a highly successful business. If you can stand there, say nothing and look someone in the eye (especially if it's Randolph Shuron) not threateningly and yet get across that nothing in this world has more weight and importance than this silent moment, then you too can join her elite company. Martin and Mona; what did their parents feed them? She points to the crusty fireplace. Above the mantle is a bare spot on the wall where clearly a picture had hung, and judging from the clean square patch of Fleur de Lis wallpaper, it was taken down recently.

"He was here," Mona says.

"This," she pointed to the bare wall, "is where Marty came from." She had spoken about the "Marty Portrait," during our days and nights of driving and dropped the name Knox along the way. I'm beginning to think that the stress of entrepreneurship and the lack of sleep are draining the sanity out of this woman. So, with my limited knowledge of handling the unstable, I gently nod in agreement with every comment she makes lest any further conflict send her into some knife-wielding rage.

Like the slow chewing of Saltines, there comes a scratching from the wall beside the fireplace. Mona calls out, "Marty!" No reply, just scraping. Randolph assumes a pose that's half Kung Fu, half sprinter waiting for the starter's pistol. I can hear bits of plaster coming apart behind the wall, and Mona takes a step toward it. Soon it's a bulge behind thin wallpaper and then

PLOP, SCKREEEEK, like intestines falling out of a wound, sharp wet and pink noses burst through. They splash to the floor.

The brown skeletal rats pour into the room. We backpedal to the door and outside the ground comes to a boil with hundreds more. Randolph screams, "AAHHH!" and swats at one dangling from his ass by its teeth. It swings like a piñata and hangs on. He swipes again and it goes flying. I freeze, picturing them crunching to their death under my feet as I flee. My stomach seizes and the desire to avoid such unpleasantness overpowers that of my flesh being nibbled and ripped by hundreds of starving swampland vermin. *I actually think it* as they unhesitatingly close in. Marty, how do you account for this? Randolph grabs my arm and Mona screams, "To the car!" Yes, the squeals of their last breath being squashed out of them, toothpick ribs puncturing tiny lungs, is indeed horrible, even under the vain attempt of visualizing the whole event as fleeing a burning crouton factory and the crackling death under my heels is merely squares of seasoned cooked bread.

In the back of the car as we're speeding away from Dick Berg's private property, Randolph says between breaths, "Did you look at this guy's resume before you hired him?"

Even under the fat heat, nobody dares to crack a window lest some flying equivalent of a rat—like a bat or pigeon—comes soaring in straight for the throat. The sweaty dust on the windows smears our view of the dusky landscape. The sun isn't round. It's not even a shape.

Except for the movement of the steering wheel, Mona is completely rigid, still on guard. She's somewhere else, and Randolph is squirming and moaning in the back seat.

"Did you see that?" he says, interrupting his groans of pain with wide-eyed laughter. "I got bit! Bit! A rat colony. Do you think I'm going to need to get this looked at? Ohhh! Those things eat their own shit you know."

"Shut up!" I say.

Randolph keeps on as if only his babbling powers the car.

"Shut the fuck up," I repeat.

He stops and looks at me.

"I'm trying to think," I tell him.

He bares his teeth at me, and this is what I learn about myself: I'm more afraid of stepping on rats than getting ripped apart by them, or by Mr. Universe. That's got to mean something.

Mona rolls down all the windows at once. The wet wind lifts a few strands of hair from my sweaty scalp. Before, I would smear it back down with my own spit, keep it put, but now I leave it be. Moss hangs from trees like forgotten laundry. There's a house every hundred or yards or so. What do those people do all the way out here? Are they all self-employed? Tour guides? Hiding out from the law? Florida had potential at some point, but now it's California's booger-eating kid brother. The folks that wind up here—the elderly, desperate, beautiful and dangerous— sought Ponce de Leon's dream hanging off the end of America and promptly stopped looking upon arrival.

We find a sub-class motel that hasn't been abandoned for pursuit of a greater calling or undergone transformation into something that could be described as "rustic." An Indian family runs it. The office furniture is permanently soaked with the sweet smell of exotic spices. The woman behind the counter wears way too much clothing for the heat. We pay for a single room with two beds (Randolph and I get to share) and we bribe her to give us some of whatever's cooking. She shakes her head no but Randolph begs, and she scoots out of the room. She returns carrying a blackened pot and hands it over. We scrape together the rest of our cash, twice the cost of the room and hand it over. The woman smiles and tells us to be careful as the food will "burn our brains out."

Our room. Duct tape performs the role of curtain rods, holding up Kleenex-like curtains on the window that looks out into the gravel parking lot. The bathroom windows are the same. Cigarettes snubbed-out on the bedstand along with a burn blister on the telephone receiver. Mona says, "I've seen worse," and sets about spreading her own blanket atop the spotty comforter like she's done this many times before. "Imagine this urine stained comforter," she continues, "Nailed, yes *nailed* over that front window. You know," she pauses almost wistfully, "different fleabag hotels have their own distinct smell. It depends on what part of the country you're in. The southeast has a sweaty, barbecue aroma, almost pleasant, while up north urine has a strong presence. Out west it smells like fire." She lets out a sigh and takes the food outside to the courtyard with its empty pool. Next to the diving board are an old washer and dryer, each with a pile of bricks stacked on top. Randolph picks up the phone. He hunches over it as we leave, his voice low. He later joins us outside as we eat the manager's food.

"My business is no more," he says. "Everybody, except that half-wit of a salesman Alan Westerly, has gone to seek their fortune. He says he'll be leaving soon to become a prince. How do you become a prince?"

Mona says, "Mmm-hmm," as she chews. She offers Randolph some of the dark orange stew.

"I can't eat that stuff," he shakes his head. "Too spicy. How do you guys do it, in this heat?"

"It makes you sweat," Mona says.

Randolph walks to the rusted out washing machine and plays with the knobs. It's sad to see someone deflated like this, but worse that it's a six foot something guy with shoulders the width of a doorframe, blighted and sunken. I'm struck with the impulse to walk over and put my arms around him, but that would get me killed.

"Motherfucking Marty," he says and turns to Mona who is looking down at her food as she eats. She takes another bite and sets down her plastic fork.

"Everybody's winning except us," she says smiling.

"Before we were the winners, except maybe you, Joe," Randolph says. "I don't know. Maybe in your own way you were." Randolph does a little rhythmless drum roll on the aluminum washer and spins back around to face us, as if in the middle of a presentation. He's before a packed and sweaty cotton candy-smelling stadium. Puffing his chest out like a rooster. "But isn't this exactly what we need?" he announces. "For hindrances like this will only make tomorrows victories sweeter."

"That sounds like Martin," I say. Mona nods in agreement.

"Nope, that's mine," Randolph says. "I just came up with it."

"Randolph, that's a Martin line," Mona says with her mouth full of Asian spice.

"Mine," Randolph says. "It just came to me. Just now."

"I don't think so, Randolph."

"That's a unique quote, and it came from me, Randolph Shuron. Not from Martin. He never said it. This situation, us, here, in this motel, without a prospect in sight, inspired it. This is all a test, and I answered the first question by that poignant off-the-cuff comment. I thrive in these situations."

Mona stops chewing and swallows. "Okay, it's yours."

"I'm gonna copyright it," Randolph warns wide-eyed.

We're in bed with the TV on low. I expect Randolph to turn into my grandfather, grandpa Clement, in his pajama bottoms with his arm around me reading to me the Sunday comics. Explaining stuff I never inquire about. "You see, Joe. Beetle Bailey's in idiot, the way the whole military'll go if they don't look out." Grandma's in the other bed, wearing way more clothing than necessary. But Randolph flops down beside me and is soon asleep, smacking his lips and mumbling curse words.

When we awaken, Mona says we're going to Martin's estate, "Excelsior." With no money and no credit, at least we'll be able to live in relative comfort overlooking the crisp blue waves that go on forever. It will act as headquarters now that the Romaine Enterprises campus is all but abandoned. From there, we shall hunt down Marty, Misty, and Joe Junior.

I don't care to go back to the house I had broken into where, impersonating the owner, persuaded the 2nd largest American automobile manufacturer to sell out, all the while wearing Martin's snug bathrobe and Jockeys. I slink back under the covers as Randolph complains about his dry mouth, chills and fitful sleep.

Mona surrenders the wheel to me for the drive south. Randolph sits crooked in the back favoring his rat-bitten ass cheek (earlier he had dropped his drawers and insisted I inspect the wound). The radio's on, keeping our radar open to any sound of Marty. We dial in a few imitators who have his shtick down well: vaulting ambition wrapped it laid-back wisdom. "The only thing you should be busy doing is getting someone else to be busy working for you." These casual preachings are effective; much more than the guy with the veins like thick cords running down his neck breathing fire on stage, leaving you wondering which drug he's on, and how long he's been on it. I find myself, the way I always do, lost in these Martyisms and how they simultaneously make you feel better and worse about yourself. "Imagine yourself in the place you want to be. Just sit back and see yourself at the end of a huge mahogany desk flanked by a board of directors whose sole purpose is carrying out your commands. Do you see it? Good. You're nine-tenths there." And my brain goes, wings spread, back to Conflict Control Systems, answering to no one, smiling big as I stride down the hallways. Billy Emmons is whisked away, and it's now me sitting at his gleaming crystal office giving commands over the phone... I awaken to a waxen Randolph shivering in the rear-view mirror. The dynamic assurances pour from the radio. These guys are really, really good.

Now that we're on our way to Excelsior, Mona is much more relaxed. Like Randolph's claim of inventing that rather generic Martin quote, she tells a story of her childhood that seems plucked from my own past. Had I recounted it one night on stage?

She says, "When I was, I think, ten or eleven, and Martin was seven or so, mom and dad pulled the car to the side of the road and made us walk home. We had been jumping around the back seat, screaming like monkeys, and I seem to remember a battle with cheese chips. It made an orange dust in the air you could taste. Mom swatted at us from the front seat while dad threatened to pull the car over. We'd quiet down for a minute, but went right back at it. Then my father said, 'All right,' and I could tell straight off that by his calm manner he was handing down an irreversible decree. He turned to us, not like he was speaking to his children, but rather to an employee who showed up at the pharmacy drunk, and he said, 'You're walking the rest of the way home.' There was a finality to it, the decision was made, and I shut up. But Martin couldn't accept it. He tried begging his way out of it, as he always did. 'Dad, no, please!' Father turned around again to face us (something I didn't want to see) and mom screamed. The street lamp we hit snapped straightaway and down it went. A silver flash. We stopped halfway up somebody's lawn. The aluminum lamppost stretched across the street, the end of it tangled with more metal, a bicycle, and a small motionless arm stuck straight up out of it. Martin bolted. I sat there until mother turned to me and screamed, 'Go get your brother!'

"I jumped out of the car, making certain to keep my eyes far from the end of that pole. I ran through this unfamiliar neighborhood with people mowing lawns, taking out the trash, getting home from work. Despite what I had just seen, I was too shy to call out my brother's name. I deliberately stayed clear of the accident and soon I heard the whine of an ambulance in the distance.

"It turned onto a rather pleasant little walk. The sun was setting but it was still warm out. I had been circling the same half-mile of neighborhood for some time. The sirens had stopped. I strolled about until I thought my parents would begin to get worried about us. I called out weakly, "Martin. Martin!" And then I saw him in the front window of a house. His back was to me while he gestured wildly. I thought, 'God. He's describing this terrible accident to strangers.' I was nervous about going up to this strange house—that's how self-conscious I was—but as I reached the door I heard laughter. The owners let me in, wiping laugh tears from their eyes. They were a couple—what kid can tell a person's age—thirty? Seventy? Martin was standing there, a sandwich in his hand, doing his 'Friends from Inside the Body' routine he made up that my parents didn't allow. It's about a lonely boy who befriends his bodily fluids. Yeah. Ear wax, pee, and the rest. They live in France and go on grand adventures. So there's Martin with a mouth full of sandwich narrating the tale of the little boy fighting the Japanese (who Martin still thought were enemies) alongside his bodily fluid companions. Beuregaard the Booger being one of them. 'What a talented brother you have,' the couple gushed. 'He seemed hungry, so we made him a little snack.' I said our parents were waiting, and Martin started whining that his story wasn't finished, but I know he was improvising.

"A tow truck was hitching up my parent's car when we got back. The lamppost was moved to the sidewalk. Bystanders were dispersing. Mom and dad said nothing when we returned, which was surprising. We all squeezed into the tow truck and nobody spoke on the way home. The incident about the kid crushed under the lamppost never came up. Nobody talked about it. I don't even know if it was a boy or a girl under there, or whether he or she survived. Martin never mentioned it, so I guess he never saw it or he repressed it or something. And me, as a kid being too embarrassed to talk about anything, never brought it up. My parents are both dead, so it's too late to find out."

Mona's pause in reflection seems artificial, as if we're to reflect upon it as well. The air feels drier as the Florida swampland begins to thin out. Refreshing even. "How about that story?" she says.

"That's *my* story," I tell her.

"Uh?"

"That happened to me," I say. "My parents got into a wreck. They hit the pole and it landed on a kid and I took off. They couldn't find me for hours."

"Joe, I didn't make it up."

"I saw the kid and I took off. I ran into somebody's house and hid under their breakfast table. They lured me out with some grape juice. I don't know where you came up with that bodily fluids story. I remember telling them about wanting to be a professional baseball player when I grew up. A catcher. They wanted to know why I wanted that position, and I said because wearing all the padding made me feel like a Knight."

Randolph is leaning on his one good ass cheek, trying to distract himself with the steady palm trees backlit by the setting sun. "Shit. I think I've got an infection," he says. "Come on, Joe, take a look and tell me if its oozing."

"I can't imagine anyone still wanting to be a doctor," Mona says. "Maybe just hunky pediatricians with composed skill and deep compassion who pat kids on the head and make mothers swoon."

Sleek glistening automobiles pass us on both sides, their drivers glancing over at our modest sedan like it's a foreign insect. "I don't know where you heard that story, Mona," I say. "The kid that got hurt. I knew what happened to him. A broken collarbone and he received permanent damage to his inner ear. He would get dizzy spells and he suffered Tinnitus. He was a couple years younger than me."

"Maybe it's a common occurrence," Randolph says spastically. "The same thing happened when I was a kid, except that kid who got hit by the falling lamppost wasn't hurt, he received special powers. He can now command animals to do his bidding."

"Fuck off," I say. "Did you get that story from Marty, Mona?"

Mona shakes her head. "Let's just forget it."

But I don't want to. If a person can't claim the traumatic, life altering stories from his childhood, then anything's game. I feel something inside me slipping. Now if Mona recalls a tale about Martin wanting to change his name to Constance when he was a kid (because he thought it sounded regal), then I'll lose it.

"No, I won't forget it. That happened to me," I say.

"What do you want?" Mona says. "Maybe different people can share identical experiences." Randolph is beginning to groan, either from our argument or the rat bite that has infected him with rabies.

The road becomes more populated with cars (all of them luxurious), but my initial jealousy is soon eclipsed by the uniqueness of owning the only clunker on the road. And what we're driving isn't a clunker by old standards; I would have been proud to drive this to and from work, as it's well beyond my income to afford. So now I'm proud to be driving it for totally different reasons. Randolph, of course, doesn't share this pride. He sinks down into the seat to avoid being noticed in this mid-priced import.

We drive through the outskirts of Miami. It's rush hour, but traffic keeps its brisk pace. It gets denser the closer we get to the city. We keep on the freeway and see the tall chrome downtown buildings framed by endless blue skies. And soon the city's gone, blending into the suburbs. Just a couple lifetimes ago Miami was a simple trading post, essentially cut off from the rest of America. All it took was a bouquet of unfrosted citrus blossoms sent from the wife of an industrialist to a railroad baron up north to get tracks down there the very next year. That started the boom. Now it's America's diving board, the final step you'll take from being too rich, too desperate or too old. A family of SEVEN in a Rolls Royce slows down to take a look at our Japanese anomaly as they pass. The father is shirtless and wears a baseball cap. The wife next to him is poking at her shiny black hair, and the kids in the back climb over each other to get an eyeful and give us the finger.

Like my last time here, but much faster, the suburbs thin out and eventually disappears. The highway narrows down to two lanes and we turn off. Plunging into the stringy wilderness, Mona says, "We'll soon be in Excelsior. Martin had in mind a Mediterranean-style villa, and it started that way until he discovered mid-century modern. You'll see." The deeper we plunge into the royal pines bathed in strangler figs, the less self-assured I feel. Like my confidence is in rewind.

We arrive. The limousines are still parked out front.

"Beautiful, beautiful limousines," Randolph says. He is now limping from his wound.

Mona pulls out a key and opens the door to the main house. I bounce on my feet in playoff game anxiety. In the middle of the foyer, under a chandelier of thousands of bladed raindrops, is a giant ceramic upraised fist. It would take all three of us holding hands to encircle it.

"What is *that*?" I say.

"It's a fist," Mona says. "It represents the indomitable spirit, or something like that. The same artist who did the big praying hands at a Christian university designed it. Martin first had it outside in front, but it made the place look like a dictator's stronghold."

No stairs going up. It all goes down, in levels, towards the shore. Mona leads. "This house was built on the closest thing to a cliff that Florida has to offer. There's a lot of rooms to choose from, or you can stay in one of the guest cottages."

"The world is falling apart," I say, "And we're staying here."

"This is considered middle of the road by today's standards. Besides, *people* seem to be doing well," Mona says. "They're getting what they want."

"Except us," Randolph grunts.

"Yeah," Mona says and waves her hand. "These are all bedrooms. At the end of the hall is an entertainment den. Martin brings the guests there for drinks and a nice view of the ocean before dinner is served, which is downstairs."

We walk downstairs. I feel great doors inside me slamming shut, and I don't know what to think, except, perhaps, things are all right. And as Mona gets out, "This is the kitchen," there's Marty, looking tanned, well fed and healthy in a terrycloth bathrobe (a one-in-eight chance the one I had worn), sitting alone at the counter eating a sandwich. "Hi," he says and smiles.

Mona stops. She squints as if identifying someone recognizable flash by on the news. "Martin?"

He takes a bite of his sandwich and nods.

"Martin, buddy," Randolph calls out. He takes quick limping strides to him. Marty stays seated and grins.

"Something happened to the air conditioner when I was out," he says. "And someone broke in downstairs, busted in the window, got it repaired, and stuck me with the bill. Nothing was taken but the furniture was re-arranged. How about that? The toilet water evaporated." He looks down at his sandwich and the dill pickle on his plate.

"Where's Mona?" I demand.

Randolph is standing behind Marty, a hand on his shoulder. "Martin," is all he says, beaming as if Santa were real.

"How are you, Randolph?" Marty says absently while looking at Mona. It's like I'm finally back at Conflict Control Systems, at a meeting and making no impact. Anonymity was my method of conflict control.

Mona takes a tentative step toward Marty like he's a feral cat. "You've been here?" she says.

"Yes, in Excelsior," Marty says with a flourish and looks at me.

I'm suddenly nervous about confronting my mentor, and I remember back, before Marty, to Martin and the temporary inspiration (and courage) that his writings gave me. I step forward.

"I want Misty, Marty. Where is she?"

"We need to talk, Martin," Mona says. "Alone."

Marty pops the last bite of sandwich into his mouth, takes dainty slurps of his fingertips and bites the end off the pickle.

Footsteps come up the stairs, from Martin's bedroom. The first thing I recognize is the least recognizable part of Misty, her new bladed nose. And those boobs. The rest of her seems to follow a few seconds behind. She's carrying a sleeping baby in her arms.

"Wait!" Randolph howls and sends Marty flying off his stool squeaking along the tiles in his half-opened bathrobe.

Randolph takes two broad steps and stands over him sprawled on the floor. "You cost me my company, Marty!"

I had imagined what I was going to say and do once I found Misty. And I imagined a lot. A few of the scenarios, starting with the most popular:

- At first glance I realize how pathetic she is in her nouveau-riche, plastic surgery, tummy-tuck, smothered in faux-Cherokee turquoise finery and I snatch Joe Jr. from her. I walk away with the apple-cheeked youngster in my arms, ignoring Misty's wailing, black streaks of mascara running down her cheeks, and it strikes her that she made the biggest mistake of her life. She falls to her knees in cataclysmic regret.
- Upon seeing me, it occurs to her that I was the one who stuck with her during the bad times (when getting to the bottom of a pint of ice cream a night was her only goal), and without me she wouldn't have reached these stratospheric heights. We walk away together; me, her and the child, into the future.
- She resists me at first, but my dogged persistence (despite Marty's contrary beliefs) pays off. I send her love letters, the baby clothing and toys, and (even better) she cannot ignore the success I have achieved. She comes back to me and refuses to take Marty's desperate calls.
- The instant I find them, Marty is pulling the struggling Misty by the arm. I crack Marty across the jaw. Misty shrieks and both she and the baby fall into my arms. The reason this scenario was last is because I hardly thought for a second that she went with Marty against her will.

Randolph lifts Marty to his feet by the collar, one fist raised to send his skull down into his torso. Marty squeaks out,

"Randolph, I hired you," and Mona leaps to stop Randolph's blow. She clings to his oak tree arm, hanging by it, her toes scraping the floor.

Misty adds to the pile, baby in arms.

Randolph lets out a bark from somewhere down deep, letting Marty and Mona fall to the floor. Mona reaches out and brushes Marty's cheek. Misty squats down next to him. "Marty," she says. "It'll be okay."

Mona recoils; her legs flayed out like a fallen ballerina.

"Martin?" she says, squinting.

He squeezes out a half smile. "You did a hell of a job."

Mona looks at my baby, staring out into space trying to make out all those colors. Or maybe it's just a wash of gray light, swirling to become something. I don't know if it's a boy or a girl.

"Shouldn't you be watching the company?" Marty says, and then puts on an overdone southern twang. "Mindin' the store?"

Misty sniffles, "Marty..." but he keeps looking at Mona, waiting for something. I go up to Misty and force her to look at me, and she does. I will her to show even a faded tinge of shame, and I think I see it. She looks down and rubs the baby's head.

"Cute kid," I say to her. She gives a heartbreakingly weak smile.

"Joe," she says as if that's all she can get out.

"You named the baby after me?"

"Oh, Joe," she shakes her head and looks back at Marty.

The half-eaten pickle lies on the tile floor. The sun is high and cooking us through the broad window overlooking the sea. It's a beautiful view. Florida's got the most shoreline of any US state. Alaska doesn't count.

Using sweat as a hold, I smear down my hair. The baby gurgles and nobody talks. Mona moves a leg and it squeaks against the floor.

Randolph swats the air. He's at a boil. "All right. Just tell me who the hell this is, God dammit? Martin or Marty?"

Mona takes a quick look at Marty and back down to the tile. She runs a finger along the grouting as if admiring the work. We all look at that finger. She doesn't look up. "It's Marty," she says.

"Great!" Randolph shouts flatfaced. He leaps towards Marty and drops his fist straight down upon his head. You wouldn't think it, but it sounds like a bound stack of newspapers dropping on the floor. Marty's head wobbles, looking at Mona, and Randolph yanks him to his feet by the collar of his terrycloth robe. Randolph quickly composes himself with a calm pre-deadlift breath, and sprints with Marty to the broad window overlooking the beach. Randolph lets out a shriek for momentum, and with a few more strides hurls Marty to the golden sands.

Instead of flying through the kitchen window, arms and legs flailing in the white robe amongst a shower of glass like a downed bird, he bounces off with a KA-THUNKA and lands on Randolph.

A wide crass smear of blood is left on the window. It's glowing red in the sun. Marty is atop Randolph, neither one moving. Misty runs to the pile and drops. I take the baby, and Joe Jr. begins gurgling. Misty tries to get at Marty. The two bodies are tangled in Marty's bathrobe. "Marty! Marty!" she screams.

I pat the baby's head as if that will prevent him from crying. It seems to work. Such a well-behaved kid. Mona is still sitting splayed-out on the floor; her finger had stopped moving along the tiles and rests in one place.

Misty is whimpering, trying with all her might to move Randolph off Marty.

The baby jerks in my arms. I don't want *him* to start crying. That would be too much.

*

Martin woke up with his throat on fire and gasping for breath. His voice now had a distinctive crackle and it would stay that way. And with the strength from his full belly came his mental clarity. Martin strolled back to the house thinking. He thought about the eighteen solid days it took to finally hunt down something to eat. Was this the way Dick Berg had done it? Eighteen days for a rat! How long would it take to gather the fixings for gator stew? Or start up a crop to live off? The jungle cleared and the house blending in secretly with the swamps came into view. It must have taken Berg years to build it. And there's so much more. Electricity. Car repairs. Cooking. Plumbing. Farming. Mulching. Weeding. The Law. Your Rights. Entertainment. So much God Damn work. Marty stared at the portrait of Dick, the only surviving visual document of the man, leaning back and spitting fire, his iron jaw set.

Martin decided that he didn't much care for Dick Berg's life. But he sure liked his style. He went back to the rental van and drove to Cooperation City. Speeding along, he still felt like Berg, stiff-arming the wheel, crooked grin in place. That's what he needed. The smell of American sweat. Unspoken achievements. But it didn't keep him from spending hundreds of dollars on some real food and a bottle of Bordeaux, a room for the night, and chartering a two thousand dollar limo ride back to headquarters.